Ghost in the Ashes

Jonathan Moeller

EPIGRAPH

You conceive chaff, you give birth to straw; your breath is a fire that consumes you. The peoples will be burned to ashes; like cut thornbushes they will set ablaze.

-The Book of Isaiah 53:11-12

OTHER BOOKS BY THE AUTHOR

Child of the Ghosts

Ghost in the Flames

Ghost in the Blood

Ghost in the Storm

Ghost in the Stone

Ghost in the Forge

Demonsouled

Soul of Tyrants

Soul of Serpents

Soul of Dragons

Soul of Sorcery

Soul of Skulls

CHAPTER 1
KNIVES IN THE NIGHT

Caina Amalas opened her eyes.

Something was wrong.

She turned her head, her hair rustling against the pillow. A pale shaft of moonlight leaked through the balcony doors. In the gloom she saw the table that held her mirror and cosmetics, a wooden stand for Corvalis's weapons and armor, and the wardrobe that contained her disguises. Corvalis lay next to her, eyes closed, chest rising and falling with his breath.

It was utterly silent.

Yet Caina was certain that she had heard someone scream.

She pushed aside the blankets and stood, her bare feet silent against the floor, her hair cool and dry as it brushed her shoulders. Her right hand slid under her pillow and retrieved a dagger, the razor-edged blade glinting in the moonlight.

She had a hard time sleeping without a weapon close at hand.

Caina crossed to the balcony doors and pushed them open a few inches, looking into the street below. Thick fog choked Malarae's streets, transformed into a pale silver haze by the full moon overhead. Successful merchants occupied this district of the Imperial capital, merchants with money enough to purchase townhouses separate from their shops, but not enough to imitate the lifestyles of the high lords. Through the silvery fog, Caina glimpsed the houses across the street, tall and narrow with small courtyards encircled by iron fences. The smell of brine and rotting fish filled her nostrils, carried by the fog rolling off the harbor.

Yet the street was deserted.

She shook her head in annoyance, still certain she had heard someone scream.

Caina stepped away from the doors and saw Corvalis Aberon standing behind her.

He was tall and lean, his arms and chest heavy with muscle, his eyes like cold jade disks. Strange, spiraling black tattoos marked his pale torso. Inked by an Ulkaari witchfinder, the tattoos gave him a measure of resistance to sorcery, which had saved his life more than once.

A dagger gleamed in his right hand. Like Caina, he always slept with weapons at hand. Unlike Caina, he was unable to sleep at all unless he had a weapon nearby.

His training had been rather more brutal than hers.

"There was a time," said Caina, "when I would have been alarmed to find a naked man with a dagger in my bedroom."

Corvalis barked his short, harsh laugh. He ran his free hand over his face, the blond stubble rasping beneath his callused palm. "What is amiss?"

"I heard someone scream," said Caina.

Corvalis looked out the balcony doors and back at her.

Caina shrugged. "Perhaps I dreamed it."

"No," said Corvalis. "A dream wouldn't fool you."

"One of the servants?" said Caina. They had a pair of maids, a cook, a seneschal, and a footman who doubled as the night watchman. Had someone attacked the house? Any number of people wanted Caina dead, and Corvalis's father would never forgive his defeat at Catekharon ten months earlier. "No. If they screamed, it would have awakened both of us."

Corvalis shook his head. "Eight months we've played this game, and I still cannot get used to the idea of servants."

Caina shrugged. "If it helps, think of them as Anton Kularus's servants, not yours. A man like Anton Kularus has servants."

She looked into the fog-choked street. It was still deserted.

"True," said Corvalis. "I'll go speak with them and see if anything is amiss, let them know you heard someone screaming."

Caina smiled. "They'll think I'm flighty and irrational."

"Ah," said Corvalis, "but you are Anton Kularus's mistress, and a man like Anton Kularus has both servants and a flighty, irrational mistress." He put a quick kiss on her lips. "Go to sleep. I'll speak with the servants. If there's anything wrong, I'll come get you. Otherwise you'll want to be rested when we speak with Master Basil tomorrow."

Caina nodded. "He has news about the new Lord Ambassador from Istarinmul, I am sure…"

She shivered, and not just from the cool air against her bare skin. She remembered the last time she had seen a Lord Ambassador from Istarinmul, the day that Rezir Shahan had come to Marsis. But his arrival had been a trap. Rezir Shahan had allied with Andromache of New Kyre and smuggled troops into the city. Caina remembered the ambush, women and children screaming as lightning fell from the sky, the shouts of fighting men, Nicolai sobbing for his mother, the cold blue glow in the Immortals' eyes...

She looked back at the street and saw a gleam of blue light in the mist.

Caina went rigid.

"Caina?" said Corvalis.

For a dreadful moment Caina thought she was dreaming, that her nightmares had come to life. A man walked on the street below, moving at a rapid pace. He looked like a caravan guard out for a night of drinking, clad in leather armor and a ragged cloak. Yet there were no taverns nearby, which made it an odd place for a caravan guard to go after dark.

But his eyes reminded Caina of her nightmares.

Specifically, the blue glow coming from his eyes..

"Corvalis," whispered Caina. "His eyes."

Corvalis frowned.

"He's an Immortal," said Caina.

"So," said Corvalis, "what is one of the Padishah of Istarinmul's elite soldiers doing in Malarae?"

They looked at each other, and Caina knew what they had to do next.

Caina had taken many names and disguises in her life. Countess Marianna Nereide, a minor noblewoman. Marina, the maid of Theodosia, the leading lady of the Grand Imperial Opera. Marius, a caravan guard. Anna Callenius, the daughter of the wealthy master merchant Basil Callenius. Sonya Tornesti, the mistress of the rakish merchant Anton Kularus.

But she changed names and identities as easily as she changed clothing, for she was a Ghost nightfighter, one of the spies and agents of the Emperor of Nighmar.

Caina moved to the wardrobe, catching sight of her reflection in the mirror as she did. In the moonlight she looked lean and pale, the muscles in her arms and legs visible, the scar below her navel an ugly gash across her belly. The moonlight caught her pale blond hair and turned it silver.

Blond hair. She was just vain enough to find that an irritation.

But dyeing it had made sense. There were many among the nobles and the magi of Malarae who would kill a black-haired, blue-eyed woman of the Ghosts on sight, and Caina needed to disguise herself.

She opened the wardrobe, lifting out the false bottom, and all thoughts of her appearance fled her mind.

Caina dressed in black boots, trousers, and a black jacket lined with steel plates to deflect knife blades. Black gloves covered her hands, and a mask concealed everything except her eyes. Daggers went in her boots, throwing knives up her sleeves, and a belt holding more knives and other useful tools went around her waist.

Last came the cloak.

The cloak was a marvelous thing, woven of both spider-silk and shadow by a method known only to the nightkeepers of the Ghosts. It blurred around her, merging with the shadows. Additionally, the cloak also protected her from mind-affecting sorcery, and rendered her undetectable to divinatory spells.

It had saved her life more than once.

She turned just as Corvalis finished dressing. He had clothing similar to hers, a shadow-cloak over his shoulders, but he wore black chain mail beneath a leather jerkin and carried a sword at his hip.

She nodded, and Corvalis headed for the balcony with a slender rope in his hands. He hooked the grapnel to the iron railing and tossed the rope to the street below. Corvalis scrambled down the rope, bracing his boots against the wall, and Caina followed him.

"Most women," said Corvalis, releasing the rope and stepping onto the street, "want a house with a balcony for the view."

"I never cared much for scenery," said Caina. She peered into the mist for a moment. There was no sign of the Immortal. Or of anyone else, for that matter. "This way."

Corvalis nodded and let her take the lead, his hands remaining near his weapons. He was stronger than Caina, and better with his blades. But she was far more observant.

And this damnable mist and the narrow alley presented ideal conditions for an ambush.

She scanned the walls and the windows, looking for any sign of the Immortal, while the rest of her mind turned over the possibilities.

Why was an Immortal in Malarae? The Empire and Istarinmul had been at war ever since Rezir Shahan's attack, and Caina had spent months hunting Istarish and Kyracian spies through the Empire's capital. The Immortals were the most ferocious soldiers in Istarinmul, yet their vicious temperaments made them poor spies.

To say nothing of the glowing eyes.

Was the Immortal an advance guard for the new Lord Ambassador? Or had the Immortal gone renegade? Caina thought...

She heard a yelp in the fog ahead, followed by the sound of a fist striking flesh.

Caina came to a stop, as did Corvalis. She listened for a moment, the fog cold around her, and again heard a shout, followed by the sound of scuffling. She beckoned, and they moved forward in silence. They turned a corner, and the alley ended in a courtyard shared by several different houses. No lights shone in the darkened windows overhead, but the moonlight and the fog illuminated three figures.

The first was the Immortal, glowing eyes narrowed in thought. The second was a lean man in servant's livery, a dagger in his hand. He held the dagger at the throat of a brown-skinned Istarish girl of about eighteen, his free hand clamped over her throat. The girl wore a ragged gray shift, her black eyes rolling back and forth in terror.

She was also at least eight months pregnant, her belly tight against the thin cloth of her shift.

"You have found her, then?" said the Immortal in Istarish, his voice a rasping rumble.

"Yes, master," answered the man in the servant's livery. "The girl fled out the back door as her father fought. A pitiful sacrifice. As if a pregnant slave girl could escape the grasp of the Kindred."

Caina saw Corvalis's hand move to his sword. She knew of the Kindred, the outlaw families of assassins that terrorized their victims. She had crossed paths with them more than once.

And Corvalis's father had sold him to the Kindred.

"Good," said the Immortal. "Take her to the harbor. We shall secure her until we contact the master."

"What of her father?" said the Kindred assassin. "He killed several of my brothers. The blood of the Kindred must be avenged."

The Immortal growled, and the assassin took a prudent step back, dragging the slave girl with him. The alchemical elixirs the Immortals ingested made them stronger and faster than normal men. They also induced fits of murderous fury.

"Your brethren were paid to take the girl," said the Immortal. "If they were foolish enough to fall beneath an old man's rusty sword, that is not my concern. Now. Gag the girl and come."

The assassin nodded pulled a gag from his pocket.

"Gently!" said the Immortal. "If she miscarries your life shall not be worth two copper coins."

Caina looked at Corvalis, and he nodded.

He disappeared into the fog, moving with the stealth of a master Kindred assassin.

Unsurprising, given that he had been one for years.

Caina strode forward, letting her shadow-cloak billow behind her.

"Hold!" she roared, using the rasping, snarling voice she employed while masked.

Both the Immortal and the assassin whirled to face her.

"Help me!" the slave girl screamed in Istarish. "Oh, gods, please, please help…"

"Shut up!" said the assassin, striking her across the face with the handle of his dagger. Her head snapped sideways, blood flying from her lips.

"Let her go," said Caina.

"Be off with you," snarled the Immortal. "This is not…"

"Fool," said the Kindred. "Don't you recognize the cloak? That's a Ghost, one of the Emperor's pet rats."

"The Ghosts?" said the Immortal. "The Ghosts are a myth."

"And one is standing before you in the flesh," said the Kindred. "Kill him now, or else we'll never get out of Malarae alive."

"Very well," said the Immortal, drawing his sword with a steely hiss. The Immortal strode towards her, and Caina remained motionless, eyes fixed on the Kindred assassin.

An instant later the Immortal let out a shocked gurgle, and a foot of bloody steel blade erupted from his chest.

Corvalis's gloved hand gripped the Immortal's shoulder, the other twisting the blade of his sword. The Immortals were some of the most dangerous and ferocious soldiers in the world, and only a skilled fighter could prevail in a fight against one.

So better not to fight at all.

The Kindred snarled a curse and shoved the girl aside. She fell with a cry, twisting so she landed upon her rump rather than her belly. The assassin ran at Caina, yanking a second dagger from his belt. Caina rolled her right wrist, a throwing knife dropping from its sheath to her gloved hand. She took a step forward and flung the knife, her entire body snapping like a bowstring. The assassin jerked to the side, but the knife raked the right side of his jaw, and the man stumbled with a cry of pain.

Caina yanked the daggers from her boots and charged. The Kindred assassin recovered his balance and came at her, both his daggers a blur of steel. But Caina had fought Kindred assassins before, had learned many of their secrets from Corvalis, and knew what to expect. She blocked the thrust of his right dagger, ducked under the swing of his left, and rammed her right dagger into his belly.

The Kindred doubled over with an agonized groan, and Caina grabbed his hair and opened his throat. Blood sprayed over the damp cobblestones, and the assassin pitched forward onto his face and lay motionless.

Caina let out a long breath Corvalis as joined her. The dead assassin's blood pooled on the ground, seeming to drink the light. She had killed a lot of men in her time as a Ghost, and it troubled her how easy it had become for her to kill without hesitation, without remorse…

The slave girl sobbed, taking a step back.

Caina pushed aside her doubts. She had more immediate problems.

"Please, please," said the girl. "Do not hurt me. I…please, do not kill me the way you killed my sisters. Please, dark ones. Please!"

"What is she saying?" said Corvalis.

Caina blinked, and remembered Corvalis could not speak Istarish. "She thinks we're going to kill her the way someone killed her sisters."

She stepped forward, wiped her daggers clean on the dead assassin, and lifted her hands. "We're not going to hurt you."

"Please," said the girl, shivering. "Please, just let me go."

"What happened to you?" said Caina. "Why were these men trying to kill you?"

"I don't know!" said the girl. "I don't know why they wanted me, and I don't know why they killed my sisters." She rubbed a hand over her eyes. "I…please, let me go."

"Where will you go?" said Caina.

"I don't…I don't know," said the girl, shaking her head. "Anywhere. Someplace where they can't find me."

"I can help you," said Caina.

"No," said the girl. "Please…don't hurt me."

Caina realized the Istarish girl only saw them as cloaked shadows, as armed wraiths who had cut down an Immortal and a Kindred assassin in the space of a few heartbeats.

Little wonder she feared them.

Caina decided to take a gamble, and drew back her hood and pulled off her mask.

The girl's eyes widened. "You…you are a woman?"

"I am," said Caina. "I can take you somewhere safe. You must be expecting the child soon."

The girl gave a hesitant nod. "Any day."

"Then come with us," said Caina. "You do not want to be alone when your time comes." She gestured at the corpses. "And these men had allies, I'm sure. You don't want them to find you."

The girl shook her head. "No."

"What is your name?" said Caina.

"Mahdriva," said the girl. She hesitated. "The assassin…the assassin said you were a Ghost. Is that true?"

"We are," said Caina. "We can help you, if…"

"My father!" said Mahdriva. "Please, save my father. We were hiding at the Inn of the Broken Wheel when they came for me. My father fought them off and told me to run. I went through the back door and ran as fast as I could, but the men caught me here. Please, Ghost, help my father."

Caina knew the Inn of the Broken Wheel. It was at the edge of the district, and catered to the moderately successful merchants that lived nearby. But if the Kindred and the Immortals had come for Mahdriva and her father in force, then the man was likely dead.

"He is still alive!" said Mahdriva, as if she had guessed Caina's thoughts. "My father is the mightiest warrior in Istarinmul. It will take more than assassins to kill him. But, please, he must have aid."

"She's asking you for something," murmured Corvalis in Caerish, "isn't she?"

Caina nodded, thinking. Mahdriva's father, whoever he was, had likely perished. Yet why send Kindred assassins and Immortals to kidnap one pregnant girl?

A pregnant girl, Caina suspected, who had escaped from slavery in Istarinmul.

Why go to that much trouble to recapture a pregnant slave girl?

An odd coincidence, with the Istarish Lord Ambassador arriving within a week.

And Caina did not like coincidences.

She looked at the girl, remembering the day her own father had died before her eyes.

"Yes," said Caina. "We will save your father, if we can."

"Thank you," said Mahdriva, her voice shaking. "Thank you."

"Ah," said Corvalis. "We're going to help her, aren't we?"

"You told me you liked challenges," said Caina. She pulled her mask and cowl back into place. "Well, get ready for a challenge."

Corvalis laughed. "Best we move on before the militia finds the corpses."

Caina left the courtyard and headed for the Inn of the Broken Wheel, Corvalis and Mahdriva following.

CHAPTER 2
THE GLADIATOR

Something was amiss at the Inn of the Broken Wheel.

It was an impressive five-story building of mortared stone and timber, its wings encircling a courtyard containing a fountain and a small garden. Usually lamps holding enspelled glass globes illuminated the courtyard at night. Yet now the iron lamps were dark, and Caina saw glittering shards strewn about their base.

Someone had smashed the lamps.

The Inn stood dark and silent.

"Where were you and your father staying?" said Caina.

"On the second floor, in one of the cheaper rooms," said Mahdriva, shivering in the damp. Caina wished there had been time to find Mahdriva a cloak. Or to secure her in one of the safe houses the Ghosts had hidden throughout Malarae.

Yet if there was any chance of saving Mahdriva's father, Caina could not delay.

And she suspected Mahdriva's father knew far more about what was happening than Mahdriva herself did.

"The footman at the door is dead," said Corvalis, pointing at a dark shape slumped against the wall. "Looks like they did it quietly, too. Smashed the lamps so no one could see them, and then slipped inside. I'd wager most of the guests at the Inn are still asleep."

"You ran through the back door?" said Caina.

"Yes," said Mahdriva. "In the kitchen. The assassins…the assassins came through the door to our room. My father overpowered them, and had me run while he fought."

Caina nodded. Likely Mahdriva's father had escaped through the back

9

door in pursuit of his daughter.

Assuming he was still alive.

"This way," said Caina, and they slipped around the side of the Inn, past the stables, and into the alley behind the building. The Inn's back wasn't nearly as polished as its front, with raw brick and rough timber showing in place of the facade's polished stone. The air smelled faintly of garbage, rotting food, urine, and...

And blood.

The door to the Inn's kitchen stood open, and a pair of bodies lay motionless in the alley.

Caina hurried closer, her dagger ready in her right hand. One of the corpses wore servants' livery identical to the assassin in the courtyard, and the other the clothing of a common laborer. Both men were dead, slain by a sword thrust through the heart.

"Kindred, most likely," said Corvalis, nudging one of the corpses with his boot.

"Mahdriva," said Caina in Istarish. "Are either of these men your father?"

Mahdriva gave a ragged shake of her head, arms wrapped tight around herself. "No. But they broke into our room."

"Looks like they were facing that way," said Caina, switching back to Caerish. "I think Mahdriva's father was backing away and fighting."

"You're right," said Corvalis. He pointed with his sword, and Caina saw a third corpse. "There's another one."

Caina hurried to the next corpse. The dead man wore dark clothing, his chest torn and bloody from multiple puncture wounds. The eyes gazed sightlessly up at Caina, and in their depths she saw a fading blue glow.

"Gods," said Corvalis. "He killed an Immortal."

"So did you," said Caina.

"I stabbed an Immortal in the back before he noticed me," said Corvalis. "This Immortal's wounds are in front."

Caina looked at Mahdriva.

"Father," she said, "is the mightiest warrior in Istarinmul."

"Plainly," said Caina, looking down the alley. "He must have gone this way."

She hurried down the alley, Corvalis and Mahdriva following. They passed two more slain Kindred. Mahdriva's breath came in harsh, short bursts, her face going gray. Caina wondered how much father she could go. Perhaps they ought to turn back and find a safe place for Mahdriva to rest.

But Mahdriva kept going, her teeth gritted.

The alley opened into a street leading to Malarae's vast maze of docks and warehouses. The Imperial capital's harbor accommodated both ships from the Bay of Empire and barges from the River Megaros, and merchant vessels from a score of nations filled Malarae's quays.

Or, at least, they had, before the Kyracians had started sinking half the ships in the Cyrican Sea.

Caina looked around. Where would Mahdriva's father have gone? Perhaps he had slipped into an empty warehouse and eluded his pursuers. Or had he lured his foes into a trap? If a man had the skill to fight and defeat an Immortal of Istarinmul, he might have the cunning to draw his enemies into a trap...

Even as the thought crossed her mind, she heard the clang of steel on steel, heard men shouting. The noise was coming from an alley between two brick warehouses.

"Go!" said Caina, running for the alley.

She ran into the alley, Corvalis following, Mahdriva staggering after. The sounds of fighting grew louder, and Caina heard a man scream and fall silent. Mahdriva groaned and came to a stop, one hand clutching her belly.

"Wait here," said Caina, grabbing her shoulders and steering her to a narrow doorway in the side of the wall.

"But," said Mahdriva, her face glistening with sweat, "but my father...my father..."

"You won't help him if you miscarry and bleed out," said Caina. "Wait until we come for you."

Mahdriva nodded.

Caina helped her to sit and rejoined Corvalis.

"How is she?" said Corvalis.

"Not well," said Caina. "But she'll do worse if her father dies in front of her. Come on."

Corvalis nodded and followed her.

The alley ended in a yard between three warehouses. Stacks of crates and barrels stood scattered at intervals, and countless white streaks of gull dung marked the brick walls. Three dead men, two Kindred and one Immortal, lay sprawled near the edge of the yard.

Another shout and the clang of steel on steel reached Caina's ears, followed immediately by the sound of another body striking the ground.

Caina beckoned to Corvalis, and he nodded. They crept around one of the stacks of crates, their boots making no sound, and Caina peered around the edge.

An Istarish man in his fifties stood in the center of the yard, clad in boots, trousers, and a leather vest. His hair and beard were the color of iron, and his arms bulged with muscle. Fine wrinkles lined the dark skin of his face, and he reminded Caina of an ancient oak tree, hard and tough and unyielding.

In his right hand he held a scimitar, and his left he carried a steel trident.

"Come!" roared the man in Istarish, banging the trident and the sword together with a clang. "I know you skulk in the shadows, creeping in the darkness like rats! Come and die, dogs!" He spat upon the ground. "Are you so afraid of one pit slave? Do the mighty Immortals and the Kindred cringe in fear of one gladiator?" Again he struck his trident and sword together. "Come and I shall send you to join your brothers down in hell!"

And as he spoke, men emerged from the fog. Six men, wearing the livery of servants or the rough clothes of dockhands. Yet all moved with the balance and grace of trained Kindred assassins, swords and daggers in their hands. At their head walked a gaunt man in leather armor with a salt-and-pepper beard and a hooked nose. His eyes narrowed at the sight of the middle-aged Istarish man, his scowl deepening.

"I know him," whispered Corvalis. "Nalazar. From the Kindred family in Istarinmul."

That surprised Caina. Malarae had its own Kindred family. So why had Istarish Kindred pursued Mahdriva and her father to Malarae? For that matter, the Immortals served only the Padishah and Istarinmul's College of Alchemists.

Someone of great power and influence in Istarinmul clearly wanted Mahdriva.

"Enough, Muravin," Nalazar said. "You have made this far more difficult than it needs to be. Where is Mahdriva? This needn't be painful."

Muravin spat again. "Do not weary me with your lies. Do you think me stupid enough to believe them? You have already spilled the blood of my daughters!"

Nalazar gestured with his sword. "Where is the girl?"

"Where you shall never find her," said Muravin.

"Enough," said Nalazar. "One pregnant girl cannot elude the Kindred. Kill this fool and let's be on our way."

Muravin hefted his weapons, and the Kindred advanced on him, spreading in a half-circle. Muravin turned back and forth, his trident darting forth like a serpent's tongue. He would take at least two or three of them with him, but in the end, Nalazar and the Kindred would kill him.

And Caina had told Mahdriva she would save her father, if she could.

She looked at Corvalis, who nodded, and they slipped around the stack of crates.

Muravin backed away, the Kindred following him. Which made it so easy for Caina to glide up behind the assassins, Corvalis at her side. She darted forward, seized the hair of the nearest assassin, and ripped her dagger across his throat. The hot blood splashed across her gloves, and the man toppled with gurgling moan. In the same instant Corvalis plunged his sword through the back of another assassin, killing the man in an instant.

The remaining four Kindred whirled in shock.

"We are attacked!" shouted Nalazar. "Defend…"

Muravin surged forward with a roar, stabbing with his trident. One of the Kindred caught the trident on his sword blade, but Muravin ducked under the locked weapons and stabbed, his scimitar taking the assassin in the gut. Caina snatched a throwing knife from her sleeve and flung it at the nearest Kindred. The assassin dodged the spinning blade, but Corvalis lunged, his bloody sword taking the assassin in the chest.

Nalazar whirled and sprinted away, the remaining Kindred assassin following him. In an instant the two men vanished into the fog. Muravin lowered his sword and trident, breathing hard, and Caina saw a spasm of exhaustion go over his lined face.

Then the hardness returned as he looked at them.

"I know not whether you are living men or shadows of the netherworld," he said, looking at their cloaks, "but I thank you for the aid. But I must find my daughter. Aid me or not, but do not think to hinder me."

"Your daughter," said Caina in Istarish, making sure to keep her voice disguised. "She is named Mahdriva, and great with child?"

"Aye," said Muravin, a flicker of hope in his hard black eyes. "You have seen her?"

"Yes," said Caina. "And we shall aid you, if we can. Follow me, quickly. Explanations can come later."

Muravin nodded. "Then lead on, shadow. But I have slain Kindred and defied Immortals to come here. Betray me or harm my daughter, and I swear you shall sup with your ancestors before the sun rises again."

"What is he saying?" said Corvalis in Caerish.

Caina walked from the yard, the men following "That if we betray him or hurt his daughter, he'll cut off our heads."

"How touching," said Corvalis. "Tell him he fights well. Not many men can face an Immortal and live."

"My companion praises your valor," said Caina in Istarish, as Muravin gave Corvalis a suspicious look. "Few men can defeat an Immortal unaided."

"Bah!" said Muravin. "The Immortals are strong, yes, but they trust overmuch in their strength. A true warrior does not place too much trust in any weapon, lest it be turned against him."

Caina found that she agreed.

They returned to the alley, the fog cold and cloying. Caina headed for the doorway, hoping that Mahdriva was still there, that the girl hadn't fled terrified into the night, or that Nalazar had been bright enough to send some men to search the alley.

But Mahdriva huddled in the doorway, arms wrapped tight around herself.

"Father!" said Mahdriva, staggering to her feet.

"My girl," said Muravin, his voice rough. "You were very brave."

"They saved me, Father," said Mahdriva, nodding at Caina. "The shadows. One of the Immortals caught me, and they would have taken me if the shadows had not come."

"Who are you?" said Muravin, turning to Caina. "And why have you aided us?"

"Questions can come later," said Caina. "For now, we must decide upon a course of action. A moment."

She turned back to Corvalis and switched to Caerish.

"We have to get them somewhere safe," said Caina. "Nalazar got away, and I'm sure he has more men hidden in the city."

"Aye," said Corvalis, "and he's not the sort to give up easily."

"How do you know him?"

"Later," said Corvalis. "Perhaps we should take them to the townhouse."

Caina shook her head. "It's too close. If Nalazar is still searching the area, he might think to look there."

"The Grand Imperial Opera?" said Corvalis.

"It's too far across the city," said Caina. "And Muravin would stand out at the Opera like a wolf in a flock of peacocks." Caina lowered her head and thought for a moment. The Ghosts' various safe houses were all too far away, and Caina had no doubt that Nalazar had other groups of men searching the city. If they ran into another group of Kindred or Immortals, they might well be overpowered. They needed a safe place, one they could reach without...

The answer came to her.

"The foundry," said Caina.

Corvalis snorted. "The Champion will be delighted, I'm sure. Who doesn't enjoy unexpected guests in the middle of the night?"

"The Champion is one of us," said Caina, "and he understands his duty." She glanced at Muravin, who stood glowering at her, Mahdriva huddled against him. "And both the Champion and his wife will aid an escaped slave."

"So you think our new friend is a gladiator?" said Corvalis.

"Almost certainly," said Caina. "He called himself a pit slave when he challenged Nalazar. And a man of that age who survived as a gladiator...he'll know his way around a sword."

"Plainly," said Corvalis.

Caina nodded and turned back to Muravin.

"Well?" said Muravin, his eyes wary, his posture tense. "You have decided our fate, then?" He had one arm around Mahdriva, his scimitar at his belt, his trident slung over his shoulder. Yet Caina had no doubt he could have his sword in his hand and through her heart in an instant.

"Your foes still hunt you," said Caina. "We will take you to a safe location. From there, you can rest and recover your strength, and decide how best to keep your daughter safe."

"We are strangers in a foreign land," said Muravin, "and so we must place ourselves in your hands." He scowled. "But why are you helping us? Before we go anywhere with you, you will tell me who you are."

"We are the Ghosts," said Caina, "the eyes and ears of the Emperor of Nighmar."

Muravin's eyes narrowed. "So the Ghosts are real. The emirs and the Alchemists always claimed the Ghosts were myth."

"They are fools," said Caina.

Muravin snorted. "They are. But why would the Emperor's Ghosts help us?"

"Because we hate slave traders," said Caina, "and I would kill every last one of them with my own hands, if I could."

Muravin's black eyes glittered. "That I understand. Lead on."

CHAPTER 3
THE CHAMPION OF MARSIS

Malarae's newest foundry loomed out of the fog.

It was a tall, blocky building of stout brick and concrete, constructed with reinforced walls in the event of an explosion. Six thick smokestacks rose from the roof, smoke rising from their crests to mingle with the fog. A sullen glow came from the high, narrow windows, casting a harsh orange light over the fog. The foundries of Malarae labored day and night, manufacturing arms and armor for the Legions, or producing pots and pans and horseshoes to sell across the Empire.

"A foundry?" said Muravin.

"The Ghosts have friends in many places," said Caina.

Muravin scowled. "A foundry is no place for my daughter."

"Fear not," said Caina. "She'll be comfortable enough."

They circled to the foundry's rear courtyard, where iron carts held heaps of coal and raw ore. A night watchman patrolled the yard, a man in his middle forties whose close-cropped hair and tattooed right arm marked him as a veteran of the Imperial Legions. He turned at their approach, a loaded crossbow in his arms.

Muravin bared his teeth and reached for his weapons.

Caina raised a gloved hand to forestall him.

"Let the tyrants beware the shadows," said the watchman in High Nighmarian.

"For in the shadows wait the Ghosts," said Caina in the same language.

The watchman looked them over, grunted, and jerked his head to let them pass. They passed the carts of iron and coal and came to the foundry's corner. A flight of wooden stairs climbed twenty feet up, ending in a thick, iron-banded door. Caina took the stairs, knocked, and waited.

After a moment the bolts released and the door swung open.

Caina found herself looking at the tip of a crossbow bolt pointed at her face. The crossbow rested in the arms of a bald man of about forty, with cold gray eyes and the build of a blacksmith. He wore a ragged red tunic and trousers, a Kyracian sword at his belt.

"It's late," said the man. "Business can wait until tomorrow."

"Not this business, Ark," said Caina in Caerish, dropping her disguised voice. She reached up, drew back her hood, and tugged off her mask.

She heard a startled curse from Muravin. Undoubtedly he had believed her to be a man.

Arcion of Caer Marist, the Champion of Marsis, friend of Lord Corbould Maraeus, and owner of Malarae's newest foundry, lowered his crossbow. "Countess. I wasn't expecting you until later this morning, when Halfdan arrives. You have a knack for surprises."

"It's a gift," said Caina. "I need your help." She gestured at Muravin and Mahdriva. "I think they're escaped slaves. They've got the Kindred of Istarinmul and the Immortals after them."

Ark frowned. "Immortals? In Malarae?"

Caina nodded.

"You must have left quite a few corpses behind," said Ark.

"Aye," said Caina. "The civic militia is going to have a busy morning. This is the safest place I could reach at short notice." Indeed, it would be hard to find a more secure place to hide Mahdriva and Muravin. Ark preferred to hire veterans, and most of his workers knew how to fight. The Kindred could not burn down the brick foundry, and there was only one entrance into Ark's apartment.

And, more, she trusted Ark. They had entered some very dangerous situations together and managed to come out alive at the end.

Ark glanced at the stairs. "I suppose you have your pet assassin with you?"

Corvalis rolled his eyes.

"Ark," said Caina. "He does come in handy."

Ark grunted. "Come inside."

He turned and vanished into the apartment, and Caina beckoned for the others to follow.

They entered a large, comfortable sitting room, with wide windows overlooking the foundry's courtyard. The view was hardly scenic, but the windows would admit ample sunlight. A thin boy of about seven years stood near the door, watching them with wide gray eyes.

He grinned when he saw Caina.

"Countess," he said.

Caina smiled and ruffled his hair. "Nicolai." A blur of memories shot through her. She had taken Ark's son with her on a walk on the day Rezir Shahan attacked. They had been trapped in the Great Market by the Istarish troops, and the slavers had taken Nicolai.

Caina had gotten him back, but to save his son, Ark had rallied the remaining defenders of Marsis and wound up killing Kleistheon, a Kyracian stormdancer, winning the title of the Champion of Marsis.

If the slavers had not taken Nicolai, Marsis might well have fallen to the Istarish and the Kyracians.

"You have brought guests," said Nicolai, looking at Mahdriva and Muravin with wide eyes.

"I did," said Caina, pushing aside the memories. "Your mother makes the finest cakes in Malarae, and they wished to taste them."

"Nicolai," said Ark, "go wake your mother."

"She's up anyway," said Nicolai. He wrinkled his nose. "The baby was crying again."

Caina laughed. "Babies do that."

Nicolai ran back into the apartment's inner rooms. Muravin walked to one of the couches and helped Mahdriva to sit. The girl looked wet and cold and exhausted. Muravin hovered over her, his touch gentle, and she leaned against him.

Strange to contrast that with the man's brutal fighting prowess.

"Where have you taken us?" said Muravin to Caina in Istarish, voice low. He watched her warily, no doubt still surprised that she was a woman.

"The house of a friend," said Caina. "He owns this foundry, and his workers are veterans of the Emperor's Legions. I do not think the Kindred followed us, but if they did, they will find this place well-protected."

"Give him my thanks," said Muravin. "For he has put himself at risk by taking us into his home."

"No need," said Ark in Istarish. "I understand you well enough. And your thanks are unnecessary." His eyes hardened. "I think you are escaped slaves...and I do not care for slavers."

Muravin nodded. "The woman of the shadows said as much." He looked Ark up and down, a warrior measuring another warrior. "You were in the Legions, no? That is how you know the Padishah's tongue?"

"I was the first spear centurion of the Eighteenth Legion," said Ark. "The Eighteenth spent several years guarding the Empire's southern border against the tribesmen of the Argamaz Desert."

"Ha!" said Muravin. "Then we are well-protected. The tribesmen of the Argamaz are vicious..."

The inner door opened, and Tanya walked out, wrapped in a robe. She looked a great deal like Caina, with blue eyes and black hair, though she was six inches taller and a bit heavier. She stopped, looked at Muravin and Mahdriva, and then at Ark.

"Husband," she said in Caerish. "We have guests?"

"Aye," said Ark. "I suspect they are escaped slaves."

"Oh, you poor dear," said Tanya, sitting next to Mahdriva. "You're half-frozen, I shouldn't wonder. Let us get you some warm clothing and food. That will help. And a comfortable bed upon which you can sleep."

Mahdriva blinked and looked at her father.

"She only speaks Istarish, I think," said Caina. She switched to Istarish and addressed Muravin. "This woman has borne two children herself. She will know how to care for Mahdriva."

"Daughter," said Muravin, getting to his feet, "go with this woman, and let her tend to you." He started to step forward, swayed, and grabbed at the back of the couch for support.

"Father!" said Mahdriva, grabbing his hands.

"I am well," said Muravin, shaking his head. "I…"

"I suspect you spent all night fighting and running," said Caina, "and even the mightiest champion needs rest. Go with your daughter. You have earned your rest, and we can decide how to proceed in the morning."

Muravin managed a weary nod. "You speak wisdom, however strange you seem to me. I will rest."

"Wife," said Ark in Caerish. "Put them in the guest room. Make sure the shutters are closed. I suspect dangerous men wish them dead."

Tanya smiled. "If I know anything, husband, it is how to be discreet in the face of danger. Nicolai, come and help me bring food to our new friends."

She took Mahdriva's arm and led the girl from the room, Muravin and Nicolai following, leaving Caina and Corvalis alone with Ark.

"What the hell is this about?" said Ark.

"I don't yet know," said Caina. "We saw an Immortal moving through the streets, and I thought it odd. We followed him and found the Kindred and the Immortals trying to take Mahdriva alive. Muravin held them off while Mahdriva tried to flee."

"The old man must be formidable with a blade," said Ark, "if he managed to hold off Immortals."

"He is," said Corvalis, voice quiet. "And if he survived Nalazar, that makes him all the more formidable. The Istarish Kindred are not to be trifled with."

"Who is Nalazar?" said Ark.

"A Kindred from Istarinmul. Which reminds me," said Caina. "How do you know Nalazar?"

Corvalis sighed. "When I was a member of the Kindred family in Artifel, Nalazar and some Kindred from Istarinmul came to our Sanctuary. An emir who gained the Padishah's disfavor had fled north, and Nalazar had been sent to hunt him down. The Elder of Artifel helped him in exchange for a cut of the profits."

"Did this Nalazar succeed?" said Ark.

"He did," said Corvalis. "He's good at what he does."

"Would he recognize you?" said Caina.

"Maybe," said Corvalis. "I was in the room when he met with the Elder, but I don't know if he would remember me."

"A more important question," said Ark, "is why the Istarish Kindred came north in pursuit of this gladiator and his daughter. And with Immortals."

"I don't know," said Caina. "The Immortals serve the Padishah, but the College of Alchemists creates them. My best guess is that Mahdriva is pregnant with the bastard heir of some emir or another."

"She said the Kindred had slain her sisters," said Corvalis.

"Perhaps the Kindred killed her sisters," said Ark, "and Muravin took her and fled north before they could find her."

"That seems likely," said Caina. She yawned and rubbed her face. Gods, but it had been a trying night. "We can get more information out of them tomorrow. When Halfdan meets us here, we can tell him what happened, and perhaps he'll know more…and he might be able to get Muravin and Mahdriva to talk."

"You think they'll lie to us?" said Ark.

Corvalis shrugged. "Why would they not? They have no reason to trust us."

"And it is indeed odd," said Ark, "that this happens the week before a new Lord Ambassador arrives from Istarinmul."

"We will find out more tomorrow," said Caina.

Ark grunted and crossed to the shutters. "It is tomorrow." Caina saw that the night sky had begun to brighten. "Halfdan will be here soon. Why don't you two rest here? I'll have Tanya bring you some food once she's finished with Muravin and Mahdriva."

"Thank you," said Caina. "For everything."

Ark offered a tight smile. "I don't like slavers any more than you do."

He disappeared through the inner door, leaving Caina alone with Corvalis. She sat on the couch Mahdriva had vacated. The soft cushions felt pleasant against her legs and back, and a wave of weariness went through Caina. It had indeed been a long night.

She looked at Corvalis and smiled.

And she hadn't gotten that much sleep before seeing that first Immortal, either.

Corvalis stared at the inner door as he sat, his face grim.

"What is it?" said Caina.

"I wonder if Muravin would have tried to kill me," he said, "if he knew what I really was."

"What you used to be," said Caina. "You're not Kindred any longer."

"True," said Corvalis. He sighed. "A man like Nalazar. That's what I would have become. If not for Claudia." He looked at her. "If not for you."

"You're a better man than you think you are, Corvalis Aberon," said Caina. "I've told you that before. Perhaps someday you shall listen."

"Perhaps," said Corvalis. His frown faded. "Though I wonder how Nalazar found them at the Inn of the Broken Wheel. Malarae has a thousand inns. Muravin could have chosen any one of them. How did Nalazar find them?"

"With luck," said Caina, "we'll discover that tomorrow."

He took her hand, and they lapsed into a comfortable silence.

"There is one thing," said Corvalis, "I enjoy about this ridiculous charade of Anton Kularus. He has quite a comfortable bed."

Caina laughed. "If you're tired enough, you can sleep anywhere."

She proved it by drifting off to sleep.

A pounding at the door awoke Caina.

She lifted her head from Corvalis's shoulder, her hand reaching towards her knives out of habit. More sunlight streamed through the opened windows.

The inner door opened, and Ark came out, crossbow in hand. He stepped to the front door, opened it a crack, and spoke for a while in High Nighmarian. Then he laughed and stepped aside. A man in the furred-lined robe of master merchant walked into the sitting room, a beret with a silver badge on his head. He had iron-gray hair and a close-cropped beard, and the thick arms of a man accustomed to physical labor.

"Well," said the man in the robe, his voice thick with a Caerish accent, "you've been busy, haven't you?"

"Halfdan," said Caina.

He was one of the high circlemasters of the Ghosts, and she had known him for over ten years, ever since he had rescued her from Maglarion's lair near Aretia. He was one of the four or five most knowledgeable men in the Empire – and one of the most dangerous.

Few others knew as many secrets.

"I will never get used," said Halfdan, "to the sight of you with blond hair."

Caina sighed. "Don't remind me."

"It suits you," said Halfdan. "But we have more pressing concerns. The civic militia is in an uproar, Theodosia tells me. A dozen dead men, found scattered from the merchants' district to the docks, most of them Istarish. I've heard some say that a gang of Istarish slavers ran amok, others that a group of assassins sent to kill the new Lord Ambassador turned on each other."

"Fanciful tales," said Corvalis.

"Indeed," said Halfdan. "What really happened?"

"You just assume we were involved?" said Corvalis.

Halfdan snorted. "I stopped by the home of Anton Kularus on my way here, and the servants told me that Master Kularus had stepped out with his mistress. Kindly credit me with at least some brains between my ears, my boy."

So Caina told him. She described how they had seen the Immortal, rescued Mahdriva, and helped Muravin escape from Nalazar and the Kindred.

"I don't know what was happening," said Caina. "My best guess is that Mahdriva is carrying the bastard child of some emir or another, and one of the emir's wives sent assassins to kill off the threat to her own children." She shook her head. "But that doesn't explain why the Immortals came with the Kindred."

Halfdan crossed to the windows and gazed down at the foundry's courtyard. "It doesn't."

"And the timing is suspicious," said Caina, "since the new Lord Ambassador from Istarinmul is arriving within a week."

"It is," said Halfdan. "Especially since the Lord Ambassador will sue for peace."

For a moment silence fell over the sitting room.

"For peace?" said Ark.

"The war against New Kyre is a stalemate," said Caina. "The Empire cannot defeat them on sea, but the Legions can crush them on land."

"Aye," said Halfdan, "but the war against Istarinmul is different. I doubt the Padishah really wanted it, and Rezir Shahan convinced him that he could win a quick victory in Marsis. Well, Rezir is dead, and the Empire still holds Marsis. Lord Corbould's eldest son Conn has been leading the Legions south against the armies of Istarinmul, and he has won victory after victory. He has pushed deep into the Argamaz Desert, and the Istarish armies have fallen back to Istarinmul itself. The Padishah's power comes from his ability to close the Starfall Strait, but Lord Conn is almost close enough to build forts overlooking the Strait itself."

"And if he does," said Caina, "the Padishah will lose a great deal of power."

"More likely, the Padishah will find himself with a Kindred dagger between his ribs," said Halfdan. "The emirs of Istarinmul are a ruthless lot, and do not tolerate weakness in their rulers. The Padishah wants peace, now, before he loses any more prestige."

"Why not finish it?" said Corvalis. "Push on to Istarinmul and take the city itself?"

Ark shook his head. "The city's walls are too strong. Every Legionary in the Empire, gathered together, could not take Istarinmul."

"And Istarinmul is impossible to besiege in any event," said Halfdan. "The Padishah could bring a constant supply of fresh soldiers and food from the lands of his southern emirs. Our army would starve before the most wretched slave in Istarinmul felt the slightest pang of hunger. No, better to secure peace now, while the Padishah is willing to deal. And with Istarinmul at peace, the Emperor and the Legions can turn their full attention to New Kyre."

"So the Padishah wants peace," said Caina. "Who is he sending as his Lord Ambassador? Not Callatas, I hope." She had met the cold, arrogant Master Alchemist at Catekharon.

"No," said Halfdan. "You remember Rezir Shahan?"

"Better than I would like," said Caina.

"You should, given that you killed him," said Halfdan.

"You did?" said Corvalis. "You never mentioned that."

"No," said Caina. She did not like to discuss what had happened in Marsis. "Actually, I lured him into a trap, blew off his hand, set him on fire, cut his throat, and threw his head into a crowd of his soldiers." Thinking back, it seemed...surreal. As if it had happened to someone else. Yet she hated slavers, and Rezir Shahan had tried to enslave Nicolai and thousands of others.

And the dramatic way she had killed him had given rise to the legend of the Balarigar, the story so beloved among tavern jongleurs.

"I see," said Corvalis. "Remind me not to anger you."

Caina smiled. "Wise man." She looked at Halfdan. "But why mention him?"

"Because," said Halfdan, "Istarinmul's new Lord Ambassador to the Emperor is also the new emir of the Vale of Fallen Stars. Tanzir Shahan, Rezir's younger brother."

"Then is the Padishah truly serious about peace?" said Caina. "Rezir was the architect of the attack on Marsis. Surely his brother is cut from...no, poured from the same alloy."

Ark chuckled.

"One would think so," said Halfdan. "But Rezir was one of the most powerful emirs of Istarinmul and a hardened battle commander. Tanzir, it seems, is young and inexperienced. The Padishah wants peace, and is sending Tanzir because Tanzir will do exactly as he is told."

"Ah," said Caina. "That's why you're here."

Both Ark and Corvalis looked at her, puzzled.

"Because the Padishah wants peace," said Caina, "but I doubt that all his emirs feel likewise. Or all the nobles of the Empire. Or the Kyracians."

"Or the Shahenshah of Anshan," said Corvalis, understanding. "Anshan profits while the Empire and Istarinmul are at war."

"And if you want to keep the Empire and Istarinmul at war," said Caina, "what better way to do it than by murdering the Padishah's Lord Ambassador in the capital of the Empire?"

"Indeed," said Halfdan. "As you have discerned, my dear, there are any number of powerful people who want the war between the Empire and Istarinmul to continue, people who have the means to murder Tanzir Shahan while he is in Malarae. Our task, therefore, is to keep the good emir alive long enough to sign a treaty of peace with the Emperor. I will need your help for this, Caina. You are more observant than anyone I have ever met...and you have a gift for improvisation in life-and-death situations." He smiled. "As a few Kindred found out last night, I expect."

"You have it," said Caina.

"And you, Master Corvalis," said Halfdan, "or should I say Master Anton? You know how assassins operate. We will need your help to keep the emir alive. And as Malarae's rising young merchant prince of coffee, you'll have access to the social circles Tanzir will visit during his time in Malarae." He winked at Caina. "Along with Master Anton's mistress, of course."

"I am yours to command," said Corvalis.

"Splendid," said Halfdan, looking back at Caina. "When you asked Zalandris to give you Khaltep Irzaris's coffee beans as your reward, I thought it a good idea...but I did not dream it would be as successful as it has been. You and Corvalis have done the Ghosts are a great service."

"Thank you," said Caina, a flush of warmth spreading through her. Halfdan was a hard, fair man...but compliments from him were as rare as jewels.

"Given that the Emir Tanzir will arrive soon," said Corvalis, "doesn't that make it all the more peculiar that some Istarish Kindred and Immortals were pursuing a pregnant slave girl through the streets of Malarae?"

"I agree," said Ark.

"Why, thank you, Lord Champion," said Corvalis.

Ark shrugged. "If you want an expert on killing, consult a Kindred assassin."

"Indeed," said Halfdan. "This Muravin. Is he awake?"

"He's asleep," said Ark, "but I knew men like him in the Legion. He sleeps with one eye open."

"Not surprising, if he is indeed a gladiator and a slave of the fighting pits," said Halfdan. "Corvalis, wait here. Caina, please come with me. I think it is the time we got to the bottom of this little mystery."

CHAPTER 4
THREE SISTERS

Ark led them into the inner rooms.

Caina saw Tanya's touches everywhere. Cloths of Szaldic design hung upon the wall, and in the windows stood the little painted wooden statues designed to ward away the demons of Szaldic legend.

Of course, not all the demons in the Szaldic tales were legendary.

Caina knew that too well.

Tanya stood at the table in the dining room, looking over several plates of food. Nicolai sat at her left, eating a bowl of porridge. A baby girl of three months rested in Tanya's right arm, eyes closed.

"Halfdan," said Tanya with a smile. She crossed the room and kissed him on the cheek. "You old rascal, you stormcrow. Wherever you go, trouble follows."

"My dear," said Halfdan, "I fear you have it backwards. I simply go to the trouble."

"Aye," said Tanya, grinning at Caina, "and then you have the Balarigar end it."

Caina smiled. She had told Tanya not to call her the Balarigar, but it never seemed to take.

"This is Natasha?" said Halfdan, looking at the baby.

"She is," said Tanya. "I had wanted to name her Mihaela..."

"No," said Caina, remembering the Forge in Catekharon's heart. "You really didn't."

"But Natasha is a fine name as well, one of the great Szaldic queens of old," said Tanya without missing a beat. "Caina." She reached down with her free hand and picked up a clay cup. "Here. I thought you might like this when you woke up."

Caina took the cup and drank. It was full of hot coffee, and it warmed her throat and lifted some of the tired haze from her mind.

"Thank you," said Caina. "You have the hospitality of one of the great Szaldic queens of old."

"We bought it from the House of Kularus, of course," said Tanya.

Caina laughed. "Corvalis will approve."

"Given that the House of Kularus is merely a front for spies," said Tanya, "it certainly sells fine coffee."

"Of course it does," said Halfdan. "The best lies are always true. Where is Muravin? It's time we have some answers."

"The guest room," said Tanya. "Careful around him, Master Halfdan. He's a bit...prickly."

Halfdan nodded. "Caina, with me. Tanya, Ark, thank you for your help."

He walked to the guest room door and opened it, Caina following him. Muravin lay upon the bed in the guest room, his eyes closed. Yet he sat up at their approach, his scimitar appearing in his hand, his eyes hard and cold.

Halfdan closed the door behind him.

"A light sleeper, I see," said Halfdan in flawless Istarish.

Muravin grunted. "Men can sleep deeply when they are dead. And I am not yet dead."

"Unlike those Immortals and Kindred," said Caina.

"As you say," said Muravin. He looked back at Halfdan. "And who are you, merchant?" He snorted. "Though if you are a merchant, I am the Padishah."

"A keen eye," said Halfdan. "You can call me Basil Callenius."

"And you are a chieftain of the Ghosts," said Muravin.

"Something like that," said Halfdan. "As you can imagine, I am curious why Immortals and the Istarish Kindred were chasing an escaped slave and his pregnant daughter through the streets of the Emperor's capital city."

Muravin snorted. "You are almost right. I was a slave. Now I am a freeman. Though more people are trying to kill me now than when I was a slave."

"Perhaps you should tell me more," said Halfdan, "if we are to keep you alive."

"I don't know if I can trust you," said Muravin.

"Then decide," said Halfdan. "Because you need my help. You are alone in a foreign city where most of the people do not speak Istarish, and you have a daughter who will give birth soon. Additionally, there are powerful men who want your daughter. You need help, or you're going to die and the gods only know what will happen to your daughter."

Muravin scowled. "And what do you want for your help? I have no money."

Halfdan smiled. "You can pay us in secrets, for secrets are the business of the Ghosts. Secrets can be a weapon. And I am very interested in the secret of your story."

"Very well," said Muravin. "It seems I have no choice. And the woman of the shadows saved my life. If she has a name."

Caina thought for a moment. "Sonya. You can call me Sonya."

"Sonya, then," said Muravin. "And you have given me no reason to distrust you...so this is what I know. I was a gladiator for many years, fighting in the pits of Istarinmul." He drew himself up. "I was the best. Again and again I was victorious, and no man could stand against me. The most powerful men in Istarinmul purchased me, and I fought in the Arena of the Padishahs itself. Three times I was the champion, and at last my freedom was purchased."

"By who?" said Halfdan.

"By the Seneschal of the College of Alchemists," said Muravin. "As his bodyguard. Former slaves are despised in Istarinmul, but the champion of the Arena of the Padishahs has some prestige. Within five years I found husbands for all three of my daughters, and soon all three were with child."

"And you have no wife?" said Halfdan.

Muravin's eyes grew a little distant. "She died, many years ago."

Halfdan nodded. "I am sorry. Why did you flee to Malarae?"

Muravin scowled. "They killed my daughters."

"Why?" said Halfdan.

"I do not know!" said Muravin, slapping his hand against the bed in frustration. "They sent the Kindred dogs to strike at us in the night. They slew my two oldest daughters, Ardaiza and Ranai, and cut the children from their wombs."

Caina felt a chill. "What?"

"They slew my daughters and their husbands," said Muravin, his tone flat, "and cut the children from their wombs. After they were dead. I suppose that was a mercy."

"A small one," said Caina.

But his words brought back memories of her time as a prisoner in Maglarion's lair, of the lectures Maglarion had given to his students. Necromancy drew upon blood and death for its power, and Maglarion had said the blood of unborn children could fuel certain powerful spells.

"How did Mahdriva survive?" said Halfdan.

"She and her husband were with me when the Kindred found us," said Muravin. "I slew the Kindred, but not before they killed Mahdriva's husband." He sighed. "He was a good man. I went to the Seneschal to warn him, but he was slain, too."

"The Kindred killed the Seneschal as well?" said Caina.

"Aye," said Muravin. "He was a fat, pompous braggart, but a decent master."

"Perhaps the Seneschal was the target," said Halfdan, "and you and your family were merely in the way."

"Unlikely," said Caina. "Else why go to the trouble of…taking the unborn children? The Kindred can be cruel, but only if they are paid to be so."

"And you know the Kindred well, woman of the shadows?" said Muravin.

She did. Riogan, a former assassin of the Kindred, had trained her in weapons and stealth. She had fought against Kindred assassins in Malarae and Cyrioch. And she now shared a bed with a former assassin of the Kindred.

But Muravin didn't need to know that.

"I do," said Caina.

"So the Seneschal was slain," said Halfdan, "and you decided to flee for Malarae."

"I did," said Muravin. "The Seneschal was my patron, and someone powerful obviously wanted my daughters dead. If we stayed in Istarinmul we would perish. Getting out of the city unseen was a challenge, but we managed it. It was easier once we reached the great desert of the Argamaz. The war between the Padishah and your Emperor has thrown the desert clans into chaos, and it was easy for me to find work as a caravan guard. We made our way to Malarae with a caravan." Muravin shrugged. "I thought to travel north, to the Imperial Pale. It is said fighting men are always in demand there, and I hoped to find a strong husband for my daughter, one to take care of her when I am dead."

"Instead the Kindred found you," said Halfdan. "Do you know how?"

"I know not," said Muravin. "They must have followed us."

"The first attack," said Caina. "When the Kindred killed Ardaiza and Ranai. Were there any Immortals then?"

"No," said Muravin. "I did not see any Immortals until they attacked us at the Inn of the Broken Wheel."

"Thank you," said Halfdan. "A few more questions. Do you know the name Rezir Shahan?"

Muravin snorted. "Of course. He was the emir of the Vale of Fallen Stars. He led the attack on Marsis…but some Szaldic demon called the Balarigar slew him. Or so the story goes."

"Did you ever meet Rezir Shahan?" said Halfdan. "Or speak with him?"

Muravin shook his head. "I saw him once or twice when he attended the fights at the Arena, or when he visited the College of Alchemists. But I was beneath his notice."

"What about the new emir," said Halfdan, "his brother Tanzir?"

"I never saw him," said Muravin. "Do you think House Shahan slew my daughters? I doubt it. Rezir never knew me...and Tanzir, rumor holds, is a coward dominated by his Anshani mother."

"Tanzir, in fact," said Halfdan, "is the Padishah's new Lord Ambassador to the Emperor."

Muravin laughed. "Truly? Then the Padishah must indeed desire peace."

"And it is a strange coincidence, is it not?" said Halfdan. "A week before Tanzir is set to arrive in Malarae, you are attacked by Immortals in the streets."

"It is peculiar," said Muravin, "but I doubt it has anything to do with Mahdriva. Why would the Padishah care about my daughters? I was a gladiator, and the bodyguard of a high-ranking servant. We are beneath the notice of such powerful men."

"Perhaps," said Halfdan. "Nevertheless, someone took an interest in your daughters."

"I know it well," said Muravin. "That is all I know. So, chieftain of the Ghosts. Will you help me?"

"If I can," said Halfdan, "if you will aid me."

"I will," said Muravin. "But understand this, Basil Callenius of the Ghosts. Do you know when a man becomes truly dangerous?"

"When he has nothing left to lose," said Halfdan.

"He does," said Muravin. "But a man who has only one thing left to lose is even more dangerous. Understand me well. My wife is ten years in her grave. Ardaiza and Ranai are slain. Mahdriva and her child are all that is left to me in this world. I will do whatever I can to save them." He glared. "If I have to kill you, Sonya, and everyone else in this foundry to save them, I will do it."

"I would expect no less," said Halfdan. "We will help you, if we can. Please wait here, Muravin."

He beckoned, and Caina followed him into the dining room. Ark and Tanya waited there, as did Corvalis, who was drinking a cup of coffee and chatting with Tanya. For all that Ark remained suspicious of the former Kindred, Tanya had developed a sort of maternal fondness for Corvalis.

"Well?" said Halfdan. "Do you think he was telling the truth?"

"He was," said Caina, remembering the cold, unyielding pain in Muravin's grim black eyes. "He doesn't know why this happened to his family. But he'll fight to his last breath to defend Mahdriva."

"Is Mahdriva awake?" said Halfdan.

"No," said Tanya. "I would recommend not questioning her until after she's had some decent rest. She is utterly exhausted, both physically and mentally. It is a miracle that she did not lose the baby. If you must discuss these grim things with her, please wait until she has rested."

"Very well," said Halfdan. "I doubt she'll know why the Kindred are after her."

"Necromancy," said Caina at once. "The blood of an unborn child can be used to empower a potent spell. One the Alchemists must have hired the Kindred."

Maglarion's words echoed in her head.

"Perhaps," said Halfdan with a frown. "Though it seems unlikely. Istarinmul's College of Alchemists does not have the same tradition of necromancy as our Magisterium. The Alchemists use sorcery to cause the transmutation of physical substances, not to control the body and mind as the magi do."

"A renegade, then," said Caina. "Like Maglarion. And perhaps an Alchemist happens to be dabbling in necromancy."

"If that is true," said Corvalis, "wouldn't it be easier simply to buy a slave girl? Fertile slave girls are cheap enough on the auction blocks of Istarinmul. If a necromancer required the blood of an unborn child, surely it would be far easier to buy a slave and impregnate her rather than murder the daughters of a freed man."

"For that matter," said Halfdan, "why the unborn children of sisters? Muravin said all three of his daughters were pregnant at the same time."

"I don't know," said Caina. "But there is more going on here than Muravin knows, that is plain."

"And the Immortals," said Halfdan. "Only the Padishah, the emirs, and the Alchemists can command the Immortals. If the Kindred alone had pursued Muravin north, I would say this is a coincidence. But Immortals in Malarae a week before Tanzir Shahan arrives? An unlikely coincidence."

"Then the question is," said Corvalis, "what do we do about it?"

"Muravin and Mahdriva cannot stay here," said Caina. "It is not safe for Ark and Tanya and the children."

Tanya frowned. "We would be happy to shelter them."

"And the foundry is defensible," said Ark. "My workers know how to handle themselves."

"I have no doubt of that," said Halfdan, "and your kindness does both of you credit. But if this Nalazar tracked Muravin and Mahdriva to the Inn of the Broken Wheel, he might be clever enough to follow them here. I don't want to take that chance. No, better to find a new hiding place."

"Where, then?" said Corvalis.

"I think," said Caina, "that I know just the place." She looked at Halfdan. "Did you bring your coach?"

"Of course," said Halfdan. "Basil Callenius, master merchant of the Imperial Collegium of jewelers, can hardly walk the streets like a common peddler, can he?"

"Does it have enough room for Mahdriva and Muravin?" said Caina.

Halfdan nodded.

"Then we had better go," said Caina.

CHAPTER 5
THE HOUSE OF KULARUS

A short time later Caina stood before the mirror in her bedroom.

She had bathed quickly, just enough to wash away the sweat and blood from last night. Now she donned a red gown with a tight black bodice, tighter than she would have preferred, black scrollwork adorning the sleeves and skirt. She put golden earrings in her ears and several rings on her fingers, the stones large and gaudy. She arranged her blond hair in a simple style to display the earrings and the golden chain around her throat, and stepped back to examine the results in the mirror.

She looked exactly like the pretty mistress of a wealthy merchant, of a woman who had suddenly come into more money than she had the wit to handle.

In short, she looked exactly like Sonya Tornesti, mistress of Anton Kularus.

Though, of course, she kept the daggers hidden in her high-heeled boots and the throwing knives up her sleeves.

She left the bedroom and descended to the front hall, where Corvalis stood speaking with their seneschal, a skinny, humorless Saddaic man named Talzain.

"Master Anton," said Talzain, dry-washing his hands. "I do wish you would notify me before you and...ah, Mistress Sonya departed unexpectedly in the night. It does so play havoc with breakfast."

Corvalis shrugged. "It cannot be helped." He wore black boots and trousers and a fine black coat over a stark white shirt, the very image of a rapacious young merchant. Though he did have a belt with a sheathed sword and dagger. But merchants had to guard against thieves and unscrupulous rivals. "My lady had a whim to take a walk by the water...and

I am ever powerless before her desires."

"Why, Anton, how very sweet of you," said Caina, walking towards them, the heels of her boots tapping against the polished floor. She spoke with a thick Szaldic accent, as Sonya Tornesti was Szaldic.

She took Corvalis's hands and kissed him.

"Will you be taking lunch with us today, sir?" said Talzain.

"I fear not," said Corvalis. "Business calls, I am afraid. Basil Callenius has some...interesting proposals, and I will meet with him at the House of Kularus. I do not expect to return until tonight."

"Commerce," said Talzain, "is ever a harsh taskmaster."

"Truly," said Corvalis, and he took Caina's hand and led her from the entry hall.

They stepped outside. The fog had burned away, the sun rising in the eastern sky. Traffic moved back and forth before the house, mostly couriers carrying messages and maids and cooks on their way to the markets.

"It always amazes me," murmured Corvalis, closing the front door behind them, "how perfectly you can imitate an accent."

Caina shrugged. "It is merely practice, no?"

"And you sound," said Corvalis, "exactly like Tanya."

"But of course," said Caina. "Where do you think I learned the accent?"

"You don't even speak Szaldic," said Corvalis.

"I speak more than I did," said Caina. "And Sonya Tornesti grew up in Varia Province, surrounded by Szalds, even if her family spoke Caerish."

Corvalis laughed. "You think of everything."

"Halfdan was right," said Caina. A fine coach rattled towards the townhouse, pulled by two brown horses. "The best lies are true."

"Speaking of which," said Corvalis, brushing some dust from the sleeve of his coat, "it's time for me to go lie." The coach stopped before the house, and Corvalis extended a hand. "Shall we?"

He led Caina to the coach and opened the door. She climbed inside, red skirts gathered in her hands, and saw Halfdan sitting upon one of the seats. Muravin sat across from him, between Mahdriva and the door, and glowered at Caina.

"Is this why we must stop, Basil Callenius?" said Muravin. "So you can acquire prostitutes to comfort you?"

Caina heard Corvalis chuckle and resisted the urge to kick him.

"She is no prostitute," said Halfdan.

"Indeed not," said Caina in Istarish, settling next to Halfdan. "Or do you forget our first meeting in the courtyard, when Nalazar and his men pursued you?"

Muravin looked at her for a moment, and then his eyes widened. "The woman of the shadows?"

Caina nodded.

"By the Living Flame," said Muravin. "I would never have recognized you."

"I have heard it said that the Ghosts vanished into the shadows," said Mahdriva, her face tired. She wore one of Tanya's dresses, and though her belly bulged against the front, it was too long and loose for her. "But if you can disguise yourself so well, you have no need of shadows."

"Shadows," said Caina, "have their uses."

"Where are you taking us?" said Muravin.

"A safe house," said Halfdan.

"What kind of safe house?" said Muravin.

"The kind of safe house," said Halfdan, "where you can get the best coffee in Malarae."

Muravin looked puzzled.

A short time later, the coach stopped in the Imperial Market.

A million people lived in Malarae and the surrounding villages, and the city had hundreds of markets and thousands of shops. The Imperial Market was the richest and the most prestigious in the city and perhaps the Empire. The market sat at the base of the rocky crag that supported the Imperial Citadel itself. Marble paved the square, and statues of gods and heroes and long-dead Emperors lined the market or stood before the buildings. The richest merchants' collegia kept their halls here, lining the square in glittering marble facades. Smaller shops sold luxuries from across the Empire, wives of wealthy merchants and the seneschal of powerful lords examining the wares.

And at one end of the square, overlooking it all, sat the House of Kularus.

"What is this place?" said Muravin, peering through the coach's windows.

"The only place," said Halfdan, "to purchase coffee in the city of Malarae. Or the Empire itself."

Mahdriva blinked. "In Istarinmul, even slaves drink coffee. Why is it so popular here?"

"About a year ago," Caina heard herself say, "I did a favor for some powerful men in the south. They asked if I wished a reward."

"What did you ask for?" said Mahdriva. "Riches?"

"All the coffee beans in the warehouse of a dead merchant," said Caina, "and the freedom of one slave. And this," she gestured at the House of Kularus, "is the result."

The coach stopped, and Muravin and Mahdriva donned hooded

cloaks. Corvalis opened the coach's door and climbed out, and Caina followed him.

The House of Kularus rose over them, five stories topped by a small dome. Statues stood in niches along the walls, showing various victorious lords and Emperors from the Empire's long history. The statues looked marble, but Caina knew they were plaster, painted over to look like stone.

It was cheaper.

The smell of roasting coffee filled her nostrils, along with the low murmur of conversation from within the House.

"It sounds as if business is good," said Corvalis.

"A coffee house?" said Muravin. "You think to hide us in a coffee house? Madness."

"We do, but it is not madness," said Caina. "Follow us."

She slipped her arm into Corvalis's, and footmen opened the doors at their approach. Inside, sunlight fell from the oculus in the dome overhead, supplementing the light from the enspelled glass spheres lining the walls. Tables and chairs filled the floor, and five stories of balconies climbed the walls, providing booths where men could converse in privacy. Servants hurried to and fro from the kitchens, carrying trays of coffee and food.

"It is larger," said Muravin, "then I expected."

"It is," said Caina.

It had worked better than she had thought. While in Catekharon, she had seen how the Anshani and the Istarish conducted business in coffee houses. No doubt a great many secrets were discussed over coffee, secrets that could benefit the Ghosts. Caina had brought Khaltep Irzaris's coffee beans back from Catekharon in hopes of starting a coffee house in Malarae and gaining new information for the Ghosts.

The cover story had been easy enough to arrange. Anton Kularus, a mercenary guard in the employment of Basil Callenius, had received the coffee beans as a reward for saving the lives of the Sages during Mihaela's mad attempt to create the glypharmor. In gratitude, Basil Callenius had arranged for his friends in the Imperial Curia to give Kularus the exclusive right to sell coffee in Malarae. Kularus had opened his House...and business had boomed. Now many prominent lords and wealthy merchants preferred to conduct business at the booths and tables at the House of Kularus. Anton Kularus also controlled the coffee trade into Malarae, and that income combined with his coffee house had made him a wealthy man.

And every last one of the maids, servants, porters, footmen, and cooks reported everything they saw and overhead to the Ghosts. Already the Ghosts had stopped assassination attempts on Lord Titus Iconias and some of the other lords who supported the Emperor using the information gleaned from the House of Kularus, and Caina had tracked down two different rings of Istarish spies.

Of course, the capital thought the coffee house belonged to Anton Kularus, but in truth, it belonged to Caina...and it had made her wealthy. But she had little use for money.

She looked at Mahdriva, at the curve of the girl's belly.

Money could not buy her what she really wanted.

"Master Anton!" said a voice.

A short man of Anshani birth hurried towards them, clad in an immaculate black coat and trousers. He was not much older than Mahdriva, but already he had dark circles under his eyes and a hint of gray in his jet-black hair.

Given that his sister had been murdered and transformed into an enspelled suit of armor, Caina was not surprised.

"Shaizid," said Corvalis, greeting the former slave who managed the House of Kularus. "How is business?"

"Well, Master Anton," said Shaizid with a bow. "Many fine lords grace your House, and we are pleased to serve them."

"And to take their coin, eh?" said Corvalis.

"Well," said Shaizid. "That is the purpose of commerce." He turned to Caina and offered a bow, deeper than the one he had given to Corvalis. "And you, Mistress Sonya. It is always good to see you."

"And you, Shaizid," said Caina, keeping her Szaldic accent in place. She had avenged his sister's death at the hands of Mihaela and Torius Aberon, and he would do absolutely anything she asked of him. Just as Tanya and Ark would do anything she asked of them, for saving Nicolai from the Moroaica and the slavers.

That troubled her, for the cold part of her mind, the part trained by the Ghosts and hardened by experience, saw how she could use her friends as weapons.

But today, at least, she need not ask anything so demanding of Shaizid.

"Shaizid," she said, "these are my kinsmen, visiting from Varia Province." She gestured at Muravin and Mahdriva, swathed in their cloaks. "They are tired from travel, and wish to rest. Anton said they could use the guest quarters."

"Ah," said Shaizid, nodding. He, too, was a Ghost. "This way, mistress."

"Anton," said Caina to Corvalis. "I must make sure my kinsmen are comfortable."

"Go," said Corvalis. "I have business to discuss with Master Basil anyway."

Caina wagged a finger at Halfdan, the jewels on her hand flashing. "And do not let him drink too much coffee, yes? Otherwise he shall be up all night, and I will not get any sleep."

"My solemn word upon it," said Halfdan, amusement in his eyes.

"This way, mistress," said Shaizid. Caina beckoned, and Muravin and Mahdriva followed them across the floor. Shaizid took them through the kitchens and into the cellar. Sacks of coffee beans stood against the wall, harvested and shipped north from the great plantations of Anshan. Shaizid stopped before the wall and slid aside a brick, revealing a hidden lock. He opened it with a key, and a hidden door swung open to reveal a concealed room. Within was an armory and a workshop, the shelves on the walls stocked with weapons, armor, and other useful supplies.

"A curious inventory," said Muravin, "for a coffeehouse."

"I told you," said Caina, dropping her accent and switching to Istarish, "the Ghosts have safe houses. This is one of them."

Shaizid opened another door on the far side of the armory, revealing a room furnished as a barracks. "You should be comfortable enough here, sir," he said to Muravin in Anshani-accented Istarish. "I assume Mistress Sonya wishes your presence kept secret, yes? Well, within the House of Kularus, her wishes are law. You will be well-fed while you are here, and we shall keep you hidden."

Mahdriva crossed to one of the cots and lay down at once.

"It is good that Mahdriva can rest here," said Muravin. "But I shall need to keep watch."

Caina nodded. "I expected as much. But Nalazar and the Kindred will be looking for you, and there are materials you can use for a disguise on the shelves in the armory. I suggest you disguise yourself as an Istarish mercenary. If anyone asks, say Anton gave you a job as a guard."

"We can find livery to fit him, mistress," said Shaizid.

Muravin chuckled. "From pit slave to Arena champion to guard at a coffee house. The wheel of fate spins in peculiar directions. But it shall be as you say." He hesitated. "Sonya Tornesti...thank you for your kindness. I admit, you are a most peculiar woman, but without your aid, Mahdriva and I should surely have perished."

"I told you," said Caina. "I don't like slavers. Rest here for a while. We will speak later."

She left the barracks and stepped into the armory, closing the door behind her.

"Who are they, mistress?" said Shaizid. "If I am allowed to know."

Caina shrugged. "A former gladiator and his pregnant daughter. The Istarish Kindred murdered his other daughters and their husbands. I need a safe place to hide them."

"They shall be kept safe, mistress, I swear it," said Shaizid. "And the Ghost circles of Malarae know the identities of several of the local Kindred, though we have been unable to find their Sanctuary. We will not permit any of them to come near the House of Kularus."

"I doubt the assassins from the Malarae family will be involved," said

Caina. "The Istarish Kindred pursued them north."

"It will be difficult to watch for them," said Shaizid, "with the new Lord Ambassador visiting the city."

"I know," said Caina. Had the Kindred merely wanted to use Tanzir Shahan's arrival to mask their attacks? Yet they couldn't have known that Muravin would flee to Malarae. "But, please, watch for them anyway. And make sure Muravin stays out of trouble."

"It will be as you say, mistress," said Shaizid.

They returned to the main floor. Shaizid bowed once more and returned to his work, and Caina paused for a moment, looking over the balconies of the House of Kularus. Men and women sat at the tables and booths, laughing and talking. Some of them were enemies of the Emperor, and yet they came here to drink coffee and exchange news and negotiate contracts. To enjoy themselves in the company of others.

Caina looked at them, an odd feeling settling over her.

She had done this. Shaizid managed it, and Corvalis acted as a figurehead...but the House of Kularus was hers. She had masqueraded as many things since joining the Ghosts nearly eleven years ago – a merchant's daughter, a Countess, an opera singer's maid, a mercenary soldier, an Istarish soldier, and a score of other disguises. Yet she had always thought of herself as a nightfighter of the Ghosts.

She had never thought she would become a woman of commerce.

And to her surprise, Caina liked it.

Theodosia had told her that no one could remain a Ghost nightfighter forever. Could Caina do this instead? She enjoyed this life, the intrigue and the plotting and the work required of business. And she could continue to gather information and knowledge for the Ghosts.

For a moment she saw herself wed to Corvalis, the two of them ruling Malarae's coffee trade together.

But she pushed aside the vision and joined Corvalis and Halfdan at their table.

For now, she was a nightfighter of the Ghosts, and she had work to do.

"Our guests are comfortably settled," said Caina, sitting next to Corvalis.

"Good," said Halfdan. "They should be safe enough here. It would take a bold assassin to sneak past so many witnesses."

"And bold assassins," said Corvalis, "are usually dead assassins."

"You're bold enough," said Caina.

He grinned and squeezed her thigh underneath the table. "Oh, aye, but I'm not an assassin any longer."

"Speaking of assassins," said Halfdan, "we need to keep watch. Tanzir Shahan arrives within a week. He'll likely stay at the Lord Ambassador's official residence, a mansion not far from the Imperial Citadel. That would be the likely place to kill him."

"Aye," said Corvalis. "An arrow from a rooftop would be too chancy. Better to slip some poison into his breakfast and have done with it."

"It would have to be a potent poison," said Halfdan. "The Alchemists are the best apothecaries in the world, and the emirs have access to antidotes that can do everything short of raising the dead."

"And a poison might be too subtle," said Caina, her eyes wandering around the balconies. "The point is to have Tanzir murdered in Malarae and cast the blame upon the Emperor. A poison can always be mistaken for a sudden illness, but it's hard to misinterpret a dagger through the..."

She blinked.

"What is it?" said Corvalis.

Caina peered at the third-floor balcony, trying not to make it look obvious.

"What is it?" said Corvalis again, glancing over his shoulder.

"I think," said Caina, "that I just saw Nalazar."

Corvalis whispered a curse. "Should we kill him?"

"No!" said Caina. "Not here, at least. It would look a bit odd if Anton Kularus started killing patrons at his coffee house."

"Perhaps he followed us here," said Halfdan.

"No," said Caina, thinking it over. "He wouldn't recognize either me or Corvalis. We had our masks on when we fought him. He probably didn't even realize he was fighting a woman." A thought came to her, and she laughed out loud.

"What?" said Corvalis.

"Our own reputation works against us," said Caina. "All men know both coffee and secrets can be bought at the House of Kularus...and so Nalazar came here to find our friends." She stood. "Wait here. I'll see who is meeting with him."

"Do as you think best," said Halfdan.

"Slap me," said Corvalis.

"Why?" said Caina.

"If you simply walk after Nalazar, it will look suspicious," said Corvalis. "But if you storm off to sulk after we've had a quarrel, no one will think anything of it." He grinned. "Sonya Tornesti has a bit of reputation for...tempestuousness."

"Good," said Caina. "I've worked hard at that."

"Then I can walk after you to apologize," said Corvalis, "and give you assistance, should you need it."

Caina smiled. "Clever man."

She took a deep breath, drew back her arm, and slapped Corvalis as hard as she could manage. His head snapped around, his eyes bulging wide, and he rubbed his jaw, though she saw the amusement in his green eyes. A sudden silence fell over the surrounding tables, and Caina felt every eye on her.

There was no need for additional histrionics. She lifted her chin into the air with a sniff of contempt, turned, and strode away, making sure her heels clacked loudly against the floor. The murmur of conversation rose again from the floor, and Caina headed for the stairwell. She climbed the stairs to the third level, keeping her expression angry and hurt.

But her mind remained cold and focused, and she felt the weight of the throwing knives within her sleeves.

The third-floor balcony was crowded with merchants and minor nobles speaking in low voices. No doubt Nalazar preferred a crowd. It made it easier to hide. She swept along the aisle between the rows of booths, chin raised, but her eyes scanned back and forth for Nalazar.

She saw him disappearing down the stairs at the other end of the balcony. Caina whispered a curse through clenched lips and started after him, moving as fast as she dared. She wanted to run, but that would draw too much attention.

Not that she could have run anyway in these damned boots.

Caina descended the back stairs and returned to the main floor just as Nalazar and another man strode through the front doors. Nalazar did not look the part of an assassin. He wore a close-fitting black coat, brown trousers, and gleaming black boots. He looked like a merchant of middling prosperity, perhaps the seneschal of a minor lord. The man with him wore polished chain mail and carried an expensive sword. He looked like an officer from an elite mercenary company.

They walked through the doors and strode into the crowds of the Imperial Market. Caina wondered if she should pursue them, but there was no guarantee she could find them again in the crowds. For that matter, her red gown and jewelry would stand out, and they might realize she was following them.

That could prove fatal.

But Caina doubted that Nalazar had realized Muravin and Mahdriva were hidden in the cellar. He had come here for information, seeking clues on where Muravin might have gone...and where better to go than the House of Kularus?

And, she realized, he would be back.

Shaizid appeared at her side. "Mistress? One of the Kindred was here."

"Where?" said Caina.

"Talking to the Istarish merchant in the black coat," said Shaizid.

"That was Nalazar, one of the Istarish Kindred," said Caina. "You know the man with him?"

"Yes, mistress," said Shaizid. "He calls himself Tasca, though I suspect that is not his real name. He is a Kindred of the Malarae family, and arranges meetings with clients."

"And fellow Kindred, it seems," muttered Caina. So Nalazar had turned to the local Kindred for help. That meant Nalazar would have more men at his disposal. On the other hand, the Ghosts knew many of the Malarae family's members, and it gave them a better chance of tracking Nalazar's movements.

And perhaps it would keep the Malarae Kindred from going after Tanzir Shahan, if someone hired them to kill the new Lord Ambassador.

"If they return, mistress, shall I have them killed?" said Shaizid.

"No," said Caina. "Just have them followed. Discreetly. See where they go. Once we know more, then we can act."

"It will be as you say," said Shaizid with a bow.

Caina returned to the table where Corvalis sat with Halfdan. A few of the nearby merchants watched her from the corners of their eyes. No doubt they wanted to see how the little drama with the slap played out.

"Well?" said Halfdan.

Caina sat down. "That was Nalazar. Shaizid says he was with one of the local Kindred agents, a man named Tasca."

"A Speaker," murmured Corvalis. "A brother who negotiates with the clients, or arranges deals with the other families, is a Speaker."

"Then it would seem," said Halfdan, "that Nalazar has decided to engage Malarae's Kindred family for help."

Corvalis frowned. "Then he didn't follow Muravin here?"

Caina shook her head. "As far as I can tell, he came here for information and to meet Tasca."

Halfdan laughed, long and loud.

"What is it?" said Caina.

"This," said Halfdan, gesturing at the tables around them. "What a perfect little trap you have constructed for us, my dear. Tracking down the secrets of our foes is hard work. Yet now they come to the House of Kularus to plot, and we need only sit and wait for them." He lifted his cup. "All while drinking fine coffee. Though truly civilized men prefer wine, of course."

"Thank you," said Caina. "I had Shaizid keep watch for them. I suspect both Nalazar and Tasca will return. When they do, Shaizid can have them followed...and we'll know where Nalazar is hiding. Then we can settle with him, and Muravin and Mahdriva can go on their way."

"Good," said Halfdan, finishing his coffee and standing. "Well, we have work to be about."

Corvalis stood and took Caina's hand. "Kiss me."

"What?" said Caina.

"We quarreled, you slapped me, and you ran off," said Corvalis. "Now you are overcome with desire for me, and have returned to my side once more." He smiled. "Our audience deserves a resolution to our little drama, do they not?"

"Oh, of course," said Caina. "And the fact that you would enjoy it is a mere coincidence?"

"A fact of no consequence whatsoever," said Corvalis.

Caina laughed, took his head in both hands, and kissed him long and hard upon the lips. She heard the murmurs of amusement from the nearby tables, but did not care.

It was part of her disguise as Sonya Tornesti.

And masquerading as Sonya Tornesti did have some compensations.

CHAPTER 6
THE GARDENERS

Eight days after leaving Muravin and Mahdriva at the House of Kularus, Caina awoke before dawn and practiced the unarmed forms.

She moved over and over again through the forms Akragas had taught her at the Vineyard, years ago. The high block. The middle palm strike. The unarmed throw, the middle kick, and the leg sweep. Between sets she stood balanced upon one leg, her other foot raised above her head, or gripped a rope set into the bedroom rafters and pulled herself up by the strength of her arms over and over again.

When she finished, her breath came fast and quick, her heart pounded, and sweat soaked her thin shift, but she felt better. Even if the knowledge of unarmed combat had not saved her life again and again, she would still practice the unarmed forms for the clarity they brought to her mind.

After she bathed and dressed in another red gown. It was going to be a hot day, so she picked a gown with a neckline lower than she would have liked, but at least it was cooler. The sleeves and tight bodice were adorned with black scrollwork, and she put a black leather belt around her waist.

She clipped her sheathed ghostsilver dagger to the belt. The curved blade had been fashioned by from ghostsilver, harder and lighter than normal steel. The weapon also had the ability to resist almost all forms of sorcery.

That, too, had saved her life more than once.

She paused one more time to check her jewelry and her makeup – she wore too much of both – then donned a pair of high-heeled sandals and left the bedroom.

Corvalis awaited her in the front hall, working his sword through a number of forms. He wore his usual black coat, boots, and trousers over a white shirt, and looked very good.

He saw her, grinned, and slipped the sword back into its scabbard. "You look lovely."

Caina laughed. "I look like I have poor taste and spent too much of your money on ill-suited jewelry."

"Well," said Corvalis. "Technically, it is your money. You may spend it on as much ill-suited jewelry as you wish."

"How gracious," said Caina. She touched her hair. "And on bad dye."

"I would say it suits you," said Corvalis, "but I know you hate it, so I will not."

She laughed. "You listen to me so closely, then?"

Some of the amusement drained from his eyes. "As I should have done."

"You should stop blaming yourself for that," said Caina.

"It was my fault," said Corvalis. "What happened in Catekharon."

"It was," said Caina, "but it was just as much my fault. If I had not gone after Sicarion by myself, if I had gotten help from Halfdan or Kylon first…maybe I would have been killed anyway."

Odd that she had never blamed Corvalis for the near-disaster in Catekharon. But he had been listening to his sister, to the only family he had left. If Caina's father had still been alive, if he had told her to do something against her better judgment, she would have heeded him.

"Corvalis," said Caina. "I could have died a hundred times in the last ten years. And I could die of a hundred different things today." She shook her head. "Maybe this damned dye will poison me for all I know. So we must use the time we have as well as we can."

She leaned up and kissed him.

"Aye," said Corvalis. "Let's go meet the Lord Ambassador."

Crowds of nobles, merchants, magi, and priests lined the stone quay.

A portion of Malarae's vast complex of docks was reserved for warships of the Imperial navy. Many of the quays were empty, since Kylon Shipbreaker had sent most of the Emperor's warships to the bottom of the western sea. The notables of Malarae stood on the empty quays, watching the Lord Ambassador's ship maneuver to the docks. Some commoners stood watching from the streets leading to the warehouses, held back by lines of black-armored Imperial Guards.

For a moment Caina remembered Rezir Shahan's ambush in the Great Market of Marsis, remembered the screaming people fleeing from the Immortals, and went cold despite the hot sun overhead.

She shivered.

"Are you all right?" said Corvalis.

"I'm fine," lied Caina. Malarae was not Marsis, Tanzir Shahan had come to make peace, not to start a war, and Nicolai and Tanya and Natasha were safe at the foundry. Some of the dark memories faded away.

But they did not go away, not entirely.

"It's just as well we are so close to the quay," said Caina, hoping to change the subject.

Corvalis snorted. "Anton Kularus has friends. Specifically, Master Basil Callenius of the Imperial Collegium of jewelers. Master Basil is friends with Lord Titus Iconias after our little adventure in Catekharon. Since Lord Titus is greeting the emir at the quay, we get to stand and watch."

And, hopefully, they would keep any assassins from reaching the Lord Ambassador.

Corvalis and Caina walked onto the quay, past the more powerful lords surrounding Lord Titus himself. A few of the lords gave Corvalis irritated looks, which he ignored with blithe indifference. The nobles regarded Anton Kularus as an upstart, as a peddler of coffee who had no place among the councils of the mighty. Yet nonetheless Corvalis looked like a gaunt wolf among the plump nobles in their robes and finery.

Caina could only imagine what they thought of her. No doubt they believed her a scheming whore drawn to Anton for his sudden rise in wealth and status.

But that made it all the easier to steal their secrets.

She spotted Halfdan standing next to Lord Titus Iconias and a knot of black-armored Imperial Guards. Lord Titus was a stout man in his middle forties with a perpetually disgruntled expression. He was a strong supporter of the Emperor and one of the most powerful men in the Empire.

"Master Basil," said Corvalis. "Thank you for inviting me."

"Master Anton," said Halfdan. "Good of you to come."

"Eh?" said Titus, looking away from the Istarish ship. "Who's this, Basil?"

"Anton Kularus," said Halfdan, "our rising young master of the coffee trade."

Titus looked at Corvalis, at Caina, took a longer look at Caina's neckline, and then back at Corvalis. Caina stifled a laugh. Titus had seen them both a dozen times in Catekharon, but he did not recall either of them.

"Yes, of course," said Titus. "My seneschal is buying some of your wares. A pity I didn't think of starting the coffee trade in Malarae myself. I could have made a fortune."

"Business favors the bold, my lord," said Corvalis.

"Indeed, Master Anton," said Titus. "I may bring the emir to your establishment. The protocols of diplomacy require that I entertain him for a few days, and I understand they are fond of coffee in Istarinmul."

"I should be honored, my lord," said Corvalis. "All men of good will desire peace between our noble Emperor and the Padishah."

Titus snorted. "And peace will make it all the easier to ship coffee from the plantations of Anshan and Cyrica?"

"Well, yes, that too."

The Istarish warship pulled up to the quay, and Titus fell silent. The Istarish ship was a huge wooden galley, propelled by three masts and two banks of oars, its decks lined with ballistae and Istarish soldiers in spike-topped helmets. The ship came to a stop, and dockhands rushed forward with mooring lines. The crew lowered a gangplank, the soldiers stirring.

The Immortals came ashore.

Caina kept her face calm. The Immortals wore black chain mail and plate armor, their face-concealing helmets worked in the shape of grinning skulls so that the Padishah's enemies might know death came for them. A pale blue glow shone in the depths of the skulls' eye holes, a result of the sorcerous elixirs the Immortals consumed. Caina remembered running from the Immortals in the streets of Marsis, remembered fighting them...

She wondered again why Nalazar had brought Immortals in pursuit of Muravin and Mahdriva.

A score of Immortals assembled upon the quay, carrying lances with the Padishah's banner, a crimson field with a black sword and crown. An Istarish soldier stepped forward, clad in the cloak of a khalmir, an Istarish officer. He took a deep breath and began to shout.

"Hearken!" he yelled in Istarish, his voice rolling over the docks. "He comes! He who is the Emir of the Vale of Fallen Stars! He who is Captain of the Southern Towers! He who is Lord Ambassador to the Empire of Nighmar, and high in the favor the Most Divine Padishah! Tanzir Shahan comes!"

Caina remembered Rezir's herald shouting those words in the Great Market moments before the fighting began.

The similarities were eerie, and made her skin crawl.

She looked to the top of the gangplank as Tanzir Shahan himself appeared.

And just like that, the similarities stopped.

Rezir had been a warrior, tall and strong and hard with muscle. He had almost killed Caina, had almost strangled her to death one-handed in front of Andromache and Kylon. He had come within a hair's breadth of seizing Marsis.

Tanzir Shahan Lord Ambassador of the Padishah, was nothing like his brother.

He was short and fat, at least two hundred and fifty pounds, a thick black beard masking his double chin. Unlike Rezir, he wore elaborate ceremonial robes of red and gold instead of armor, possibly because no armor would fit him. A jeweled turban rested askew atop his head, and his nervous black eyes darted back and forth in his face. He was younger than Corvalis, no more than twenty-three or twenty-four.

He hesitated atop the gangplank, and a long, awkward silence fell over the quay.

Halfdan muttered something, and Lord Titus cleared his throat and stepped forward.

"Emir Tanzir," said Titus in High Nighmarian, "I am Titus, Lord of House Iconias and an emissary of our Emperor. In the name of the Emperor Alexius Naerius of Nighmar, I greet..."

Tanzir took a deep breath and started forward.

Then his foot slipped, and to Caina's horror Tanzir tumbled down the gangplank, coming to a hard landing on the stone quay. She stepped forward, expecting to see a Kindred assassin atop the ship, hands extended from a shove.

But the Istarish soldiers atop the ship gaped at Tanzir, and Caina realized the emir had simply slipped.

For a moment no one moved.

Then Tanzir sat up with a groan, and the khalmir barked a command. Two of the Immortals stooped and helped the sweating emir to his feet. Titus blinked, nodded to himself, and stepped forward.

"My lord emir," he said in High Nighmarian, "are you injured?"

"I...I am well, I think," said Tanzir in the same language. His voice quivered with nervousness. "Yes. I am well. These robes. Very long. I tripped. You understand."

"Ah...yes," said Titus. "On behalf of the Emperor of Nighmar, I bid you welcome to Malarae. If you will permit, it will be my honor to escort you to the residence of the Padishah's Lord Ambassador."

"Ah," said Tanzir. "Yes. That is a...good idea, yes. To the residence. Um." He looked back at the ship. "Ah...the rest of my party. We should wait for them."

"Of course," said Titus with smooth aplomb, and the rest of Tanzir's men began to make their way down the gangplank.

Caina felt a sudden icy tingle against her skin, the muscles of her stomach clenching.

The presence of sorcery.

Ever since Maglarion had wounded her all those years ago, she had gained the ability to sense the presence of sorcery. The ability had become sharper as she grew older, and now she could often distinguish the degree and intensity of spells.

A man of about forty descended the gangplank, his gold-trimmed white robes gathered in one hand. He had a stern, hard face, with short black hair and a close-cropped black beard. The robed man reminded Caina of Rezir more than Tanzir did. Yet the robed man was not an emir or a soldier, but an Alchemist, a brother of Istarinmul's College of Alchemists. The Padishah ruled in Istarinmul…but the foundations of his power rested upon the sorcerous knowledge of the Master Alchemists.

Perhaps Tanzir had been sent as a figurehead, and this Alchemist would do the real negotiating.

Yet an oddity caught Caina's attention.

She had not seen many Alchemists, but she knew the patterns of their robes. A Master Alchemist wore a ceremonial white cloak with a gold-trimmed cowl. This man only wore a gold-trimmed white robe without a cloak. A full Alchemist, then, but not a Master.

Odd, that.

"My lord Titus," said Tanzir, regaining some of his poise, "this is my advisor, Ibrahmus Sinan, a full brother and Alchemist of the College."

Sinan bowed. "An honor, my lord." His High Nighmarian was flawless. "I hope that your wisdom shall help bring an end to this senseless war."

"That is my Emperor's hope as well," said Titus.

Several minor Istarish nobles disembarked from the ship, and Tanzir introduced them to Lord Titus. Titus in turn introduced his advisors and minor lords, and Halfdan as Master Basil Callenius. Tanzir listened with a distracted expression, while Sinan watched with cold black eyes.

"And this," said Titus, "is Master Anton Kularus, a merchant of coffee, and his, ah, companion…"

"Sonya Tornesti," said Halfdan.

"Yes, Sania Tornost," said Titus.

Tanzir had not been paying attention, but his eyes brightened at the mention of coffee. "Coffee? You have coffee in Malarae? I was under the impression that the noble drink was unknown in Istarinmul."

A brief flicker of irritation went over Sinan's face.

"It was until recently, my lord emir," said Corvalis with a bow, "but I completed a journey into the lands beyond Anshan and did a favor for Lord Titus, and obtained exclusive license to import coffee into Malarae."

"Splendid!" said Tanzir. "I wish to visit your establishment, Master Anton. I thought I would have to make this miserable trip without any coffee. And do you have bookshops in Malarae? I am a bit of a collector, you see, and…"

"My lord emir," said Sinan with a tight smile, "we have duties."

"What?" said Tanzir. "Yes, yes, of course. Until later, Master Anton." He looked at Caina once, opened his mouth, closed it, and turned back to Titus. The lord and the emir turned from the quay and began the long walk to the Imperial Citadel and the Lord Ambassador's residence, trailed by their followers. On the ship men in gray tunics began to unload chests from the hold. Slaves, Caina realized, her lips pressing into a hard line. Tanzir Shahan had brought his slaves with him to Malarae.

"Well," murmured Halfdan, moving alongside Caina and Corvalis. "What do you think of the Padishah's new Lord Ambassador?"

"My heart almost stopped when he fell," said Caina. "I thought someone had decided to assassinate him by pushing him off the damned ship."

Corvalis laughed. "Clumsy of him."

"He's no Rezir Shahan," said Caina, "that's plain."

Halfdan shrugged. "From all reports, Rezir's and Tanzir's mother Ashria dominates their family. Rezir ruled while he lived, but since Rezir met an untimely end at the Balarigar's hands," Caina scowled, "I believe the dowager amirja rules the family."

"Tanzir doesn't seem the sort to defy his mother," said Corvalis.

"Or anyone, really," said Halfdan. "I suspect most of the actual negotiating will fall to one of the other nobles."

"Or that Alchemist," said Caina. "Ibrahmus Sinan. Do you know anything about him?"

Halfdan shrugged. "Little enough. The College is a like our Magisterium, in that the Alchemists renounce their previous affiliations when they join the College. In theory, anyway. Sinan is no one of particular note, but he's apparently associated with House Shahan. Rezir relied on him as an advisor, as does Ashria, but that's all the Ghost circle in Istarinmul knows about him."

"He's not a Master Alchemist," said Caina.

"From what I understand," said Halfdan, "it's rather difficult to become a Master Alchemist. The Masters of the College can live decades, even centuries, longer than most men. You remember Callatas? He was at least two hundred years old. The Master Alchemists have some method of staving off aging and death...and as far as we know, that method itself is the test. If an Alchemist learns the method, he becomes a Master Alchemist."

"And if he fails, he dies of old age," said Corvalis. "Efficient, I suppose."

"Or the method kills him outright," said Caina. "Sorcery is rarely kind to an incompetent wielder."

"True," said Halfdan. He glanced at the procession making its way from the docks. "We should follow the emir to the Lord Ambassador's residence. It would be a bold assassin indeed who would strike Tanzir down in front of so many eyes..."

"And bold assassins are usually dead assassins," said Corvalis.

"Unless, of course, the assassin is smarter than we are," said Halfdan, "and has some clever plan we have been unable to foresee. Keep your eyes open."

Caina nodded, and followed Halfdan from the quay, her arm linked with Corvalis's. The procession wound its way through the docks, past the maze of warehouses, and to the Via Triumphalis. The broad, wide street led from the docks to the gates of the Imperial Citadel itself, and statues of ancient commanders upon horseback stood in the median, their stone faces stern and forbidding. In ancient times, victorious Emperors had enjoyed triumphal processions along this street, riding in a ceremonial chariot with gangs of Caerish captives bound behind them.

"A good view," said Corvalis, looking at the Imperial Citadel upon its mountain spur. "I can see why the Emperor wants to have new ambassadors march this way."

"Yes, the might of the Empire and all that," said Caina, looking at the surrounding buildings. Modest shops lined this part of the Via Triumphalis, with several levels of apartments rising above. Caina found herself scanning the rooftops, watching for any sign of movement.

"You keep looking up," said Corvalis.

"Yes," said Caina. "No one ever looks up. If I had been hired to kill Tanzir Shahan and I knew a good archer, I would split the fee with him and have …"

Even as she spoke, she saw a flicker of movement on one of the nearby rooftops.

Caina turned her head, trying not to make the movement obvious, and scanned the building. The shop on the first floor sold boots and sandals, while the remaining four stories of the building held apartments with balconies. She did not see anyone on the balconies or the roof. And any event it would not be unusual for someone to be on the roof. Malarae's summers were hot, and people often slept upon their roofs to escape the day's accumulated heat. But it was almost noon. No one would be sleeping on a roof in the middle of the day.

"What is it?" said Corvalis.

"Maybe nothing," said Caina. "Maybe not." It would look odd if she broke away from the crowd to dash into a shop. "Tell the others that a pair of sandals caught my eye, and I simply had to buy them." It was the sort of thing that Sonya Tornesti would do. "I'll catch up to you later."

"You should not go alone," said Corvalis.

"You're right, but you should stay with the procession," said Caina. "Anton Kularus cannot acquire the reputation as the kind of man who runs off after his mistress every time she decides to buy a new pair of sandals, not if he wants to keep the respect of the merchants."

Corvalis scowled, but nodded. "Be careful."

She slipped her arm from his. "I'm always careful."

"You," said Corvalis, "are usually a better liar than that."

He turned, walked to join Halfdan, and started complaining about Sonya's predilection for spending his money like water.

Caina hurried towards the shop, moving as fast as her gown and her sandals allowed. She avoided the shop itself and slipped into the alley next to the building. A narrow door stood in the brick wall, recessed in an alcove, and Caina tried the handle.

The door was unlocked.

That did not mean anything by itself. Most of Malarae's landlords preferred to avoid the expense of installing locks on their main doors. Yet Caina realized that this building stood in exactly the right place to command a view of the Via Triumphalis as it turned towards the Imperial Citadel itself. The rooftop would make an excellent platform for an archer who wanted to shoot someone in the procession.

Caina entered the hallway beyond the door. The interior was gloomy, the only illumination coming from a skylight atop the building's central stairwell. Caina slipped off her sandals and hurried forward, her bare feet making no sound against the stairs' worn boards. She reached the top floor and saw a ladder leading to a trapdoor.

The trapdoor stood open, sunlight falling into the corridor. Caina drew a throwing knife from her sleeve, tucked it into her teeth, and climbed to the roof. The flat tiles of red clay felt warm beneath her bare feet, a few barrels scattered here and there to catch rainwater.

Otherwise the rooftop was deserted.

Then she saw a flicker of motion near one of the barrels.

A man crouched there, clad in rough clothes and thick sandals. His clothes marked him as a common laborer, and he looked Istarish or Anshani. Yet he moved with the slow, expert stealth of a trained assassin.

A common laborer did not generally carry a quiver of arrows and a short recurved bow.

The weapon was Anshani, favored by Shahenshah's nobles on their endless hunts over the plateaus and plains of Anshan. Caina watched as the man moved around the barrel to the edge of the roof. He was trying to make up his mind, she realized, about whether or not he would take a shot at Tanzir.

Best not to give him the chance.

Caina glided forward, throwing knife in one hand.

And she did, the assassin apparently changed his mind and turned, bow still in hand.

For a moment he stared at her, stunned.

He raised the bow, in his hands a blur, and loosed an arrow.

Caina dodged and heard the buzzing hiss as the arrow shot past her head, the resonant thud as it sank into the ladder. She caught her balance and flung the throwing knife at the assassin. The man swung his bow like a club, deflecting the weapon. Caina stepped back and drew her ghostsilver dagger from its sheath, preparing herself for the assassin's attack.

But instead the man stepped back, snatching an odd-looking leather cord from his belt. Why would he do that? He had left himself open to another throwing knife. He would only do that if…

The assassin spun the cord over his head, and Caina saw the blur of lead weights at either end.

A bola.

If that thing hit her legs, it would entangle her long enough for the assassin to kill her. Or, if his aim was good enough, it could strike her throat, snap her neck, and kill her in the space between two heartbeats.

The assassin flung the bola, and Caina collapsed her legs, dropping hard to the clay roof tiles. The leather cord slammed hard into her stomach, and the impact felt like a blow from a wooden rod. But the lead weights struck the roof and bounced, and the cord did not entangle her.

The assassin lunged, raising his foot to crush her throat.

Caina slashed her ghostsilver dagger, the shining blade ripping into the assassin's right calf. The man hissed in pain, and Caina rolled sideways as the assassin fell. He landed hard upon his right knee, and Caina slashed her dagger.

The blade sliced through the assassin's throat, blood spraying from the wound. Caina stepped back and rammed the dagger between the assassin's ribs. The man stiffened, loosed a gurgling groan, and fell as Caina wrenched the weapon free.

She looked around, breathing hard, her stomach throbbing from the bola's impact. No had noticed the fight, and she heard no sounds of alarm from the street.

Nobody ever looked up.

Caina looked at the dead man and whispered a curse. If she had taken him alive, perhaps he would have provided useful information. On the other hand, he might well have disposed of her and then turned his attention to Tanzir.

Still, killing assassins did not trouble her.

But Corvalis had once been an assassin…

She pushed aside the tangle of emotions and examined the dead man. She found nothing in his pockets, save for a pair of daggers strapped to his thighs. His thick sandals were the sort favored by the Anshani. His bow and his arrows, likewise, were of Anshani make. He had no tattoos or identifying marks that Caina could see.

She straightened up with a grunt, cleaning her bloody dagger on his shirt. Her eyes fell upon the discarded bola. Something about that weapon scratched at her mind, recalled to her thoughts something she had read long ago ...

Then it clicked.

"Oh," said Caina.

With a chill she realized that she was very, very lucky to be alive.

If she had been even a half-second slower, she might lie dead upon the roof instead of the assassin.

Caina gathered her weapons, descended to the stairwell, retrieved her sandals, and checked her reflection in a rain barrel in the alley. She looked disheveled, but that could not be helped.

Considering how close she had come to death.

She went in pursuit of the procession, the bola coiled in her left hand.

"Gardeners," said Caina, rejoining Corvalis and Halfdan.

Corvalis raised an eyebrow. "You interrupted some poor soul tending a garden on his roof?"

"Something like that," said Caina, lifting the leather bola, the lead weights swinging.

Halfdan and Corvalis looked at the cord, and then both cursed in unison.

"You killed a Bostaji?" said Corvalis.

"One of the personal assassins of the Shahenshah of Anshan," said Caina. "I would have taken him alive, but..."

"Don't bother," said Halfdan, voice grim. "The man would have cut out his own tongue before betraying the Shahenshah."

"I am surprised you are alive at all," said Corvalis, his voice calm, but she knew him well enough to see that he had been shaken. "The Shahenshah's Gardeners are more dangerous than the Kindred." He shook his head. "Do you know what the Shahenshah does to nobles who betray him? They are taken to the heart of the Shahenshah's gardens, and left alone with one Bostaji. If the traitor can run to the gate before the Bostaji catches him, he's allowed to live. If not...the Bostaji strangles him with a bola."

"You've dealt with the Gardeners before?" said Halfdan.

"Aye," said Corvalis. "In Arzaxia, years ago, before I met Claudia again. An Anshani occultist defected to the Magisterium, and the Shahenshah sent the Bostaji after him. My father dispatched me to keep the occultist alive."

"Did you?" said Caina, curious. She had never heard this story.

Of course, there were things she had never told Corvalis.

"Barely, but yes," said Corvalis.

"Just as well," said Halfdan. "We'll need your knowledge. If the Bostaji are here, the Shahenshah does indeed want to assassinate Tanzir to prevent the Empire and Istarinmul from making peace." He glanced towards the procession. "The Emperor himself is receiving Tanzir at the Imperial Citadel tonight. I have secured an invitation from Lord Titus for myself, Anton Kularus…and Master Anton's chosen guest."

Caina shook her head. "Which is a polite way of saying Master Anton's mistress."

"Indeed," said Halfdan. "We must be there to keep watch over the emir."

Caina nodded.

"Out of curiosity," said Halfdan, "what did you do with the body?"

"I left it there," said Caina. "Someone will find it in a few days and report it to the civic militia."

Corvalis snorted. "We've left a lot of corpses for the civic militia lately."

"Aye," said Caina, looking at the procession.

She shivered.

There might be more corpses before this was done.

CHAPTER 7
THE ALCHEMIST

A few hours later, Caina strode through the doors of the House of Kularus.

The coffee house was quiet now, between the morning crowd and those who preferred to conduct business in the evening. By nightfall, Caina knew, the balconies would be filled with merchants and minor lords holding court.

Shaizid hurried over with a bow. "Mistress Sonya! This is a pleasure. How may I be of service?"

"Master Anton sent me," said Caina, using her Szaldic accent. "He says that the emir may be visiting the House of Kularus. Everything must be made clean, yes? The floors shiny, the railings polished, the tables free of crumbs."

Shaizid blinked. "Master Anton already sent the message."

Caina stepped closer and dropped her accent.

"I know," she said in Anshani, voice quiet, "but I wished to see our guests."

"Ah. Of course," said Shaizid. "This way, mistress."

He led her to the cellar and the secret armory.

"How have they been?" said Caina.

"As well as can be expected, given the grievous losses they have suffered," said Shaizid. "Muravin is grim, and speaks but little. And I have heard Mahdriva weeping in the night. Yet neither one has despaired, which is good." He sighed. "I know what it is to lose a loved one to violence."

"We all do, I fear," said Caina, thinking of her father. "How is the baby?"

"Imminent, I believe," said Shaizid. "Mistress Tanya visited at your behest, along with a physician from the temple of Minaerys. The child could come at any time. In the name of the Living Flame, I hope it is soon. It will give Mahdriva something to consider other than her grief."

"Has there been any sign of Nalazar?" said Caina.

"None," said Shaizid. "Neither he nor any members of the Malarae Kindred known have entered the House of Kularus. Nor have the footmen seen them outside. Possibly they are watching the House at night, out of sight of the watchmen, but if so they are exceedingly cautious."

"The Kindred know what they are about," said Caina. "Master Basil sent word to the other Ghost circles in Malarae. None of them have seen Nalazar, and they have reported nothing unusual from the local Kindred."

"Perhaps Nalazar has given up," said Shaizid.

"If only," said Caina. "No, he's Kindred. He will not stop until either he is dead or he captures Mahdriva." Again the riddle gnawed at her. Why would anyone spend so much money to steal the unborn child of a freedman's daughter? She had wondered if Mahdriva's husband had been a man of standing, the kind of man with powerful enemies, but he had been a freeborn carpenter employed by the College of Alchemists, and Ardaiza's and Ranai's husbands had both been masons. Certainly they were not the kind of men someone would hire the Kindred to kill.

So why kill them and take their unborn children?

It made no sense.

"I would like to see them," said Caina. "I have a few questions for Muravin."

"Of course, Balarigar," said Shaizid, crossing to the far door.

"Don't call me that."

Inside the barracks Mahdriva sat on one of the cots. She now had a proper dress of deep blue and looked healthier, though her cheeks were still drawn and dark circles ringed her eyes. Several spools of yarn rested next to her, and a pair of knitting needles clicked in her hands.

Muravin stood nearby, polishing a suit of chain mail on a stand. He had asked for weapons, and Caina had obliged. The former gladiator now had weapons enough to fight an entire army on his own.

Mahdriva started to stand. "Mistress Sonya."

"No, no, stay sitting," said Caina in Istarish, putting a hand on Mahdriva's shoulder.

Muravin put down his cloth and walked over to join them. For all his age, the former gladiator moved with the same efficiency and economy Caina had seen in Corvalis and other skilled fighters. If she had faced Muravin and not a Bostaji atop that roof, Caina doubted she would have survived the encounter.

"How are you?" said Caina.

"Very tired," said Mahdriva. "I am ready for this child to come, I think." She touched her stomach. "To pass the time I am making a blanket for him." She held up the cloth dangling from her needles. When finished, it would be a blue blanket adorned with yellow lions, worked with cunning skill.

"It's beautiful," said Caina, touching the soft yarn with one hand.

"I choose lions," said Mahdriva, "because they are brave, like my child shall be. Just as my husband was, before..."

She looked away.

"It will be a fine blanket," said Caina.

"It is kind of you to speak to us," said Muravin, "but I suspect you have questions for me."

He was clever. "Yes. For you, specifically, if you can spare the time."

Muravin snorted. "I am doing nothing but waiting. Come. We shall speak." He led Caina into the corner of the barracks, and she heard the tap of Mahdriva's needles resume.

"How are you?" said Caina.

Muravin shrugged. "I am as I always am. I do what I must." He looked at her and nodded. "You killed someone today."

"How did you know?" said Caina, looking at her hands. Had she missed a blood spot? She didn't think any of the Bostaji's blood had gotten on her, but...

"Your eyes," said Muravin. "I know what the eyes of a killer look like. Do I not see them every time I look into a mirror?"

"I did," said Caina. "It was necessary."

"I do not doubt that," said Muravin, "but we are still killers." He glanced at Mahdriva. "Which is why I do not want her to overhear us. Such talk...upsets her, and she has endured enough suffering."

"Wise words," said Caina, looking at Mahdriva. That could have been Caina, waiting for her first child. But then Maglarion had come...and her life had taken a very different path. "I came to talk about something else."

"Has there been any sign of Nalazar?" said Muravin.

"None," said Caina. "He's lying low, I think, waiting for you to show yourself. Do you know a man named Ibrahmus Sinan?"

Muravin frowned. "Why?"

"He arrived with Tanzir Shahan today," said Caina. "His advisor, I think."

"I do know him," said Muravin. "He is an Alchemist of the College, and not as cruel as some of them."

Caina blinked. "Indeed?"

"He was once a slave, I believe," said Muravin. "When the power manifested in him, he was taken to the College, as are all who display arcane power. So he is not as cruel or lordly as many of the Alchemists."

"He knows you, then?" said Caina.

Muravin nodded. "Not well, but we have spoken in passing. Perhaps I should go to him. He might know who has hired the Kindred to attack my daughters."

"I would not recommend that," said Caina.

"Why not?" said Muravin.

Because Sinan was a sorcerer, and sorcerers were not trustworthy. But Caina stopped herself from saying that. That argument had not persuaded Corvalis during their disagreement about Claudia's plan to ally with Mihaela, and that disagreement had almost led to disaster. Muravin would see Sinan as a potential patron and a powerful protector, not as a dangerous sorcerer.

"Because it would put you and Mahdriva at unnecessary risk," said Caina. "The emir has at least three hundred men in his embassy. Any one of them could be Kindred. If one of them sees you talking to Sinan, they might well follow you back here."

Muravin frowned. "But the Alchemist might know who hired the Kindred to attack us."

"Would he?" said Caina. "Do you think whoever hired the Kindred to murder your unborn children announced his plans to the College of Alchemists? Would Sinan be able to protect Mahdriva from the Kindred? Truly? Could he hide you from the assassins the way the Ghosts have done? Would he care that much?"

Muravin said nothing for a long moment.

"No," he said at last. "He would not. He would be sympathetic, I think...but here in Malarae, he could not help us as he could in Istarinmul." He sighed. "Assuming he would help us in Istarinmul. But why have you helped us so much, Ghost?"

"Because," said Caina, "I don't like slavers."

"Well and good, but I am not a slave any longer," said Muravin, "and neither is Mahdriva."

Caina frowned, caught off guard. "Because I do not wish to see her child murdered. Is that not enough?"

Muravin looked at Mahdriva. "It is. Do not think me ungrateful, Mistress Sonya." He snorted. "Though if that is your real name, I am the Padishah himself. I am grateful, Ghost...but life has taught me that nothing comes without a price. And I am curious what price you and Master Basil shall extract for your aid."

"Oh, there will be a price," said Caina. "You're going to become one of us."

Muravin frowned. "A Ghost?"

"The Ghosts always have need of talent and skill," said Caina, "and how many men fight as well as Muravin, the champion of the Arena of Padishahs? That is what Master Basil does, you know." She thought of Riogan and Komnene and Ark and Annika and Marzhod, all the men and women Halfdan had rescued over the years...and then reshaped in his own image, just as he had done with her. "He rescues people…and then he recruits them."

"As he did with you?" said Muravin.

"Yes," said Caina. "And you will have need of employment, will you not? Champion or not, you're a little old to hire out as a caravan guard."

"Cruel," said Muravin, "but true." He hesitated. "A favor to ask of you, Ghost."

"Ask," said Caina.

"The Emperor is offering a feast to welcome the emir Tanzir?" said Muravin.

"He is," said Caina.

"And you and the other Ghosts shall be there, to keep the emir safe from assassins?" said Muravin.

Caina frowned. "How do you know about that?"

Muravin shrugged. "It is obvious. Why else would you question me so closely about Sinan and Tanzir Shahan? I know how the emirs scheme and plot against each other. Many wish the war with the Empire to end…but some wish it to continue, and how better to continue the war than by murdering the Padishah's ambassador in the Emperor's capital?"

"That is so," said Caina. "What favor do you wish to ask?"

"Permit me to accompany you," said Muravin.

"Absolutely not," said Caina. "If anyone recognizes you, Mahdriva will be danger."

"You can disguise me," said Muravin. "I have seen how easily you shift from a merchant's concubine to…whatever you truly are."

Caina decided to let that pass. "I have had practice. Can you masquerade as anything other than a former gladiator?"

"No," said Muravin, "but I can pass as your bodyguard. Master Anton seems like the sort of man who would hire a former gladiator as his guard."

That could work.

"Perhaps," said Caina. "But why take the risk?"

"I wish to see the embassy for myself," said Muravin. "It occurs to me that whoever brought this woe upon my family might have come north with the emir's companions. Once we escaped Istarinmul and eluded Nalazar, our enemy might have come to Malarae to take a hand in the search."

"That makes sense," said Caina. "Though we still don't know how Nalazar found you at the Inn of the Broken Wheel."

"He must have followed me," said Muravin. "I ask this of you, Ghost. I am useless caged here. Let me aid you. I know more of Istarinmul than any of your Ghosts. Perhaps I shall be of use to you."

It was a risk. Muravin could pass as a former gladiator turned bodyguard easily enough, but that was exactly the sort of man Nalazar would be hunting. But surely there were hundreds of such men in the Imperial capital, and Malarae was a city of a million. Nalazar could not find Muravin overnight.

And Muravin's knowledge might prove useful. The Bostaji proved that the Shahenshah wanted Tanzir dead...but that did not mean the Shahenshah was the only man who wanted Tanzir dead. Muravin might see something useful.

It was a risk...but a calculated one, and it might have a useful payoff.

"Very well," said Caina. "Come along, then. You're going to have to dress for a banquet."

CHAPTER 8
THE IMPERIAL CITADEL

Caina had been a Ghost for eleven years, half of her life, and she had never set foot within the Imperial Citadel.

Caina's tasks for the Ghosts had taken her from Rasadda in the east to Marsis in the west and Cyrica Urbana in the south, and yet for all the time she had spent in Malarae, she had never entered the Imperial Citadel, the heart of the Empire, where the Emperor lived and the Imperial Curia met.

She had to admit the vast fortress was much more impressive up close.

Caina walked arm-in-arm with Corvalis, climbing the broad stone ramp that cut its way up the mountain spur to the Citadel's outer wall. The ramp would make a tempting target for an invading army, but anyone foolish enough to attack would face the archers and war engines lining the Citadel's towering outer wall. Little wonder the Imperial Citadel had never fallen to an invading army.

Corvalis laughed.

"What is it?" said Caina.

He glanced over his shoulder at the guests making their way up the ramp to the gates. "Cruel of the Emperor to make them leave their coaches at the foot of the ramp."

Halfdan shrugged. "It is traditional."

"Though unpleasant," said Corvalis, "to make those accustomed to riding everywhere to walk up the ramp."

"The exercise does them good," said Halfdan.

Muravin grunted. Thanks to Caina's efforts, he looked quite a bit different. He had dyed his beard and hair black. The careful application of makeup gave the left side of his face a series of scars, his lip drooping from the damage. He wore gleaming chain mail beneath the livery of the House

61

of Kularus, and carried a broadsword and a dagger at his belt, rather than his preferred weapons. She only hoped no one would recognize him.

They reached the massive arch of the Citadel's outer gate. A centurion of the Imperial Guard stood there, flanked by a half-dozen Guards in their black armor and purple cloaks.

"Ah, Tylas," said Halfdan to the centurion, "you've come up in the world, I see."

Tylas looked at Halfdan, his expression hard beneath the black helm, and nodded. The man was a centurion of the Imperial Guard…but he was also a Ghost.

"Master Basil," said Tylas, looking at Corvalis and Caina.

"These are my guests," said Halfdan, "Anton Kularus and Sonya Tornesti, both of Malarae. How are matters here?"

"Well enough," said Tylas, lowering his voice. "There are Guards at all the entrances, and I have a century of trustworthy men assigned to watch over the Lord Ambassador's residence in the city."

"Stay vigilant," said Halfdan. "There already was one attempt on the emir's life at the Via Triumphalis. The Bostaji of Anshan are after him, and it is possible he has other enemies as well."

Tylas nodded. "The emir will remain safe, Master Basil." He looked at the line of nobles and merchants and magi climbing the ramp and waved his hand. "You may enter. Next!"

Caina walked through the gates and into the Imperial Citadel's outer courtyard. The great white mass of the Citadel rose up before her, domes and towers and basilicas and ramparts blended together in a huge mass of stone. The banners of the Empire, a golden eagle upon a purple field, flew from the towers. Already hundreds of guests filled the courtyard, lords and merchants and master magi in their stark black robes. Many guests had brought a few servants and bodyguards of their own, but Imperial Guards stood everywhere, keeping watch from the walls and the entrances into the Citadel proper. Globes of enspelled glass threw bright light from the ramparts. It would take a very bold assassin to try anything here.

Just as it would take a bold assassin to shoot Tanzir Shahan upon the Via Triumphalis.

"There is the Emperor," said Halfdan.

For the first time, Caina looked at the Emperor she served.

Alexius Naerius, Emperor of Nighmar, stood on the steps to the main doors of the Citadel proper, Tanzir at his side. He was a tall man in his sixties, clad in the white-trimmed purple robe of the Emperor. Caina thought he looked…tired. Sad, even. The most powerful lords in the Empire stood clustered around him. Caina saw Corbould Maraeus, Titus Iconias, and a dozen others, along with the heads of the merchant collegia and several of the high magi.

Corvalis grunted. "Shorter than I expected."

"Who?" said Caina. "The Emperor?"

"Aye," said Corvalis. "But my father hates him, so he must be a decent fellow."

"The emir should be safe enough," said Caina, looking at the score of scowling Imperial Guards near the Emperor, hands on their sword hilts, eyes scanning the crowds with ceaseless vigilance. "Anyone who tries for the emir will have to deal with the Imperial Guards."

And the Immortals, for that matter. Six of the skull-helmed soldiers stood near the emir, no doubt a concession to his rank.

"True," said Halfdan. "Unless, of course, the Shahenshah decides the best way to continue the war is to have both the Emperor and the emir murdered in the Imperial Citadel."

Caina hadn't considered that. "Someone is always trying to kill the Emperor."

"Aye," said Halfdan. "Tanzir is as safe here as anywhere in Malarae...but there is no such thing as perfect safety. Remain vigilant. Come, Master Anton. It's time to mingle."

They moved through the crowds, Halfdan and Corvalis greeting the other merchants, Caina keeping an expression of vapid boredom on her face. She was glad she had taken the time to bathe and change her gown after fighting the Bostaji. Now she wore a sheer cloth-of-gold gown that utterly failed to match her dyed hair...though Sonya Tornesti would think it matched her hair. Jewels glittered on her fingers and at her ears, a silver chain dipping into the gown's low neckline. The sleeves and bodice felt tight against her skin, too tight to conceal weapons, though she had knives hidden in her boots, and the curved ghostsilver dagger rested in a sheath at her belt.

She listened as Halfdan and Corvalis discussed the state of trade with the merchants, nodding in the right place, laughing at the jokes whether or not they were funny. But her eyes roved over the crowds, watching for any sign of the Bostaji or other assassins. Both native-born Anshani and Istarish men usually had bronze-colored skin and dark hair and eyes, and an Anshani Bostaji could pass unnoticed among the emir's guards and advisors. But like the Kindred, the Bostaji recruited men from every nation and tribe. For all she knew an assassin could look like one of the cold-eyed barbarians from beyond the Imperial Pale in the far north.

Muravin played his part well. He stood expressionless at Corvalis's left, his eyes likewise scanning the crowds for any sign of threat. Once Ibrahmus Sinan drew near, his white robes glittering in the light from the globes, and Caina feared that he would recognize Muravin. But Sinan's eyes passed over them without recognition, and the Alchemist continued through the crowd.

Caina caught Muravin's eyes as Corvalis and Halfdan listened to a grain merchant discuss the cost of shipping, and the former gladiator gave a tiny shake of his head. He had not seen anyone he suspected of sending the Kindred after him, nor had he seen any potential assassins. That was a relief.

Still, if it came to violence, Caina was glad she had brought the former gladiator.

"And the rate of shipping from Cyrioch has increased by at least nine and a half percent," said the grain merchant, his voice dour.

"Egregious," said Halfdan with a shake of his head.

"Truly," said the merchant, "and…"

The Emperor climbed to the top of the steps to the Citadel's main doors, and a hush fell over the crowd.

"Men of the Empire," said Alexius Naerius, his voice hoarse, yet still commanding. "Men of Istarinmul. I bid you welcome to the Imperial Citadel, to the very heart of the Empire of Nighmar. In the last year our Empire has been ravaged by war, both upon the land and the sea. Yet our Legions have defended us with stern valor, and we have not surrendered an inch of land to our foes."

That overlooked the fleet Kylon Shipbreaker had destroyed upon the western sea. But truth, Halfdan often said, was of only limited utility in politics.

"But enemies can once again become friends," said the Emperor, "and the Padishah of Istarinmul has seen wisdom, and dispatched his cousin Tanzir Shahan, the emir of the Vale of Fallen Stars, to negotiate a treaty of peace between our two nations."

The Emperor beckoned, and Tanzir stepped to his side.

The emir licked his lips, looking back and forth over the crowd, and Caina saw the sweat dripping from beneath his turban. The man was plainly terrified, and for a moment of awful embarrassment Caina wondered if he would lose his balance and fall down the stairs in front of the assembled high nobles of the Empire.

"Yes," said Tanzir in High Nighmarian at last. "Yes, peace. Our Padishah desires peace. With you. The Empire, I mean. But all of you are part of the Empire…so, yes, peace. Because the Padishah is wise. Very wise. And peace is good. So…ah, peace."

He fell silent, and the Emperor coughed.

A smattering of polite applause went up from the crowd. Caina glanced at Sinan, saw a hint of contempt on the Alchemist's face.

"Thank you for your wise words, emir," said the Emperor without a hint of levity. "I look forward to hearing the results of your discussions with Lord Titus." He turned back to the guests. "Meanwhile, I urge you to enjoy the hospitality of the Empire, as we prepare to inaugurate this new era of peace."

The guests returned to their conversations.

"What shall we do now?" said Corvalis.

"Now?" said Halfdan. "Now we shall eat and drink." He took a flute of wine from the tray of a passing servant. "This is the finest Caerish wine, and I urge you to avail yourself of the opportunity." He smiled. "If drinking coffee all day hasn't ruined your palette."

"I can get drunk with the best of them," said Corvalis.

"That is exactly what I mean," said Halfdan. "Wine is…"

He fell silent, and Caina saw a man in a white robe walking towards them.

Ibrahmus Sinan.

Muravin looked away, as if scanning the crowd.

"Good evening, honored sir," said Halfdan, switching to High Nighmarian. "You are a member of the honored emir's party, if I may be so bold?"

"I am," said Sinan. "You are?"

Halfdan bowed. "Basil Callenius, a merchant of the Imperial Collegium of jewelers." He gestured. "This is Anton Kularus, an associate of mine, and his…companion, Sonya Tornesti."

Corvalis bowed, and Caina gripped her skirts and did a curtsy.

"Indeed," said Sinan, ignoring Caina. "I am Ibrahmus Sinan, a full brother of the College of Alchemists of Istarinmul. Fame of your coffee house has spread far and wide, Master Anton. It seems the emir himself wishes to visit."

"Truly?" said Corvalis. "He would be welcome. All are welcome at the House of Kularus."

Sinan smiled. "Provided they have coin to spend, of course."

"Well," said Corvalis. "A man must make a living however he can."

"Might we be of service to you, learned one?" said Halfdan. "Do you wish to purchase some gems from me? I understand Alchemist can make potent arcane objects from the proper gemstones. Perhaps some emeralds, cut just so…"

"No," said Sinan. "Rather, I have come with a warning for Master Anton."

"Oh?" said Corvalis, lifting his eyebrows. Caina recognized the dangerous smile on his face. "I always appreciate warnings."

"You should," said Sinan. "Not all the nobles of Istarinmul approve of our Padishah's wisdom in making peace with your Emperor."

"From what I understand," said Halfdan, "Rezir Shahan started the war, and lost both Marsis and his life. The wisdom of peace should be apparent."

"It should be," said Sinan, "but it was not apparent to Rezir, and it is not apparent to many in Istarinmul. Or in the Empire or Anshan, I imagine.

And how easy to continue the war by murdering the Lord Ambassador in Malarae?"

"I confess," said Corvalis, "such a thought had occurred to me, but such matters are far beyond a simple merchant of coffee."

"They are," said Sinan, "unless the Lord Ambassador is murdered at the simple coffee merchant's establishment. The emir has taken quite an interest in your establishment, and wishes to visit tomorrow. An excellent opportunity for an assassin."

Corvalis shrugged. "I have guards, and the emir has his Immortals. I'm sure Imperial Guards will accompany him as well."

"Nevertheless," said Sinan, "be on your guard. Make certain your workers are trustworthy." He peered at Muravin. "Such as this disreputable fellow. What is your name?"

Muravin turned, blinking, and for an alarmed moment Caina was certain Sinan would recognize him.

"He is mute," said Caina, making sure her Szaldic accent was thick. "He was once a slave, yes? His cruel master, he cuts out his tongue to make sure his secrets are safe. Then he flees to Cyrioch, and Anton finds him, gives him a job."

Sinan gave her an annoyed look, his lips pressed together.

Corvalis shrugged. "I don't own slaves, but I have secrets that must be kept."

"Yes, the price of coffee in Malarae," said Sinan. "A dire secret, I'm sure." He looked at Muravin, and for an instant seemed so angry that Caina thought he might attack. "Heed my warning, Master Anton. It is amazing how quickly a merchant can fall into penury when a nobleman is murdered under his roof. If you will excuse me."

He strode away, his robes flowing behind him.

Muravin let out a long breath. "I fear he recognized me. He seemed most wroth."

"Have you forgotten that you are mute?" said Halfdan. "Good thinking, by the way."

"Thank you," said Caina. "And I don't think he recognized you, Muravin. You said he used to be a slave?" Muravin nodded. "I think…I think he doesn't like to be reminded of what he was. That sometimes happens when a man climbs from poverty to wealth. Anything that reminds him of the past infuriates him, because it reminds him of who he used to be."

"That was quite profound," said Halfdan.

"Why, thank you," said Caina.

"And likely accurate," said Halfdan. "Still, he thought to warn us against assassins. We can be confident he is not involved in the plots against Tanzir's life."

Caina shrugged. "Or he is, and his warning was to disassociate himself from any attacks on the emir."

"Regardless, we will heed his warning," said Halfdan. "And speaking of the emir..."

Caina saw Tanzir Shahan walking towards them. The emir's ceremonial robes of red and gold glittered in the light from the enspelled globes, and for an uncharitable moment Caina thought it made him look like a polished apple. Two Immortals followed him, grim and silent in their skull-faced helms, the blue glow of their eyes glimmering deep within the eyes of the black skulls.

Caina felt herself tense, and fought to keep her expression calm. She had never been this close to an Immortal without fighting for her life.

Halfdan bowed and spoke in High Nighmarian. "My lord emir. You honor us with your presence, and I am pleased to see you again."

"Yes," said Tanzir. He swallowed. "It is good to see you again, ah..."

"Basil Callenius," said Halfdan, smoothly stepping into Tanzir's lapse of memory. "A master merchant of the Imperial Collegium of jewelers. And this is..."

"Anton Kularus!" said Tanzir. "Master of the House of Kularus."

Corvalis bowed. "At your service, my lord emir."

"Your establishment," said Tanzir. "I would like to visit it on the morrow."

"I would be honored," said Corvalis.

Tanzir's eyes lit up, and for a moment he reminded Caina of a child promised a treat.

"We could talk...business, yes, that is how you say it?" said Tanzir. "There are many coffee plantations in the Vale of Fallen Stars. For Istarish coffee is the finest coffee in the world."

"I had heard," said Corvalis, "that the men of Anshan grew the best coffee."

"Nonsense!" said Tanzir. "Once we have peace, we shall have new opportunities. You can buy coffee from my plantations to sell in Malarae, and we shall both be rich. There is no finer pleasure than sitting with a cup of Istarish coffee and reading a book." He looked wistful.

"You mentioned, lord emir," said Halfdan, "that you might wish to visit a book shop as well? There are several near the House of Kularus."

Tanzir brightened again. "Are there? That would be splendid. It is hard to find works in High Nighmarian in Istarinmul, especially since the war began."

"Of course," said Corvalis. "If you have no objection, I would be happy to show you some of Malarae's book shops."

"Truly?" said Tanzir, smiling. "I did not think you would appreciate books, Master Anton." He flinched. "Forgive me. I did not mean...well, it is rare for a merchant to spend time reading for pleasure..."

Corvalis laughed. "I fear your observation is correct, my lord emir. I have never held much interest in books." He put his right hand on Caina's back. "But Sonya has something of a passion for them."

Tanzir looked at Caina in surprise. "A woman? Truly?"

Caina shrugged. "I must have something to amuse myself while Anton is busy making money, no?"

"Indeed," said Tanzir. "I suppose...I suppose that makes sense. In Istarinmul it is rare for women to read. In fact, if any of the female slaves are caught reading, Mother has them whipped and sold to the first dealer who will take them." He swallowed. "Mother has strong opinions on the matter."

She sounded, Caina thought, a great deal like Caina's own mother.

"While I will be occupied with business," said Corvalis, "I am sure Sonya would be happy to show you the book shops of Malarae. If, of course, it would not be beneath the dignity of an emir."

Caina appreciated his cleverness. If gave Caina a chance to keep an eye on Tanzir, and hopefully keep him away from any assassins. And perhaps she could learn if anyone else had targeted the hapless emir.

Tanzir's eyes kept twitching, and Caina realized he was trying very hard not to stare at the low neckline of her gown.

Well. That would be awkward.

Caina would have to make sure she stayed in public with him.

Though she suspected Tanzir might well faint from nervousness if he ever found himself alone with a woman.

"I would be delighted, of course," said Caina. She reached over and patted Muravin's arm. "But only if you let me borrow your bodyguard, Anton. I feel ever so much safer with him. And he is mute, yes? So my lord emir need not fear that he shall reveal any of your secrets."

"Of course," said Corvalis. "Your safety is ever my first concern, my dear."

And if more Bostaji came after Tanzir, Muravin's skill with weapons would prove useful.

"Propriety," said Tanzir. "Yes, we must keep to propriety. And books. I look forward to the books. Also the coffee."

He stammered a few more words, turned, and marched away, the Immortals following like steel shadows.

Corvalis lifted his hand to cover a cough, but Caina saw him laughing behind his palm.

"The emir seems rather taken with you, Sonya," said Halfdan.

"Gods save me," said Caina. She looked at Corvalis. "You had to mention the books, didn't you?"

Corvalis shrugged. "It worked, didn't it? You can keep an eye on

Tanzir more easily, at least for a few hours. And I'll find some excuse to accompany you. With the help of our mute friend here," Muravin glowered at him, "we should be able to keep the emir safe from assassins."

Caina nodded, her eyes following Tanzir as he crossed the courtyard.

"Sinan seems to have a great deal of contempt for him," said Halfdan.

"It's not hard to see why," said Corvalis. "The emir is not the sort of man to inspire respect."

"No," said Caina, watching the servants following after the Immortals. "No, he's not. With a brother like Rezir Shahan, it's not surprising he learned to avoid drawing attention to himself." She felt a moment's pang of sympathy for Tanzir. Having Rezir as an elder brother, as the head of a noble House, could not have been a pleasant way to grow up. "Likely he never expected to become the emir, and hid himself away on his family's estates with coffee and books. Now he has to negotiate peace between the Empire and the Padishah."

"Little wonder the Padishah sent him," said Halfdan, "if he truly desires peace. Lord Titus will conclude negotiations in no time."

Caina nodded. "I think..."

Her voice trailed off.

One of the servants following Tanzir, a short, muscular man, carried a tray of food in his hands. He looked little different than the other servants, and wore the same black livery. Yet his belt looked longer than the others, knotted at the side...and a pair of lead weights hung at the end of his belt.

"A bola," hissed Caina. "That servant's Bostaji."

"Follow him," said Halfdan, his face calm as he glanced at the servant. "Don't kill him, not unless Tanzir is in danger. If you attack him, the Imperial Guards might kill you both before they bother to ask questions."

"I will," said Caina, and touched Muravin on the shoulder.

The former gladiator nodded, the fake scars making him look fiendish.

"Anton," announced Caina loud enough for the others to hear. "I am not feeling well. I think I shall lie down."

"There is a garden in the outer courtyard," said Halfdan, "where guests can rest."

"Go," said Corvalis with an irritated flip of his hand. "Take my bodyguard, too."

"As you wish," said Caina with a sniff. She set off through the crowd, Muravin trailing after her...and kept her eyes on the disguised Bostaji. The servant broke away from the crowds and circled around the great stone mass of the Imperial Citadel.

"Where is he going?" muttered Muravin.

"The kitchens, most likely," said Caina. "His tray is empty."

"Might he have fed poisoned food to the emir?" said Muravin.

"I doubt it," said Caina. The Bostaji headed with brisk strides towards a narrow door in the side of the Citadel. The entrance to the kitchens, Caina suspected. "The emir will not eat until the banquet proper starts. So that Bostaji might be slipping off to poison his food."

"If we go any closer, he will see us," said Muravin.

"I know," said Caina. "Wait a moment."

She paused at the edge of the crowd, and the Bostaji vanished into the servants' door.

"Go," said Caina.

They crossed the courtyard. Caina reached for her ghostsilver dagger and loosened the weapon in its sheath. No one moved in the servants' entrance, and Caina realized that she had seen no one else go in and out of that door.

Muravin reached for the door's handle.

Caina put a hand on his forearm. Muravin stopped, looked at her, and Caina put a finger to her lips. She gestured to the side, and Muravin nodded and stepped to the right of the door.

Then Caina stepped forward, gripped the handle, and pulled open the door, ducking behind it as she did so.

And a throwing knife flashed out of the doorway.

Muravin sprang forward, sword leaping into his hand. Caina caught a glimpse of the Bostaji, his face a cold mask as he raised a dagger. But Muravin slammed the hilt of his sword into the Bostaji, staggering him. Before the assassin could cry out or raise his weapon, Muravin slapped his free hand over the assassin's mouth, drew back his sword, and rammed it into the Bostaji's chest just below the breastbone.

The assassin went rigid, but Muravin drove him against the wall inside the door. A moment later he went limp, and Muravin eased him to the floor and tugged his blade free.

There was quite a lot of blood.

"I regret killing him," said Muravin, in the same tone of voice he might have used to regret dropping a glass of wine. "Master Basil said we were not to kill him."

"He would have killed us," said Caina, looking around. No one had seen the fighting. She stepped into the corridor, taking care to keep her skirts away from the pool of blood, and searched the corpse. Again, as with the Bostaji on the roof, she found nothing useful. He wore his bola in place of a belt, and it had been disguised so well that hardly anyone would have noticed the lead weights. Caina found three more throwing knives in his pockets, but nothing else.

No clues, no hints, nothing. Save for his unusually muscled build, the dead assassin looked like any other servant of the Imperial Citadel. The Bostaji knew how to blend into their surroundings.

She shook her head and straightened up, and Muravin cleaned his sword on the dead man and sheathed his blade.

"Come," said Caina. "We'll have to tell Basil to let Tylas know about the corpse…and to keep watch for any additional assassins."

But no Bostaji showed themselves for the rest of the night.

CHAPTER 9
DIPLOMACY

The next morning Caina awoke, tired and groggy.

The Emperor's banquet had dragged on until midnight, and Caina had kept watch for any additional assassins. Yet Tanzir had returned to the Lord Ambassador's residence at the foot of the Imperial Citadel safe and sound, and Caina and Corvalis had retreated to their townhouse for a few hours of sleep.

She was alone when she awoke. Corvalis often slept worse than she did. She climbed to her feet and worked through the unarmed forms until sweat dripped down her face and her arms trembled from exertion. After she bathed and arranged her hair in an elaborate crown, noting that she would need to apply more of Theodosia's vile-smelling dye soon. She dressed in a teal gown, again cut lower than she would have preferred, the curved dagger on her hip and knives hidden in her boots, jewels flashing on her fingers and in her ears.

She examined herself in the mirror and gave an approving nod. She looked quite good, which pleased her...and that thought troubled her.

For she was not truly Sonya Tornesti, mistress of Anton Kularus. She was Caina Amalas, Ghost nightfighter, and she had disguised herself as everything from a countess to a scullery maid. The gowns and jewelry were only another disguise and nothing more. She was a Ghost, and she would use whatever disguise served her best, whether rags or a fine gown.

But she liked wearing the gown, in a way she had not liked wearing the armor of a caravan guard.

And she liked that Corvalis could see her like this.

She pushed aside the thought and went join Corvalis.

He awaited her in the entry hall, sword in hand as he worked through a number of thrusts. Like Muravin, he moved with the brutal efficiency of the trained killer. Unlike Muravin, he looked good doing it. It was odd that she had fallen in love with an assassin, a former member of the Kindred. Yet he had left the Kindred, had risked everything to save his sister's life. And now he helped the Ghosts to fight against the magi and the corrupt lords, the men who had turned Corvalis into what he was.

She descended the stairs and kissed him.

"Well." Corvalis grinned, sliding his sword back into its sheath. "You are glad to see me."

"If you brought a book with you," said Caina, "you could read while you waited."

He laughed. "Books are your amusement, not mine. Reading is…a tool, like a whetstone or a hammer. You use it when you need it, and then set it aside. Like when I receive a letter from Claudia at Caer Magia. I read it to learn what she says, not for the pleasure of the act itself. I will never fathom how you can do it for amusement."

"It would give you something to occupy your time while you wait for me to prepare," said Caina.

He grinned. "You could prepare more quickly."

She raised an eyebrow. "It takes more work for a woman to make herself ready for a gathering than a man. You need only put on a coat, shine your boots, and make certain you don't have any cheese stuck in your teeth."

"Well," said Corvalis. "You do look lovely."

"Thank you," said Caina.

His hands slid down her hips and tugged her closer. "Though you would look lovelier with nothing on at all."

She smiled. "Bold man. Later." Her smile faded. "After we've kept Tanzir alive for another day. Thank you for coming along."

"He is visiting my coffee house," said Corvalis. He barked his harsh laugh. "Though it is actually your coffee house. I just playact as the owner. Theodosia would be proud."

"I hope that does not trouble you," said Caina.

"Why would it?" said Corvalis. "Certainly it is an improvement over murdering my father's enemies."

"And thank you for coming along to the book shops later," said Caina. "I confess I would not enjoy fending off Tanzir's advances all afternoon, but I doubt he would have the nerve with you nearby."

"I doubt he would have the nerve if you were alone with him in a locked room," said Corvalis. "Our emir does not seem the bold sort."

"No," said Caina. "With a brother like Rezir, can you blame him? And if his mother is anything like Rezir…little wonder Tanzir prefers not to put himself forward."

"You sound sympathetic," said Corvalis.

"I am," said Caina. "His mother reminds me of mine."

"He is besotted with you, that is plain," said Corvalis. He made a show of looking her up and down. "Not that I could blame him."

"Flatterer," said Caina. "Come. Let us welcome the Lord Ambassador to the House of Kularus."

She turned to go.

"Caina," said Corvalis, voice quiet.

She looked back at him. She remembered the first time she had met him in Cyrioch, when he had been hunting the master magus Ranarius to save his sister Claudia from her prison of living stone.

"Be careful," said Corvalis. "I would be…upset if anything happened to you."

She felt a pang.

Something would happen to her, sooner or later. Caina had taken tremendous risks as a Ghost, had gambled her life again and again. So far, she had won out in the end. But someday she would be a half-step too slow, and then she would die.

Or the same thing would happen to Corvalis.

She shivered, and suddenly understood the deeper allure of the gowns and the jewelry.

Because she did not want to give up the life she now shared with Corvalis. Not for any reason.

"I love you," said Caina.

He smiled. "I love you, too." He extended his arm. "Shall we?"

Tanzir Shahan arrived an hour and a half late, which was earlier than Caina had expected.

Merchants and nobles packed the House of Kularus, filling every booth and table. Caina suspected most of them wanted to speak with the Lord Ambassador to gain some advantage in trade or prestige. Shaizid's team of servants and maids hurried back and forth, carrying trays of coffee and food, and the smell of roasting coffee and baking cakes filled the air.

"Here they come," murmured Corvalis.

Caina stood with Corvalis and Halfdan on the main floor, near the table they had reserved for the emir and his companions. The footmen pulled open the main doors, and a pair of black-armored Immortals strode into the House of Kularus, the eerie blue glow shining from deep within their black skull helms.

A hush fell over the coffee house.

Shaizid hurried forward and bowed. "Master Anton, I wish to present

Lord Titus of House Iconias and the Lord Ambassador of Istarinmul, the emir Tanzir Shahan."

Lord Titus walked through the doors, followed by a pair of Imperial Guards. Tanzir walked at his side, breathing heavily, sweat glistening on his face. The day was growing hot, and Caina suspected the walk had not been pleasant for him.

Corvalis bowed. "My lords, I welcome you to the House of Kularus."

"Master Anton," said Titus, looking around. "So this is where my seneschal has been buying all that marvelous coffee."

"Indeed, my lord," said Corvalis. "Your patronage honors us."

Tanzir's expression brightened as he took in the coffee house. "That smells...yes, that smells delightful. Master Basil. I am surprised to see you here. I thought you sold jewels."

Halfdan shrugged. "Master Anton is a friend of mine. And I do enjoy coffee. Though I much prefer wine."

Titus laughed. "A man of taste!"

"Wine has its place," said Tanzir, "but there is nothing better than coffee in the morning."

He looked at Caina, started to say something, and then closed his mouth.

"I cannot disagree," said Corvalis. "My lords, we have a table waiting for you."

Tanzir and Lord Titus seated themselves first, while Halfdan and Corvalis followed, and then Caina sat next to Corvalis. Shaizid clapped his hands, and a small army of maids and servants issued from the kitchens, bearing trays laden with food and drink.

"For you, my lord emir," said Shaizid with a bow, "Istarish coffee, grown on the plantations in the Vale of Fallen Stars."

Tanzir blinked, and for the first time, Caina saw a genuine smile on the young emir's face. "Truly? How did you obtain this? Trade between Istarinmul and the Empire has stopped since the war began."

"I have my sources," said Corvalis. "It did cost a small fortune."

"Superb," said Tanzir, taking a sip. "I did not think to find proper coffee so far from civilized lands."

"Among us northern barbarians?" said Titus.

Tanzir flinched. "I...I did not mean any offense, my lord. I..."

Titus laughed. "Forgive my small joke. I suppose we are all uncivilized barbarians to our neighbors."

"Perhaps," said Tanzir, some of his nervousness fading. "But that was a brilliant idea, Master Anton. Opening Malarae's first coffee house, I mean. We of Istarinmul have enjoyed coffee for centuries, as have the men of Anshan...but it never made its way north. You were clever to think of it."

"Thank you, my lord emir," said Corvalis. "The person to think it up was clever indeed."

He squeezed Caina's hand under the table.

"Indeed," said Tanzir. He waved a hand at the crowds. "I imagine…well, I suppose all sorts of plotting and intrigue goes on here. The coffee houses of Istarinmul are rife with such things."

That was a more astute observation than Caina had expected.

"I'm sure I wouldn't know about such things," said Corvalis. "I am only a simple merchant of coffee."

Titus snorted.

"A gift for you, my lord," said Corvalis, sliding something across the table. "A book, since you seemed fond of them. A history of the emperors of Nighmar, written in High Nighmarian."

Again Tanzir smiled. "A thoughtful gift, master merchant. Thank you. I shall read it with great pleasure and remember your kindness."

"Sonya picked it out," said Corvalis.

"Indeed?" said Tanzir, picking up the book. "I am grateful. Yes. Grateful." He took a deep breath and looked at Caina. "A question. I would like to ask you a question. About the book. If you please?"

"Of course," said Caina. "What do you wish to know?"

"Um," said Tanzir. "I would like to ask you a question out of earshot of the others." He looked at Corvalis. "It is…nothing untoward, nothing forward. But it is improper for an Istarish emir to show too much interest in Imperial history. So just a brief question."

That was perhaps the single clumsiest seduction attempt Caina had ever heard.

"Of course, my lord emir," said Corvalis. "If you do not object, Sonya?"

"I would be honored," said Caina, rising and smoothing her skirts. Her mind worked, trying to find a way to turn him down in a way that would spare his pride. If he took offense at her rejection, that would make it all the harder to keep him alive. "We can speak quietly over here."

Tanzir rose, grunting with the effort, and followed her to a corner of the House near the kitchen doors. If they spoke quietly, no one would overhear them. Yet they were within sight of Corvalis and the others.

"What did you wish to ask, my lord emir?" said Caina, bracing herself.

Tanzir looked at her, licked his lips, and Caina saw dread, utter dread, in his black eyes.

"Help me," he whispered.

"My lord?" said Caina.

"Help me find the Ghosts," said Tanzir.

Of all the things he could have said, Caina had not expected that. For an irrational instant she was annoyed that he had not tried to seduce her, and then dismissed the thought as absurd.

"I'm sorry?" she said at last.

"The Ghosts," said Tanzir, clutching his book to his chest like a shield, "the spies and assassins of the Emperor of Nighmar."

"The Ghosts are just a story," said Caina.

"They're not!" said Tanzir, his tone urgent. "I know they're not. And I know they're here." For a terrible instant Caina wondered how she had given herself away, but Tanzir kept talking. "In Istarinmul spies frequent the coffee houses. Everyone in Istarinmul has their spies. The emirs have spies, the Alchemists, the slavers' brotherhood, everyone, and they all come to the coffee houses. Why else would the Emperor allow a coffee house to open in Malarae? So the Ghosts can spy." He lifted a finger. "I know the Ghosts are real. Rezir was so sure he would conquer Marsis...but instead the Balarigar appeared and freed the slaves and slew Rezir. Who else could the Balarigar be but a Ghost nightfighter?"

Caina realized she had underestimated him. "Even if you are right," she said, "why are you talking to me? Do you think I am a Ghost?"

"Are you? I don't know," said Tanzir. "I don't even know if there are women among the Ghosts. But I am certain that Master Basil knows some of the Emperor's spies. Or, at least, Master Anton does. I dared...I dared not approach them, nor Lord Titus. They might betray me, or spread rumors about me. But if I approached you and you were not a Ghost ...I could say that you tried to seduce me, and I rebuffed you as beneath me."

"How flattering," said Caina.

"But...please, tell me," said Tanzir, still clutching his book. "Can...can you contact the Ghosts for me?"

"Let us say, for the sake of argument, that I can," said Caina, dropping her Szaldic accent. Tanzir's eyes widened at that. "If you could contact the Ghosts...what would you say to them?"

"That my mother," said Tanzir, "is going to kill me."

"Your mother," said Caina. "Why?"

"Because she rules House Shahan," said Tanzir. "She never questioned Rezir. He was a strong man, a man who made House Shahan respected and feared. But now that he is dead, the dowager amirja does as she wishes...and I am only still alive because she needs a public figurehead."

"So if she needs you as a public figurehead," said Caina, "why is she trying to kill you?"

"Because she wants the war to continue," said Tanzir. "Our foes among the nobles of Istarinmul held wide lands near the Argamaz Desert, lands your Empire has now seized. The Emperor might grant those lands to the Padishah in exchange for peace...which will strengthen the enemies of our House."

"If your mother kills you, won't she need a new figurehead?" said Caina.

Tanzir sighed. "She already has one. My younger brother Morazir. He's like Rezir, but crueler and stupider. He will do whatever Mother tells him, so long as he has enemies to kill and slaves to torture."

"So your mother sent assassins after you," said Caina.

"It is much worse than that," said Tanzir. "Mother is Anshani, a cousin of the Shahenshah himself, and since the Shahenshah wishes for the war to continue, he has given my mother the aid of the Bostaji." His fingers tightened against the book's leather cover. "I do not know if you have heard of them, but they are the Shahenshah's personal assassins, the most lethal killers in the world. They will come after me any day."

"Actually," said Caina, "they've come after you twice."

Tanzir flinched. "What?"

"The first time was as you walked along the Via Triumphalis with Lord Titus," said Caina. "There was a Bostaji upon the roof of an apartment building, preparing to shoot you with an arrow. The second attempt was last night at the Emperor's banquet. One of the servants was a disguised Bostaji. We don't know what he planned, but we suspect he intended to poison you."

Tanzir looked a bit sickly. "It seems...it seems that I already owe the Ghosts my life."

"Why come to us with this?" said Caina. "Why not tell the Immortals, or Sinan?"

Tanzir scowled. "The Immortals are fierce warriors...but they are none too bright. And Sinan...Sinan is my mother's creature. He has been loyal to her for years, ever since he settled in the Vale of Fallen Stars." He snorted. "He is giving the Bostaji every detail about my actions, I expect, but there is nothing I can do about it. So you see why I have come to the Ghosts for aid. And why I had to do it covertly."

Caina nodded. "Then you wanted to visit the book shops just to talk to me alone?"

Tanzir bobbed his head. "Yes. I wanted people to think I would seduce you...then I would be safe to ask you questions." He hesitated. "Please do not be offended. Not...not that I wouldn't want to seduce you. Ah. You are very lovely. I mean..."

"I find it difficult to believe," said Caina, "that you are Rezir Shahan's younger brother."

Tanzir sighed. "He said the same thing. Often. But...will you speak to the Ghosts for me? Will they help me?"

"They will," said Caina. "Lord Titus invited you to the Grand Imperial Opera tonight?" Tanzir nodded. "Then ask him to invite Master Anton with you."

"Why?" said Tanzir.

"Because," said Caina. "The Ghosts have been watching over you, but it will be all the easier if you cooperate with us. We also want the war between the Emperor and the Padishah to end."

"Anton Kularus," said Tanzir, "is a Ghost?"

Caina smiled. "Do you truly expect me to answer that? Suffice it to say that Master Anton can help protect you."

As Caina could, but she preferred for people to underestimate her.

"But he is a coffee merchant!" said Tanzir. "If the Bostaji come for me...how will a coffee merchant help?"

"Master Anton," said Caina, "was not always a coffee merchant. He has some skills that might surprise you. These are your choices, my lord emir. You may take your chances with the Bostaji...or you can come to the Ghosts for help."

Tanzir swallowed. "When you put it that way, it seems I have little choice at all. Very well."

"Come, then," said Caina, resuming her Szaldic accent. "We should return to the table, yes? Otherwise they will think you are trying to seduce me. And Anton is ever so tedious when he is jealous."

"How do you do that?" said Tanzir, bewildered. "The accent, I mean. Are you an actress?"

"Of a sort," said Caina, and she walked back to the table, Tanzir following.

"Well," said Halfdan, looking up from his coffee, "that must have been quite a spirited discussion."

"It was," said Caina. "The emir is quite taken with his book." She looked at Corvalis. "Anton, the emir has invited us to join him at the Grand Imperial Opera tonight."

"Ah. Unless you have...objections, my lord Titus?" said Tanzir, and he looked like a boy asking permission from a stern teacher.

Titus shrugged. "Certainly not. I have my own box at the Opera, and there is room enough for both Master Anton and his companion."

"Splendid," said Tanzir. "I'm sure it will be a pleasant evening."

"Interesting," said Halfdan.

Corvalis had excused himself from the table, and Caina had followed with Halfdan. They had retreated to the cellar to discuss their plans, free from any risk that anyone might overhear.

"We ought to have Tanzir keep the Immortals around him," said Corvalis.

"No," said Halfdan. "This isn't commonly known, but the sorcerous elixirs that the Alchemists give the Immortals to enhance their strength and speed also allow the Alchemists to control them. The Immortals might serve the Padishah…but if an Alchemist knows the proper spells, those same Immortals will cut down the Padishah in a heartbeat."

"Then why not just have the Immortals kill Tanzir?" said Corvalis.

"Because," said Caina, thinking it over, "because that would defeat the purpose. The point is to kill Tanzir and cast the blame upon the Emperor. If Tanzir's own Immortals cut him down, well…that cannot be used as an excuse to continue the war."

"It's just as well that Tanzir is going to the Grand Imperial Opera tonight," said Halfdan. "Many of the Opera's workers are Ghosts, and Theodosia has eyes and ears everywhere. It will be harder for the Bostaji to move against him at the Opera."

"We'll need to get him away from the Immortals," said Caina. "I suspect the dowager amirja put Sinan in charge of seeing Tanzir dead. If he gets desperate, he might have the Immortals kill Tanzir without any witnesses and hope to lay the blame upon the Emperor."

"Harder to do without any witnesses," said Corvalis.

"Harder," said Halfdan, "but not impossible. I will speak with Tylas and have extra Imperial Guards assigned to the Lord Ambassador's residence. Once he has concluded the treaty of peace and left the city, the danger against his life will subside."

"Not entirely," said Caina. Tanzir's mother seemed like the sort of woman who could keep a grudge.

"His life is his own concern then," said Halfdan. "Meanwhile, we need to keep him alive long enough to conclude peace with Istarinmul. Which means you get to prepare for a night at the opera."

CHAPTER 10
THE GRAND IMPERIAL OPERA

Caina prepared for the opera.

She exchanged her teal gown for one of dark green with black scrollwork. Again she chose golden jewelry, intended to clash with the color of her dyed hair and the gown. Tanzir might suspect that there was more to her than met the eye, but the rest of Malarae knew her as Sonya Tornesti, Anton Kularus's flighty and temperamental mistress, and she wanted to keep it that way.

The looser sleeves allowed her to carry more throwing knives, and she strapped two to each of her forearms. She chose high-heeled boots with concealed sheaths for long daggers, and kept her curved ghostsilver dagger at her belt.

She did not think the Bostaji would try anything at the Grand Imperial Opera…but it never hurt to be prepared.

Caina joined Corvalis, and they took his coach to the opera.

The Grand Imperial Opera's massive domed edifice loomed overhead, its polished marble façade gleaming in the light of the enspelled lamps lining the square. A mass of coaches stopped before the Opera, footmen helping lords and ladies descend from their conveyances. Men and women of all classes came to the House of Kularus, though most of the House's patrons were merchants and minor nobles. But the opera was the high lords' and powerful merchants' favorite. The Grand Imperial Opera's company was the most prestigious in the Empire.

"You're smiling," said Corvalis, offering her a hand as she descended from the coach.

"I suppose I am," said Caina, looping her arm through his. "I have...pleasant memories of this place."

She had trained here, working under Theodosia, the Grand Imperial Opera's leading lady...and also the circlemaster of a Ghost circle. Caina owed her skill at accents to Theodosia's training, along with her abilities in disguise. Theodosia had taught her to disguise herself as anything from a highborn countess to a common mercenary guard.

"And Theodosia approves of you," said Caina, "which is a point in your favor."

"Frightening woman," said Corvalis. "I suspect she could order a man's death in the morning and then sing upon the stage in the evening."

"Probably," said Caina, who had seen Theodosia do just that.

A short time later Lord Titus's splendid coach arrived. A screen of Imperial Guards and Immortals surrounded the coach, and the nobles cast wary eyes at the Immortals. Lord Titus descended from the coach, and Tanzir followed. His Istarish robes and turban drew even more eyes.

"My lord emir," said Corvalis in High Nighmarian, bowing as Caina gripped her skirts in a curtsy, "we are pleased and honored to accept your invitation."

"Ah!" said Tanzir. "Master Anton and Mistress Sonya. I am pleased you could come." He looked at Caina, and looked away again. "Yes. Very pleased."

"I take it," said Caina, "that the learned Sinan will not be joining us?"

"No," said Tanzir. "Um. He said that opera was not a fit entertainment for a noble of Istarinmul and...ah, he said many other things as well. But I've come all this way, and I should really see an opera. And in...in reliable company as well."

"Come," said Titus, gesturing to the Imperial Guards. "If you wish to see an opera, my lord emir, let us take our seats."

He strode towards the great doors, Caina, Corvalis, and Tanzir following, flanked by Immortals and Imperial Guards. The lesser nobles hastened to get out of Titus's way, though a few of the noblemen cast venomous stares at Caina and Corvalis. The Grand Imperial Opera was for the nobility, not for an impudent coffee merchant and his mistress.

Caina hid her smile.

A page led them to Lord Titus's private box. The main theatre was a vast space, the acoustics perfectly pitched to hear the singers upon the stage. Those commoners who obtained admittance sat on the benches before the stage, while wealthy merchants took seats in the highest balcony. The wealthy lords kept their boxes in the middle balcony, close enough to have a view of the action upon the stage, yet far enough away to converse quietly.

Merchants went to the House of Kularus to haggle…but lords visited the Grand Imperial Opera to scheme.

Lord Titus took his seat, the Imperial Guards and Immortals standing in the aisle. Caina sat next to Corvalis, and a maid in the black and gold livery of the Grand Imperial Opera stepped forward with a tray of wine glasses. Caina took a glass for the sake of appearances, though she had no intention of drinking and muddling her wits. She had once worn that same livery herself, working as a maid in the opera and listening to the nobles speak their secrets, heedless of the nearby servants.

Idly, she wondered how Tanzir and Titus would react if they knew.

Tanzir drained his wine glass in two gulps and gestured for another. "What opera shall we see tonight?"

"The story of the founder of House Maraeus," said Titus. "He was a knight in the First Empire who ventured into the mountains to save his lady love from barbarians, and wed her upon his return. A good opera needs two elements. A tale of valor and martial boldness, to remind us of the virtues of our Empire." He chuckled. "And a tale of romance to please the ladies."

"We do enjoy romance, my lord," said Caina. "But we appreciate valor and courage as well. For who will admire a man who is craven? Or a woman, for that matter?"

"True enough," said Titus. "What say you, my lord emir? Should an opera have more romance, or more tales of valor?"

Tanzir opened his mouth, closed it, opened it again. "I…confess, my lord, I have given the matter no thought. In Istarinmul there is no opera. The nobles amuse themselves by hunting or playing chess or…attending the gladiatorial games. Mostly the gladiatorial games. The most popular games are to the death, with wagers laid upon the outcome." He shuddered. "I have never cared for it. I have seen men die, yes…but I found no joy in it, and I would not seek it out for entertainment." He sighed. "The other nobles call me weak…but I have no taste for blood sport."

"I think that speaks well of you, my lord emir," said Caina, "and more poorly of your fellow Istarish nobles."

Tanzir blinked. "Thank you." He looked almost absurdly pleased. She suspected he had not received many compliments in his life.

The lights dimmed, pulleys creaked as the stagehands raised the curtains, and the opera began.

Caina sat motionless in the darkness, listening to the opera with one ear, scanning the nearby crowds with her eyes. Theodosia herself stood upon the stage, singing the opening aria. She was a tall woman in her forties with long blond hair, and wore the antique costume of an ancient Nighmarian noblewoman, singing forlornly of her long-lost love, the distant ancestor of House Maraeus. Her voice was rich and strong, and she filled the aria with power, the words ringing off the roof and walls of the theatre. Theodosia was a gifted singer, perhaps the best Caina had ever heard.

She was so good that the nobles stopped plotting long enough to listen to her. Tanzir stared at her, open-mouthed.

Theodosia finished her aria to ringing applause, and the leading tenor of the opera took the stage, surrounded by chorus singers wearing ancient Nighmarian armor. Marcellus was stunningly handsome, with a rich voice that like thunder, and had absolutely no brain whatsoever. Still, he sang well and looked good in his costume, which Theodosia had said were the chief skills of an opera's leading man.

Caina watched the nearby boxes as the maids carried food and drink for the nobles and their guests, the footmen hurrying back and forth as they carried messages for the lords. The nobles came to the opera to plot, and Caina supposed the messages contained the details for any number of schemes. But for the moment, that was not her concern.

Would the Bostaji make an attempt on Tanzir here? Caina watched as Tanzir ate the refreshments the maids brought, his eyes fixed on the stage. She doubted the Bostaji would use poison – too much risk that it would look like a sudden illness. Violence, then? But violence at the Opera seemed like an even greater risk. Dozens of nobles filled the boxes, and all of them had bodyguards. A Bostaji who drew a sword might not make it three steps.

Perhaps the Bostaji would try nothing here, and wait for a more opportune moment.

Nonetheless Caina did not relax.

An hour later the chorus finished a song, and the lights came back on as the intermission began. Caina saw hundreds of men and women rise and make their way to the theatre's latrines, and she was grateful that she had not consumed any wine.

"I have to say," said Tanzir, "that is rather more impressive than I expected."

"Yes," said Lord Titus. "Theodosia is quite renowned for her voice. Though she does have a bit of a scandalous reputation for luring noblemen into her bed. Old Lord Macrinius, for one…and his downfall came soon after. Of course, he was kidnapping Imperial citizens and selling them into slavery, so he brought his fate upon his own head."

A maid stopped at their box and bowed. "A message for you."

"Leave it here," said Titus with a wave of his hand.

"Pardon, my lord," said the maid, "but it is for Sonya Tornesti."

Caina frowned. "What is it?"

"The leading lady wishes to speak with you," said the maid.

Titus grunted. "You know Theodosia?"

"I do not," said Caina. She had known Theodosia for years, but Sonya Tornesti and Theodosia had never met. "She wishes to meet me after the opera?" Perhaps Theodosia had learned something about the Bostaji, and perhaps Nalazar and the Kindred.

"Pardon," said the maid, "but Mistress Theodosia would like to speak with you now, if it is convenient."

Caina hesitated, glanced at Corvalis.

"Go," said Corvalis. "Perhaps Theodosia wishes to purchase some coffee from the House of Kularus." He grinned. "I hear she is a stern taskmistress, and runs her maids ragged with unreasonable demands. I can keep the emir company while you are gone."

Which meant he would keep the Bostaji from killing Tanzir.

"Of course, Anton," said Caina. She rose and followed the maid through the aisles, down the stairs, and into the cavernous workshop below the main stage. It looked much as she remembered. Stagehands and carpenters swarmed over the scenery, preparing for the next act. The chorus singers stood in one corner, while the costumers cursed ferociously at them. Caina recognized many of them from her time at the Grand Imperial Opera, but none of them recognized her. She had been Marina, Theodosia's black-haired, quiet maid. Marina was nothing like Sonya Tornesti, Anton Kularus's blond, haughty mistress.

She felt a brief twinge of satisfaction at that.

Theodosia had her own dressing room off the workshop, and stood before her mirror and table of cosmetics, scrutinizing her reflection.

"Mistress," said the maid. "This is Sonya Tornesti."

"You wished to speak with me?" said Caina in Caerish, keeping her Szaldic accent in place. "Though your singing, mistress, it was most lovely. Even Anton listened, and Anton is not the sort of man to listening to singing."

"Thank you," said Theodosia to the maid. "You may go."

The girl scurried away, and Caina stepped into the dressing room and shut the door behind her.

Theodosia grinned and hugged Caina. "You can drop the accent, if you want. Though you do it quite well, my dear, especially since you don't even speak Szaldic."

"I've had some lessons," said Caina. "The opera is lovely."

"Of course it is. I am singing it, after all," said Theodosia with a laugh. "And I must say you look very fine sitting next to that strapping young coffee lord of yours. Not at all like Marina...who was the most competent maid I ever had." She gave a very unladylike snort. "This new girl...ah, I ask for the rouge, and she brings me the face powder."

"Be gentle on her," said Caina. "You have fifteen different kinds of rouge."

"Well, everyone must start somewhere, I suppose," said Theodosia. Her smile faded. "There is something you should know."

"What?" said Caina. "You know something about the Bostaji or the Kindred?"

"Perhaps," said Theodosia. "Someone broke into the opera this morning and ransacked the carpenters' shop."

Caina frowned. "The shop? Why? There's nothing valuable in there. The carpenters' tools, maybe. Some of the elixirs used to make smoke or flashes. A lot of paint. Unless." She thought it through. "Unless someone wanted to look around the theatre, to find the ideal spot for an assassination…and make it look like a common theft."

Theodosia nodded. "You see my fear."

"Was anything taken?" said Caina.

Theodosia scowled. "We don't actually know. The carpenters are not terribly good about keeping an accurate inventory. The seneschal was most distressed."

"The best place to kill someone here," said Caina, "would be in one of the workshops." She ought to know, given that she had once lured a Kindred assassin into the workshops and tricked him into consuming his own poison. "The trick would be luring the emir into the workshop. I can't think of any reason he would come down here."

"Nor I," said Theodosia. "The best I can tell you is to be on your guard, and since you are always on your guard, it is pointless to repeat it."

Caina laughed. "But I appreciate the thought." She took Theodosia's hands. "Once this is all over, you ought to come to the House of Kularus. I'll see to it that you have the best table in the House."

Theodosia smiled. "A kind thought. But, really, you should call it the House of Amalas. It is yours, and I've never understood why you play this shell game with Corvalis."

Caina shrugged. "I am a nightfighter of the Ghosts, and I need to keep my anonymity. Opening Malarae's first coffee house in my own name is hardly the way to do that."

"But you won't be a Ghost nightfighter forever," said Theodosia. "You could return to the city in your own name, as Countess Caina Amalas, and run a Ghost circle centered out of the House of Kularus."

Caina said nothing.

It was…a compelling thought She was twenty-two years old, but she could not remain a Ghost nightfighter forever. Sooner or later she would slow down, or take an injury severe enough to keep her from fighting. Yet that did not mean she had to leave the Ghosts. She could run the House of Kularus, turning it into the center for a network of Ghost circles.

She could wed Corvalis, with her own name.

And that thought was compelling.

Caina had thought she would never marry, both because of her inability to bear children and her place among the Ghosts. But Corvalis did not care about children, and she loved him.

"That is," said Caina at last, "that is a very interesting idea."

"Oh, child," said Theodosia. "After all you have suffered, all the people you have saved, I think you deserve a little joy in your life. Why…"

The door swung open, and Marcellus stepped inside, blinking.

"Marcellus," said Theodosia, "what have we discussed about knocking?"

"Oh," said Marcellus. "Is this your daughter?"

"I have two sons, Marcellus," said Theodosia. "No daughters."

"Yes, that's right," said Marcellus. He frowned for a moment. "Which opera are we singing tonight?"

"Look at your costume," said Theodosia.

Marcellus looked at his elaborate armor, and then nodded. "Oh, yes, of course. The origins of House Maraeus. Ah. I think intermission is almost over." He looked alarmed. "We should return to the stage!"

"Indeed we should," said Theodosia. "I will join you shortly."

"Good," said Marcellus. "It was nice meeting your daughter."

He left the dressing room.

"A dear man," said Theodosia, "but I swear if the city burned down around our ears, he wouldn't notice until the maids failed to bring his wine. And why does he think you were my daughter? We looking nothing alike."

Caina touched her hair. "I suspect the dye has something to do with that."

Theodosia laughed. "You miss your proper color, don't you? Well, consider this. If you declare yourself openly, you can go back to it. And speaking of that, you ought to get back to your assassin and that great hulk of an emir." She paused. "Be careful."

"You, too," said Caina.

"I'll send a maid to escort you back to Lord Titus's box."

Caina grinned. "No need. I think I know the way."

She left the dressing room, climbed the stairs back to Titus's box, and seated herself next to Corvalis. Titus and Tanzir were deep in a discussion of the opera. Corvalis gave a slight shake of his head when she looked at him.

There had been no sign of the Bostaji or of other assassins.

Perhaps Caina had been overcautious. Perhaps the Bostaji would not make an attempt on Tanzir's life tonight, and perhaps the burglary had been nothing more than a simple attempt at theft.

But Caina hated coincidences, and she would stay vigilant.

The lights dimmed, and the opera resumed.

Caina listened as Marcellus and the chorus sang of storming the barbarians' stronghold, complete with a stylized battle and copious amounts of stage blood. Theodosia sang of love and longing and hope and despair.

At last they sang a duet together as Maraeus rescued his lost love, the barbarians defeated.

And then the opera was over, and thunderous applause filled the theatre. Lord Titus rose to his feet, clapping, and the less influential nobles looked at him and followed suit. Tanzir heaved himself to his feet with a sigh, though he applauded no less enthusiastically. Caina looked around the theatre. If someone was going to attack Tanzir, this would be the perfect moment, when the singers and chorus took their bows.

But the singers and the chorus departed from the stage, the applause faded away, and no attack came.

"I thank you, my lord Titus," said Tanzir. "That was...that was a remarkable experience. Again it is a pity we have no opera in Istarinmul, only blood sport and chariot racing."

"Well, it is a refined taste," said Titus. Around them the commoners started to move for the exits, the murmur of conversation filling the Grand Imperial Opera. "And we..."

There was a flash of light from a nearby box, and a plume of thick gray smoke erupted towards the ceiling.

A stunned silence fell over the theatre. Corvalis reached for his sword, and Caina's hand slipped into her sleeve for a throwing knife.

Three more flashes went off, throwing columns of gray smoke up, and the air in the theatre grew hazy.

"Fire!" screamed a man's voice. "Fire! Fire! Fire!"

"Fire!" said a woman.

"No," said Caina, "no, that's not fire. That's..."

"Run!" screamed someone else, and the sound of panicked chaos filled the theatre. The light from the globes threw eerie beams through the swirling smoke.

"The theatre is on fire!" said Titus. "We must get out of here at once. We..."

"No, my lord!" said Caina, grabbing his arm.

Titus looked at her, affronted. "Do not presume to touch..."

"That isn't real smoke," said Caina. "It's stage smoke. Someone's creating a diversion. My lord, the assassins are coming for Tanzir."

The emir made a strangled noise.

"Well, they shall find a stern reception if they do," said Titus. "Imperial Guards! Prepare to..."

Something clinked at Caina's feet.

She saw a glass bottle, its interior filled with a boiling gray fluid.

Titus hurried out of the box, the Imperial Guards falling in place around him, while the Immortals stepped forward.

"Watch out!" said Caina, and she felt Corvalis seize her shoulders and pull her back, putting himself between her and the bottle.

She covered her eyes, and there was a brilliant flash and a crack. When Caina opened her eyes, gray smoke filled the world, and she could not see more three feet in front of her.

"Are you all right?" said Corvalis.

"Fine," said Caina. "We've got to find Tanzir..."

"Here!" said Tanzir. He staggered forward. "I'm..."

A whistling noise cut through the sound of the panic, and a blurring shape slammed into Tanzir. The emir screamed and toppled to his knees, and Caina saw the leather cord of a bola pinning his arms to his torso, the lead weights bouncing off his chest.

A man jumped upon the railing of the box, clad in the fine coat and polished boots of a successful merchant. A short sword gleamed in his hand, and his eyes fixed upon Tanzir.

A Bostaji.

CHAPTER 11
ROPES AND LADDERS

The Bostaji jumped from the railing, sword angled to plunge into Tanzir's back.

Caina flung a throwing knife. The Bostaji was moving too fast for her to aim well, but the knife clipped his shoulder and sliced into his coat. The Bostaji staggered and lost his balance.

Corvalis attacked, sword in his right fist. The Bostaji tried to meet the attack, but Corvalis ripped his sword across the assassin's throat and shoved, and the Bostaji toppled backwards over the railing and landed in the neighboring box.

"What is happening?" said Tanzir, struggling against the bola.

"The Bostaji," said Caina, yanking her ghostsilver dagger from its sheath, "are trying to kill you." She cut the leather cord, and Tanzir staggered back to his feet. There was no sign of Lord Titus. But there was no sign of anyone, despite the screams and shouts filling the theatre. The smoky haze kept Caina from seeing more than a few paces in any direction.

"Go," said Caina, pushing Tanzir away from the aisle and towards the railing of the box, "right now. Over the railing."

"Why?" said Tanzir.

"Because," said Corvalis, "the Bostaji know where you are, but if you move, they'll have a hard time finding you in this haze."

"Ah!" said Tanzir, his face brightening with comprehension, and he heaved himself over the railing into the next box.

The trap had been perfect. Tanzir had remained in Lord Titus's box throughout the opera, giving the Bostaji time to distribute the smoke bombs. Then when the bombs went off, they knew exactly where Tanzir would be, allowing them to strike at once.

If Caina and Corvalis had not been there, Tanzir would be dead.

Caina vaulted over the railing and landed next to Tanzir.

"We've got to get out of here," said Corvalis.

"The exits," said Tanzir, pointing. "We…"

"No," said Caina. "They'll be waiting at the exits. We'll go towards the stage. They might not expect that." And Caina knew the maze of passages and workshops below the Grand Imperial Opera's main stage. With luck, they could lose the Bostaji there and escape into the streets. "This way."

The haze had not thinned, but Caina had spent months serving wine and food at the Grand Imperial Opera, and she knew how to find her way around in the dark. She made her way to an aisle, Corvalis and Tanzir following, and headed towards the stage. The sounds of panic grew softer as they drew closer to the stage. Most of the audience had likely escaped through the main entrances. She hoped no one had been trampled in the chaos.

Though as more people escaped, that would make it easier for the Bostaji to find them.

Armor clattered, and a dark shape appeared behind them.

Caina whirled and saw an Immortal step towards them, the blue light from the depths of the skull helm painting the smoke with an eerie glow.

"You!" said Tanzir. "Assist us! The Bostaji are attempting to kill…"

The Immortal raised his scimitar and advanced at Tanzir, and Caina remembered Halfdan's warning about the Alchemists. Tanzir stumbled back in terror, his boot coming down on the hem of his ornamented robe, and that alone saved him. The emir stumbled, and the Immortal's scimitar blurred through the air his head had occupied an instant earlier.

Caina sprang forward, ghostsilver dagger in hand, and stabbed. Chain mail and plate covered the Immortal's head and torso and arms, but there was a gap in the armor above the boots. Her dagger bit into flesh, drawing blood, and the Immortal bellowed in fury. The soldier whirled to face her, scimitar blurring for her head, and Caina just barely got out of the way.

She dodged to the left, and the Immortal pivoted to follow her. Yet the movement put the Immortal's weight onto his bad knee, and the soldier stumbled. That gave Corvalis all the opportunity he needed to act. He drove his shoulder into the Immortal, and the soldier fell upon the floor, his black armor clattering. Corvalis sprang forward, his sword flashing, and drove the blade into a gap in the black armor.

The Immortal shuddered and went still.

"Mercy of the Living Flame," said Tanzir, his voice quavering, "my own bodyguards are trying to kill me."

"They're not your bodyguards, but Sinan's," said Caina. "Go."

They had to keep moving. The haze blocked sight but not sound, and the Immortal's death had been loud. Tanzir stumbled along, and Caina urged him forward, her ghostsilver dagger in her right hand. The stairs to the workshop were next to the stage. From there, it would be easy enough to escape ...

"Look out!" shouted Corvalis.

Caina shoved Tanzir to the side, knocking the emir onto one of the commoners' benches. A thrown dagger flashed overhead, so close that Caina felt the breeze of its passage. Another Immortal sprang out of the smoke, the glow from his eyes reflecting on the steel of his scimitar. Corvalis met his attack, sword clanging in his hands. The Immortal growled and bulled forward, and Corvalis gave ground.

Caina darted forward and stabbed, and the Immortal blocked her attack, moving with the unnatural speed granted by the sorcerous elixirs in his blood. Corvalis landed a blow, but his blade rebounded from the Immortal's black armor. Caina snarled a curse. The longer they delayed, the more likely it was that more Immortals or the Bostaji would find them.

If they did not get away now, they were dead.

Corvalis launched a flurry of blows, his strikes ringing against the Immortal's helmet. The Immortal backed away, trying to regain his footing, and Corvalis thrust again. But the Immortal's left fist lashed out, the punch catching Corvalis in the chest. The sheer power of his blow knocked Corvalis off his feet, and he landed with a grunt.

Caina threw herself at the Immortal, angling her dagger for a gap in the side of his breastplate. The blade bit into flesh, and the Immortal threw her aside. She struck the floor with a bone-rattling thump, the pain stunning her into immobility.

"Die!" spat the Immortal, raising his scimitar for a two-handed blow.

Corvalis surged forward, leaping to his feet in a single fluid motion, and drove his sword into the Immortal's exposed armpit. The elite soldier staggered, and Caina jumped to her feet and thrust her dagger into the eye hole of the skull helm.

That made a mess, but the Immortal dropped to his knees, and then fell on his face.

"Are you all right?" said Caina. Corvalis nodded, and she helped Tanzir to his feet. "And you?"

"Not particularly," said Tanzir.

"Get moving," said Caina, giving him a push. "Or you're going to be worse."

"I can see that," said Tanzir. "This is..."

"There he is!"

The smoke had begun to lift, drifting towards the ceiling, and she saw a pair of men in the clothing of merchants standing in Lord Titus's box.

Bostaji.

The assassins pointed, and beyond them Caina saw several blue lights glimmering in the thinning smoke. More Immortals appeared, and even as she looked, the black-armored soldiers raced down the aisles.

"Run!" said Corvalis.

Caina hurried to his side, and Tanzir ran as fast as he could manage, which was not very quick. Caina shot a glance behind her. They might reach the stairs before the Immortals, but that would not matter. They would be trapped on the stairs, and either the Immortals or the Bostaji would cut them down.

Unless…

An idea came to Caina.

"Onto the stage!" she yelled.

"The stage?" said Tanzir, panting. "Are we to be opera singers now?"

"Listen to her!" said Corvalis, tugging the emir towards the stage. "Go!"

Caina scrambled onto the stage, and Tanzir grabbed the lip and heaved himself up, rolling onto his knees. Corvalis jumped up, and together they hauled the panting emir to his feet and ran across the stage, the planks thumping beneath Caina's boots. Her eyes scanned the boards, her mind racing.

Yes. There.

The Immortals surged past the lords' boxes and into the commoners' benches.

"Stop!" said Caina. "Right here, stop!"

She yanked the dagger from her left boot and reversed her grip, the blade tucked between her fingers. Her eyes swept over the sides of the stage, at the intricate mass of ropes and pulleys that controlled the curtains and the scenery. The rope, where was the damned rope?

The Immortals jumped on the stage, scimitars drawn back to kill. Four Bostaji followed them, short swords in their right hands, bolas dangling in their left.

And Caina still couldn't find the rope.

She needed a distraction.

"Stay back!" she roared, drawing herself up in a commanding pose. "Do you worms truly think to threaten me?"

The Immortals paused, and the Bostaji looked at her with cold eyes.

"This man is under my protection!" said Caina, gesturing with the dagger as her eyes traced the maze of ropes hanging along the wall. "For I am a sister of the Imperial Magisterium, and sorcerous powers are mine to command! Yet I am merciful, and will give you one chance to save your lives. Turn and flee now, fools, while you still can."

For a moment no one said anything. Caina felt sweat trickle between her shoulder blades, soaking into the cloth of her gown. If she did not find that rope, she was going to die along with Tanzir and Corvalis.

Odd that in all her musings about the future, she had never considered that she and Corvalis might die together.

"She's lying," said one of the Bostaji in a flat voice. "Kill them all."

Caina spotted the rope, and the Immortals started forward.

"You had your chance!" said Caina, and flung the dagger with all the strength and accuracy she could manage. For a dreadful instant, she thought she would miss, but the spinning blade sheared through the rope.

"You missed," said Tanzir, voice faint.

"Actually," said Caina, "no."

There was an ominous creaking noise, and then the floor fell away beneath her boots.

An instant of spinning, wrenching disorientation, and Caina slammed into something soft and yielding. An enormous stack of old pillows, piled to catch the actors and chorus singers who dropped through the trapdoor. She looked around and saw that she was in the workshop, the stage fifty feet overhead. Caina heaved herself to her feet, saw the Immortals staring down at her, and raced across the workshop before the Immortals realized they could jump after them.

She yanked another rope dangling from the wall, and the trapdoor swung shut with a bang.

Corvalis staggered back to his feet, laughing. "That was clever."

"Clever?" said Tanzir, standing with a groan. "Clever? We could have been killed! What if we had missed those pillows?"

"Then we would be dead," said Caina, looking around the workshop. "Of course, if we had stayed up there, we would be dead anyway. Let's go. We don't have long before those assassins figure out how to get down here."

"Sonya!"

She saw Theodosia hurrying towards them, still clad in her stage costume.

"What the devil is going on?" said Theodosia. "I came down to my dressing room for some wine, and the next thing I know the theatre is filling with smoke and the audience is running in every direction."

"The Bostaji made smoke bombs," said Caina, gesturing at Tanzir, who stood gaping at Theodosia, "and tried to kill the emir in the chaos."

"Dreadful," said Theodosia. She sniffed. "At least they had the good taste not to do it during the performance."

"Yes, that was my chief worry as well," said Caina.

"Don't be snide," said Theodosia. "Well, let's get you out of here before the assassins catch up to the lord emir. They'll be watching the main doors, but I doubt these Anshani thugs thought to guard every exit from the Grand Imperial Opera. This way."

She led them from the main workshop to the maze of smaller shops, the only light coming from the occasional enspelled globe set into the stone walls. Caina followed, her eyes scanning the shadows. The Immortals wore heavy armor, and she would hear their approach. But the Bostaji knew how to move with stealth, and might be unable to take them unawares…

"I do not understand," said Tanzir. "We are following an opera singer?"

"An opera singer?" said Theodosia, not looking back. "My lord emir, I shall have you know that I am the leading lady of the Grand Imperial Opera, and that I have sung before the Emperor himself upon multiple occasions."

"Er…yes," said Tanzir, "but…but I appealed to the Ghosts for help! For protection! Now I am skulking through the darkness with an opera singer…"

"Leading lady," said Theodosia, stopping before a door.

"And a coffee merchant and his mistress!" said Tanzir. "Do the Ghosts have nothing better to offer?"

"Not really, no," said Corvalis with a laugh.

"We've kept you alive so far," said Caina. "You can go back and take your chances with the Immortals…or you can come with us. If you come with us, you might die, yes. But if you go back, you will certainly die. So. Which shall it be?"

Theodosia opened the door, and Tanzir sighed.

"You sound like my mother," said Tanzir.

"If your mother is anything like mine, I certainly hope not," said Caina.

"It seems I have little choice," said Tanzir as they walked through the opened door. "I don't want to be here. I never wanted to come to Malarae. Gods, I don't even want to be the emir. Why couldn't they have just left me alone in the library with my books?" The room beyond was a small vault, sacks piled up against one wall.

"They could have, but they didn't," said Caina. "You didn't want to be the emir, but you are. Now shut up and do what we tell you. You might want to lie down and die, but the Emperor needs you alive, so by all the gods we are going to keep you alive."

Tanzir opened his mouth, closed it again.

"You are," he said, "a lot like my mother."

"Here we are," said Theodosia, pushing one of the bricks in the wall. There was a low grinding noise, and a portion of the wall slid aside to reveal a stone stairwell spiraling into darkness. "This leads to the old catacombs beneath the original city. The way is marked, and the exit opens near the Imperial Market. You can get the emir to safety from there. Don't stray from the marked path. The magi buried their failed experiments in the catacombs, and some of them might still be down there." She pushed aside some of the sacks and passed Caina a lantern. "Good luck."

"Thank you," said Caina. "For everything. Make sure to stay out of sight. It will take the Bostaji and the Immortals some time to figure out that we've left. If you stay out of their way, they will likely ignore you."

"I know," said Theodosia. She smiled. "The civic militia is on its way to put out any fires, I'm sure, and the Bostaji won't wait for them." She turned to Corvalis. "Do take care of her, Master Anton. I will be most put out if anything happens to her."

Corvalis gave her a mocking little bow. "Who could defeat the Balarigar? But as always, I shall heed your wisdom and experience."

"Infuriating man," said Theodosia. "Go."

Caina lit the lantern and led the way into the darkness.

An hour later Corvalis heaved aside a rusted iron sewer grate, and Caina pulled herself up, looking around a narrow alley. Her gown had been thoroughly ruined by the trek through the catacombs and then Malarae's sewers, the cloth stained with blood and dirt and worse things.

But she was still alive.

"It's clear," said Caina.

Corvalis pulled himself into the alley with a grunt, and then turned back towards the hole into the sewers. He squatted, as did Caina, and she grabbed Tanzir's right arm and Corvalis grabbed his left.

"Jump on the count of three," said Caina. "One, two, three!"

Tanzir jumped, and Caina pulled on his arm, as did Corvalis. They got the emir a few feet off the tunnel floor, and Tanzir grabbed the edge of the alley. With Caina's and Corvalis's help, the emir pulled himself up and flopped onto the ground, breathing hard.

"That," wheezed Tanzir, "that was horrible. If I live through this, I am going to stay in bed for a week."

Caina crept to the edge of the alley and peered into the street. They were not far from the Imperial Market, and the streets were deserted. Not surprising, since it was almost midnight by now. She saw no patrols of the civic militia, no doubt because most of them had gone to deal with the "fire" at the Grand Imperial Opera. Theodosia had a lot of clout with them, which was not surprising, since her eldest son Tomard had just been promoted to a tribune of the militia.

"It's clear," said Caina.

"Good," said Corvalis. "So. What now?"

Caina looked at Tanzir, who sat sweating and trembling against the wall.

That was an excellent question.

"We have to keep him alive," said Caina.

"Yes," said Corvalis, "but that is your field of expertise, not mine. I'm good at killing people." He grimaced. "Not so good at saving them."

"You saved Claudia," said Caina.

"With your help."

"Any ideas?" said Caina.

Corvalis shrugged. "The best way to defend against a foe is to have no foes at all. If we sit back and keep reacting to the Bostaji, sooner or later we will make a mistake and they'll kill the emir. Better to strike first and eliminate the Bostaji."

"So we find the Bostaji," said Caina, "and eliminate them. But that will take time, and they could use the time to kill Tanzir. Which means…"

She nodded and walked over to Tanzir.

"Get up, my lord emir," said Caina. "You're going to need to disappear for a few days."

CHAPTER 12
SAFE HOUSE

Corvalis unlocked the House of Kularus's narrow back door. The kitchens were dark and quiet. The servants had not yet arrived to begin baking the next day's cakes and preparing the coffee. Caina beckoned Tanzir into the kitchens and closed the door behind him.

"This...this is Master Anton's coffee house?" said Tanzir, blinking.

"It is," said Caina.

"I'll get Shaizid," said Corvalis. "He's usually up at this hour going over the books anyway."

Caina nodded. "We'll wait here."

Corvalis strode into the main floor of the coffee house, leaving Caina alone with Tanzir. She leaned against one of the counters and closed her eyes. It had been close, very close, at the Grand Imperial Opera. If she had not remembered the trap door, if she had not cut the correct rope, they would all have died...

"Thank you."

Caina opened her eyes. Tanzir stood nearby, his hands brushing the front of his robes.

"For saving my life, I mean," said Tanzir. "I'm not...I'm not any good at this sort of thing. At the running and the fighting, I mean. Istarish nobles are supposed to be warriors and hunters...but I cried the first time I saw a horse, and I wouldn't even try to get in the saddle until Rezir and Morazir beat me black and blue. I almost gutted myself the first time I held a scimitar. Eventually they left me alone, and I would hide in my father's library."

"Your father," said Caina. "What was he like?"

"Just like Rezir," said Tanzir. "He hated me. If he knew I was now the emir of the Vale of Fallen Stars, he would be furious." He shook his head. "He was right to hate me."

"Why?" said Caina.

"Because I am useless," said Tanzir. "An emir of Istarinmul is supposed to be a bold hunter and a fearless warrior and a merciless ruler…and I am none of those things."

"Perhaps you ought to take pride in that," said Caina. "I have seen the Istarish slavers' brotherhood kidnap men and women and children from their homes and drag them away in chains. The Istarish nobles could benefit from practicing a little mercy."

"My father always said otherwise," said Tanzir. "He kept trying to make me harder, to make me into a warrior." His voice dropped. "When I was fifteen he sent a slave woman to my bed, in hopes that she would inspire me to manly lust. She did…but not in the way he hoped." He looked away. "I told her I loved her…and my father had her strangled for it."

"I'm sorry," said Caina. It reminded her of the story Corvalis had told her, how his father had sent a woman to seduce and kill him. "I would not wish that on anyone."

"Thank you," said Tanzir. He sighed. "After that…after that, I confess I stopped caring. My father tried to turn me into a proper nobleman for a few more years, and then decided to ignore me. He died and Rezir became the new emir, and he also ignored me. I spent most of my time in the library at our palace…and eating, I fear." He brushed his robe again. "And then Rezir got himself killed in Marsis…and now I am the new emir. And my mother is trying to kill me to spite her enemies."

"We will keep you alive," said Caina, "if we can."

"Because you need me to have peace with Istarinmul," said Tanzir.

"Obviously," said Caina. "But…you are not a cruel man, Tanzir Shahan, from what I have seen of you. Not like your brother. I would not leave you to die at the hands of the Bostaji."

"Thank you," said Tanzir. "Though if I had known I would one day flee assassins in the streets of Malarae, I might have paid more attention to my father's weapons masters." Again he sighed. "Then perhaps I would not feel like dying after running a few yards."

"The threat of death," said Caina, "has a marvelous way of focusing the mind."

They stood in silence for a moment.

"Mistress Sonya," said Tanzir. "Might I…might I ask you something?"

"What is it?" said Caina.

"Did you kill Rezir?"

Caina frowned. "Why do you ask?"

"Because Theodosia and Master Anton mentioned the Balarigar," said

Tanzir, "and I think they were talking about you."

For all his timidity, Caina reminded herself, Tanzir was not stupid.

"I did," said Caina.

"How did he die?" said Tanzir.

Caina remembered that awful night in the streets of Marsis, remembered fleeing from the Immortals and Rezir himself. She remembered Rezir lying stunned on the floor of that burned-out warehouse, his sword hand burned away, his eyes full of horror and agony as she approached. The chaos as she flung his head into the mob of his soldiers.

"Not well," said Caina at last.

Tanzir looked away for a long moment.

"Good," he whispered, his voice full of loathing. "He strangled her, you know. My father told him to do it."

"I have done many things I regret," said Caina, "but that wasn't one of them."

Again they fell silent. Caina wondered what was taking Corvalis so long. She wondered why Tanzir was pouring his heart out to her. Perhaps she was the first one to ever listen to him.

"The Balarigar," said Tanzir, frowning. "If you are the Balarigar…"

"The Balarigar is a legend and nothing more," said Caina. "It's a Szaldic word. Means 'demonslayer', or 'destroyer of darkness', something like that. I happened to free some Szaldic slaves and kill a few sorcerers, and they decided the Balarigar walked among them once more. That's all."

"But if you're the Balarigar," said Tanzir, "does that mean the Moroaica is real?"

Caina felt a chill.

"How do you know that name?" she said.

"There was a book of Szaldic myths in my father's library," said Tanzir, "allegedly written by one of the solmonari, the old sorcerer-priests of the Szaldic nation. Many of the tales described the Moroaica."

"What did they say?" said Caina, curious. She knew more about the Moroaica than any other living mortal, save perhaps Talekhris of the Sages. Not surprising, given that the Moroaica's spirit had lurked within Caina's body for almost a year and a half. But Caina hardly knew all of Jadriga's secrets.

Tanzir shrugged. "The stories were…inconsistent. In some she was an old woman in the woods, a witch who lured the unwary with promises of power. In others she was a young woman of stunning beauty who promised to make the world anew, but her every effort always led to destruction. I assumed that was an allegory for hubris."

"An allegory," said Caina, recalling Jadriga's promises to remake the world and make the gods pay for the suffering of mankind.

"But is she real?" said Tanzir. "I mean...not merely a story?" He frowned. "You look more disturbed by what I just said than anything else that has happened tonight."

"She is real," said Caina, "very real, and dangerous. Pray that you never meet her. She..."

The kitchen door opened, and Caina reached for her dagger. But it was only Corvalis, Shaizid following after him.

And after Shaizid came Halfdan.

"Master Basil," said Tanzir, surprised. "You, too, are a Ghost?"

"Correct, Lord Ambassador," said Halfdan. "I am pleased you are unharmed."

"If I am," said Tanzir, "it is because of the efforts of Master Anton and Mistress Sonya. Is Lord Titus unharmed? He was...well, he was kinder to me than I expected."

"He is well," said Halfdan, "though alarmed at the attack. Once I heard word of what had happened at the Grand Imperial Opera, I came immediately. After it became clear that you were no longer there, I suspected Anton and Sonya might have taken you here."

"They did," said Tanzir. "Ah...are you going to kill me now?"

Halfdan looked surprised. "Why would we do that? We've gone to extreme lengths to keep you alive."

"Well...I know that you're a Ghost," said Tanzir. "And that Anton and Sonya are Ghosts, and I suspect your seneschal is as well. You might want to kill me to keep your secret."

"We might," said Halfdan, "but we won't. You will simply owe us a favor or two. We won't task you to betray the Padishah, or your family, but...well, a favor is often more valuable than a chest full of gold coins."

"What will you do with me now?" said Tanzir.

"I think it is best," said Halfdan, "if you disappear for a few days. It will throw the Bostaji off your trail."

Tanzir frowned. "Won't that...won't that defeat the purpose? If people think I am dead?"

"Oh, they won't think you're dead," said Halfdan. "We'll spread the story that there was an accidental fire at the opera, and you were injured in the resultant panic. You're simply resting to recover your strength before resuming negotiations with Lord Titus. That will keep the Immortals away from you while we seek the Bostaji."

"Where shall I hide where the Bostaji cannot find me?" said Tanzir.

Caina looked at Corvalis.

"Oh," said Corvalis, "I think we can accommodate you."

"Shaizid?" said Caina.

"This way, please, my lord emir," said Shaizid, beckoning. He led them down the stairs to the House of Kularus's cellar, and then through the secret door to the armory. Muravin stood outside the door to the barracks, cleaning and sharpening the swords and daggers one by one. He did not seem to sleep very much. Caina suspected she knew why.

She knew all about nightmares.

"Master Basil," said Muravin. "An eventful night, I trust?" He looked at Caina's disheveled, stained gown and grunted. "A very eventful night."

"Aye," said Halfdan. "The Bostaji came in force for the emir. So the emir shall stay here for a few days, if it will not trouble your daughter."

"It will not," said Muravin, "though Mistress Tanya says her time is very near."

"I will not trouble your daughter, I swear," said Tanzir.

Muravin looked him up and down. "I suspect not."

"I remember you!" said Tanzir. "You were...you were Master Anton's mute bodyguard. But...you had a scar..."

"Makeup," grunted Muravin. "Mistress Sonya insisted. I have learned to trust her judgment."

"Muravin has the Kindred after him for some reason we haven't been able to discern," said Caina, "and he came to the Ghosts for aid."

"Aye," said Corvalis, "and we didn't want that Master Alchemist of yours to recognize him, so..."

"Sinan?" said Tanzir. "He's my mother's creature. And he's not a Master Alchemist. He hasn't created an Elixir yet."

"Anyway," said Halfdan, "if we..."

"Wait," said Caina. "Wait." Something scratched at her mind. "Tanzir. Wait. What was that about an Elixir?"

Tanzir shrugged. "Well...it's how an Alchemist becomes a Master Alchemist. It's not widely known."

"It's not," said Halfdan. "I would be grateful if you would share the details."

"Oh," said Tanzir, "well, the Alchemists study a branch of sorcery that deals with transmutation. Altering the base properties of substances."

"Like lead into gold," said Caina.

"True," said Tanzir, "but from what I understand, the cost of the materials for the spell makes transmuting lead into gold financially prohibitive. So the Alchemists make elixirs to enhance strength and speed, like the ones they give the Immortals. Or they make cloth that is as strong as steel. Or they transmute flesh into crystal or stone, if you can believe such a thing."

"I think I can," said Corvalis.

Tanzir shuddered. "The College of Alchemists is filled with statues of people who offended the Alchemists. But I am rambling. To become a Master Alchemist, an Alchemist has to create and consume a vial of Elixir Rejuvenata."

"Elixir Rejuvenata?" said Caina. "That's how Master Alchemists live for centuries, isn't it?"

Tanzir nodded. "It's also a test. Apparently the formula for creating the Elixir is incredibly dangerous, and involves rare ingredients...ingredients obtained from powerful creatures that are not willing to give them up."

"So if an Alchemist creates the Elixir, consumes it, and it doesn't kill him," said Caina, "then he's a Master Alchemist?"

"He is," said Tanzir. "Or if the Elixir doesn't turn him into a monster. Even the slightest error in preparing the Elixir can cause...problems. There are not many Master Alchemists, I am afraid. Either the process of creating their first Elixir kills them, or they make an error and kill themselves later on. Or they kill each other. The Master Alchemists are as ruthless and competitive as the emirs."

Caina looked at Muravin, a thought occurring to her. Three pregnant sisters, all attacked at the same time... "Do you know anything about the ingredients? What components go into the Elixir?"

"No," said Tanzir. "The Master Alchemists guard the secret quite closely. Part of the test, I suspect."

"Regardless of the vagaries of alchemy or sorcery, Lord Ambassador," said Halfdan, "we will need to keep you here for a few days. Away from your Immortals, if you trust us that far."

"Given that my Immortals tried to kill me a few hours ago at Sinan's bidding," said Tanzir, "I can live with that."

"Good," said Halfdan. "Shaizid, please see to the emir's comfort."

"Of course, Master Basil," said Shaizid with a bow.

"The accommodations will be a little more...austere than you are accustomed to," said Halfdan, "but you ought to be safe here."

Tanzir shrugged. "Since an Immortal's scimitar in my belly would be even more uncomfortable, it would be churlish to complain."

"Excellent," said Halfdan. "Sonya, Anton, a word, please."

"Mistress Sonya," said Tanzir as Caina turned to go.

She paused.

"Thank you," said Tanzir. "For my life, I mean. And I shall think on what you said."

"You are welcome," said Caina, and followed Halfdan and Corvalis into the armory.

"What was that about?" said Halfdan, closing the door behind him.

"He hates himself," said Caina, "because he's inept with weapons and incapable of mustering the necessary level of cruelty to be a proper Istarish emir. Given that proper Istarish emirs tend to be men like Rezir Shahan, I suggested that it was not a bad thing."

Halfdan nodded. "Well, so long as he cooperates, he can believe whatever he likes. Meanwhile, we have to find the Bostaji as soon as possible."

"How long do we have?" said Caina.

"A few days," said Halfdan. "Maybe a week at most. I will speak to Lord Titus, and he will circulate the story that Tanzir hit his head during the panic and needs a few days to recover. Any longer, and people will get suspicious…and this entire thing might fall apart."

"So we need to find the Bostaji," said Caina. "Any idea of where to start looking?"

"None," said Halfdan. "None of the other Ghost circles in the city have reported anything unusual. The Bostaji could be holed up in the catacombs or the sewers. Or in an abandoned warehouse. Or they might well have rented rooms at an inn somewhere. The only thing we know is that some of them are Anshani…but there are at least ten thousand Anshani in the city."

Caina nodded. Malarae was huge, the largest city in the civilized world. Nearly a million men, women, and children lived in its districts, lords and merchants and beggars and craftsmen and priests and soldiers and countless others. A few dozen Bostaji, if they were clever, could hide themselves almost anywhere, just as Nalazar and his Kindred had done.

And the Bostaji had proven themselves to be clever.

"We had better get started," said Caina.

CHAPTER 13
BLADES IN THE NIGHT

Caina traded the silk and linen of her gown for leather and wool.

She donned the clothing of a common caravan guard, with mud-crusted boots, ragged trousers, a steel-studded leather jerkin, and a ragged brown cloak. A short sword and a dagger went in scabbards at her belt, and she strapped a pair of leather bracers to her forearm. She rubbed sweat into her hair, let it fall in greasy blond curtains around her jaw, and used makeup to create the illusion of stubble on her jaw and chin.

When she finished, she looked like a ragged, disreputable mercenary, the sort of man who might either guard a caravan or rob it.

She joined Corvalis in the alley behind the House of Kularus. He had put aside his merchant's finery for clothing similar to hers, though he wore chain mail under his leather jerkin.

"You look disreputable," said Corvalis.

"You look downright villainous," said Caina.

"It is a gift of mine," he agreed with a smile. "Shall we find the Bostaji?"

Caina nodded, and they went searching. Halfdan had set all the Ghost circles of Malarae seeking the hiding place of the Bostaji. Caina hoped they might also find where Nalazar and the Kindred of Istarinmul had their lair. They were connected somehow to Tanzir and the Bostaji, she was sure of it.

Caina and Corvalis went to the dockside district, moving from inn to inn, from tavern to tavern, from brothel to brothel. They used the guise of couriers from Anshan, claiming to have news about a rich inheritance in the south. Caina saw dozens of Anshani men, but most were dockworkers, escaped slaves, and petty caravan guards.

They found no trace of the Bostaji.

Dusk fell, and after finding nothing, they returned to the House of Kularus.

###

Caina left the kitchen and walked to the main floor of the coffee house. A few of the servants moved through the upper balconies, wiping down the tables, but the House was otherwise deserted. Halfdan sat at one of the tables on the main floor, sipping from a glass of wine.

Caina and Corvalis sat across from him.

"Where did you get wine?" said Corvalis.

"Shaizid brought it for me," said Halfdan. "He really is a sturdy fellow. You did well, Caina, hiring him as your manager."

"I'm surprised he doesn't go into business for himself," said Corvalis.

"He can't," said Caina, voice quiet. "I tried to encourage him to do it, but refused to even consider it. He was born a slave, he was raised a slave…and he thinks like a slave. He's smart and diligent, but he needs someone to tell him what to do." She made a fist. "They put chains in his mind, and he'll never be rid of them, not entirely."

"I take it," said Halfdan, "that your search was unsuccessful?"

"It was," said Corvalis. "Did the other circles find anything?"

"No," said Halfdan. "Inquiries are underway, but nothing has turned up. Still, we shall keep looking. Malarae is a large city, and we'll also search the surrounding villages and villas. Sooner or later…"

"Master Anton!"

One of the servants sprinted down the stairs from the balcony.

"What is it?" said Corvalis.

"There are armed men outside," said the servant, pointing at the doors. "At least thirty of them."

"Mercenaries?" said Caina.

"I don't know," said the servant, "but they have swords and shields and chain mail, and…"

Caina ran to one of the narrow windows overlooking the Imperial Market. Through the glass she saw the dark shapes of armed men standing outside the House of Kularus. They wore chain mail and bore heavy shields, broadswords at their belts. Mercenaries, most likely. Caina saw another group of men standing behind the mercenaries, clad in dark leather armor and cloaks.

In their midst she saw Nalazar.

"Oh, damn," breathed Caina.

One of the mercenaries raised something.

A crossbow.

Caina shoved herself away from the window and hit the floor as the glass shattered in a rain of glittering shards. A crossbow bolt skipped off the floor next to her and came to a stop.

She scrambled her feet and saw Corvalis and Halfdan with swords in their hands, Shaizid hovering behind them.

"Nalazar and the Kindred," said Caina. "Looks like they hired a mercenary company."

"How the devil did they find us?" said Corvalis. "Mahdriva hasn't come out since she arrived..."

"This is my fault," said Caina. "One of the Kindred must have seen Muravin at the Imperial Citadel. I..."

"We may assign blame," said Halfdan, "once we have completed the more important business of staying alive."

Caina nodded. "Shaizid. Get your people, and get them ready to run."

"Shall we go out the back, mistress?" said Shaizid.

"No!" said Caina. The Kindred and the mercenaries would have moved to seal off the back door as soon as possible. "No, get them to the cellar. We'll have to use the escape tunnel."

"What about you, mistress?" said Shaizid.

"We'll be fine," said Caina, hoping it wasn't a lie. "Get everyone into the cellar. Now." Shaizid nodded. "Go."

Shaizid sprinted away, yelling orders to the remaining maids and servants.

"If the Kindred have someone watching the escape tunnel..." said Corvalis.

"If they do, we're dead in any event," said Caina.

"The tunnel was to remain a secret," said Halfdan, raising his eyebrows.

"I won't leave Shaizid and his people here to die," said Caina.

Halfdan nodded. "Good. However, if we don't have a plan, we're all going to die anyway."

"I have one," said Caina. "Go to the cellar and get Shaizid's people and Mahdriva and the emir ready to move. Muravin wanted a chance to fight, well, he's got it. We prepared for something like this...and it's time to put those preparations to the test."

Halfdan looked at her, as did Corvalis, and Caina realized that she had just given commands to Halfdan, something she had never done before.

"If you think that is best," she added.

Halfdan grinned. "I do. When you are a circlemaster yourself one day, my dear, you'll find it's best to let your subordinates come up with good ideas. It saves you the trouble of having to come up with them yourself. Be careful."

He headed for the cellar.

"Corvalis," said Caina. "The bottles."

"What are you going to do?" said Corvalis, stepping towards the wall. He popped off a wooden panel, revealing a hidden compartment.

Several bottles of multicolored fluid gleamed within the hidden space.

"Buy time," said Caina, running for the stairs. She dashed up to the second-floor balcony and crossed to the window. Below she saw the mercenaries standing before the doors. She spotted Nalazar standing behind the mercenaries, sword in hand, next to a middle-aged man Caina recognized as Tasca, the contact for the Malarae Kindred Shaizid had pointed out.

Caina took a deep breath and opened the window.

At once several mercenaries pointed their crossbows in her direction.

"Nalazar of the Kindred!" she roared in Istarish, using the disguised, rasping tone she employed while wearing her shadow-cloak. "I know what you seek!"

Nalazar scowled and raised his hand, and the mercenaries lowered their crossbows. Caina let out a sigh of relief. Hopefully this would buy enough time for Halfdan and Shaizid to get everyone into the secret tunnel.

"Oh? Is that so?" said Nalazar in Istarish. "And just what do I seek, hmm? Perhaps I simply want a cup of coffee."

"Or you are seeking Mahdriva," said Caina, "and what grows in her womb."

"Maybe I am," said Nalazar. "Might you know where I can find her?"

"I do," said Caina, "and you are wasting your time. She is not here."

Nalazar laughed and looked at something in his left hand. Caina caught a flash of metal and glass in his grasp, and then he tucked the object into a pouch at his belt. It had looked like a jewelry box.

"You're lying, Ghost," said Nalazar. "The girl is inside the coffee house, or perhaps a little below it. The cellar, I think. You will hand her over to us."

"Perhaps we can negotiate," said Caina. She noted some of the mercenaries with crossbows changing position.

"Oh?" said Nalazar.

"One pregnant girl is of no particular importance," said Caina. "But she is well-defended, and you will take significant losses if you try to take her by force. Perhaps we can reach an agreement that will allow you to claim her without bloodshed."

"Or," said Nalazar, "I could simply kill you all and take the girl. Yes, I think I like that plan. Kill him!"

The mercenaries raised their crossbows.

But Caina had anticipated the attack, and threw herself backwards as they lifted their weapons. The glass of the window shattered as the quarrels hammered into it. Caina rolled back to her feet and sprinted down the stairs, the scabbard of her sword slapping against her left leg. She reached the main floor, and heard the crack of axes biting into wood.

The mercenaries were cutting down the door.

Caina felt a stab of irritation. Hiring glaziers and carpenters to repair the damaged windows and doors would not be cheap, and...

She pushed aside the thought and joined Corvalis at one of the tables. He had mixed the contents of the bottles in a metal bowl. He held the final bottle in his left hand, his drawn sword in his right.

"There were some flasks left," said Corvalis, pointing at a pair of small clay flasks on the table.

"Good," said Caina, taking them. "They might be useful."

"Now?" said Corvalis.

"Not yet," said Caina, looking at the doors. They shook and heaved beneath the axe blows. One of the panels popped out and clattered across the floor. Caina glimpsed the mercenaries standing outside, axes rising and falling.

Corvalis moved the bottle over the bowl, standing in the loose, ready posture that indicated imminent violence.

The doors burst open, and the mercenaries stormed into the House of Kularus.

"Now," said Caina.

Corvalis threw the bottle into the bowl, and they whirled and sprinted for the kitchen.

An instant latter a dazzling flare filled with coffee house, a massive plume of smoke erupting from the bowl. The mercenaries came to a stunned halt as smoke billowed through the coffee house, more brilliant flashes throwing stark shadows against the wall. Caina had taken the formula for the concoction from the papers of the Kindred Sanctuary in Cyrioch. Among the documents had been the plans for making the smoke bombs the Kindred assassins of Cyrioch had employed, and Caina had put them to good use.

She and Corvalis hurried into the kitchens, leaving the mercenaries and the assassins to fight their way through the smoke and confusion. Caina crossed to the cellar door, her mind working through the next steps. The escape tunnel from the armory led to the catacombs of Malarae, and from the catacombs they could make their way to the streets. But what then? They needed to find a new safe house, both for Tanzir and for Muravin and Mahdriva. They certainly could not come back here, not after Nalazar had found their hiding place. And no doubt Nalazar would be happy to kill Tanzir and claim the reward as a bonus.

All this flashed through her mind as she reached for the cellar door.

The door to the alley exploded open, and three mercenaries in chain mail burst into the kitchen, broadswords in hand and shields upon their arms. They took one look at Corvalis and Caina and charged.

"Flask!" said Caina.

Corvalis closed his eyes, and Caina flung one of the clay flasks she had taken from the table and screwed her eyes shut.

It shattered against the leading mercenary's shield.

Even through her closed lids, she still saw the flash.

She opened her eyes and charged as the mercenaries screamed, blinking and shaking their heads to clear the afterimage from their eyes. Corvalis lunged forward, sword flashing, and his blade plunged into the first mercenary before the man could recover. Caina stepped past the falling corpse, snatched a dagger from her belt, and stabbed. She opened the throat of the second mercenary, his blood flowing over her fingers.

The third man lunged at her with a snarl, sword reaching for her chest.

Corvalis beat aside the thrust and launched a swing of his own, the tip of his sword opening the man's jaw. The mercenary staggered, and Caina drove the heel of her heavy boot into his knee. His leg buckled, and Corvalis sidestepped and brought his sword down onto the back of the mercenary's neck.

The man collapsed in a pool of his own blood.

She looked at the mess. It would take ages to clean up the kitchen.

The clatter of armor rose from the alley door, and she heard the shouts and cries of the mercenaries on the main floor.

"Go!" said Corvalis, and Caina threw open the cellar door. They hurried into the stairwell, Corvalis barring the door behind them. Hopefully it would slow the Kindred long enough for Caina to escape with the others.

They ran into the hidden armory. Halfdan waited with Shaizid and a dozen servants and maids. Muravin stood before Mahdriva, who looked tired and strained. Tanzir waited nearby, dry-washing his hands as his eyes darted back and forth.

"Oh, mistress," said Shaizid, "the Living Flame be praised that you are unharmed."

"None of us will be unharmed if we don't hurry," said Caina. "The door, Shaizid."

Shaizid nodded and pulled a hidden lever beneath one of the shelves. Another portion of the wall swung back, revealing an ancient stairwell that spiraled down into the earth. It had once been an entrance leading to Malarae's catacombs, until the city's growth had built over the old temple that once stood on the House of Kularus's location. The entrance had been forgotten...but Halfdan had remembered it, and arranged for the builders to include it as a secret exit.

"This way, all of you," said Shaizid. "Quickly. There is not much time."

Corvalis went first to scout the way, sword and lantern in hand.

Shaizid and the servants followed, then Muravin, helping his daughter along. Tanzir went next, hand grabbing at the wall for support, and then Halfdan followed the emir.

Caina went last, closing and locking the door behind her. Nalazar might not find the hidden door at all. But if he did, it was stout and thick and would resist for a long time. By then, Caina hoped to have gotten Muravin and Mahdriva to safety. She started down the stairs, following the light of the retreating lanterns.

The stairs ended in a long galley, the vaulted roof supported by thick brick pillars. The dancing lights of the lantern revealed hundreds of niches lining the walls, stuffed with moldering bones. Small niches held funerary urns, some of age-tarnished bronze, other of stone, and still others of brittle clay. The air smelled musty, and Caina heard the distant skittering of rats.

"This is an ill-omened place," said Mahdriva, voice faint.

"It is," said Caina, "but it will let us get away. We..."

A crossbow bolt hurtled out of the darkness and slammed into Tanzir. The emir fell with a strangled shout of pain.

"Take them!" roared a voice in Istarish, and a half-dozen black-cloaked men appeared from around the pillars, weapons in hand. "Kill them all, but leave the girl alive!"

The servants fled back towards the stairs, Shaizid shouting at them. Corvalis and Halfdan raced to meet the assassins, swords in hand. Muravin stood before his daughter, brandishing weapons in either hand and bellowing curses at his attackers. Caina ran after Corvalis as four of the Kindred converged upon him. Two faced Corvalis and Halfdan from the front, while the others circled to stab him from behind.

Caina lunged, dagger in hand, and buried the blade in the back of the nearest Kindred. The man stiffened, and she ripped the weapon free and stabbed him twice more before he fell. She stepped back, the blade wet with blood, and the assassin toppled to the damp stone floor. A second assassin charged at her, his sword a blur. Caina jumped back, but not fast enough, and the tip of his sword raked across her chest and belly. Her leather armor kept the blade from reaching her skin, but the sheer force of the blow knocked her to the floor.

The assassin loomed over her, raising his sword for a killing blow.

Caina snatched the last flask from her belt and flung it into his face.

She slammed her eyes shut and rolled to the side, the assassin's scream filling her ears. Caina sprang to her feet as the assassin fell to one knee, sweeping his blade back and forth as he sought her.

She stepped out of reach, drew her ghostsilver dagger, and plunged the blade into his side. The man stiffened, and Caina seized his hair and opened his throat. The assassin fell to join the dead of the catacombs.

Caina whirled, seeking new enemies, and saw that Corvalis had cut down one of the Kindred, and he and Halfdan drove their remaining foe back. Muravin faced two of the assassins at once, and Caina ran to aid him.

But he hardly needed the assistance.

The assassins fought with skill and grace, but Muravin met them with power and brutality. His fist slammed into an assassin's face, and the man's head snapped back. Muravin stepped into the opening, driving his scimitar through the assassin's chest. He spun to face the remaining assassin, and Caina drew a throwing knife and flung it. It struck the Kindred in the hip, and the assassin staggered. Muravin's free hand darted out, seized the wrist of the Kindred's sword arm, and twisted.

There was a hideous crackling noise, and the assassin fell with a scream.

Muravin's sword descended and ended the fight.

Silence fell over the catacombs once more, save for the terrified whimpers of the maids and Tanzir's moans of pain. Caina saw that Corvalis and Halfdan had slain the last assassin. Corvalis looked untouched, save for the blood of his foes, while Halfdan had a cut on his jaw and a patch of blood upon his left sleeve.

"You're hurt," said Caina.

"It will keep," said Halfdan. "Shaizid, are your people all right?"

"Yes, Master Basil," said Shaizid, his voice shaking. For all his other skills, Shaizid was not a fighter.

"Get them together," said Halfdan. "We need to move. Muravin?"

"I am unharmed," said Muravin. "As is Mahdriva." He spat upon the corpses. "Bah! These foolish men fight for money and think it makes them warriors. A man is not a warrior until he has fought for his life!"

"Indeed," said Halfdan. "My lord emir?"

Tanzir groaned, and Caina cursed and hurried to his side. The crossbow bolt had clipped his right shoulder, drawing quite a bit of blood, but as far as she could tell, it had not struck an artery or a vein.

"I'm going to die," said Tanzir.

"Not from this," said Caina, examining the wound. "Not if we get you to safety. Get up, my lord emir. We need to…"

"Leave me," said Tanzir. "It's useless. Mother is right to hate me. Leave me, Ghost. I will only slow you down. Leave me here to die in the darkness like I should."

"We are not going to let you die," said Caina, glancing at the others. Shaizid herded his workers together, while Muravin looked at Tanzir with ill-concealed disgust. "You can still stand. Get on your feet."

"No," said Tanzir. "It is futile. I can't escape my mother. I can never escape my mother." He was crying. "Just let me die. Let me die! Let me…"

Caina slapped him as hard as she could manage.

Tanzir sat up, gazing at her in shock.

"Stop whining and get up," she spat. "Those assassins weren't even trying to kill you, my lord emir, they were trying to kill Mahdriva. A pregnant girl, and she is handling this better than you are. Now get up, or I swear by all the gods that I will have Shaizid and his workers tie you up and drag you along like a sack of flour."

"You hit me," said Tanzir.

"Yes, I noticed," said Caina. "Are you going to get up or not?"

Tanzir staggered to his feet, breathing hard, one hand on his wounded shoulder.

"Thank you," said Caina.

"Would you have really…really had them drag me?" said Tanzir.

"She would have," said Corvalis.

"If we are all quite finished," said Halfdan with a hint of asperity, "perhaps we can move along?"

"Aye," said Caina, stepping over one of the assassins Muravin had killed. "We…"

She stopped.

She felt the faint prickle of sorcery.

"What is it?" said Corvalis, recognizing her expression.

"Wait a moment," said Caina, kneeling next to the dead Kindred. She pushed the corpse onto its back and waved her hand over it. Again she felt the tingle of sorcery.

"We must go!" said Halfdan, one hand clamped to his wounded arm.

He was right. But Caina felt arcane force…

"There," she breathed, opening a pouch on the dead man's belt. Inside was a flat, round metal box, one side faced with glass. It looked a bit like a smaller version of a mechanical Strigosti clock. Yet instead of a clock, the metal case held a single crimson needle that spun back and forth wildly.

Like a compass, perhaps.

And the thing absolutely vibrated with sorcerous power.

"We have to go, now," said Halfdan.

Caina nodded, tucked the compass into her belt pouch, and followed the others into the catacombs' gloom.

CHAPTER 14
HUNTERS

"Push!" said Corvalis.

"I am pushing!" snarled Muravin.

They shoved once more, and the stone door swung open, moonlight spilling into the catacombs.

Caina gave a sigh of relief.

"Oh, good," said Mahdriva, a faint quaver in her voice. One thin hand rested upon her swollen belly. Caina was sure that Mahdriva was in pain, but the girl had not complained as she marched through the catacombs in grim silence. She was indeed her father's daughter. "I feared we would wander this evil place forever. It is ill to offend the dead."

"I do not think the dead mind very much," said Halfdan. "Perhaps they are even glad for the company." He beckoned with his lantern. "These stairs should open up near the Imperial Citadel."

"I'll go first," said Corvalis, drawing his sword. He climbed the spiraling stone stairs, Halfdan following. Muravin came next, standing before his daughter like a shield, and then Shaizid and his workers. Tanzir followed them, one hand gripping his wounded shoulder, face glistening with sweat. Caina brought up the rear, shooting one last glance over her shoulder. Nalazar had been clever enough to set an ambush at the secret tunnel, but hopefully he had not been able to follow them through the stone maze of the catacombs.

Still, best not to dawdle.

Caina followed Tanzir up the stairs.

The door at the top of the stairs opened at the base of the Imperial Citadel's mountain spur, near the great stone temples to the gods of the Empire. Caina took a cautious look around, but the street was deserted.

Malarae's taverns and brothels did a brisk business after dark, but the temples were empty.

"Well," said Halfdan, "we seem to have eluded our foes."

"But not for long, I fear," said Muravin. "How did they know where to find us?"

"We can worry about that later," said Halfdan. "Meanwhile, we need to get you, your daughter, and the emir," he glanced at Tanzir, "to safety."

"What did you have in mind?" said Corvalis. "If Nalazar tracked Mahdriva to the coffee house, he might be able to track her anywhere."

"If he can do that," said Halfdan, "then we need to take them to a place with defenses strong enough that Nalazar will need more than common mercenaries to enter."

"And you have just the place in mind?" said Caina.

"Why, I do," said Halfdan. "This way."

A short walk brought them to the mansions below the Imperial Citadel. The chief magistrates of the Empire lived here, along with some of the more powerful lords. The various Lord Ambassadors from the surrounding nations also maintained residences in the shadow of the Imperial Citadel.

"The Lord Ambassador's mansion?" said Tanzir.

The official mansion for the Lord Ambassador of Istarinmul rose before them. It had been built in the Istarish style, a sprawling-three story mansion with gleaming whitewashed walls. It looked unassuming, but most houses in Istarinmul and Anshan were built with whitewashed walls to reflect the harsh sun.

"Aye," said Halfdan.

A large pool, easily three times the size of the mansion itself, stretched next to the house, the waters rippling in the moonlight. It fed into Malarae's aqueduct system, drawing the snowmelt from the mountains and draining it into the city's public fountains.

"Muravin and Mahdriva will be safe here," said Tanzir, "but the Bostaji will find me easily."

"They will," said Halfdan, "but they will have a harder time reaching you through the three centuries of the Imperial Guard I've stationed here."

He strode up to the polished double doors and knocked. A moment later they swung open, revealing a man in the black armor and plumed helm of a centurion of the Imperial Guard.

"Tylas," said Halfdan.

"Master Basil," said Tylas. "Everything has been prepared as you instructed. We have refused to allow the Immortals entry."

"Good," said Halfdan.

"There is a problem, though," said Tylas.

"We can discuss it in private," said Halfdan, glancing back at Shaizid and the servants. "Shaizid, take your people to the dining hall and see to their injuries. Tylas, Anton, Sonya, Muravin, Mahdriva. Please follow me. My lord emir, if you will accompany us?"

Tanzir gave a rueful glance at Caina. "It seems that I have little choice in the matter."

The entry hall was grand, built in Istarish style with an elaborate mosaic of a garden upon the floor, the walls adorned with frescoes showing emirs hunting beasts in a tangled jungle. Beyond was a wide dining hall with a long, low table, ringed with cushions so the guests could recline in comfort. A huge, gleaming mirror stood over the table. Shaizid led his workers to the dining hall, while Halfdan opened a narrow door in the wall. It led into a small guardroom with a bench. Tanzir started towards the bench, but Mahdriva sat down first, breathing hard. Muravin turned a glare just short of murderous towards Tanzir, and the emir took a prudent step back.

"Well?" said Halfdan. "What is the problem?"

"You've taken wounds," said Tylas, looking at Halfdan's bloodstained robe.

"I have," said Halfdan, "but we have more immediate concerns. What is the problem?"

Tylas took a deep breath. "That Alchemist is here. Ibrahmus Sinan."

"He wants to kill me!" said Tanzir.

"I told you to keep him out," said Halfdan.

"He insisted," said Tylas, "and we would have needed to use force to keep him out. And since killing an Alchemist of the College would be as bad as killing the emir himself," he shrugged, "I figured I had better let you decide what to do. He's probably realized you're here by now."

"Thanks," said Halfdan.

"Rank has its privileges," said Corvalis.

Halfdan gave him an annoyed look and opened the door.

Sinan waited in the entry hall, staring at them.

"My lord emir," said Sinan. "How good to see you are safe." He strode forward as Tanzir and Halfdan stepped into the hall, his gold-trimmed white robes rustling against the floor. "I feared these northern barbarians had done you some harm."

"The only reason I am still alive is because of these northern barbarians," said Tanzir. "My own Immortals betrayed me, Ibrahmus. If not for the northerners, I would be dead on the floor of the opera."

"Impossible," said Sinan with a thin smile. "Immortals do not disobey the commands of their superiors. Your attackers must have been impostors clad in stolen Immortal armor."

"Perhaps," said Tanzir.

"Come with me, my lord emir," said Sinan. "I will take you to safety."

Tanzir hesitated, licked his lips, and looked at Caina.

She gave him a tiny nod.

"No," said Tanzir. "I would rather stay here for a time. If you do not mind. At least until any traitors among my Immortals are discovered."

"You would trust your safety to foreigners?" said Sinan.

"Forgive me, learned one," said Halfdan, stepping forward, "but I believe the emir is quite safe with us. You see, if the emir were murdered while in Malarae, people would believe that the Emperor had him killed. Why, an unscrupulous person could use that to continue the war between the Emperor and the Padishah. Though I'm sure the thought of such perfidy never crossed your mind."

Sinan glared at Halfdan. "Indeed not." He looked at Tanzir. "Come with me, now. This discussion is over."

Tanzir looked at Caina, and she nodded again.

He drew himself up. "I am Tanzir Shahan, emir of the Vale of Fallen Stars and the Padishah's Lord Ambassador to Istarinmul. I come and go at my pleasure, Alchemist. Er. Not…not yours."

Sinan drew himself up, his fingers flexing…and Caina's skin crawled as she felt the surge of arcane force.

He was preparing to cast a spell.

"Basil," said Caina.

"I should point out, learned one," said Halfdan, utterly calm, "that you are surrounded by three hundred of the Imperial Guard. Not quite as ferocious or supernaturally strong as your own Immortals, true, but better disciplined and just as tenacious. Even an Alchemist of power might find it difficult to overcome three hundred men."

Sinan offered a tight smile. "Difficult, but not impossible."

He flexed his fingers again…and then froze, his eyes fixed on Caina.

She stared back at him without blinking.

"But made more difficult," said Sinan, and the sense of power faded from the air, "by the presence of the sorceress you have among your number. A good evening to you, Basil Callenius. Do keep the emir safe. It will go quite badly with you if you do not."

He turned and strode for the doors without another word.

"Let him go," said Halfdan to Tylas. "Don't admit him again, even if he tries to force his way inside."

"What was that about?" said Corvalis to Caina. "Why did he think you were a sorceress?"

"I think," said Caina, reaching into her belt pouch, "because of this thing."

She held up the peculiar compass and held it flat, the needle spinning.

"What the devil is that?" said Halfdan.

Muravin stepped out of the guard room. "It looks like a ship's compass."

"I don't know what it is," said Caina. "One of the Kindred in the catacombs had the thing. It's enspelled powerfully."

"Why would the Kindred take a compass with them into the catacombs?" said Corvalis.

Caina shrugged. "It's easy to get lost down there." The needle began to slow. "But I don't think this is actually a compass."

"It looks like one," said Muravin.

"It is enspelled," said Caina, "and it's not pointing north." The needle had stopped to point at the guard room. "That's…south, I think. Due south."

"Oh," said Tanzir, staring at the compass. "Oh, that's not good at all."

They looked at him.

"I think," said Tanzir, "I think that is a blood compass."

"A blood compass?" said Caina.

"The Alchemists make them to bind useful slaves or servants," said Tanzir. "They take a sample of blood from a slave and use sorcery to fuse it to a steel needle. The device acts like a compass, but the needle always points towards the slave."

A dark thought occurred to Caina, and she walked past the others and into the guard room. Mahdriva sat on the bench, leaning against the stone wall.

"Is something wrong?" said Mahdriva.

The needle pointed at her, quivering.

"Probably," said Caina. She walked in a slow half-circle around Mahdriva, holding the compass flat on her palm.

The needle rotated as she moved, continuing to point at Mahdriva.

"It's her," said Caina. "The compass is pointing at her." She took a deep breath. "I think we know that an Alchemist wants your daughter dead, Muravin. Maybe even Sinan himself."

"But why?" said Muravin. "Why would an Alchemist want to harm my family? I was the seneschal's bodyguard for years, and the College bore me no ill will."

"For that matter," said Tanzir, "where would they have gotten her blood?"

"Any number of places, if she grew up near the College," said Caina. "When she got a cut, maybe. Drugged her and stole it from her while she slept. Menstruation, maybe." She thought for a moment. "Tanzir. Would the blood of a near relative work for the blood compass?"

Muravin scowled. "Like a sister or a nephew, perhaps?"

"I…I don't know," said Tanzir. "I'm not an Alchemist, or even a sorcerer. I don't know how the blood compass works."

Caina turned, still watching the needle…and the tingling presence of sorcery grew stronger, harsher. She looked around, wondering if Sinan had decided to launch an arcane assault after all. But as she turned, the tingling faded. She turned again, and the sensation strengthened anew. Was it sharpening as she drew nearer to Mahdriva? Caina stepped past the girl, towards the wall of the guard room, and still the tingling grew stronger.

Odd. But why was it happening?

"Then perhaps we are safe," said Muravin. "If the Kindred lost their blood compass."

"No," said Caina, turning away from the wall. "Nalazar had one. And if he gave one to the ambushers in the catacombs, it is safe to say that he has at least a few more to spare."

"Then I shall never be free of this," said Mahdriva, her voice tired. "They will hunt me to the ends of the earth."

"No," growled Muravin. "I shall find them, kill them, and smash their compasses."

"Assuming we can find them," said Halfdan. "You and Mahdriva should be safe here for now, as will you, my lord emir. But we have not gained much of a respite. Neither the Bostaji nor the Kindred will stop. Not until we find them and eliminate them."

"We will start looking at once," said Caina. "I'll have Shaizid and the others close the House of Kularus tomorrow and contact the civic militia. We'll claim that thieves broke into the House and killed each other." That would provide an explanation for the corpses in the kitchen. "Perhaps examining their bodies will tell us something useful."

"Return here tomorrow night," said Halfdan. "We'll decide how to proceed from there." He turned to Tylas. "If you could find some bandages, thread, and boiling wine, I would be most obliged."

Caina left the Lord Ambassador's house, Corvalis at her side, Shaizid and his servants walking before them. They passed alongside the reservoir pool, their reflections dancing on the dark water.

"Fear not, mistress," said Shaizid. "We will repair the damage to the House of Kularus, and it shall be as splendid as before. If not more so."

"I know," murmured Caina, feeling the cold weight of the blood compass in her left hand. "I have complete confidence in you, Shaizid."

She moved the compass before her, feeling the tingling of sorcery grow weaker and stronger as she did so.

It meant something, she was sure of it.

But what?

###

A short time later Caina and Corvalis returned to their townhouse.

There was some risk in that, she knew. Given that Nalazar knew that Mahdriva had been hiding in the House of Kularus, he might decide to raid Anton Kularus's home. Yet Caina doubted Nalazar would bother. With a blood compass, he knew where Mahdriva was. Most likely he would focus his efforts on finding a ruse that would allow him to enter the mansion and kidnap Mahdriva.

Still the question of the compass gnawed at her.

The blood compass's presence meant that an Alchemist, perhaps even Sinan himself, wanted Mahdriva. Yet Sinan must have seen Mahdriva in the entry hall of the mansion, and he had not left until he sensed the presence of the blood compass. Perhaps he recognized the compass's maker, a more powerful Alchemist he did not want to offend.

"But why?" muttered Caina, putting the blood compass on the windowsill of their bedroom. The street outside, the street where she had first seen the Kindred in the fog, was empty and deserted.

"You truly do want to save her," said Corvalis, "don't you?"

"Who? Mahdriva?" said Caina. "Of course. She doesn't deserve what's happened to her, Corvalis."

"No," said Corvalis, his hand resting on the small of her back. "But many people have suffered things they did not deserve."

"True," said Caina, "but I can keep her from suffering worse. She can have her child, Corvalis. The Ghosts can find a place for her in Malarae, both for her and Muravin. We just have to find who wants to kill her."

"And who wants to kill Tanzir," said Corvalis.

"That's no mystery," said Caina. "His mother wants him dead, and Sinan and the Bostaji came to carry out her wishes." She shook her head. "Though even that is connected to Mahdriva somehow, I'm sure of it. I wish I could see how." She leaned against him. "But I will. I will find a way, Corvalis...and I will save her. Both her and her child."

They stood in silence for a moment, his arm curled around her shoulders.

"You know what this is about," said Corvalis, "don't you?"

"Oh?" said Caina. "Enlighten me."

"The Kindred killed her sisters," said Corvalis, "and their unborn children. They're trying to take her unborn child, the gods know why. And that's why you care so much. You can't have children yourself, so you're going to save Mahdriva's child for her."

Caina laughed.

"What?" said Corvalis.

"Give me credit for having some self-awareness," said Caina. "I know who I am, Corvalis. I know why I do what I do. I would help Mahdriva and

Muravin anyway…but I see myself in her. Or myself as I could have been, had things been different. I can't have children. I've made my peace with that. I won't have a family of my own…but I can save the families of others."

His arm tightened around her. "The way you saved Claudia."

"Yes," whispered Caina. "And I will save Mahdriva and her child, if it is in my power."

Corvalis laughed. "Caina Amalas. Claudia used to talk about saving the world. But you could do it." He snorted. "I suppose you have, if even half the stories Halfdan has told me about you are true." He turned her to face him. "You may not have a family, but you're not alone."

"No," said Caina, "no, I suppose I'm…"

He silenced her with a long kiss, and a short time later they were in bed together, despite the long and trying day. Nothing fired Corvalis's blood like a brush with death…and she had been surprised to discover that the same was true about her, as well.

After they finished she slumped back against the pillows, sweating and breathing hard, and soon dropped into a black and dreamless sleep.

Caina awoke with the sun in her eyes.

She sat up with a yawn, pushing lank hair from her face. Corvalis lay on his back next to her, breathing slowly. Caina stood, the floorboards chill against her bare feet, her joints stiff and sore. She had pushed herself hard yesterday. Caina moved through a series of stretches, working the knots from her arms and legs.

Corvalis remained sleeping, and he usually awoke at the drop of a pin. Yesterday had indeed been exhausting.

Of course, she had helped wear him out.

Caina took a carafe of wine from the sideboard and took a swallow, washing the dryness from her mouth. She took a sheet from the bed, wrapped it around herself, and padded to the window. It was well past sunrise, later than she had wanted to sleep. Well, Mahdriva and Tanzir would be safe at the Lord Ambassador's mansion, and Shaizid could handle matters at the House of Kularus. The blood compass still sat upon the windowsill, its needle pointing towards the ambassador's house.

Caina picked up the compass with her free hand, gazing at the blood-colored needle. The metal felt cold and heavy in her grasp, and the faint tingle of active sorcery washed over her hand.

But it was fainter than it had been last night.

She turned in a circle, holding the compass before her.

And again the tingling grew stronger as she turned to the south. No –

more to the southwest. But as she turned north, the tingling faded.

She paused, faced south again, and felt the tingling strengthen.

Caina shook her head, and saw Corvalis standing near her.

"I would ask," he said, "why you are wearing a sheet and waving that compass about, but I'm sure you have a good reason."

"There is something odd about it," said Caina. "It's designed to point at Mahdriva. The needle never wavers from that." She swung the compass to the southwest and felt the tingling sensation grow sharper. "But the sorcery feels...stronger, somehow, whenever I point it to the southwest. I can't figure out why."

Corvalis shrugged, the black lines of the tattoo on his chest twitching. "Maybe it's reacting to something."

Caina blinked. "Reacting..."

Then she understood.

"Corvalis," she said.

"What is it?" he said, looking around in alarm at her tone.

"I think," said Caina. She took a deep breath. "I think I know how to find Nalazar."

Caina usually did not resent the time it took to don whatever disguise was most appropriate, but the delay as she pulled on a gown and arranged her hair and put on jewelry grated on her. Still, it was necessary. Anton Kularus and Sonya Tornesti could hardly wander around Malarae like a pair of vagabonds...and a pair of ragged mercenaries would not gain entrance to the Lord Ambassador's house.

But the delay chafed as they rode in Anton Kularus's coach to the Lord Ambassador's house. The blood compass rested in a leather pouch at Caina's belt. If she was right, if she had puzzled out the mystery, perhaps she could find the Kindred and save Mahdriva from them before the end of the day.

The coach stopped before the Lord Ambassador's residence, the whitewashed walls gleaming in the morning sunlight. Caina saw a dozen Imperial Guards standing before the mansion's doors, more standing guard on the roof and patrolling around the mansion. The Bostaji would find it hard to get at Sinan...and the Kindred would find it just as difficult to reach Mahdriva.

Four of the Guards approached as Caina and Corvalis climbed down from the coach. "Halt and identify yourself."

Corvalis smiled. "Anton Kularus."

"Your business?" said the Guard. "The Lord Ambassador's residence is closed while the emir meets with Lord Titus."

"Actually, I'm here to see Master Basil Callenius," said Corvalis. "He should be with Lord Titus, and I suspect he'll want to speak with me. I have news about an urgent matter."

"A moment," said the Guard, and one of the men vanished into the mansion.

He turned a moment later.

"You may enter," said the Guard. "Master Basil awaits you in the guard room. Attempt to enter any other part of the Lord Ambassador's residence, and we will cut you down."

"I wouldn't dream of it," said Corvalis.

Caina put her arm in Corvalis's, and the Guards led them into the entry hall. Halfdan awaited them in the guard room, clad in a fresh robe and cap. He looked almost cheerful.

"You must have slept well," said Corvalis, once the Guards had closed the door behind them.

"Not really," said Halfdan, "but success is almost as refreshing as sleep. I persuaded Lord Titus to conduct most of the negotiations here."

"Isn't that a concession of weakness?" said Corvalis. "Meeting with the ambassador in his residence?"

"It is," said Halfdan, "but given that the Padishah wants peace, and is willing to cede large portions of the Argamaz Desert to the Empire, a concession here costs the Emperor nothing. And it may keep the emir alive. The Bostaji can't get to him here, not as long as the Imperial Guard watches him, and once the negotiations are complete, the Bostaji will no longer have any reason to kill him." He looked at Caina. "What have you found?"

She took the compass from her belt pouch. "I think I can use this to locate the Kindred."

"How?" said Halfdan.

"The...aura of power around it feels stronger whenever I point it towards the southwestern corner of the city," said Caina. "I'm not sure why. But I think it's reacting to the blood compass Nalazar still holds. The enspelled needle was fused to Mahdriva's blood, and it reacts to her presence. So why shouldn't the two needles react to each other?"

"Then you think the aura will grow stronger the closer the two blood compasses get?" said Halfdan.

"I believe so," said Caina. "And unless Nalazar has the ability to sense the presence of sorcery, he won't realize what is happening. If we're careful, we can figure out where the Istarish Kindred are hiding...and then get rid of them."

"Do it," said Halfdan. "If you can find Nalazar and the Kindred, I will arrange to strike them at once."

Caina nodded, and she and Corvalis left the mansion.

CHAPTER 15
SERPENT'S NEST

"It's getting stronger," said Caina, her hand thrust into the pocket of her coat.

She and Corvalis walked down a narrow lane in Malarae's dockside district. Corvalis had again traded Anton Kularus's finery for the rough grab of a wandering mercenary. Caina wore her caravan guard disguise, blond hair hanging loose and ragged around her head, but she also wore a ragged gray coat over her leather armor. The thing was damnably hot and made her arms itch, but it did have deep pockets.

Which allowed her to hold the blood compass unseen.

"That's just as well," said Corvalis. "We're not in a safe part of the city."

This part of the dockside district held seedy taverns, pawn shops, brothels, the sort of apothecaries that sold poisons under the table, and tenements towering six or seven stories over the street. Men sat on the stairs of the tenements and shops, drinking wine and watching Caina and Corvalis with cold, predatory eyes.

It was not the sort of place Caina would want to visit alone, even while disguised as a man.

It was also the perfect place for the Kindred to hide. A few bribes to the local gangs of thieves, and no one would speak a word to the Ghosts. And since those who betrayed the Kindred tended to wash in with the morning tide, the locals had plenty of motivation to keep their mouths shut.

But Caina had the blood compass.

"Think we'll get mugged?" said Caina.

"Doubtful," said Corvalis. "Two caravan guards planning to spend their pay on drink and whores aren't good targets. After we're drunk and can't defend ourselves, aye. But not until then, and not during the daylight." He glanced at a group of men who stood in an alley. "But if some of them are bold enough and drunk enough, I might have to kill a few."

"Try to avoid that," said Caina. "That will draw attention."

Corvalis nodded, and they kept walking, Caina feeling the compass's pulse of sorcery. It was strong here, and grew stronger the further they walked southwest. The other blood compass had to be near...

They turned a corner, and Caina saw the tavern.

It looked little different than the others she had seen, a ramshackle building of brick and wood with a sagging roof of clay tiles. The top floors held rented rooms, while the bottom floor held the tavern itself. The sign hanging over the door had been painted with a twisted green serpent.

"The Serpents' Nest," said Corvalis, reading the sign.

"It's there," said Caina.

The blood compass vibrated in her grasp, and when she pointed it at the tavern, she felt a low thrum that went down into her bones.

"Truly? They're hiding in a tavern named the Serpents' Nest?" said Corvalis. "That's bold."

"This is it," said Caina. "Don't turn around, but I think there's a sentry on the roof of the warehouse across the street."

"There would be," said Corvalis. "And I bet there's one in that room on the top floor overlooking the street. You're right. This has to be the place. Do we go back and tell Halfdan?"

"Not yet," said Caina. "Not until we've had a look around."

"It's dangerous," said Corvalis.

"Of course it is," said Caina. She thought for a moment. "Caerish mercenaries?"

"Ones looking for work," said Corvalis. They had used the ruse before. "I'll do the talking. You look around. You're better at it than I am anyway."

Caina nodded, and they strode into the Serpents' Nest.

A flight of stone stairs dropped into a cellar, and they walked into the tavern's common room. The room was dim and smoky, lit only by the smoldering glow of twin hearths. Battered chairs and tables stood strewn about the dirt floor, and men sat in the corners, speaking in low voices over clay cups of beer. A bar ran the length of one wall, and an enormously fat man in a leather apron stood there, his bushy black beard hanging halfway down his chest.

Every eye in the room turned towards Caina and Corvalis for a moment, weighing them, and then looked away.

"Well?" said the landlord with a surly glare. "What do you want?"

"Beer," said Corvalis with a thick Caerish accent, "and work, if you have it."

He slapped some copper coins upon the bar. The landlord squinted at them, made the coins disappear, and handed over to clay cups of beer. Corvalis took a drink, and Caina sipped from hers, trying her very best not to grimace at the taste.

"Work, you say?" said the landlord. "I'm not looking to hire any bouncers. Everyone here is a well-behaved gentleman, don't you know it."

He snickered at his own joke.

Corvalis grinned. "Oh, aye, I'm sure your patrons are the lords of the Imperial Curia. But I'm looking for a job, and I figure a well-connected fellow like you might know of work for a fighting man like myself."

The landlord grunted. "Why don't you have work now?"

"I did," said Corvalis, "yesterday. My brother and me," he jerked his head at Caina, "helped escort a merchant caravan out of the Mardonish provinces. Came to Malarae, and the merchant decided to hire some damned Anshani for guards instead of us." He spat upon the floor. "Serves the cheap bastard right if the Anshani take his goods and gutted him like a pig."

The landlord looked Caina up and down. "This scrawny little fellow is a mercenary?"

Corvalis shrugged. "He's not very good in a fight, but I promised our mother I would look out for him."

"Go to hell," said Caina.

Both Corvalis and the landlord laughed.

"Aye, I might know where you can get some work," said the landlord. "War with the Istarish is ending, or so they say, so the lords won't be hiring mercenaries for the campaign in the south. You could try one of the established companies – they're always looking for fighting men. Or you could head up the Megaros valley to the Imperial Pale. They always need swords up there."

Corvalis snorted. "I'd prefer not to end up in a frozen grave."

The landlord laughed. "Don't be so picky. You're a fool with a sword, not a lord of the Empire. Either fight, go toil on a farm, or beg."

"What about something more local?" said Corvalis. "Some merchant whose caravans need guarding?"

The landlord snorted. "Does it look like wealthy merchants frequent my tavern?"

"Or," said Corvalis, "someone who needs things done…quietly, on the side."

"I might have something," said the landlord, "for a man who can keep his mouth shut."

They kept talking, insulting each other with friendly indifference, and Caina put a bored expression on her face. Her eyes roved over the common room of the Serpents' Nest, seeking for anything unusual. The patrons looked like common thieves and workers, and she saw nothing exceptional about them.

Except...

Years of practice kept the surprise off her face.

Except that one of the men wore a bola at this belt.

The Bostaji were here, too? Were they working with Nalazar and the Kindred?

"To hell with that," said Caina. "Let's go."

Corvalis scowled at her. "He might have work for us."

"What, washing his floors?" said Caina. She pushed away from the bar. "I need a piss."

"Up the back stairs and into the alley," growled the landlord. "You piss on my floor, I'll beat you black and blue."

Caina gave him a rude gesture, walked across the common room, and climbed the stairs at the far end of the cellar. The stairs ended in a narrow wooden door that opened into the alley behind the tavern. To judge from the stench, the alley had an opening directly into the city's sewers. But the stairs continued towards the upper levels of the Serpents' Nest.

She shot a quick glance over her shoulder, saw that no one had followed her, and reached into her coat pocket for the blood compass. The tingling grew stronger as she lifted it, so strong it felt as if tiny knives stabbed into her skin.

Nalazar, she suspected, was somewhere above.

Caina took a deep breath, ignoring the smell, and glided up the stairs, taking care to keep her boots from making any sound. She went up one flight of stairs, and then the next, following the feel of the blood compass until she came to the top floor. Corvalis had seen a lookout keeping watch over the street, and she wondered if the Kindred had made their lair up here.

She crept down the hallway, straining not to make a sound, waving the compass back and forth.

There. The tingling was strongest in front of that door. She suspected it opened into the lookout's room.

And she heard voices coming from within.

Caina hesitated, decided to take another gamble, and pressed her ear against the door.

She heard Nalazar's voice.

"We need more men to pull this off, Tasca," said Nalazar. "The Ghosts moved the damned girl to the Lord Ambassador's residence, and they've got three or four hundred Imperial Guards crawling around the place."

"Then send a lone assassin to take her," said Tasca, "rather than this nonsense about open attacks. Which, I should point out, I told you was a bad idea at the House of Kularus."

"Don't remind me," snapped Nalazar. "And there are too many Guards for an infiltration. We can't get at the girl, and we're running out of time. The client wants the girl, alive, with her child yet unborn. She will give birth any day."

"Why does the client want an unborn child, anyway?" said Tasca.

"Do I look foolish enough to ask?" said Nalazar. "But I need more men."

"And you will not have them," said Tasca. "The Elder of Malarae is…sympathetic to your plight. But you already lost the men he loaned you at the House of Kularus, men that represented years of training. Their skills are now lost to the Kindred of Malarae, and you will have no more help from us."

"Damn it," said Nalazar. "That is not good enough."

Caina could almost hear Tasca's shrug. "That is not my concern, nor is it the Elder's. If you had wished to avoid this difficulty, then you should have taken the girl alive while she was still in Istarinmul."

Nalazar barked a curse. "I would have, if not for her damned father. Who knew one old man could put up such a fierce fight?"

"You ought to have killed him in his sleep first," said Tasca.

"Thank you for that helpful advice," said Nalazar, his voice heavy with annoyance. "If the Elder will not spare any more brothers, then perhaps he might assist with coin? With proper planning, a small team of skilled mercenaries could break into the Lord Ambassador's residence and steal away the girl before the Imperial Guards react."

"Perhaps," said Tasca, "though such mercenaries would require a great deal of coin. The Elder would like to see some return on this investment."

"He will," said Nalazar, "once we are successful. The client is desperate for the girl's child, and will pay any sum we ask."

"The best kind of client," said Tasca with a laugh. "Why not ask the Bostaji for help?"

"No," said Nalazar. "Absolutely not."

"Why not?" said Tasca. "You both need to get into the Lord Ambassador's mansion. And the Bostaji want that fat buffoon of an emir, not the girl. You can work together to obtain your goals, and then go your separate ways."

"Because the Bostaji are madmen," said Nalazar. "We are Kindred, Tasca. We are the wolves that cull the weak from the herd of humanity, making the race of man stronger and fitter. But the Bostaji are fanatics and nothing more. They believe their Shahenshah is the chosen of the Living Flame, the representative of the divine on earth, and they will do anything in his name. If they think it necessary to kill us all to reach Tanzir Shahan, they would do it. I could see the Bostaji agreeing to a joint attack with us, only to betray us and kill the emir while we're busy getting slaughtered by the Imperial Guards."

"Then the answer is obvious," said Tasca. "Speak to your client and ask for his assistance. Surely he has certain…skills that could aid you."

"He does," said Nalazar, "but I am not particularly eager to ask him."

"He made those blood compasses for you," said Tasca.

"He only did that," said Nalazar, "grudgingly, once Mahdriva eluded us. A sorcerer like him, Tasca…no one in their right mind trifles with such a man. Bad enough to admit failure to him once. But twice? He might decide to kill us all and hire someone else for the task."

Tasca laughed, long and loud. "Surely one man is incapable of posing such a threat."

"This man is," said Nalazar. "He is not the most powerful sorcerer I have ever encountered, true…but he is desperate, and desperation mated to power is a dangerous combination."

"Desperate enough," said Tasca, "to aid you? If he so desperately needs the girl and her unborn brat for some sorcerous purpose, then he will give you whatever aid you require. It's all a matter of phrasing, brother Nalazar. Simply tell him that you have a plan for success, but it requires some arcane assistance. Your client will fall over himself to aid you. Desperate men do not think clearly."

"Perhaps you are right," said Nalazar. "I shall think on it."

"Think quickly," said Tasca. "As you said, the girl shall give birth any day…and if she does, this will all have been for nothing."

"Indeed," said Nalazar. "Come! Let us get some food. This wretched landlord is incapable of preparing any meal without boiling it into tasteless mush…"

Caina pushed away from the door and moved towards the stairs as fast as she dared. She had no doubt that other Kindred were resting in the nearby rooms, and they would wake at Nalazar's call.

If Nalazar saw her, she was going to die.

She glided down the stairs, back to the cellar and the common room. Caina hesitated for a moment, hand on her dagger hilt. But no one appeared on the stairs.

Nalazar and Tasca had gone for food…and they had not noticed Caina.

She let out a long breath, thanking Halfdan for all those years he had made her practice stealth at the Vineyard.

Then she strode into the common room, making no effort to muffle her footfalls. Corvalis still leaned against the bar, gesturing with his cup of beer. The landlord scowled up at her.

"What the hell took so long?" he said.

"I ate a lot of cabbage," said Caina, using her disguised voice. She jerked her head at the door. "Let's go. The stench of this place is turning my stomach."

Corvalis shrugged, set down his cup, and followed her into the street.

They walked in silence for a moment, waiting until they were out of earshot and sight of the Serpents' Nest.

"I did get a job," said Corvalis. "It seems our landlord has a lucrative sideline in stolen goods, and wished to hire me to steal items from his rival. I trust your time was as profitably spent?"

"It was," said Caina. "I overheard Nalazar and Tasca. They're both here, Corvalis, the Bostaji and the Kindred. They're here, and they don't know that we know they're here. We've got them caught like rats in a trap."

"Or snakes in a nest," said Corvalis.

"Droll," said Caina. "If we move at once, we can take them all. Both Mahdriva and Tanzir will be safe. And perhaps we can find who hired the Kindred to murder Muravin's daughters and their husbands."

"I don't suppose Nalazar gave a name?" said Corvalis.

"No," said Caina. "But they mentioned him. Some kind of sorcerer. Apparently he wants all three unborn children for some sort of spell. Though it sounds like the spell, whatever it is, will only work if the child is unborn. So if we can keep this sorcerer away from Mahdriva for a little while longer, she should be safe once the baby is born."

"A sorcerer," said Corvalis. "Sounds like the work of a necromancer."

"Aye," said Caina, her voice full of loathing. "Maybe one of Maglarion's old students. Or another disciple of the Moroaica."

"Like Ranarius," said Corvalis, his voice distant.

"Like Ranarius," said Caina. "We stopped Ranarius, and we'll stop this sorcerer, too."

"Once Nalazar tells you who he is," said Corvalis.

"Or we find out," said Caina, "from his papers." She looked back at the receding shape of the ramshackle tavern.

"I suspect," said Corvalis, "that Nalazar might not live out the night."

"I'd prefer not to kill him," said Caina. She had grown weary of killing. "I'd prefer that he tells me whatever he knows." She shrugged. "But if he doesn't...if he doesn't, he killed two innocent women and their husbands, along with their unborn children. He killed Mahdriva's husband and tried to kill her. I wouldn't shed any tears for his death."

"Then," said Corvalis, "let's get started."

They walked back to the townhouse.

CHAPTER 16
PATHS

"Well done," said Halfdan. "Well done, indeed."

Caina smiled.

They stood in the solar of the Lord Ambassador's residence. Like every other room in the mansion, it was furnished lavishly in Istarish style, with pillows encircling a low round table. A brazier sat on the center of the table for burning incense. Caina again wore the gown and jewels of Sonya Tornesti, while Corvalis had returned to his fine black coat and trousers and boots.

She would, she suspected, wear more utilitarian clothes tonight.

"And they suspected nothing?" said Halfdan.

"I don't think so," said Corvalis. "In fact, the landlord of the Serpents' Nest thinks I'm meeting him tonight to help rob a rival."

"Yes, I know him," said Halfdan. "Cornan Bascaii, petty thief, fence, and trader. I suspect he ran slaves for Haeron Icaraeus a few years ago, but he was clever enough not to get caught. And now with Lord Haeron dead, it seems he has found a new patron with the Kindred." He nodded. "Renting his tavern to the Kindred is exactly the sort of thing he would do."

"And the Bostaji," said Caina. "The amirja Ashria might have sent Sinan to make sure that Tanzir dies, but I'm certain he has something to do with the Kindred as well." Perhaps he had hired the Kindred himself. Or perhaps he was the student of another, more powerful sorcerer, and had been sent to seize Mahdriva at his master's bidding.

"Either way," said Halfdan, "we shall end it tonight. I've sent word to our friend Tomard in the civic militia. He will send a cohort of the militia to surround the Serpents' Nest. When they do, we'll flush out both the

Kindred and the Bostaji."

"And send them running into Tomard's waiting arms," said Caina.

"That is the plan," said Halfdan. "I would prefer to take as many of them alive as possible. They may know useful things – the location of the Kindred Sanctuary in Malarae, for one, or who hired the Kindred to go after Mahdriva." He shook his head. "But I suspect most of them will fight to the death. The Kindred will not want to face the wrath of their Elder. And the Bostaji are glad to die in the service of the Shahenshah."

Caina nodded. "How are the negotiations?"

"Proceeding well, from what I understand," said Halfdan. "Most of it is a formality at this point...a river there, a hill there. But a necessary formality. Neither the Emperor nor the Padishah want to lose face, and this treaty is the way to accomplish it. It will be finished in a few days, and then the war with Istarinmul will be over."

"And no one will have any more reason to kill Tanzir," said Corvalis.

"His mother might," said Caina, "mostly out of spite."

"Once he returns to Istarinmul, that is his responsibility, not ours," said Halfdan. "Incidentally, Tanya is here, if you want to speak with her."

"What is she doing here?" said Caina.

"She's checking on Mahdriva," said Halfdan. "Apparently the two of them have become fast friends."

"I'll talk to her," said Caina.

"I will head back to the townhouse," said Corvalis, "and get our equipment. I suspect it is going to be another long night."

Caina walked alone through the upper corridor of the Lord Ambassador's mansion.

It was, she had to admit, a splendid house. The narrow windows admitted sunlight, illuminating the mosaics upon the floor and the frescoes upon the wall. They showed stylized scenes from nature, or Istarish nobles upon horseback hunting lions and hippopotamuses.

Though, she noted sourly, the nobles were often attended by their slaves.

An odd emotion swept over her, and Caina stopped for a moment.

She had almost died last night. But she had almost died many times, had come within a hair's breadth of death more times than she could even remember. And if she had died, it would have been in a worthy cause. Caina had risked her life to free slaves before, so often that the ridiculous legend of the Balarigar had grown up around some of her deeds.

The thought of death did not trouble her. For she would die one day, no matter what she did, and perhaps it was better to die in pursuit of a noble cause than alone in bed decades from now.

Yet Corvalis had almost died, too.

And that troubled Caina a great deal. The thought of losing him burned like a knife in her flesh. Worse, what would happen to him if she were killed? So many people had betrayed Corvalis. His father had turned him into a brutalized killer. Nairia, the one woman he had loved before her, had tried to kill him. Claudia had led him astray and almost gotten them both killed at Catekharon.

If Caina died tonight, if she left him alone, would that be a betrayal?

She leaned on a windowsill for a moment, surprised at the intensity of the emotion that washed through her.

Perhaps the time had come to stop risking her life so often.

She had become a Ghost nightfighter in rage and pain, determined to avenge her father's death at Maglarion's hands, to avenge the children she would never bear, to keep others from suffering as she had. Yet even after Maglarion was dead she had continued to serve the Ghosts as a nightfighter, driven by the fury and the hate that burned in her chest.

But time had passed, and then she had met Corvalis.

And she no longer felt so angry.

The pain of her father's murder would never leave her. Yet she had grown accustomed to it, the way a woman could grow accustomed to a missing finger or a constant limp. It would always be part of her, but she could live with it.

But she wanted to live, and to live with Corvalis. Caina had been a Ghost nightfighter her entire adult life. Could she leave it and do something else?

If she declared herself openly, as Theodosia suggested, she certainly would not leave the Ghosts. She could become a Ghost circlemaster, could command her own circle of eyes and ears and nightfighters. And with the prestige of a Countess's rank and the wealth of Anton Kularus, she could do great things for the Empire. She could smuggle escaped slaves out of Istarinmul and Anshan, could foil the plots and schemes of the magi, could place bounties upon the heads of renegade sorcerers.

She could wed Corvalis.

The vision of that life floated before her eyes, and she wanted it as badly as anything she had ever wante …

Caina realized she was standing alone in a corridor, lost in her own thoughts while there was work to be done. She rebuked herself and kept walking, pushing aside the dream for now.

But it still lingered.

She came to the guest room. Mahdriva lay upon the overstuffed bed, propped up with pillows, her face wan but relaxed. Tanya stood next to the bed, wearing a blue dress that matched her eyes, and Muravin stood on the other side, arms folded over his massive chest.

"You are certain she is well?" said Muravin in Istarish. The sight of the hulking gladiator, the brutal killer, hovering over his daughter like a concerned bird was so incongruous that Caina almost laughed.

But it spoke well of him.

Tanya nodded. "Yes, Master Muravin." She spoke perfect Istarish. Given that she had spent five years imprisoned by Naelon Icaraeus's slavers, that was not surprising. "She is as well as can be expected. I think the delivery will go as well, and my friends at the temple of Minaerys will come as soon as we receive word."

"Will it hurt?" said Mahdriva.

"Quite a lot, I am afraid," said Tanya, "but it passes." She shrugged. "Like many things worth doing, there is a lot of pain…but all pain passes, in time."

Caina walked closer to the bed.

"Sonya," said Tanya.

"Tanya, it is good to see you," said Caina, speaking Istarish with her Szaldic accent. "And it is very kind of you to look after Mahdriva."

Tanya laughed. "Your accent is flawless. Which is astonishing, since you don't even speak a word of Szaldic."

Caina shrugged. "More than I used to. I learned most of the profanities from Ark."

"Arcion should watch his tongue around the children," said Tanya.

"It is funny," said Mahdriva, "how you can change your voice so completely."

"I had a good teacher," said Caina. "How are you feeling?"

"Tired," said Mahdriva. She yawned. "And sleepy." She smiled. "I think I stayed up too late last night."

"We all did," said Caina.

"I am frightened, too," said Mahdriva.

"We will deal with Nalazar and the Kindred," said Caina. "We know where they are now, and…"

"Well, I am frightened of that, too," said Mahdriva, "but right now I am mostly frightened of…the baby. Not the baby, not really, but…"

"Of what is about to happen," said Tanya. "The pain, the blood. Your life will never be the same again."

"No," said Mahdriva. "I suppose not. I just wish that my husband was here."

"He should have been," said Muravin. "But he died bravely, saving you from the Kindred."

"I know," said Mahdriva. "I still wish that he were here, though. Along with my sisters."

"As do I," said Muravin. "But we are still alive, daughter, and we must carry on." He looked at Caina. "And it is thanks to this Ghost."

Caina shrugged. "I was in the right place at the right time."

"You are falsely modest," said Muravin. "If not for your aid, Nalazar would have killed us in the streets of Malarae. He would have slain us in the cellar of your coffee house." He raised his chin. "I told Master Basil I would serve the Ghosts in exchange for our lives. I assumed it would be no different than serving any other master, whether the masters of the fighting pits or the seneschal of the College. But you, Ghost...your wits and kindness have saved us. And I will serve the Ghosts gladly."

"Nor is it the first time she has done such deeds," said Tanya. "She saved my husband while I was still a captive of a wicked sorceress. She rescued my son from the sorceress's knife, and saved me and hundreds of others from the chains of slavers. When Rezir Shahan and the Istarish attacked Marsis, she snatched my son back from the slavers and slew Rezir Shahan himself. She is the Balarigar..."

"That..." said Caina.

"She is the Balarigar," said Tanya, "whether she believes it or not. The solmonari of the Szalds once taught that every generation, the gods in their mercy send one to oppose wicked sorcery and cruel lords. The breaker of chains, the slayer of demons, the Balarigar. And the woman who calls herself Sonya Tornesti is the Balarigar, whether she knows it or not."

"I could call myself the Queen of Anshan as well," said Caina, "but that would not make it so."

But they would not believe it. She had employed Theodosia's lessons in theatrics entirely too well. They believed in the legend of the Balarigar, and that was that.

And she had saved their lives.

She did not feel she could take credit for the things she had done, the lives she had saved. Sometimes she had gotten lucky. Other times she had managed to outwit her foes by barely half a second. But she had saved those lives. If she had not acted, Maglarion would have killed everyone in Malarae. Kalastus would have burned the people of Rasadda to ashes. Cyrioch would have drowned beneath the waves.

All those people dead, if not for the choices she had made.

She had become a nightfighter in rage and pain, seeking revenge for her father's death...but she had, indeed, kept so many people from suffering the same pain she had endured.

So many people.

And looking at three of the people she had saved, Caina found that she was not ready to stop being a nightfighter. Not yet.

"I am glad," said Caina, "that you are all safe. Even if you give me too much credit for it."

"Ghost," said Muravin. "A word with you."

Caina nodded and stepped into the hallway, leaving Tanya to discuss the mechanics of childbirth with Mahdriva.

"You are moving against the Kindred tonight?" said Muravin.

Caina frowned. "How did you know that?" If the Kindred and the Bostaji got word of what Halfdan planned, they might well flee.

"Master Basil told me," said Muravin. "You have tracked the assassin scum to a tavern near the docks, and they are lurking there like rats in their nest."

"Or snakes," said Caina.

"Or snakes," said Muravin. "I wish to join your attack upon them."

Caina frowned. "Mahdriva needs you here. Her child could be born any moment."

Muravin nodded. "I know. But I am a warrior, Sonya Tornesti. I am a killer, not a physician or a priest. A man like me has no place in the birthing room." He sighed, his dark eyes heavy with pain. "She needs her husband at her side. Or her sisters. But her husband is dead, and Ardaiza and Ranai are dead with them. Mahdriva has Tanya and the priestesses of Minaerys, and that must be enough."

Caina nodded.

"But my place is with you, for this," said Muravin. "Those assassins slew my daughters and my grandchildren before they were born. I will see that blood repaid."

"The assassins were only the tools of another man, you know," said Caina. "They killed your daughters because they were paid to do so. Some other man hired them. A renegade sorcerer, I think, a necromancer of some kind."

"And I would see him dead," said Muravin.

"It won't bring your daughters back," said Caina. "Vengeance never does. I know that well."

Muravin snorted. "Do you think me a child? Or is this some singer's tale, where I slay the evil sorcerer and live happily ever after? No, it is too late for that. But I will find this man, this sorcerer who slew my daughters, and I will kill him. To repay him for the blood of Ardaiza and Ranai, and to stop him from shedding any more blood."

Caina stared at him for a moment.

"That is as good a reason as any," said Caina, "and better than most. I will speak to Master Basil, but I don't think he will disagree." She pointed at him. "But you will do as I and Anton and Basil command, is that understood? No rushing off to die in glorious battle. Mahdriva needs you to live, and by the gods you're going to live."

For a moment Muravin looked almost amused. "For such a short woman, you are...fierce."

"Ask the Kindred," said Caina, "just how fierce I can be."

"Very well," said Muravin. "I will do as you command. If I am to be a Ghost, I suppose I should start accustoming myself to following your orders."

"Wise man," said Caina. "Arm yourself, and be ready to depart at sundown."

Muravin nodded and went to rejoin his daughter.

Caina watched him go. He might die tonight, she knew. Or she might die, or Corvalis.

But they would stop the Kindred and the Bostaji tonight, one way or another.

CHAPTER 17
BLOOD AND STEEL

Corvalis returned with their gear, and Caina prepared herself.

She donned her nightfighter garb, the black boots, trousers, gloves, and jacket lined with thin steel plates to deflect knife blades. A belt of throwing knives and other useful tools went around her waist, and daggers into the hidden sheaths in her boots. Her curved ghostsilver dagger went into its scabbard at her belt. A black mask hid everything but her eyes, and her shadow-cloak went around her shoulders.

Her father's worn gold signet ring, the only heirloom she had of his, hung on a leather cord around her neck.

She squeezed the ring once and then tucked it beneath the black jacket.

Then Caina tugged on a brown cloak and cowl, disguising the shadow-cloak, and slipped through the back door of the mansion, unseen by the Imperial Guards patrolling the corridors.

Armed men waited outside, hundreds of them, clad in chain mail and the red tabards of Malarae's civic militia, the city's guards and constables. Corvalis waited at their head, a dark shadow in his leather jerkin and shadow-cloak. At his side stood a man in his late twenties clad in the cuirass and plumed helmet of a militia tribune. The tribune grunted as Caina approached, pulling off his helmet to reveal a strong face beneath close-cropped blond hair.

Theodosia looked a great deal like her eldest son.

"Well," said Tomard, "here we are again, Ghost."

"Tribune," said Caina, using her disguised voice. "You've come up in the world since we last met."

"So I have," said Tomard, "though I'm still hunting scum in the docks.

Such is the fate of a militiaman, I suppose."

"You shall do as we ask?" said Caina.

Tomard shrugged. "Don't I always? Mother would be disappointed if I did not. Do you have a plan?"

"Aye," said Corvalis, stepping forward. Like Caina, he used a disguised voice. "We will need to surround the Serpents' Nest. The street can be blocked in two places. The Kindred and the Bostaji will try to flee, and we cannot allow any of them to escape."

"Shall we try to force them to surrender?" said Tomard.

"That would be best," said Caina, "but we doubt it. The Bostaji and the Kindred are not the sort to surrender. If any of them give up, bind them at once and take their weapons. But if they do not, kill them."

"What about sentries?" said Tomard. "I know the Serpents' Rest – I have men there every other week trying to arrest thieves. The tavern has a good view of the surrounding streets, and clever men would post at least one sentry on the roofs of the nearby buildings. There's no way I could sneak that many armed men past a sentry."

"Leave the sentry," said Caina, "to us."

She told Tomard the rest of the plan.

A short time later Caina and Corvalis stood in the shadows of the Serpents' Rest, looking up at the tavern. Light and the sound of carousing came from the tavern's common room, but most of the windows of the upper floors were dark.

Yet even in the darkened window, she glimpsed the shape of the sentry on the top floor.

"He's still watching the street," said Corvalis.

"Aye," said Caina, keeping her voice low. "And the man on the warehouse roof is still there."

"Sloppy," said Corvalis. "He should have moved." He shook his head. "Well, he'll pay for it now."

Caina nodded, discarded her brown cloak, beckoned Corvalis forward, and they moved silently into the alley behind the warehouse. She scrutinized the wall for a moment, then stepped back and unhooked a coil of slender, strong rope from her belt, one end tied around a collapsible steel grapnel. She tossed the rope, felt it catch on the clay tiles of the warehouse's roof, and gave it a few tugs.

The rope was secure.

Corvalis went up first, crouched at the edge of the roof, and beckoned for her to follow. Caina went up hand over hand, pressing her boots against the wall for traction. And as she did, a memory flashed through her mind.

She remembered climbing onto the roof of Khaltep Irzaris's warehouse in Catekharon in hopes of discovering where Mihaela had built her secret Forge. But that had been a trap. Corvalis's half-brother, the battle magus Torius Aberon, had been waiting for them, and they had barely escaped with their lives.

Both Torius Aberon and Khaltep Irzaris had been dead for ten months, but the memory lingered in Caina's mind.

She crouched next to Corvalis and saw the dark shape of the sentry watching the street. Caina gripped Corvalis's shoulder, leaned close, and whispered Torius's name into his ear. She felt him tense, and then saw him nod as he understood.

Corvalis glided forward, drawing his sword from its scabbard without a whisper of sound. Still the sentry did not notice them. Corvalis made his way across the clay tiles of the roof, weaving his way around the skylights. Caina followed, a throwing knife ready in her hands, her gloved fingers wrapped around the blade to hide its gleam.

Corvalis reached the sentry, drawing back his sword for a stab.

And as he did, a dark shadow rose from one the skylights. Another Kindred had been lying there, keeping watch, and Caina saw the man's mouth open to raise the alarm.

She slammed into him, her legs wrapping around his waist, her left hand slapping over his mouth, and her right hand ripping the throwing knife across his throat. The man went rigid, clawing at her, and then his legs collapsed just as Corvalis stepped forward to stab.

The sentry whirled, drawn by the noise of the collapsing assassin, and yanked his sword from its scabbard. Corvalis thrust his blade, but the sentry caught the attack on his own weapon. Caina kicked free of the dead assassin and threw her bloodstained knife. It hit the sentry in the leg, and the man staggered.

Corvalis wheeled, his sword a steely blur, and drove his blade through the assassin's gut. The sentry folded with a groan, and Corvalis yanked a dagger from his belt and plunged it into the assassin's neck.

The man collapsed upon the clay tiles.

"So much for doing this quietly," said Corvalis, tugging his sword free.

Caina pulled a flask from her belt, stepped to the edge of the roof, and flung it into the street. The flask shattered with a dazzling flash, bright enough to throw stark shadows in the nearby alleys and streets.

And bright enough to be visible from a distance.

The blast of trumpets rang out, and Caina heard the shout as the men of the civic militia charged towards the Serpents' Nest.

The sounds of carousing from the tavern ceased.

"Let's go," said Caina. "Nalazar isn't going to sit still after that."

They hurried down the rope and into the alley, and returned to the street just as a century of the civic militia marched to the Serpents' Nest, Tomard at their head. Muravin walked with him, wearing chain mail, a pair of scimitars at his belt and his faithful trident in his left hand. A masked steel helmet concealed his face.

If he was to be a Ghost, he would need to keep his identity secret.

"Ghosts," said Tomard. "We've got them surrounded."

"And the sewers?" said Caina.

Tomard nodded. "I sent some men down there. Doesn't look like Cornan Bascaii has a bolt hole, which is odd. But if he does, I've got steady lads watching the tunnels. If the Kindred get desperate enough, they might try to crawl down the latrines." He snorted. "I might owe my men some extra pay after that."

"Unless they heard us coming and fled," said Muravin, glaring at the tavern.

"No," said Corvalis. "They had two men watching the street from the roof of that warehouse. The Kindred would not waste men guarding an empty tavern, not after the losses they have already taken."

"Then we go in and kill them?" said Muravin.

"Most likely," said Tomard. "First we do things properly, give these fools a chance to surrender themselves."

He took several steps towards the tavern, and Caina followed him, looking at the windows overhead.

"In the name of the civic militia of Malarae," boomed Tomard, his voice echoing off the walls, "and by the authority of the Lord Prefect of the city and the Emperor of Nighmar, I command the assassins of the Kindred and the Bostaji to lay down their arms and come forth at once! Surrender, and I…"

Caina saw a flicker of motion in an upper window.

"Down!" she yelled, and shoved Tomard to the side. A heartbeat later an arrow hissed down and bounced off the cobblestones. Two more arrows shot down in quick succession, shattering against the street. The civic militiamen shouted and hurried forward, shields raised to protect the tribune.

"Those rats!" said Tomard. "Well, you can't expect anything better from assassins. Centurion!" He turned to the waiting militiamen. "Begin the attack. Break down the door, spare anyone who surrenders, and kill anyone who resists."

The centurion bawled commands to the militiamen. A half-dozen men raced for the front door, carrying an iron-topped ram. More militiamen screened them, shields raised to ward off any archers. The ram met the door, again and again. Bascaii had a thick, solid door on his tavern, but the wood splintered beneath the ram's iron head. Behind the door another century of militiamen braced themselves, shields raised as they prepared to storm into the tavern.

"Shall we stand here and watch other men do our fighting?" growled Muravin.

"No," said Caina. "Wait until the militia breaks into the common room. Then we'll circle around back and head upstairs. The Kindred might have something useful. Documents or papers they'll try to destroy before we come. Something that might tell us who hired the Kindred to come after your children."

The crack of splintered wood filled her ears, and the tavern's door collapsed.

"Forward!" shouted the centurion. "In the name of the Emperor!"

The militiamen yelled and charged for the broken door, and Caina heard the hiss of arrows and the clang of swords and spears.

"Go!" said Caina. "Now, while they're distracted!"

She raced for the alley, Muravin and Corvalis at her heels. Caina circled to the back of the building, where another squad of militiamen waited, ready to catch any Kindred or Bostaji who escaped through the back door.

"Ghosts," said the centurion in command. "The tribune said we were to do whatever you commanded."

"Stay here," said Caina in her disguised voice. "If anyone other than us comes through that door, give them one chance to surrender. If they don't, kill them."

The centurion nodded.

"Muravin," said Caina.

Muravin growled, raised his leg, and put his armored boot to the door. Four hard kicks later, the wood near the lock shattered, and the door swung open with a groan. The sounds of fighting came from the common room, screams and shouts and the moans of dying men.

No sound at all came from the tavern's upper floors.

Caina glided forward, dagger in her left hand, throwing knife in her right. Corvalis followed, sword in hand, Muravin at his side, trident raised to throw like a Legionary's javelin. Caina climbed the stairs, her boots making no sound against the splintered wood. Muravin made rather more noise than she would have liked, but she hoped the cacophony from the common room would mask their footfalls.

"The top floor," whispered Caina, and the men nodded. If anything valuable was to be found, it would be up there. They moved to the second floor, then the third, the corridors silent and deserted.

Then she heard someone thundering down the stairs. Caina raised her weapons, as did Corvalis and Muravin.

The fat landlord, Cornan Bascaii himself, ran around the landing and came to a halt, his eyes wide with alarm. He held a heavy leather sack over one shoulder. No doubt it was filled with valuables.

"You," growled Muravin, "you harbored these murderers."

He raised his trident.

An instant of fear flickered over Bascaii's bearded face, followed by a flicker of calculation.

Then he started to bawl like an infant.

"Oh, thank the gods!" he said. "Thank the gods you have come. Oh, I thought this nightmare would never end. The Kindred and the Bostaji threatened me, they…"

"Shut up," said Caina. "I'm not interested in killing you. I'll let you surrender to the militia outside, but only if you answer some questions."

Bascaii stopped crying. "Very well. What do you want to know?"

"Where is Nalazar?" said Caina.

"Nalazar?" said Bascaii. "That name is not…"

"Play dumb," said Corvalis, "and I'll cut out your tongue."

"He's upstairs," said Bascaii at once. "In the best room. He kept all his weapons and equipment there. Some papers, too, locked in a strongbox. I think he's planning to burn them."

"Go," said Caina.

"And thank you," said Bascaii, "for saving my life. It has been an ordeal, simply for ordeal…"

"For the gods' sake," said Caina. "Save it for the magistrate. Go."

Bascaii hastened down the stairs and vanished.

"You should have killed him," grumbled Muravin.

"Why?" said Caina. "If he lives, he might know something useful." Muravin had no answer for that. "Let's go."

They crept up the remainder of the stairs and came to the top floor. It looked much as Caina remembered. But the door to the room where she had heard Nalazar stood open, light spilling into the gloomy corridor. She heard the sounds of metal clanking and muttered curses from the room.

Caina peered around the edge of the opened door, gesturing for the others to wait.

The room beyond had a shabby carpet and a sagging bed against the wall, a pair of heavy, tarnished bronze lamps hanging from ropes. A long worktable ran the length of the room, holding tools, weapons, and several different glass jars of chemicals. A hearth crackled in one wall, and a man in leather armor stooped over it, throwing handfuls of paper into the flames. Another man in similar armor stood at the table, gathering the weapons. Nalazar himself waited by the window, his thin face hard with a scowl as he stared at the street below.

"Hurry," he snapped to the other two Kindred. He held a crossbow loaded with an odd combination of a winch, a grapnel, and a coiled rope. Caina realized that he intended to fire the grapnel at a nearby building and escape over the rope to an adjoining rooftop.

A bold plan, but one that might well work.

After all, no one ever looked up.

"I am hurrying," said the Kindred by the fireplace.

"The damned militiamen will be here any moment," said Nalazar. "Those Bostaji fools will fight to the death for their precious Shahenshah, but I have no wish to die in the name of our client. But if you don't burn those papers by the time the militia arrives, the Elder of Istarinmul will have our heads."

"Just burn the building down," said the Kindred at the table. "Let the Bostaji and the Ghosts burn together. Perhaps their precious Shahenshah and Emperor will save them."

Nalazar shrugged, turning from the window. "Why not? Bascaii will tell the Ghosts everything if..."

Then he saw Caina, and his eyes widened.

"The Ghosts!" he snarled, yanking his scimitar from its scabbard. "We..."

A bellow filled Caina's ears, and Muravin stepped next to her, flinging his trident. She had thought it an impractical weapon, but he threw it with such force that the tines buried themselves in the chest of the Kindred at the table. The man toppled backwards and did not move.

Caina flung her throwing knife at Nalazar, but the Kindred raised his scimitar and deflected the blade. The assassin at the fireplace vaulted over the table, his scimitar as a blur as he attacked Muravin. The former gladiator fell back on his heels, driven back by the assassin's furious attack. Corvalis leapt into the fray, sword in his right hand and dagger in his left. The Kindred danced back, avoiding Corvalis's attacks.

Muravin roared, and the assassin raised his sword to block. But instead of stabbing or slashing, Muravin punched the younger man with his free hand. The assassin's head snapped back with a spray of blood, and Corvalis struck.

The assassin collapsed, a dagger in his heart. Caina drew another throwing knife, hoping to line up on Nalazar...

Instead she saw that Nalazar held a second crossbow, the tip of the weapon's bolt gleaming with poison.

"That's quite enough," said Nalazar, gesturing with the crossbow. "Leave and close the door behind you, and you might live through this."

"Are you so sure of that?" said Caina, the crossbow turning in her direction. "You have one shot, and there are three of us."

"Oh, you can count. How impressive," said Nalazar. "So which of you shall die? Are the Ghosts as eager to die for their Emperor as the Bostaji are for their Shahenshah?"

"You will die here, Kindred dog," spat Muravin. "You will pay for the blood on your hands."

"You are one to speak, gladiator," said Nalazar. "Oh, I recognize you, even with that helmet. How much blood stains your fingers?"

"Much," said Muravin, "but I never slew a pregnant woman."

"Semantics," said Nalazar. He grinned, his black eyes flashing above his graying beard. "But that was the point. Our client wanted your daughters because they were pregnant. He wanted them for his precious Elixir. He cut the children from their wombs and burned them to ashes, and let your daughters bleed to death. The women meant nothing to him. They were only the carriers for…"

Muravin stepped forward, and Nalazar pointed the crossbow at him, but Caina lifted a hand.

"This need not end in any death," she said.

"You want to bargain then, Ghost?" said Nalazar. "Information in exchange for my life?"

"Precisely," said Caina. "Tell us who hired you to take Muravin's daughters, and I will let you go."

"He killed my daughters and grandchildren, Ghost!" said Muravin.

"He did," said Caina, "but he was just a tool. A weapon wielded in the hand of another man. I want to know the name of that man, Nalazar."

"Do you?" said Nalazar. "Very well. Ibrahmus Sinan."

Caina had suspected as much.

"Sinan?" said Muravin. "But why? He bore me no ill will."

"He doesn't," said Nalazar, "but he's an Alchemist, and he wants to live forever. And to live forever, he needs to be a Master Alchemist…"

"And to become a Master Alchemist," said Caina, "he needs to brew a vial of Elixir Rejuvenata."

"You understand," said Nalazar. "I don't know the process or the formula. But the spell involved apparently requires the ashes of unborn children. Specifically, the ashes of three unborn children taken from three sisters. Most Alchemists purchase families of slaves and ensure that three sisters are pregnant simultaneously at the appropriate time. But our Sinan, you see, is unpopular and despised for associating with that Anshani woman."

"Tanzir Shahan's mother," said Caina.

Nalazar nodded. "But Ashria is fond of her pet Alchemist, so she loaned him the money to hire us. And," he gestured with the crossbow, "here we are. Sinan hired us, and Sinan is the one you want. Information for my life. A good bargain, no? If I had any intention of allowing you to live."

He seized a glass bottle from the table, a dark fluid sloshing within, and flung it against the floor.

But Caina had recognized the liquid the stagehands of the Grand Imperial Opera used to create smoke.

"Eyes!" she shouted, closing hers, and she felt the flash even through her closed eyelids. She opened her eyes and saw that the roomed had filled with gray smoke, that Corvalis and Muravin had thrown themselves against the walls. Through the haze she glimpsed Nalazar, saw him taking aim with the crossbow…

Caina threw herself over the table, weapons and glass bottles clattering around her, and her boots slammed into Nalazar's gut. The assassin staggered back with a gasp, and the quarrel hissed from his crossbow and slammed into the wall. Caina surged to her feet and lunged at him with a dagger, but Nalazar swung his crossbow like a club. The heavy weapon slammed against the blade and wrenched the dagger from her hand. Caina stumbled, and Nalazar dropped the crossbow and threw a punch at her head. She deflected the blow, but he was strong, and the sheer force numbed her arm. Nalazar snatched his scimitar and stalked after her, drawing the blade back for a lethal thrust.

And then Muravin smashed into him like a falling mountain.

Muravin seized Nalazar's wrist and wrenched, bones snapping and crackling. Nalazar screamed and tried to pull away, but Muravin had a grasp like iron. The former gladiator's hands clamped onto Nalazar's throat and groin, and Caina heard a gristly tearing noise as Muravin raised Nalazar over his head, the assassin screaming.

"Nalazar!" roared Muravin. "When you land in hell tell the devils that I sent you in the name of Ardaiza and Ranai!"

He flung Nalazar out of the window.

Nalazar's scream terminated in a final-sounding crack.

Caina looked out at the street below, saw a ring of surprised militiamen surrounding what remained of Nalazar.

"Good throw," said Corvalis.

Muravin closed his eyes and let out a long breath. "My daughters are avenged. But this is not over. Not until Sinan has paid for what he has done." He turned towards the door. "As he soon shall."

"Stay right there," said Caina. "If you go after Sinan by yourself, you'll get killed."

"He is but one man," said Muravin, "feeble from long study."

"He is a sorcerer," said Caina, "and the gods only know what kind of powers he can bring to bear against you. The Alchemists turn their foes into statues of crystal, or so I have heard. Is that how you want to end? Have you ever fought a sorcerer before?"

"No," admitted Muravin.

"I have," said Caina, "more often than I care to remember. So heed my counsel. Do not go after him alone. We will strike before he leaves Malarae." She gestured at the table, waving away some smoke with her other hand. "In the meantime, help me gather up these papers."

"To what use?" said Muravin. "We know Sinan is my enemy."

"But Sinan may have other allies," said Caina. "Other associates. The Malarae Kindred helped Nalazar, and perhaps we can find their Sanctuary. You want more vengeance, Muravin? Think of the blow we could deal the Kindred if we find their Sanctuary."

"Very well," said Muravin. "I suspect you are accustomed to having your way in the end."

"Wise man," said Caina, gathering up the papers that the Kindred had not managed to burn. She leafed through them. Most of the papers were notes Nalazar had written to his various spies monitoring the Lord Ambassador's residence, telling them to watch for Tanzir Shahan. One was a letter written to the Elder of Istarinmul, explaining reasons for the delay in fulfilling their contract with Ibrahmus Sinan. Nalazar, Caina noted, blamed all his difficulties upon the Ghosts.

She glanced out the window. He hadn't been wrong.

One note was in a different hand. It was a letter from Sinan, dated from this morning. In it, Sinan instructed the Kindred and the Bostaji to remain at the Serpents' Nest. In fact, all available Kindred should gather together, since Sinan would have need of them.

Caina frowned behind her mask, a suspicion growing in her mind. Did Sinan plan some grand attack tomorrow?

"This doesn't make sense," said Caina.

"What is it?" said Corvalis.

Caina held out the letter.

"I don't read Istarish," said Corvalis.

"I don't read," said Muravin.

Caina shook her head. "It's a letter from Sinan, telling the Kindred and the Bostaji to gather here tonight and await his instructions. Why would he do that? It makes no sense."

Corvalis shrugged. "He knows that both the emir and Mahdriva are in the same place. Maybe he wanted to send the Kindred and the Bostaji to strike at once, use them to kill the emir and kidnap Mahdriva."

"That is a good plan," said Caina. "But why write it down? It's a huge risk. Why not send a verbal message, or tell Nalazar in person?" She stared at the letter. "The Istarish nobles are more brutal than those of the Empire, but it's still illegal to hire Kindred assassins."

"Or to hire Kindred assassins and get caught," said Muravin. Some of the fury had faded from his expression, replaced by puzzlement. "Both the nobles and the Alchemists employ the Kindred on a regular basis. That is how I knew Nalazar – he often came to the College to arrange contracts with the Alchemists. But they were never foolish enough to put anything into writing."

"Then why did Sinan do it?" said Corvalis.

Caina stared at the paper, thinking hard. "He's not stupid. Not stupid enough to make a mistake like this, so he had to have done it deliberately. But why? To gather the Kindred and the Bostaji, obviously. And why do that? Why do it in writing? Why risk the consequences?"

She tossed the letter back on the table.

"He risked the consequences," said Caina, "because he didn't care about them. And he wanted to gather the Kindred and the Bostaji together, not to prepare them, but to…"

"To do what?" said Corvalis.

Caina blinked…and the answer came to her.

"Oh, damn," she whispered.

"What?" said Corvalis.

"This was just a distraction," said Caina. "He gathered the assassins here to draw our attention away from the mansion. He sent the instructions in writing because he didn't care about the consequences…because he thinks he'll be successful by tomorrow." Her gaze snapped up from the letter. "He's making a move against Tanzir and Mahdriva tonight."

Or, she realized with a feeling of sinking dread, a move just against Mahdriva. Overpowering hundreds of Imperial Guards to reach the emir was no small task. But using sorcery to infiltrate the mansion unseen to kidnap Mahdriva would be far easier. And Caina suspected that Sinan cared more about becoming a Master Alchemist than fulfilling the amirja Ashria's wishes.

"Mahdriva is in danger?" said Muravin.

"I think so," said Caina. "And if she's not, she will be soon."

"Then I must go at once," said Muravin.

"Not alone," said Caina, her mind racing. "I'll come with you."

"As will I," said Corvalis.

"No," said Caina. "Go find Tomard. As soon as they've dealt with the assassins, have him leave some men here and march for the Lord Ambassador's mansion as fast as he can."

"You shouldn't go alone," said Corvalis.

"It is the best choice," said Caina. "Tomard won't move unless somewhere urges him to action. And if Muravin goes alone he might get himself killed."

"We must go!" said Muravin. "Come if you wish, Ghost, but I must go to my daughter."

"The two of you should not go alone," said Corvalis.

"Trust me," said Caina.

She couldn't see his expression beneath the cowl and mask, but she could guess at it. He hadn't trusted her once before, during the fight against Mihaela at Catekharon, and that had almost resulted in their deaths and a war that would have devoured the world.

"Very well," said Corvalis. "I will speak to Tomard."
She turned to follow Muravin.
"Be careful," said Corvalis.
"I'm always careful," said Caina.
But that was a lie, and they both knew it.

CHAPTER 18
ELIXIR REJUVENATA

A short time later Caina and Muravin arrived at the Lord Ambassador's residence.

At once Caina saw that something was wrong.

A ring of gray haze surrounded the mansion. At first Caina thought that Sinan must have set off more smoke bombs, or perhaps that a fire had broken out.

Yet there was something odd about the smoke.

As they drew closer, it looked less like mist and more like smoke. Additionally, the mist was motionless. A normal mist would flow with the direction of the wind. This mist stood still, save for a slight rippling.

A ring of mist now surrounded the Lord Ambassador's mansion.

It was obviously the work of sorcery, and Caina felt the crawling tingle of arcane force as she drew closer.

Muravin strode towards it, sword and trident in hand, the tines still wet with blood. As he did, Caina saw dark shapes in the mist, motionless forms lying strewn on the street below the stairs to the mansion's main doors.

"Stop," said Caina.

Muravin kept walking.

"Damn it," said Caina, grabbing his shoulder, "stop."

He glared at her. "Mahdriva is in danger. I must go to her."

"You have a good sword arm," said Caina, "but you also have a brain and eyes. Use them!" She pointed. "Look."

Muravin stopped and looked, and his dark eyes went wide.

A dozen Imperial Guards lay motionless on the front stairs of the mansion. Neither their bodies nor their black armor bore any sign of violence, though Caina could not tell if they were breathing. Their armor was dry, without any trace of the condensation the mist should have left on the dark steel.

"The mist is poisonous?" said Muravin.

"I don't know," said Caina. She waved a hand in front of the wall of mist, felt the painful tingles in her fingers. "But it's a spell."

"The work of an Alchemist," said Muravin. "They can transmute air into poison, or into a mist that puts anyone who breathes it into a deep sleep."

"Your trident," said Caina. "That Guard is right at the edge of the mist. Try to drag him out. We can see if he's still alive."

Muravin nodded, and hooked the Guard under the armpit. He dragged the man out of the mist, the black armor scraping against the cobblestones. Caina stooped over the Guard and pulled away his helmet.

"He's still breathing," said Caina. "His pulse is good." She touched his forehead, felt the tingling aura of sorcery clinging to the Guard. "But the spell is still on him. I don't know how long it will take him to wake up."

For the first time, she regretted that Halfdan had sent Corvalis's sister to work with the Ghosts in Caer Magia. Claudia Aberon had once been a magus of the Imperial Magisterium, and she might have known how to lift the spell upon the unconscious Guard.

On the other hand, Claudia did not handle herself well in a crisis.

"This is Sinan's doing," said Muravin. "We must get inside!"

He stepped back, bracing himself.

"What are you doing?" said Caina.

"If I hold my breath long enough," said Muravin, "perhaps I can reach the door."

"There has to be a better way," said Caina. "If you breathe that mist, you won't be any good to Mahdriva."

"There isn't a better way!" shouted Muravin. "If we wait for Anton to arrive with more men, Sinan will do to Mahdriva as he did to Ranai and Ardaiza! If we try to do something clever to get into the mansion, we will run out of time. I am going in there. Will you help me or not?"

She could not think of anything better.

Caina nodded. "I will. Take as many breaths as you can, quickly, and then one deep breath." She began breathing quickly and raised her right hand. "Do you remember where the doors are?"

"Yes," said Muravin, his chest rising and falling beneath the chain mail.

"Good. Take one more deep breath, and then we'll run for the doors when I drop my hand," said Caina.

She took a deep breath, sucking in as much air as she could manage, and then dropped her fist.

They sprinted into the mist, jumping over the prone Imperial Guards. The strange mist did not have the cool damp of most fogs, but she felt the arcane power tingling within it. Caina scrambled up the steps, moving through the gloom by memory, and then the gleaming double doors stood before her. Two Imperial Guards lay on either side of the doors. Which meant they had still been at their posts when the mist washed over the mansion, and that in turn meant Sinan had taken them by surprise.

Muravin was right. They had to hurry.

Caina seized the door handles and pulled.

But the doors were locked.

She tugged on them again, her stomach sinking in time to the growing burn in her lungs. She had not considered that Sinan might take the simple expedient of locking the doors behind him.

Stupid, stupid, stupid.

Muravin pushed her aside and pounded on the door, trying to kick it open as he had at the Serpents' Nest. Caina grabbed his shoulder, trying to pull him back, but it was no good. He was going to save his daughter, or he was going to die trying.

The latter seemed more likely than the former.

Caina raced back down the stairs. An instant later she heard the thud as Muravin fell unconscious. Her chest burned, black spots dancing before her eyes. Her lungs screamed for her to breathe, to open her mouth, but Caina drove herself onward. The edge of the mist was almost there...

Too late.

She could not stop herself, and sucked in a breath of the sorcerous mist.

Yet nothing happened, and an instant later Caina staggered out of the mist and onto the street.

She turned, stunned, waiting for the spell to take effect. Yet still nothing happened. She looked at the mist, baffled. It had affected the Imperial Guards and Muravin. Why hadn't it touched her? What was different?

She was the only one wearing a shadow-cloak, true. But that made no sense. The shadow-cloak shielded her from divinatory and mind-affecting spells, but the mist was neither.

But...what if it was?

Caina had thought the mist a sleeping elixir dispersed into the air. But what if it was actually a spell that commanded the mind to fall unconscious, to go to sleep? If it was, the shadow-cloak would protect her from it.

Only one way to test it.

She glanced over her shoulder. There was still no sign of Corvalis and Tomard, and it might take the militiamen another hour to get across the city. That would give Sinan more than enough time to claim Mahdriva's child.

"Damn it," whispered Caina, and stepped into the mist.

Nothing happened.

She stood in the gray gloom for a few moments, breathing in and out, and felt not the slightest trace of weariness.

If anything, she felt far too frightened to fall asleep.

She dragged Muravin out of the mist and to the street. Hopefully he would wake up in time to tell Corvalis what had happened here.

Then she took a deep breath and walked back into the mist.

The doors were locked, but there were other ways into the Lord Ambassador's residence. The windows on the first floor stood eight feet above the ground, but Caina jumped and managed to catch the sill in her gloved hands. She pulled herself up by the strength of her arms, grateful for all the hours she had spent practicing the unarmed forms.

She smashed the window, the leather of her glove protecting her hand, and climbed into the room beyond. It was a scriptorium for the Lord Ambassador's scribes, with a row of writing desks and shelves storing paper and vials of ink. The room was deserted and free of the gray mist.

Caina considered that. Most likely Sinan had brought allies with him, mercenaries or Immortals, and wanted them to move through the mansion without falling unconscious from the mist.

She would have to take care.

Caina hurried to the scriptorium door and opened it a few inches, peering into the corridor beyond.

She froze in alarm.

A man walked past the door, clad only in trousers and armored black boots, a scimitar and the chain whip of an Immortal hanging at his belt. His eyes had the usual blue glow, but much brighter, so bright that his eyes looked like blazing blue coals. His chest and arms bulged with a freakish amount of muscle, and Caina saw the veins in his arms and torso glowing with the same blue light as his eyes.

The man was an Immortal, or at least had been one. Sinan must have altered him in some way, giving him additional alchemical elixirs to enhance his speed and strength.

Caina waited until the deformed Immortal disappeared from sight, and then eased into the corridor. She looked up and down, the bright frescos of the wall gleaming before her eyes, but saw no one. The presence of both the ring of mist and the strange Immortal meant that Sinan hadn't left yet. And that meant Mahdriva was still here.

Would Sinan simply cut the child from her womb and then depart?

Mahdriva's bedroom seemed like the best place to start. Caina hurried down the corridor as fast as she dared, her ears straining for any footfalls. A pair of opened double doors on the right led to the main dining hall, and she heard movement from within. Caina stopped and peered around one of the massive doors.

The Lord Ambassador's dining hall was a grand affair, two stories tall with an encircling balcony and an intricate chandelier hanging beneath the ceiling's elaborate skylights. A dozen Imperial Guards lay motionless on the floor. Caina saw both Halfdan and Lord Titus sitting in chairs, heads slumped to their chests, their arms bound behind their backs. Tanzir sat next to them, likewise bound, though he was conscious.

Mahdriva sat tied to a chair next to him, clad in only in a shift. Tears streamed down her face, and she wept in silence, her despair plain. At least a dozen of the altered Immortals stood in the room. Caina stared at Mahdriva, trying to find a way past the Immortals…

Sinan strode into sight, resplendent in his robes of white and gold. His face trembled with rage and impatience, and in his right hand he carried something that looked like a large meat fork made from an odd silvery metal.

Caina was reasonably sure that it was not a meat fork.

"What's wrong, Sinan?" said Tanzir, trying to take a defiant tone. "It didn't work?"

"Be silent," said Sinan, coming to a stop and gazing at something.

Caina inched forward, trying to see more.

Sinan stood before the massive mirror she had seen in the dining hall earlier. The thing was at least ten feet tall and ten wide. Next to mirror stood another table, laden with jars and vials and glass tubes. But the mirror itself drew Caina's attention. She saw Sinan's scowling reflection, yet something seemed to be moving behind the glass.

And she felt the faint pulse of sorcery coming from the mirror.

Sinan turned. "I shall have to send another one."

"Why?" said Tanzir. "You just sent that poor man through."

"If he was successful, he should have returned almost immediately," said Sinan. "Time does not flow at the same rate there as it does in the mortal world. A second here can be an entire day on the other side, though the conversion is never quite precise as…why I am explaining this to you?" He beckoned to the deformed Immortals. "Bring another Guard. I shall awaken him, and perhaps he will succeed where the others have failed."

"You have already sent five men to their deaths!" said Tanzir.

"I will send as many as necessary," said Sinan.

"If you want those damned ashes so badly," said Tanzir, "then go yourself, you miserable coward."

"Coward?" said Sinan, glaring at Tanzir. "A rich choice of words from a fat sluggard who has never known want or hunger. I was born in chains, my lord emir. I clawed my way up from the dust, and I took everything I have, for nothing was given to me. And I shall take immortality as well."

"I might never have been a slave," said Tanzir, "but I am not about to murder a pregnant woman so I can live forever."

Sinan scoffed. "You are weak. Little wonder your own mother wants you dead. You were born to power, but are too feeble to keep it." He pointed at the Immortals. "Bring another Guard. I will wake him and send him through the mirror."

The mirror? What did that mean?

Still, it seemed that Caina had some time to save Mahdriva and the others, if Sinan was preoccupied with working a spell with the mirror. That gave Caina the time she needed to find Corvalis and Tomard and bring them here...

She stepped back from the door just as one of the Immortals came around the corner, an Imperial Guard slung over one shoulder. Caina froze in shock, as did the Immortal. Then the blazing blue eyes widened, and the Immortal roared, his voice unnaturally deep and rough.

As one every Immortal in the dining hall looked at her, and Sinan's black eyes widened.

That was bad.

"A Ghost!" shouted Sinan. "Take him alive!"

Caina broke into a sprint. The Immortal in the corridor roared again and pursued her, as did the Immortals in the dining hall. The Immortals were not wearing shadow-cloaks, and the sorcerous elixirs in their blood might not protect them from the enspelled mist surrounding the mansion. If she lured them outside, they would fall victim to the mist ...

The Immortal flung the unconscious Guard like a missile.

Caina tried to dodge, but the Guard's armored leg smacked into her back. The impact knocked her to the ground, the Guard landing atop her with enough force to blast the breath from her lungs.

She put both hands on the Guard's cuirass, trying to shove him off. The man was at least twice her weight, even without the bulk of his armor. At last she slid out from under him and regained her feet.

A dozen of the deformed Immortals surrounded her, scimitars in hand.

"You will," said one of the Immortals, his voice inhumanly deep, "come with us. Now."

Caina looked at the Immortals, at their gleaming scimitars, and then gave a sharp nod. They fell around her and led her to the dining hall. Sinan awaited them, the metal fork in his right hand.

The strange mirror loomed behind them, a peculiar rippling dancing in the glass. For a moment Caina had the oddest feeling that it was not a mirror but a window.

"A Ghost nightfighter," Sinan said. "Ah. A shadow-cloak. That explains how you eluded the mist...and how you may be of use to me.

Remove your mask and cowl, or I shall have the Immortals cut of your head."

Caina saw no choice but to comply, so she drew back her cowl and pulled aside her mask.

"Oh, no," said Tanzir.

"I am sorry," said Mahdriva, still weeping. "I am sorry, I am so sorry…"

Sinan's eyes widened in surprise. "A woman? You northerners have peculiar…wait. I know you." He pointed the fork at her. "Sonya Tornesti. The coffee merchant's whore."

Caina said nothing.

"Nothing to say for yourself?" said Sinan.

Caina shrugged. "You ought to surrender. The Ghosts know you are here, and they are coming for you."

"They will not penetrate the wall of mist," said Sinan. "The sorcery will hold for a few more hours, and given the well-known enmity between the Ghosts and the magi, I doubt you will have anyone capable of dispelling the mist."

"You've also got Lord Titus Iconias, a friend of the Emperor," said Caina, glancing at Lord Titus's unconscious form. "The magi might bestir themselves to help him. And I doubt even you can fight Malarae's entire chapter of magi."

"That won't be necessary," said Sinan. "I will be long gone by then."

"Of course," said Caina. She needed to delay. Sooner or later Corvalis would arrive with help. And perhaps she could trick Sinan into giving up some useful information. "With your precious vial of Elixir Rejuvenata."

"Ah," said Sinan. "Puzzled that out, did you?" Caina had the sudden feeling that she had told him more than she should have. "Very clever. Tell me, Ghost. How will I create the Elixir?"

"With the ashes of murdered children," said Caina, "carved from their mothers' wombs."

"That is part of it," said Sinan, looking at his work table. "There are numerous other ingredients as well, all of which I have gathered. The ashes of the children from related mothers are a key ingredient. But there is one more component I need, and then the Elixir will be complete."

"And just what is that?" said Caina. "The endless self-congratulation of an arrogant Alchemist?"

To her surprise, Sinan laughed. "If that were true, every member of the College would have been immortal centuries ago. No, this is something else. Something rare and dangerous to claim. All the other ingredients can be obtained with some work, but this…this kills most of the Alchemists who set upon the path of mastery." He took a step closer, and Caina wondered if she could get a knife into his neck. "Tell me, Ghost…what do you know about elemental spirits?"

A jolt of alarm went down her spine.

She knew more about elemental spirits that she would have liked. Nicasia, the slave girl of the master magus Ranarius, had been possessed by an elemental spirit of earth. That spirit gave her the power to transform anyone who looked into her eyes to stone. Claudia Aberon had spent a year imprisoned as a statue. And there were elementals of far greater power. When the fire elemental sleeping beneath Old Kyrace had awakened, it had utterly destroyed the island upon which Old Kyrace had been built. The Sages of Catekharon harnessed a greater fire elemental to fuel their sorceries. The Stone of Cyrioch, the hill upon which the city's Palace of Splendors stood, was actually a sleeping greater earth elemental. If the spirit awoke, the resultant earthquake would destroy Cyrioch and cause a wave that would drown a dozen more cities.

"Some," said Caina at last.

"There is a particular kind of spirit, an elemental of flame," said Sinan, "revered by worshippers of the Living Flame. In old Maatish and modern Saddaic, such spirits are called bannu. Among the Istarish, they are named the djinni of flame. But among your nation, the Nighmarians, they are called..."

"Phoenix," said Caina, who had read of them in her father's books. "I thought they were legendary."

"They are not," said Sinan. "They are spirits of elemental flame, and like all spirits, do not die. But when they go into...hibernation, let us call it, they revert to ashes, and from the ashes are reborn into a new form."

"And those ashes," said Caina, "are the final ingredient for your damned Elixir."

"They are," said Sinan.

"And that's what you're doing to those Guards," said Caina. "You're trying to summon up a phoenix spirit and bind it to their flesh."

Sinan smiled. "I am afraid that you have it backward. I'm not trying to summon up a phoenix. I am sending living men into the netherworld to claim the ashes."

"That's...impossible," said Caina. "A living man cannot enter the spirit world."

"Actually, he can," said Sinan. "To enter our world, a spirit needs a physical form to inhabit. However, a living man can physically enter the netherworld. Few know the proper spells, and of those who do, few attempt the journey. The netherworld is perilous beyond anything in the material world. Your Magisterium once had the knowledge, but lost it with the fall of the Fourth Empire. I suspect they have had little motivation to rediscover it, as visiting the netherworld offers much peril in exchange for little gain."

"Except for Alchemists wishing to attain mastery," said Caina. "That's why so many of them perish when trying to brew the Elixir. Murdering slave girls for their unborn children is simple enough. Any murderous thug can do it. But entering the netherworld and returning alive with phoenix ashes is harder."

"You put your finger upon the problem," said Sinan, "and those who return successfully are often killed by…errors in the preparation of the Elixir. Phoenix ashes are a potent substance, and the slightest error in the formula can cause explosive results."

"And that's why you haven't killed Mahdriva yet, is it?" said Caina, looking at the weeping girl. "You can't add the ashes of the last child to the mixture until after the phoenix ashes."

"Very good," said Sinan. "You are most clever. That will serve me well."

Caina did not like the sound of that.

"Physically entering the netherworld is a challenge, to be sure," said Sinan, walking past her, "but not beyond the abilities of a skilled Alchemist. For alchemy is the arcane science of transmutation, and with the proper materials, entry into the netherworld is possible."

He stopped before the mirror.

"The mirror?" said Caina. "What does that have to do with anything?"

"It is our entrance to the netherworld," said Sinan. "Observe."

He picked up an empty jar from the table, considered it for a moment, and threw it at the mirror.

It struck the mirror…and the glass rippled, the air shivering with arcane force. The jar sank into the mirror and vanished. For a moment Caina had a brief glimpse of a strange landscape of misshapen hills and colorless grass.

And then the mirror went still, though Caina still saw the strange rippling behind the glass.

"You see?" said Sinan. "An Alchemist can transmute a mirror of sufficient quality into a gate to the netherworld, though the elixir is rather complex, and the mirror is destroyed after the spell is finished."

"I congratulate you," said Caina. "So why aren't you in the netherworld now?"

Sinan turned from the mirror and raised an eyebrow. "Because the netherworld is dangerous. I have come too close to immortality to risk my life now."

"He's been waking up Imperial Guards," said Tanzir, "and sending them through the mirror one by one. None of them have returned."

"Perhaps you're impatient," said Caina. "I can't imagine that retrieving phoenix ashes is an easy task."

"It isn't," said Sinan, "but that is irrelevant. Time has no precise application in the netherworld. A thousand years there could be just a moment in the material world. If they had succeeded, they would have returned almost immediately, at least from our perspective. They haven't returned, so I assume they failed."

"They're dead," said Caina. "You sent those men to their deaths."

Sinan shrugged. "If they wanted to live, they should have returned with the ashes. But I should not be surprised. Soldiers are dumb brutes, used to following orders, to letting others do their thinking for them. To retrieve the ashes, I need someone of...greater cunning. Some clever and subtle."

He smirked at Caina.

"Me," she said.

"Your arrival was fortuitous," said Sinan. "You will go through the mirror and retrieve the phoenix ashes."

Caina laughed.

"You find this amusing?" said Sinan, lifting the strange fork.

"I find it idiotic," said Caina. "You're a murderer, Sinan, a man who would bathe in the blood of a child to extend his wretched life by a few months. I am not going to help you."

"I can compel you," said Sinan.

"How? Torture? A spell? An elixir to break my will?" said Caina. "You need my wits intact, and I'll do you no good injured or dead."

"No," said Sinan, "you won't." He pointed the fork, and a blue spark flared to life between the tines. "But the Imperial Guards have proven that they are of no use to me."

Caina felt a surge of arcane force.

A lance of blue-white lightning erupted from Sinan's fork and slammed into the nearest Imperial Guard. The fingers of lightning curled around the black armor, and the man's eyes popped open. He screamed in agony, his limbs thrashing in a mad dance. His skin blackened and charred, and he erupted into flames and went motionless.

Sinan lowered the fork.

The stench of burning flesh was hideous. Mahdriva gagged, and Tanzir looked like he was trying to keep his dinner down.

"You murderous dog," spat Caina.

"You will cooperate with me," said Sinan. "Or I will kill the Imperial Guards one by one. Those men have wives and children, yes? I will leave them as widows and orphans unless you help me." He pointed the fork at Tanzir. "Or perhaps I'll kill the emir. Ashria wants the little piglet dead anyway, and I would prefer to stay in her good graces. Though I imagine the stench from all that burning fat would be considerable. You Ghosts want him alive, don't you?"

"Don't do it," said Tanzir. His voice trembled, but he met Caina's eyes. "Sonya, don't do it. Let him kill me. It's not...it's not worth it, not to save my life. Don't let this bastard get his Elixir. Let him...let him kill me..."

"You," said Caina, "are far too ready to die, Tanzir Shahan." She stepped forward, and the hulking Immortals stirred, but Sinan lifted a hand. "I'll do it."

Sinan smiled. "You shall?"

"I will go into the netherworld and retrieve those damned ashes for you," said Caina.

Because she could think of no other way forward. She would not let Sinan kill Tanzir, and she certainly would not let the renegade Alchemist murder all those Imperial Guards. Going through the mirror might buy time. Corvalis was coming with Tomard and several hundred militiamen, and even the deformed Immortals could not fight them all. Corvalis would find a way past the mist, and they would defeat Sinan.

At least, Caina kept telling herself that.

"Splendid," said Sinan.

"So," said Caina. "How exactly does one obtain phoenix ashes?"

"First, take this," said Sinan, lifting a satchel and handing it to her. Caina opened it and saw a metal flask carved with arcane sigils. "That will allow you to carry the ashes safely. The gate," Sinan pointed at the mirror, "will transport you to a region of the netherworld near the Sacellum of the Living Flame."

"And what is that?" said Caina.

"It is what the worshippers of the Living Flame call the structure housing the phoenix ashes," said Sinan. "No one knows what it is called, not truly. It is a....place, for lack of a better word, that one of the greater elemental princes created. The phoenix spirits come there to die and be reborn."

"And their ashes are inside," said Caina. "I assume there are guardians? Something has to kill all those Alchemists who try to become Masters."

And the Guards that Sinan had sent to die.

"There are," said Sinan. "Spirits bound to guard the Sacellum. They are not fond of visitors from the material world. Since you will be there physically, they shall have the power to harm you. Additionally, the netherworld has its own peculiar hazards."

"Such as?" said Caina.

"The netherworld is a place of thought and spirit," said Sinan. "Your mind can reshape the environment there, if your thoughts are disciplined enough. Which can pose a problem. Your thoughts...the netherworld itself acts as a mirror to them, and your memories can take form and attack you."

"How pleasant," said Caina.

There were many dark memories in her thoughts…and she had no particular desire to see them played out again.

"Your shadow-cloak may give you an advantage," said Sinan, "and prevent the creatures of the netherworld from seeing you. But some of the more powerful spirits will be able to see through it."

"Sonya, please," said Tanzir. "Don't do this. I…"

"Silence," said Sinan. "Ghost, proceed immediately."

He gestured at the mirror with his free hand and cast a spell. Caina felt the pulse of arcane power, and the mirror rippled, her reflection writhing and bulging. It was like looking at a wall of rippling mercury.

"Go," said Sinan. "The gate is ready."

"Just walk through the mirror?" said Caina.

"Oh, the Ghosts are indeed masters of perception," said Sinan. "Stop stalling and go. I grow impatient."

Caina took a deep breath, pulled up the cowl of her shadow-cloak, and stepped towards the mirror. The wall of glass writhed in silence, and she felt the aura of sorcery radiating from it. And through the mirror she glimpsed a vast dark plain stretching away in all directions, dotted with strange, misshapen forms.

The netherworld.

She held out a hand, and it passed through the glass as if it were not there.

Caina stepped into the mirror, and gray mist filled the world.

CHAPTER 19
THE NETHERWORLD

Caina walked through an endless world filled with featureless gray mist.

The strange place was utterly silent, and the mist swallowed even the noise of Caina's footsteps. She saw nothing but mist in all directions.

It reminded her of the place she had seen in her dreams when the Moroaica had still inhabited her body.

In fact, she was certain it was the same place. Those dreams had not been dreams, but the spirit of the Moroaica speaking to her. Perhaps both their spirits had been drawn here during those strange dreams.

Then the mist vanished, and Caina found herself someplace else.

Somewhere strange.

She looked around in silence for a moment.

"Gods," she said at last.

A plain of rippling, knee-high grass stretched away in all directions. The strange grass was utterly devoid of color, and waved in a wind that Caina neither heard nor felt. Her shadow-cloak rippled behind her, blowing in the nonexistent wind.

Strange things floated overhead. Pieces of land, as if scooped from the earth by a giant hand. Images of stone and obsidian, showing men and women and creatures Caina had never seen before. Uprooted trees, some hanging upside down. Towers and stairs that went nowhere. Black clouds filled the sky, moving against the direction of the peculiar wind. An eerie green glow lit everything, and from time to time a burst of silent emerald lightning jumped from cloud to cloud.

There was absolutely no sign of the Imperial Guards Sinan had already sent through the gate.

From time to time the terrain...changed. The plains shifted to barren black trees, or a stagnant gray swamp, or a desert of black glass. Yet through it all something remained constant. A road of gleaming black stone wound over the plains and ended...

It ended at the single largest building Caina had ever seen.

She could not have said what it was. It was built from the same gleaming black stone as the road, and looked like some monstrous fusion of basilica and pyramid and fortress. It could have held the Praetorian Basilica. It could have held the entire Imperial Citadel, perhaps even all of Malarae. From within the strange building, through its vast windows, Caina saw the harsh orange-yellow glow of fire.

The Sacellum of the Living Flame.

The sight was so daunting that she had to look back away after a moment, and she saw a square of pale light behind her. After a moment she realized it was the gate back to the material world. Through the pale glow she saw Sinan and the Immortals, watching her.

Perfectly motionless.

Had something happened to them? Then she remembered what Sinan had said about time moving at a different rate in the netherworld and understood. The others hadn't frozen. She was simply moving much, much faster than them, so fast that they appeared frozen from her perspective.

Perhaps if she watched for a thousand years she might at last she Sinan draw breath, see a tear fall from Mahdriva's cheek.

She had hoped that Sinan had been wrong about the time difference, that she could simply wait just beyond the gate until Corvalis arrived. And if she returned empty-handed, Sinan would kill her...or start killing Imperial Guards until she decided to cooperate.

It seemed Caina had no choice. The best plan was to claim the phoenix ashes, return to the Lord Ambassador's residence, and delay.

Best to get on with it, then.

Caina gazed at the Sacellum of the Living Flame. She did not want to go anywhere near the monstrous black structure. She didn't even want to look at the thing. Something about its unfathomable size and the peculiar angles of its construction conspired to send a stabbing wave of pain through her head whenever she looked at it. Mortals had never been meant to gaze upon the Sacellum, let alone enter it.

But there was no other choice.

Caina took a moment to steady herself, then moved to the gleaming black road and started walking.

The strange landscape altered and shifted around her, changing from the gray grassland to the dead forest to the bleak desert and back again. Her shadow-cloak billowed behind her no matter what direction she faced, even though Caina neither felt nor heard any wind. The netherworld was utterly silent around her, and even the green lightning flashing overhead never generated any thunder. The only sounds were the click of her boots against the gleaming black stone, the slow draw of her breath, the steady drumbeat of her pulse in her ears.

The landscape changed again, and this time it became a ruined, empty city. Some of the buildings were black, and reminded her of the slums of Rasadda. Others gleamed white, like the whitewashed houses of Cyrioch. In fact, she was certain she had seen one of those houses before – it looked like the occultist Nadirah's house.

Was the netherworld reflecting her memories back at her, like Sinan had said?

That was a disturbing thought.

A golden glow overhead caught her attention.

Caina looked up, hands dropping to her weapons, and saw the winged man.

He soared overhead, great wings spread behind him, and Caina realized that both the man and his wings were wrought entirely of golden fire. He was breathtakingly beautiful, and Caina watched as he shot over the plain like a comet. The winged man rose higher, spiraling over the Sacellum of the Living Flame...and then vanished into it.

A phoenix spirit.

The creature hadn't noticed her. People never looked up...so did that mean winged spirits never looked down? Or perhaps it had seen her and dismissed her as a threat.

Or it assumed the guardians Sinan had mentioned would dispose of her.

Caina kept walking.

She saw the dead Imperial Guard a moment later.

The man lay upon the black road, blood pooling around him, his cuirass torn away. The blade of his sword jutted from his back, shiny with his blood. At first Caina thought someone had overpowered him and run him through with his own sword.

Then she drew closer, and saw the Guard's hands clenched around the sword's hilt.

He had fallen upon his sword.

Why had he killed himself?

Caina looked around, seeking some reason that would explain the Guard's suicide, but she saw only the changing terrain.

Yet something had compelled the Guard to kill himself. The Imperial Guards were the toughest soldiers in the Empire, superbly trained and disciplined combat veterans selected from the Legions. They were the sort of men to die only after surrounding themselves with a ring of slain foes.

Caina drew a throwing knife in one hand, her ghostsilver dagger in the other, and froze.

The curved blade of the ghostsilver dagger shone with pale white light, the air around it rippling and dancing. Ghostsilver was proof against sorcery. Did that mean it would be effective against the spirits of the netherworld? Caina doubted her throwing knife could harm a spirit…but the ghostsilver blade might prove more potent.

Still, the light might draw unwelcome attention. Caina sheathed the dagger, keeping her hand on its handle, and resumed walking.

A short time later she saw a dark, round shape lying on the black road. Caina drew closer and stopped with a whispered curse.

It was the helmet of an Imperial Guard, the head still inside, neatly severed at the neck. The sightless eyes gazed up at Caina, the mouth open in a silent scream. There was not a drop of blood in sight.

She looked around, but there was no trace of the Guard's body.

Caina put one hand on the helmet, titling the head to the side. The cut across the neck was smoother than anything she had ever seen. Even a skilled executioner, wielding a razor-sharp sword, could not cut through a man's neck so cleanly.

"Gods," muttered Caina, straightening up. She didn't know what had done this, and she didn't particularly want to find out.

But there was nowhere to go but forward, so she kept walking.

The Sacellum of the Living Flame grew closer, the huge, fire-lit black mass filling the eerie sky like a burning mountain. The landscape rippled and flowed around her, changing from one form to another. More and more, the terrain became an empty city, and Caina found herself recognizing many of the buildings. Marzhod's tavern in Cyrioch was one. Another was Zorgi's Inn at Marsis. A third displayed the façade of the Grand Imperial Opera.

That disturbed her. Sinan claimed the netherworld would reflect her thoughts. Was that why she had started recognizing the buildings? Maybe the netherworld wasn't quite like a mirror. Maybe it was more like wet clay, gradually molding itself to the shape of her mind…

Then the terrain changed again, half of a room appearing, and with a shock Caina saw herself.

She lay naked in a bed, Corvalis atop her, both of them groaning and panting. Caina recognized the room from the Inn of the Defender at Cyrioch, where she and Corvalis had spent the night together for the first time.

Then the room vanished, along with the bed and its occupants, becoming a dead forest instead.

Caina stared at the forest, too shaken to move. Remembering her past was one thing. Seeing it played out before her eyes was something else. That had been a pleasant memory, true…but she had others far darker.

Maybe that was why the Imperial Guard had killed himself.

Caina broke into a jog.

The plain still shifted around her, and more and more she saw buildings she recognized. And sometimes she saw figures she recognized within the buildings. In one she saw Halfdan teaching her how to pick locks. In another she saw herself running with Nicolai in her arms, Istarish soldiers chasing them. In still another she saw Maglarion, the bloodcrystal in his left eye socket shining with ghostly green light, a bloody dagger in his hand...

She looked away. No, she did not want to remember that.

The landscape changed again, becoming featureless gray grass in all directions, and a girl appeared on the road ahead of Caina.

She was about ten or eleven, short and skinny with long black hair and large blue eyes the color of ice. She wore the rich blue dress of a young Nighmarian noblewoman, and Caina recognized it. It had been her favorite dress as a child, when she had still lived with her father.

Before her mother had invited Maglarion to take her.

Caina was looking at herself as a girl.

"What are you?" said Caina, drawing her ghostsilver blade and pointing at it the girl.

"You're a monster," whispered the girl.

"What are you?" said Caina.

"I am you," whispered the girl. "I am Caina Amalas. I am you as you were, before you...changed."

"Before Maglarion came," said Caina.

The child nodded. "I wanted to be a mother. I wanted my father to pick a good and strong man for my husband, and I wanted to bear children. I would be a better mother to them than Laeria Amalas was ever to me, and someday I would be surrounded by strong sons and beautiful daughters and laughing grandchildren." Her young face twisted with loathing. "Instead I became you."

"Maglarion did this to me," said Caina. "I had little choice in the matter."

"Maglarion left you barren," said the girl, "and look what you became. You're a killer. How much blood is on your hands? How many people have you killed? Can you even count them all?"

"I've done what was necessary," said Caina. "I've killed people, but they were trying to kill me. Or they would have done worse things, had I not..."

"Excuses," spat the girl, her face crinkled with loathing. "You turned me into a monster. You turned me into you."

"Instead," said a woman's voice, dry and cold, "you should have become me."

Caina knew that voice.

It was her own.

A woman in her early twenties stepped onto the black road. She had long black hair and icy blue eyes, her thin arms and legs tight with sinewy muscle. She wore only a shift of white cloth, and her pregnant belly swelled against it.

The woman was also Caina, or at least Caina if she could become pregnant.

The sight of it hurt more than she expected.

"You should have been me," said the pregnant woman.

"I should have been her," said the girl.

"None of you," said Caina. Her voice caught, and she forced herself to start over in a calm tone. "None of you are real."

"Perhaps we are real," said the pregnant woman, resting a hand on the curve of her stomach, "and it is you who are a nightmare." She smiled. "Would you like to feel our son kick?"

Caina had taken one step forward and extended a gloved hand before she stopped herself. "I suspect that touching you would be a very bad idea."

The pregnant woman sneered. "What a contemptible creature you are. Yearning for what you can never have, desiring that which you will never touch. You wanted to be me, you wanted to be a wife and mother...and instead you are a murderer who shares the bed of an assassin with as much blood on his hands as yours. Our father would weep to see what you have become."

"My father is dead," said Caina, "because my mother and Maglarion murdered him. And I avenged him. I stopped Maglarion from killing everyone in Malarae. And I..."

"You do not need," said another woman's voice, colder and stronger than the first, "to justify yourself to anyone. You did what was necessary, and the Empire still stands today because of you."

A woman in a black-trimmed red gown stepped onto the road.

For an alarmed instant Caina thought that it was the Moroaica, and she raised her ghostsilver dagger. But the woman had long black hair and cold blue eyes, and when Jadriga appeared in Caina's dreams, she always took the form of a young Szaldic woman with wet black hair and inscrutable black eyes. Her second thought was that the red-gowned woman was her mother, which was even worse.

Then Caina realized that she was looking at yet another version of herself.

A future version. The girl was who she had been and the pregnant woman was who she wished she had been.

This was who she might become.

The woman was about fifty, with gray at her temples and hard lines upon her gaunt face, though she remained fit and trim, and the red gown clung to the curves of her chest and hips. An aura of strength and power surrounded her, and Caina realized that she felt the tingle of arcane force.

The woman was a sorceress.

A powerful one.

"No," said Caina.

"Ah," said the sorceress with a smile. "I thought you might react like this. No matter. In time, you will see the necessity. You hate sorcery for the scars it left upon your mind and flesh…but a blade can leave scars as well. Do you hate the blade, or the hand that wields it? Sorcery is but another weapon, another tool."

"I have no talent for sorcery," said Caina.

The sorceress smiled. "Neither where you born with any talent for violence, but you learned it readily enough. So it is with the arcane sciences. One day you will see the advantages of wielding sorcery to defend the Empire."

"No," said Caina.

"Pathetic," said the young girl. "You will become everything you hate and fear."

"You should have been me," said the pregnant woman with a mournful shake of her head, black hair brushing against her pale shoulders. "Instead, you shall become her."

"Do not listen to these cowardly fears," said the sorceress. "In time you shall move past them. You have always done what is necessary to save people, to destroy those who would enslave and torment the weak. And with the power of sorcery, you will do far more. You shall bring peace and order to the Empire. You will free all the slaves, force the nobles to heel, and humble the magi."

For a moment, just a moment, Caina found that a compelling vision.

"No," she said again.

"Deny it all you wish," said the sorceress, "but you will become me, in the end. You will wield sorcery. Not to achieve power for its own end, as fools like Kalastus and Ranarius did, or to pursue some foolish dream of immortality like Maglarion. No, you shall wield power to protect the weak and to humble the strong."

"And if I did that," said Caina, "I would be no better than any other tyrant."

The sorceress smiled. "You've had so many chances to claim sorcerous might already. That book you took from Kalastus and threw into the sea. The Moroaica would have taught you, made you into her disciple. You could have wielded the power of the Defender, or forged yourself a suit of glypharmor in Catekharon."

"All of that power," said Caina, "was built on the blood of the innocent."

"But what of power built on the blood of the guilty?" said the sorceress. "You have slain so many tyrants and slavers already. Why not put their lives to better use?"

Caina opened her mouth and said nothing.

Part of her, a tiny part, found the prospect alluring.

"No," she said at last, pushing aside the emotion.

"It is too late," said the girl, stepping forward. "You've gone too far down the path already. You will become everything you hate."

"You should have been me," said the pregnant woman, striding alongside the young girl. "But instead you have become a hardened killer."

"And you will become me," said the sorceress, smiling. "It is inevitable."

Terror flooded through Caina as her past, her denied present, and her potential future strode towards her. What would happen if they touched her? Would they tear her apart? Would she turn into one of them? She pointed the ghostsilver dagger, the blade like a shard of pale white light in her hand.

"Stay back," said Caina.

The others ignored her.

"I said to stay back," said Caina, "or I'll..."

She blinked.

"You're not real," she said.

The sorceress laughed. "Do you deny the obvious?"

"You're real in a sense," said Caina, "because you're part of me. All of you." She lowered the dagger and pointed at the girl. "You are my past." She shifted her gaze to the pregnant woman. "You are the woman I wish I had been." At last she looked at the sorceress. "And you are the woman I fear to become."

The three doubles stared at her, remaining silent.

"But you're only my own thoughts and fears," said Caina, "reflected back at me by the netherworld. That's all."

Had this happened to the Imperial Guards, she wondered? Had they seen their past and present and future reflected back at them, filling them with despair until they fell upon their swords?

"Perhaps," said the pregnant woman, "but we are still very real."

"My fears are real," said Caina, "but you will not rule me. And the future...I could die tomorrow." Or in the next few moments, considering the strange things she had seen in the netherworld so far. "But I can change the future, as well. Perhaps it will be like this."

She concentrated, and a new figure appeared on the road. The woman looked like somewhat like the sorceress, an older version of Caina. Yet this figure wore a gown of green and black, and stood on the arm of an older

Corvalis, clad in the garb of a prosperous merchant.

"That," said Caina, "could just as easily be me."

"Facile," said the sorceress. "You would trade the power you could have for this…this illusion of sentimentality?"

"I would," said Caina. "We're done now. My fears are part of me, but I will not listen to them, or to you."

She stepped forward, and her doubles vanished. She looked around and saw nothing but the endlessly shifting landscape and the odd objects floating overhead.

And, of course, the vast black shape of the Sacellum ahead.

It seemed her fears could harm her only if she permitted it.

Caina shook her head and kept walking. She wondered what the Imperial Guards had seen when the netherworld reflected their minds back at themselves. Every living man and woman had secrets, old scars, black memories.

And some of them were too hard to bear.

Though that didn't explain what had happened to the beheaded Guard.

The landscape rippled once again, flickering through an image of Malarae's docks and then settling upon gray grasses, and Caina saw a hooded shape standing upon the road ahead.

She tightened her grip on the ghostsilver dagger.

The figure was nine or ten feet tall, and draped from head to toe in ragged gray robes. A heavy cowl covered its face, and Caina could not see past the darkness of the hood

She did not think it was a reflection generated from her mind.

A spirit, then? Some kind of elemental? One of the guardians Sinan had mentioned?

Or something worse?

"I have no quarrel with you," said Caina. "Let me pass, and I will go on my way."

The figure said nothing, the landscape blurring into the dead forest. More of the hooded gray shapes stepped out of the trees, joining the first, until a dozen of the strange creatures stood upon the road.

"Is there something you want of me?" said Caina. "I have no wish to fight."

The first shape stepped forward and changed.

Caina stepped back, an involuntary scream coming from her throat.

When she had been seven years old, her father had gone to Aretia to consult with the magistrates, and Caina had accompanied him to get away from her mother. While there, they had walked past the docks, and an enormous dead fish, at least two feet long, floated against the quay. The thing had been half eaten away with rot, its ribs jutting through tarnished scales, its eyes swollen and black with corruption. Caina had shrieked in horror at the sight, and it had taken her father some time to calm her down. The rotting fish had appeared in her dreams for weeks after.

Later, she had acquired darker things to populate her nightmares.

Yet to this day, she still felt a little uneasy around dead fish.

The robed shape had transformed itself into a hideous, hulking amalgamation of that long-ago dead fish and a living man. It had the exact same bulging black eyes, the same swollen scales, the same ribs jutting from its rotting flesh. Gods, it even had the same stench. She dimly noted that the other robed forms had changed as well. But how? That fish had rotted away fifteen years ago...

Her mind, she realized. The spirits were reflecting some deep-rooted, primitive fear from the depths of her thoughts.

Suddenly she knew exactly what had happened to the rest of the Imperial Guards.

As one the fish-monsters charged at her.

Caina was sure their intentions were not friendly.

She turned and ran.

CHAPTER 20
A BARGAIN

Caina sprinted along the black road, her shadow-cloak billowing behind her.

The fish-creatures pursued her in eerie silence. Despite their half-rotten state, despite the fact that they should not have legs at all, they matched her speed. For a moment, despite the revulsion that clenched her stomach, Caina felt a wild urge to laugh. After everything she had survived, everything she had escaped, she was going to die at the hand of a band of spirits that had transformed themselves into giant fish monsters.

It was almost funny.

Almost.

She whipped a throwing knife at them, and it struck the lead creature with no effect. The blade sank into the gelatinous flesh and vanished.

They were gaining on her.

Caina ran off the road. The terrain shifted as she did so, morphing from grassland to the dead forest. The creatures were fast, but they were big, and the ground in the dead forest was uneven. Without the smooth road, she could outpace them, perhaps even find a place to hide until they passed. She dashed around a tree, jumped over a knot of roots, and kept running, putting more distance between herself and the creatures.

Then the land changed again to become tangled patch of swamp. A stagnant pond yawned before Caina, and she jerked sideways, hoping to avoid it. Her feet tangled in the thick grasses, and she fell hard to the ground. She jumped up in sudden fear, convinced that the creatures were going to fall upon her.

But the sudden change in terrain had affected them as well. A dozen of them had fallen into one of the stagnant pools, while others had lost their footing and struggled to stand.

And one of them towered over her, its vile stink filling her nostrils, its pale, sagging arms reaching for her…

Caina yelled in fear and reacted on instinct, slashing with the ghostsilver dagger. The shining blade ripped through the creature's torso with a wet tearing noise, and the creature stumbled back with a keening shriek. The white glow from the dagger spread into the wound, and the fish-creature dissolved into a swirling column of white mist.

Caina didn't think she had killed the creature. She doubted it was even possible to kill an immortal spirit. But perhaps the ghostsilver dagger could damage the creatures enough to keep them from taking shape for a time. If she damaged enough of the creatures, perhaps the rest would change their minds and go in search of easier prey.

But for now, the rest of the fish-creatures seemed eager to kill her.

Caina raced across the swamp, dodging around the pools of stagnant water. The swamp would give her an advantage. The creatures could move just as fast as she could, but they seemed to have difficulty turning. Caina could dodge around the pools far more easily, giving her the opportunity to outrun them.

She jumped over another pool, and as she did, the land rippled beneath her. When she landed, she stood upon a desert plain, glassy black earth stretching away in all directions.

The fish-creatures starting gaining.

"Damn it," hissed Caina between breaths.

She was starting to get tired, her breath burning in her lungs. The strange creatures seemed to have no such limitations. On this black plain, with no place to hide, they would run her down. If she had been in the narrow alleys of Malarae's dockside district, she could have eluded the beasts easily, but in this open plain she had no chance of escape.

The landscape rippled again and became a city, a strange mixture of the dockside districts of both Malarae and Marsis. The crumbling brick warehouses and sagging taverns split the pursuing creatures into a half a dozen small groups. Caina turned, surprised. She had thought about the city…and the landscape had reflected to change itself.

Did that mean she could control the terrain with her thoughts? A few years ago the power of a sorcerous relic had trapped her in a shared dream with a murderous noblewoman, and once she realized what had happed, Caina had been able to control the dream with her mind.

Could the same thing happen in the netherworld?

She reversed direction, running at the pursuing creatures.

The maneuver caught the spirits off-guard, and Caina plunged into them, the ghostsilver dagger a white blur in her hand. She slashed left and right, the white light spreading from the blade to consume the creatures. Caina cut down a third one, and then broke through, sprinting down a narrow lane that looked like a drunken mixture of the Grand Market of Marsis and the alley behind the Serpents' Nest.

She concentrated, thinking of the forests she had seen, hoping to summon the dead trees back.

And as she did, the city melted away, morphing back into the dead, leafless forest, the black trunks painted with the sky's eerie green glow. Caina dodged past the trees, making for the fire-lit shape of the Sacellum of the Living Flame. She heard the fish-monsters blundering behind her, but they sounded farther away now. The shifts in the landscape had thrown them. If she kept her wits about her, she might be able to elude them entirely...

A gray blur shot overhead.

Caina saw one of the creatures soaring above the trees. It had reverted back to its original form of a hooded gray wraith, and she felt the malevolent pressure of its gaze. It pointed at her, and a dozen more of the hooded spirits rose out of the dead trees, their ragged robes hanging eerily motionless.

The creatures plummeted towards her.

Caina cursed and summoned an image of Malarae in her mind, of the warehouse where Haeron Icaraeus had once hidden his slaves...

The dead forest morphed into the dockside streets of Malarae, though dotted with oddities. Many of the warehouses looked as if they had come from the streets of Catekharon, and bits and pieces of Haeron Icaraeus's mansion stood here and there; a fountain, a wall, a statue, a staircase that spiraled to nothing.

Clearly Caina needed practice at this.

But the warehouse stood before her, and she threw herself through the main door. The stalls that had once held slaves were dusty and empty. Caina slammed and barred the door behind her, and heard the thumping as the wraiths drove against it. She backed away from the door, the ghostsilver dagger glowing like a torch in her right fist. There had to be some way to frighten the spirits away. Perhaps if she got close enough to the Sacellum, the wraiths would not follow...

The entire wall next to the door shattered in a cloud of dust and broken brick. Caina saw dozens of the hooded forms standing in the street outside, the black pits of their cowls facing her.

They flowed towards her like a wall of gray water.

Caina ran, summoning the image of a forest in her mind as she did so. The warehouse rippled and reformed back into the dead forest. She weaved between the trees, her boots tearing at the uneven ground. Some of the wraiths blurred back into the form of the fish monsters, a shiver of revulsion rolling down Caina's spine. Others soared into the black sky like gray birds. Caina veered towards the Sacellum, trying to think of a plan.

Then she felt a surge of power, her skin crawling.

Someone was casting a spell, a powerful spell, nearby.

There was a brilliant flare of blue light, and a dozen of the wraiths ripped apart into shreds of gray mist. Caina stopped, shocked, as did the pursuing fish-creatures. Another flare of dazzling blue light, and the creatures dissolved into blue shreds. Caina stared at them, stunned, and the forest shifted back to the plain of colorless grasses.

As one of the remaining wraiths and fish-creatures fled.

A moment later Caina stood alone in the plain, her shadow-cloak billowing around her.

She let out a long breath. The creatures showed no sign of returning.

Which made her wonder if they had been frightened off by something worse. A more powerful spirit? One of the guardians of the Sacellum?

Or something even more dangerous?

Caina turned, and saw the woman in the red gown standing nearby, staring at her.

For a moment Caina thought it was another reflection from her own mind. But this woman wasn't wearing a red gown, but a robe, belted around the waist with a black slash. She looked about eighteen years old, with black hair that hung loose and wet around her shoulders. Her eyes were black and hard and old, even ancient, eyes that had seen the passage of centuries and the blood of thousands.

A spasm of fear went through Caina, and for a moment she could not decide to flee or to attack.

"Jadriga," said Caina at last.

The Moroaica stared at her, titling her head to the side.

"You dyed your hair," said the Moroaica at last.

Caina burst out laughing.

"Did I say something amusing?" said Jadriga.

"I killed you underneath Marsis," said Caina, "and your spirit inhabited my body for almost a year. Your pet assassin Sicarion tried to kill me. Your disciples almost destroyed Marsis and Cyrioch both. Mihaela tried to murder me, and wound up expelling your spirit from my body, and I haven't seen you in my dreams or in the flesh for almost a year." She shook her head. "And after all that, the first thing you ask is if I dyed my hair?"

The Moroaica frowned, and as she did, her eyes shifted from black to icy blue and back again.

"This is the netherworld," said Jadriga, "not the material world. I am not here in the flesh, and you see me as you do now because this is the form I choose to take. Should I wish it, I could appear as...almost anything, really." She gestured, and her body rippled and flowed, shifting between the forms of an ancient crone, a young Anshani woman, a proud Kyracian noblewoman, and most disturbingly, Caina herself, before returning to the shape of the red-robed Szaldic woman. "But you are not a wielder of arcane force. If your dreaming mind has cast your spirit to the netherworld, as it has before during our conversations, you would wear the form your mind believes your body to have. Black hair, not blond. Which means you have dyed your hair…and you are therefore here in the flesh."

"Aye," said Caina.

Again the Moroaica titled her head. Most of the time Jadriga affected a mask of glacial calm, the infinite patience of a creature that had seen millennia pass and empires rise and fall. Yet Caina had seen Jadriga angry, had even seen Jadriga weep after Caina had glimpsed one of the Moroaica's earliest memories.

Like Caina, Jadriga's father had been murdered in front of her.

But now there was only puzzlement on the Moroaica's face.

"Why?" said the Moroaica. "You are not a sorceress, but you are no fool, and surely you must know the tremendous danger you face by coming to the netherworld in the flesh."

Caina laughed. "We've played this game before. You set a trap for me, and now you'll offer to teach me sorcery in exchange for aiding your murderous 'great work', whatever it is."

Jadriga's red lips twitched into a smile. "Given the course of your life, I see why you think I might have had a hand in…"

"The course of my life?" said Caina. "Do you mean how your disciple Ranarius almost killed me and destroyed Cyrioch? Or how your disciple Andromache invaded Marsis to claim the Tomb of Scorikhon?" Anger flared to life in her, and the glow of the dagger burned brighter in response. "Or how your disciple Maglarion murdered my father?"

Again Jadriga's eyes flickered from black to blue, and a hint of emotion went over her face.

Regret?

That couldn't possibly be it.

"This is another trap," said Caina. "You're not the Moroaica."

She raised a black eyebrow. "Oh?"

"Your eyes," said Caina. "They keep changing color. The Moroaica would have enough control to keep a consistent disguise. And she would never express regret for anything. So who are you, really?"

The Moroaica said nothing, and her eyes turned blue and cold and hard.

"You are wrong," she said, voice quiet. "I am the woman you call the Moroaica, and there are things I regret. The death of my father, which you saw. And the death of your father. How your mother left him broken in that chair, how you killed her with that fireplace poker. How Maglarion cut his throat, and then left you in that cell."

"Stop it," said Caina.

"Or Alastair Corus," said Jadriga. "You regret his death. You regret all those you could not save at Marsis. You…"

"This is just a trick," said Caina. "You're reading my mind." She reached for the cowl of her shadow-cloak. "You won't be…"

"No," said the Moroaica. "I am not reading your mind. Just your memories. Which are now a part of my memories."

Caina froze. "What do you mean?"

"When Mihaela struck you down," said Jadriga, "and expelled my spirit from your flesh, I took a new host at once, of course. Yet there was a…side effect, something I had never before experienced. I suspect it resulted from my inability to control you while I inhabited your flesh. Your memories…"

"What about them?" said Caina.

"I have them," said Jadriga. "All of them."

Caina stared at the Moroaica. "You mean…my entire life…"

Jadriga nodded. "Up to the point Mihaela struck you down. All your memories, child of the Ghosts. All twenty-one years."

They stood in silence for a moment.

"Gods," said Caina at last. "I'm sorry."

It was an absurd thing to say, but Caina meant it. The Moroaica was an ancient horror, a creature of evil that had caused untold suffering. Yet Caina had lived through things she would not inflict upon anyone else, things she hoped no one else would ever endure.

Even the Moroaica.

Jadriga shrugged. "Life is suffering and pain. You know that as well as anyone. The world is broken, a prison the gods built to torment us while they laugh at our suffering." Her eyes flickered, becoming black and hard as the edge of an obsidian blade. "I will remake the world, and I will make the gods pay for what they have done."

But Caina had heard Jadriga say that before, and she was still digesting what the Moroaica had already said.

"All my memories?" she said. "Even when Corvalis and I…"

Again Jadriga's eyes flickered blue. "Yes."

"Oh."

"You are fortunate," said Jadriga, her voice quiet. "He loves you, and you love him in return. That is…that is a rare thing."

And with a shock Caina realized that the Moroaica's eyes were not merely turning blue. They were turning into Caina's eyes, and the Moroaica did not realize it. As if Caina's memories had left a permanent mark upon Jadriga's spirit, almost a scar.

The Moroaica was dangerous enough. What might she do with the addition of Caina's memories?

"You still haven't told me," said Caina, hoping to change the subject, "why you came here."

The Moroaica smiled, her eyes turning black once more. "I have not."

"Were you looking for me?" said Caina.

"Ah," said Jadriga, "we are now asking each other questions? You know the rules, child of the Ghosts. I will answer your question...but only if you answer one of mine."

Caina hesitated. She was reluctant to give the Moroaica any information. Though since Jadriga already had most of Caina's memories, she couldn't imagine what else the Moroaica wanted to know. And Caina did need help. She did not know the rules of this strange place, and if Jadriga had not intervened, the gray wraiths would have torn her apart.

And if she did not return with the phoenix ashes, Sinan would simply send someone else to die.

"Very well," said Caina. "I'll answer your questions if you answer mine."

Jadriga inclined her head. "In answer to your first question, I was not looking for you. I happened upon you by chance. I often send my spirit into the netherworld, for there are secrets to be gleaned here. I sensed the disturbance near the Sacellum of the Living Flame, and was curious. I saw you fighting the phobomorphic spirits, and decided to intervene..."

"Phobomorphic?" said Caina.

"They have many names," said Jadriga, "but they essentially act as...mirrors for the mind. Any mortal who looks at one sees his deepest fears reflected back at him. I am surprised you handled yourself so well. Often the mere sight of the spirits can drive a mortal to madness. And you displayed remarkable control over the netherworld. I have known sorcerers with years of experience who could not control the terrain so easily."

"It's amazing what you can do," muttered Caina, "when you're desperate enough."

"Indeed," said Jadriga. "Now. You will answer my question. Why are you here in the flesh?"

"I didn't have much choice in the matter," said Caina.

"Undoubtedly," said the Moroaica, "but an incomplete answer. The agreement, as I recall from the last time we had such a discussion, was for complete answers."

"An Alchemist named Ibrahmus Sinan," said Caina, watching Jadriga's face for any sign of recognition. There was none. "He came to Istarinmul to create his Elixir Rejuvenata, which as I'm sure you know, requires the ashes of three unborn children from related mothers and the ashes of a phoenix spirit."

"Ah," said the Moroaica, glancing at the Sacellum. "And you are cooperating with him voluntarily?"

"That's another question," said Caina.

Jadriga waved a hand. "Proceed."

"Of course I am not helping him voluntarily," said Caina. "I attempted to stop him, and rescue his last victim, and I...miscalculated. He threatened to start murdering innocent men one by one unless I helped him. So I agreed to come here and obtain phoenix ashes, hoping to stall until help arrives after I return."

"An unwise choice," said Jadriga, "given that time flows differently here."

"I already know that," said Caina. "I hope to cause a delay after I return." If she survived to return. "Now I have two questions." The Moroaica nodded. "Is Ibrahmus Sinan one of your disciples?"

Jadriga laughed. "No. I have never taken an Alchemist of the College as a disciple, child of the Ghosts. The magi of your Magisterium are proud fools, the Sages of the Scholae of Catekharon are blind fools...but the Alchemists of Istarinmul are simply fools. Like the Scholae, they are a remnant of old Maat, and once assisted the sorcerer-priests who prepared the unguents of embalming for the pharaohs and the great nobles. When Maat fell to the darkness, the men who become the College fled north, and eventually settled in Istarinmul. The arcane sciences they practice now are merely a debased shadow of the great powers their forebears wielded in Maat."

"Before you brought the darkness to Maat," said Caina.

Jadriga's smile showed teeth, and a glimmer of blue appeared in her eyes, which alarmed Caina. "I did. Once the Kingdom of the Rising Sun ruled all the land between two oceans, and the men of a hundred nations and tribes paid tribute to the throne of the pharaohs. The pharaohs sealed themselves and their slaves in their tombs to become Undying, to live in splendor and bliss forever. But I undid them, child of the Ghosts. I repaid them a thousand times over for their cruelty. I turned their cities to dust, and now only scorpions pay homage to the pharaohs' throne. I bound the pharaohs' spirits to their tombs, to let them scream forever in the waterless dark. And someday I will do the same to the gods themselves."

Caina said nothing, unsettled by the blue tint in Jadriga's eyes. Was Caina capable of that level of hatred?

"My question now," said Jadriga.

"Actually," said Caina, "that was a statement. It was kind of you to confirm it, though."

Again Jadriga laughed. "Clever! A pity you would not let me teach you. You would have made a most formidable disciple."

Caina remembered the words of her potential future self and shuddered. "Only so you could possess me when your current body dies."

Jadriga shrugged. "I tried to possess you." Her eyes faded to black. "It did not work. Clearly, you are safe from that danger. Your question."

Caina thought for a moment. "Is Sinan right? Will the phoenix ashes let him create an Elixir?"

"They will," said Jadriga. "The Elixir Rejuvenata is…crude, inelegant. The Alchemists make the mistake of Maglarion in trying to create immortality of the flesh. As well try to make a cloud immortal, or to keep the sun from setting. Flesh is a shadow that passes away, but the spirit endures. Nevertheless, the Elixir will rejuvenate him and give him at least another century of life. If he prepares it properly. If he does not, the results will be rather…less enjoyable."

"Death," said Caina.

"If he is fortunate. Now, my question." The Moroaica stared at her. "Is Sinan alone, and does he have any allies?"

"He has maybe thirty Immortals with him," said Caina. "They've been…enhanced, somehow, with sorcerous elixirs. They look like walking walls of muscle. But other than that, he is alone."

The Moroaica nodded, face glacially calm once again.

"My question," said Caina. "Why do you care about Sinan? You said you have no use for the Alchemists."

"Ibrahmus Sinan does not interest me," said Jadriga. "Whether he lives out the night or another thousand years is no concern of mine. You, Caina Amalas of the Ghosts, you interest me. You would make a valuable ally, one who could aid me in my great work."

"Your great work," said Caina, voice full of scorn. "I saw your great work in the dungeons below Black Angel Tower. Blood and death and torment and misery. I will not aid you in that. Not in a thousand years."

"A thousand years," said Jadriga, "is a long time. You are young, for all your wisdom. Only twenty-two, and you have seen so little of the world. In time, you will come to understand…and you will aid me of your own will. Which is why I shall aid you now."

"Aid me?" said Caina. "Why?"

"As I said," said Jadriga, "I have no wish for you to die. You will, one day, be a valuable ally."

"No, I won't," said Caina.

The Moroaica only smiled.

"I won't take your aid," said Caina. "Not after the things you have done."

"All I have done," said the Moroaica, "is exactly the things you have done." Her eyes flickered blue. "I have just done them on a larger scale." She shrugged. "It is within my power to aid you whether you wish it or not, but I will not force you. Go to the Sacellum of the Sacred Flame without my help if you wish." She gestured at the huge dark mass of the temple, flames shining within its vast windows. "But if you do, you will die. You will die before you go another hundred yards. The phobomorphic spirits will hunt you down. Or something else will find you. There are far more dangerous spirits than the ones you have already seen. And I am not the only wielder of arcane force to wander the netherworld."

Caina said nothing. Jadriga was right. Caina did not know the rules of this place, did not know how to fight the creatures that dwelled here. She had been clever, but also lucky…and luck was a finite quality.

Sooner or later it would run out.

And if she failed, if she did not return, Sinan would kill more Imperial Guards. And if that didn't work, he would likely cut the child from Mahdriva's womb and retreat to different location to obtain the phoenix ashes.

Caina did not want the Moroaica's aid.

But she did not want Mahdriva to die. She did not want Tanzir to die. And she wanted to stop Sinan.

And she wanted to see Corvalis again.

Caina sighed and looked at the ground for a moment.

"What," said Caina, lifting her eyes to meet Jadriga's, "did you have in mind?"

"Then," said Jadriga, "you accept that you have no choice but to take my aid?"

"No," said Caina, "I choose to take your aid. I could reject it. I could try to get to the Sacellum by myself. But if I do, I'll probably die…and other people will die. I'm not prepared to accept their deaths as a consequence of refusing your aid." She took a deep breath. "But I am prepared to accept the consequences of taking your help. Whatever those may be."

"You grow in wisdom, child of the Ghosts," said the Moroaica, her eyes as black and cold as a starless night.

"So how can you help me?" said Caina.

"First," said the Moroaica, "I will take you to the entrance of the Sacellum. The guardians and the other spirits that wander the netherworld will not trouble you for fear of my power."

"And when we reach the Sacellum?" said Caina.

"I shall tell you how to breach the defenses," said Jadriga. "There are three traps defending the Sacellum, traps that will test your skill, will, and truth."

"What does that even mean?" said Caina.

"I am not entirely sure," said the Moroaica. "I have never been within the Sacellum myself. I do know that the first challenge is one of skill. Something to test your abilities. The second challenges the strength of your will. The last, I believe, is a question that you must answer truthfully."

"And if I fail these challenges?" said Caina.

"You die," said the Moroaica. "Though that is little different than the rest of your life, is it not?"

"Fine." Caina gave a sharp nod. "Let's get moving."

The Moroaica beckoned, and they started walking towards the Sacellum of the Living Flame. The landscape rippled around them, cycling between the dead forest and the gray grassland and the stagnant swamp. Yet Caina saw new things, and realized the netherworld was also reflecting Jadriga's thoughts. She saw the gleaming white city where Jadriga's father had been killed. A desert of rolling sands, brilliant golden dunes shining in the harsh sun. A ruined temple, walls and pillars of weathered stone jutting from the moonlit sand. It was the first city, Caina realized...but after Jadriga had wrought her vengeance.

The Moroaica walked in silence, her wet hair hanging around her face like a hood.

"There is another way you could help me," said Caina.

"Oh?" said Jadriga.

"You have so much power," said Caina. "Why don't you enter the Sacellum and get the phoenix ashes for me?"

A cold smile appeared on her red lips. "Because the Sacellum is a place of rebirth."

"So?" said Caina.

"That means someone who has died as many times as I have," said Jadriga, "cannot enter the Sacellum."

"Oh," said Caina.

They walked the rest of the way in silence.

CHAPTER 21
THE SACELLUM OF THE LIVING FLAME

"I can go no further," said the Moroaica.

Caina nodded, staring at the vast entrance.

They stood at the top of the broad black stairs leading to the Sacellum's doors. The entrance itself, a huge arch nearly five hundred feet high and a hundred wide, rose over her. Beyond a vast gallery stretched into the heart of the Sacellum, a fiery glow shining in its depths.

"I don't suppose," said Caina, "that I could simply climb the walls and go through one of the windows?"

But even that wouldn't work. The huge building, she suspected, stood nearly a mile high, its vast windows five hundred feet off the ground. It would be grimly amusing to escape the phobomorphic spirits only to slip and fall to her death while trying to climb a wall.

"A good thought," said Jadriga, "but this is the netherworld, and the defenses of the Sacellum are not bound by the conventions of mere physicality. If you go through the windows, the tests will merely meet you there."

"I see," said Caina, staring into the vast gallery. "Who built this place?"

"One of the great sovereigns of the fire elementals," said Jadriga. "Spirits, like mortals, have their own hierarchies and ranks, though most of them are incomprehensible to us. The phoenix spirits are vassals of one of the greater fire elementals, and that spirit raised the Sacellum as a place for its vassals to renew themselves."

"Thoughtful of it," said Caina.

The Moroaica shrugged. "The elemental spirits have made war upon each other since before I was born, since before mortal men even walked the face of our world. To them, we are but flickers of light and shadow upon the water."

"I heard a spirit say something like that," said Caina.

"Yes, the Defender," said Jadriga.

Caina opened her mouth to ask how Jadriga could possibly know that, then remembered that the Moroaica had all her memories of Cyrioch.

She stepped towards the entrance, hesitated, and looked back.

"Thank you," she said, "for your help."

Jadriga shrugged. "Do not think of it as a gift. For I think of it as an investment."

"Never," said Caina.

The Moroaica smiled, and with a shudder Caina remembered the mocking words of her potential future self. Was taking Jadriga's help the first step on the road to becoming that woman?

Of course, she could die inside the Sacellum, so she might not live to become anything.

Caina strode into the great gallery and did not look back.

The entrance receded behind her, her boots clicking against the gleaming black stone of the floor. The high windows towered above her, rising to touch the pointed ceiling far overhead. Caina kept walking, the ghostsilver dagger glowing in her right fist, her eyes and ears seeking for attackers. Yet the interior of the Sacellum was deserted, and the gallery seemed to stretch on for miles, far longer than the exterior of the great temple itself. Yet Jadriga had said that the Sacellum was not bound by the rules of physicality...

Then the great gallery blurred around her, and Caina found herself standing somewhere else.

Specifically, in the gleaming ballroom of a Nighmarian lord, the floor of polished marble, the chandeliers of enspelled crystals shining overhead. Tables along the walls held food and drink, and a balcony ringed the ballroom, providing a place for guests to sit and talk and watch the dancers.

But the ballroom was utterly deserted.

Caina turned in a circle, watching for any danger. This had to be another illusion, but...

She heard boot heels clicking against the marble floor and spun.

"Oh, not this again," muttered Caina.

The woman that walked towards Caina was identical to her, with the same height, the same lean build, the same blue eyes, even the same dyed blond hair. The duplicate wore a shimmering green gown of rich silk, slashed with black at the sleeves and bodice, the pointed heels of her boots clicking as she walked.

"Let me guess," said Caina. "You're a ghost of my past. Or you represent what I would like to be. Or who would I like to become. Or you're going to stand there and spout prophetic nonsense about remaking the world like the Moroaica."

The duplicate raised one eyebrow, and Caina hoped she did not really look that smug when she smirked. "Actually, Caina Amalas, I am none of those things. You would call me the Keeper…"

"For you are the guardian of this place," said Caina, waving a hand around her. "The Sacellum. Which so far looks remarkably like a Nighmarian ballroom."

"The Sacellum," said the Keeper, "is beyond mortal comprehension. The minds of mortals are dependent upon metaphors, upon symbols, and so therefore your mind constructs an image of the Sacellum using symbols you can understand."

"And that is why," said Caina, "you are wearing my form."

"Indeed," said the Keeper, her smirk turning to a smile. "It is good you understand quickly. Most mortals spend more time battling the shadows of their own mind than altering the world around them." She began walking in a circle around Caina, still smiling, and Caina turned to keep the spirit in sight. "My sovereign bade me to guard the Sacellum, long millennia before your race ever walked under the sun. For my sovereign knew that our foes wished to invade the Sacellum for themselves…and in time, mortals would come to our world and seek to claim the ashes of the phoenix spirits for themselves."

"And you seek to stop them?" said Caina.

White teeth flashed behind the Keeper's lips in a predatory smile. "The spirits, yes. But the mortals may take the ashes…but only if they prove themselves worthy. Only if they are strong enough and bold enough. If you would steal our fire, mortal, you must prove yourself."

"The tests of skill, will, and truth," said Caina.

"You have prepared yourself, I see," said the Keeper. "That is good. You shall need that knowledge for what comes next.

"And what is that?" said Caina.

"Why," said the Keeper, "the test of skill."

She whirled with blinding speed, hand dipping into her sleeve, and Caina saw a gleam of steel. Caina twisted to the side just as a throwing knife blurred from the Keeper's hand. It shot past Caina's ear to clatter against the marble floor. The Keeper sprang forward, daggers in either hand. Caina yanked a dagger from her boot, gripping it in her left hand, and met the Keeper's attack. Steel clanged against steel and ghostsilver, and Caina and the Keeper traded a dozen blows in as many heartbeats. Caina lunged, feinting with the dagger in her left hand, and drove the ghostsilver blade for the Keeper's heart.

But the Keeper jumped backwards and landed a dozen feet away. Had Caina attempted to jump wearing that skirt and those heeled boots, she would have broken both her ankles. But the Keeper landed with ease, the same mocking smile on her face.

"You're cheating," said Caina, circling to the left, daggers held low.

The Keeper laughed. "I said it was a test of skill, did I not?"

Another throwing knife hurtled at Caina, and then another. She dodged both the blades and threw a knife of her own, but the Keeper danced around it. A test of skill this might have been, but it was not a fair test. The Keeper was a spirit, stronger and faster than Caina, and…

She blinked as the realization came to her, and suddenly she remembered escaping from the Immortals in the Grand Imperial Opera.

When had her fights ever been fair?

Her eyes swept the ballroom, and she nodded to herself.

The Keeper flung another knife, and Caina dodged. A rope was pinned to one of the pillars supporting the elaborate balcony, and Caina severed it with a single slash of her ghostsilver dagger.

A metallic groan echoed through the room.

The Keeper grinned and drew another throwing knife.

An instant later the chandelier, its rope severed, crashed upon the Keeper's head.

"I cannot," said Caina, "believe that worked."

The ballroom blurred and disappeared, and Caina found herself standing in a gloomy, narrow corridor. It was the upper corridor from the Serpents' Nest, the hallway lined with doors on either side.

The Keeper stood at the far end of the corridor, a closed door at her back.

"You survived the test of skill," said the Keeper, titling her head to the side. It was strange to see the spirit creature wearing Caina's face, but compared to everything else that had happened in the netherworld, it seemed downright innocuous. "Interesting. Most would have struggled against me until their strength failed. Many have struggled against me until their strength failed."

"They shouldn't have done so," said Caina.

"No," murmured the Keeper. "This, mortal, is the trial of will."

"And what must I do now?" said Caina.

"Simply walk the length of this corridor," said the Keeper, "and pass through the door behind me. This is the trial of will."

"That's it?" said Caina.

"That is it," said the Keeper. "Something so simple…but simple is not the same as easy, is it not?"

She disappeared.

Caina stood motionless, her eyes sweeping the gloomy corridor. She saw no sign of traps, no tripwires, no trapdoors, no waiting attackers. Perhaps enemies lurked behind the doors, preparing to spring upon her, but the hallway was utterly silent.

She shrugged and stepped forward.

And as she did, the door on her left swung open of its own accord.

Caina whirled to face it, dagger raised to strike. She expected more of the fish-creatures, or perhaps a room filled with shrieking knife-wielding duplicates of herself, or gods only knew what other horrors. But instead she saw…

Her dagger hand lowered, her jaw falling open.

Instead she saw her father's library, the windows behind his desk standing open, the sunlight washing over her and the salty smell of the sea filling her nostrils. Sebastian Amalas sat at the desk, pouring over his books and scrolls, and smiled at her.

"There you are, Caina," said Sebastian. "I just returned from the Imperial capital, and I brought back some books for you. A history of the Second Empire, I think you'll like that. And…ah," said Sebastian, digging through the books on his desk, "a book of old Szaldic myths. Grisly stuff, but after your mother was arrested for collaborating with that necromancer, I suppose we're used to grisly things." He blinked. "Why, you're crying! Is anything the matter?"

"Father," whispered Caina, blinking.

This was not real. She knew it could not be real.

But she could smell the sea, his dusty old books…

"Come here," Sebastian said, holding out his arms, "and we shall talk about it."

Caina took a step forward before she could stop herself. She wanted, more than anything to walk through that door and join her father in his library. But Sebastian Amalas was dead. She had seen him die with her own eyes. Whatever was happening beyond that door was an illusion.

A lie.

And her anger at that lie gave her the strength to keep walking.

More doors opened. Through one she saw herself wed to Corvalis, holding their child in her arms. Through another she saw herself as a Countess of the Imperial Court, presiding over the end of the Magisterium and the banishment of all sorcerers from the Empire. And in still another she saw herself with her mother, not with a Laeria Amalas filled with bitterness loathing, but a Laeria Amalas who loved her daughter.

For some reason, that one cut deepest of all, and Caina wanted to hurry through the door and hear that her mother had repented, that she had truly loved her after all…

Instead she wiped aside the tears, reached the end of the corridor, and threw open the door.

The shabby hallway vanished, and Caina found herself back in the vast gallery of black stone.

The Keeper stood nearby, still wearing the guise of Caina herself.

"What was the point of that?" said Caina. "To torment me with the past?"

"Hardly," said the Keeper. "You mortals are enslaved to your memories. They shape you and mold you, just as a sculptor's chisel shapes the stone. And your memories give you dreams that you are ill-equipped to resist, no matter how implausible."

"So that was the trial of will?" said Caina. "To see if I was strong enough to resist these false dreams?"

"Not many are," said the Keeper. "Look behind you."

Caina did, and flinched.

Bones carpeted the floor as far as she could see, thousands upon thousands of bones. Some of the skeletons wore rusty armor, others crumbling rags. Quite a few of the skeletons, Caina saw, wore what had once been the brilliant white robes of Alchemists. For how many centuries, Caina wondered, had people come here in search of immortality only to die?

How many millennia?

"You killed them," said Caina, voice unsteady, "if they were unable to resist the dream?"

"Certainly not," said the Keeper. "They killed themselves. Or, rather, they did nothing to preserve their lives. They fell into their false dreams, and did nothing as they perished of hunger and thirst. They could have escaped at any time, had they possessed the will to turn away from the dream."

"That's cruel," said Caina. "And you killed them as surely as if you held the sword yourself."

"I do not kill mortals for failing the trial of will," said the Keeper. "I do kill mortals for failing to endure the trial of truth."

Caina turned from the gallery of bones, her fingers tightening around the ghostsilver dagger's hilt. She wondered if she could strike the Keeper down, land a telling blow before the spirit could summon its power.

"And what," said Caina, "is the trial of truth?"

"Simply a question," said the Keeper. "Answer truthfully, and you will live. Answer falsely, and you will die."

"That's it?" said Caina. "Just a question? What if I don't know the answer to the question?"

"The nature of the question ensures that you know the answer," said the Keeper. "Whether you can speak it, whether you can admit it to yourself...that is another matter entirely."

She gazed at Caina, her blue eyes cold and hard. Caina wondered if she really looked like that, if her own eyes were as hard and cold as the spirit's guise.

"Ah," said the Keeper, stepping back and nodding to herself. "I see.

Yes. I know the question you must answer."

"Then ask," said Caina, her throat dry.

"You are a nightfighter of the Ghosts," said the Keeper, "and your actions have saved millions of lives. You do not like to think about it, and prefer to pass the credit for your victories on to others, or to mere chance. Yet if not for you, Caina Amalas, Malarae would have been destroyed, Rasadda would have burned, Cyrica Urbana would have sunk into the ocean, and Mihaela of Catekharon would have unleashed a war to drown the mortal world in blood. All those lives, saved because of your actions."

"It was chance," said Caina. "Had I been slower, or my enemies faster…"

"That was not my question," said the Keeper. "You are the Balarigar, the demonslayer, whether you wish it or not. But still that is not my question. You are a Ghost nightfighter, the Balarigar, the savior of millions…and you love a man. Corvalis Aberon, the assassin, the bastard son of the First Magus. This is my question, Caina Amalas of the Ghosts. Could you kill Corvalis?"

"What?" said Caina. "That is a stupid question. I am not going to kill him."

"Whether or not you are going to kill him," said the Keeper, "was not my question. The question was if you could kill him. If he betrayed you and took a different lover. If he betrayed the Ghosts to the Magisterium. If he returned to the Kindred and resumed his old ways. If he assisted a renegade sorcerer. Could you then kill him?"

Caina said nothing, the awful question thundering in her mind.

There had been a reason she had forgiven Corvalis after Catekharon. He had sided with Claudia over her…and because of that, Caina had almost been killed. But she had forgiven him. He had sided with his sister, his only family. She could not blame him for that.

But if he had sided with the Magisterium, if he betrayed the Ghosts…

Caina knew what she was capable of, what she could do if she felt it justified. A large part of her had grown cold and hard and merciless. Most men and women had never killed anyone. But not Caina. The innocent part of her had withered away. She could kill without hesitation, without guilt.

"Yes," whispered Caina. "Gods forgive me, I don't want to, but if it came to it, if he betrayed the Ghosts…yes, I could."

The Keeper stared at her for a long moment, then nodded.

"You could," said the Keeper. "It is a difficult thing for mortals to understand the deep darkness that lurks within their souls. For only by knowing your soul can you hope to master it."

Caina said nothing.

The Keeper lifted a hand. "Go. You have passed all three trials, and you have earned the right to the ashes of the phoenix spirits. Use the power wisely."

She rippled and vanished into nothingness, and the gallery blurred around Caina. When the blurring stopped, she found herself at the end of the gallery, in the middle of an archway opening into a vast nave of black stone.

She took a moment to steady herself, waiting until her eyes stopped stinging from the tears.

Then Caina strode into nave, looking around in wonder. The black floor and walls and columns and ceiling gleamed, and the huge windows, taller than any tower in Malarae, glowed with a fiery light. The effect was stark and strange and alien, yet nonetheless beautiful.

Thousands of stone niches dotted the floor in orderly rows, and Caina saw that some of them held glowing golden embers.

The ashes of the phoenix spirits.

She stepped forward, and a man of golden fire dropped from an opening in the ceiling, his shining wings spread around him. Caina flinched in alarm, raising her dagger, though she doubted she could land a blow before the creature burned her.

Yet the phoenix spirit ignored her. It circled the great fane twice, and then folded its wings and floated to one of the empty niches. The spirit stood motionless for a moment, flames writhing around its limbs and wings. It lifted its face to the ceiling and extended its arms.

And then golden fire exploded in all directions from the phoenix spirit.

Caina jumped back in alarm, the heat washing over her like a wave. Had she been any closer, the flames would have devoured her. She shielded her eyes from the glare, squinting as brilliant golden radiance filled the vast fane. On and on it went, the floor trembling with the power.

And at last the golden glow faded.

Caina opened her eyes, wiping sweat from her face, and saw that the phoenix spirit had disappeared.

In its place, the shallow niche had been half-filled with glowing golden embers.

The ashes of a phoenix spirit.

Caina strode forward, and knelt besides the phoenix spirit's glowing ashes. She reached for the satchel, hanging half-forgotten at her side, and drew out the metal flask. The sigils upon its side glowed with pale blue light. Caina lowered her hand towards the ashes, fearing the heat. But the ashes of the phoenix spirit only gave off a gentle, steady warmth, like fresh-baked cakes pulled from the oven.

She dipped the flask into the ashes, filled it, and returned it to the satchel.

Caina stood and looked around the fane. There was no sign of any movement, and she started the long walk back to the gallery of black stone.

She could not tell how long she spent walking through the gallery. Time did not work the same way in the netherworld as it did in the mortal world. It could have been an hour or a week, or anything in between.

But at last Caina found herself atop the stairs outside the Sacellum of the Living Flame, the vast shifting plain stretching before her.

There was no sign of the Moroaica.

It seemed that the Moroaica had kept her promise. She had helped Caina reach the Sacellum alive, and then departed.

Caina's hand dipped into the satchel, curling around the flask of phoenix ashes. Even through the metal, she felt the warmth of the ashes. Jadriga had kept her bargain.

Yet Caina still felt as if she had been cheated somehow. Or as if the Moroaica was playing a trick.

She let go of the flask and started down the stairs, and broke into a jog when she returned to the gleaming black road.

She could worry about the Moroaica later. Perhaps Jadriga had been honest, and had aided Caina in hopes of gaining her help in the future. Or maybe Jadriga had another motive.

Caina's jog broke into a loping run.

Right now she had more pressing concerns.

Like getting out of the netherworld alive before the phobomorphic spirits, or worse things, realized that Jadriga had departed.

Caina ran, the terrain rippling and shifting around her. It seemed to be changing faster now, cycling from grassland to dead forest to swamp to deserted city and back again with every beat of her heart. Was it reacting to her ragged emotional state after the ordeals of the Sacellum? Or responding to the power in the phoenix ashes?

That was a disturbing thought. The Alchemists might not be the only ones to crave the power of the ashes. The other creatures of the netherworld might desire the ashes as well.

She looked up and saw the spirits flying overhead.

More of the phobomorphic spirits in their ragged gray robes, hundreds of them, soared after her. There were other creatures as well, things that looked like winged wolves or flying serpents. Some of the creatures were unlike anything she had ever seen before, ghastly fusions of flying eyes and beating wings and writhing tentacles.

And all of them, every last one of the spirits, was heading for her.

Caina sprinted, her aching legs and hips protesting against the effort. The mass of spirits dove for her, and she saw more misshapen forms racing across the plains, creatures that looked like wolves, albeit wolves the size of oxen.

The square of white light, the gate back to the material world, appeared ahead. She saw Sinan and the Immortals standing beyond it, frozen in the space between heartbeats. Could the spirits follow her through the gate? No, a spirit needed to possess a physical body to enter the mortal world.

Perhaps that was what they wanted with her.

Or they merely wanted to rip her to bloody shreds.

The mass of spirits closed around her in eerie silence, and Caina threw herself forward with one final burst of speed.

She slammed into the square of white light, and gray mist rose up to swallow the world. Caina felt herself falling, the gray mist billowing around her.

Then light filled her vision, and she came to a staggering halt in the dining hall of the Lord Ambassador's residence, the Immortals surrounding her. Sinan took an alarmed step back, pointing that fork at her face, while Mahdriva gasped.

"By the Living Flame," said Tanzir. "That was…that was quick."

Caina looked at him, her breath rasping through her teeth.

She heard herself laughing, and could not make herself stop.

"Yes," she said. "Yes. Quick."

CHAPTER 22
THE MASTER ALCHEMIST

"The ashes," said Sinan, keeping the fork leveled at her. "Do you have the ashes?" He growled. "Stop laughing and tell me if you have the damned ashes!"

Caina managed to get herself under control.

"Yes," she said, reaching into the satchel with her free hand, "yes, I found your precious ashes."

The Immortals pointed their scimitars at her, their veins pulsing with blue light.

"Your dagger," said Sinan. "Put it away. Now."

Caina scowled and slid her ghostsilver dagger into its sheath.

"You." Sinan waved his free hand at an Immortal. "Take the ashes from her."

The hulking Immortal strode towards her, and Caina dropped the flask into the Immortal's extended hand. The Immortal turned, and Sinan snatched the flask. He examined it, and then opened it and peered inside.

"This is it," he breathed. "Yes. Well done, Ghost. Very well done, indeed. You succeeded where so many others have failed."

"Master," said one of the Immortals in a basso voice. "Kill her. Now. If she was strong enough to survive the perils of the netherworld, she is strong enough to threaten your plans. Kill her now."

Caina said nothing. The Immortal's suggestion was a good one. She would stop Sinan, if she could find a way. But that did not seem likely. Especially since the Immortals could kill her with ease.

Sinan shook his head. "Leave her alive and unharmed, for now. She succeeded in bringing back the ashes once, and she can do so again, if I require additional materials."

"I fear that is unwise, Master," said the Immortal, glowing eyes fixed on Caina. "This one is dangerous. Better to kill her now, before…"

"I said no!" said Sinan. "Do not question your master, dog. If I require your opinion, I shall ask for it. Otherwise do as I have commanded and hold your tongue."

The Immortal said nothing.

"Do not fear," said Caina, keeping her voice cold and arrogant. Delay, she had to delay until Corvalis and Tomard arrived. "Your master is wise to keep me alive."

Sinan walked towards his work table, the flask of ashes in hand. "You would say anything to save your life now."

"He is wise to keep me alive," said Caina, "because he is a pathetic coward."

Tanzir's jaw fell open in surprise, and Sinan looked at her with a glare.

"Oh?" said the Alchemist, his voice low and dangerous. "A coward, am I?"

"I have seen the netherworld, Ibrahmus Sinan," said Caina. Provoking him like this was a foolish game, but the longer she held his attention, the longer it kept him from killing Mahdriva…and the more time Corvalis had to arrive with the militia. "I have seen spirits that hunt mortals and wear the faces of your greatest fears. I have seen the Sacellum of the Living Flame, and I have faced the trials that defend the chamber of the ashes. All this I have done, Ibrahmus Sinan, and I have returned…but you have not. So your master is wise to keep me alive, Immortal. For if he botches the Elixir Rejuvenata and requires more ashes, he is too weak to claim them himself."

Sinan smirked. "Then I am the wiser. A clever man uses others as his tools, rather than exposing himself to danger."

"You would not last five minutes in the netherworld, Sinan," said Caina. "And you have the temerity to call yourself an Alchemist."

His smirk changed to a sneer. "I claimed the power of an Alchemist because it was mine by right. Just as I shall claim both mastery and immortality."

"You stole the ashes from me," said Caina, "because you were too much of a craven dog to find them yourself. Because you were too afraid to lose your precious life."

"Why should I risk it," said Sinan, "when immortality lies at hand?"

"Because all men die," said Caina, "and you are too much of a coward to see that. Whether you die tonight when you botch your Elixir or in a thousand years when your enemies finally overpower you, you will die. And you are too fearful to accept that."

"If you are so eager to throw your life away," said Sinan, "then I will have the Immortals take it."

"And if you make an error preparing your Elixir," said Caina, "will you go into the netherworld yourself to claim new ashes?"

Sinan's sneer turned into a scowl. "I will send more Guards. Or perhaps some of the Immortals."

Caina looked at the hulking Immortals and laughed. "Yes, I'm sure they'll be able to defeat the riddles surrounding the Sacellum."

"It is not a concern," said Sinan, gesturing with the fork, "since I will make no errors preparing the Elixir."

"You've done magnificently so far," said Caina. "I doubt I need to lift a hand against you. You'll kill yourself when you botch the formula."

He scoffed and turned away.

"You are not fit," said Caina, hoping to keep his attention, "to call yourself an Alchemist."

Sinan glared back at her, a dangerous glint in his black eyes. "Oh?"

"I saw the bones of Alchemists in the Sacellum of the Living Flame," said Caina. "They, at least, had the courage to risk the journey. They didn't hide behind kidnapped Imperial Guards. They didn't force a woman to go through the gate for them. They died, aye, but they were men...and you're just a cringing child."

"Be silent," said Sinan.

"You were born a slave, weren't you?" said Caina. "That is all you are fit to be. A slave for men greater and bolder than yourself. You ought to be washing their boots and polishing their floors, not..."

"Be silent!" roared Sinan.

"Not strutting about in an Alchemist's robes like a child playing in his father's armor," said Caina, ignoring Sinan's interruption. "You're a dog, Sinan. No, you're less than a dog. A dog will die for its master. You're a worm. You're not fit to be anything but a slave..."

"I said to be silent!" screamed Sinan, thrusting the fork at her, the air tingling with sorcerous power.

Caina just had time to realize that she had pushed Sinan too far, and then an arc of blue-white lightning leapt from the fork and slammed in her chest.

Everything went white.

When her vision cleared, Caina found herself on her back, her arms and legs twitching. To her surprise, she was still alive. After a moment she found that she could sit up, though her arms and legs throbbed and her chest felt as if it had been burned.

"If she interferes with me," said Sinan, standing at the work table, "kill her. If she tries to escape, kill her. If she tries to rescues the girl or the emir, kill her." He turned his head and glared at her. "Do not try my patience, Ghost. If you annoy me again, I will kill you and take my chances."

Caina stood, wincing at the stiffness in her limbs. "You make such a persuasive argument."

Sinan ignored her.

Caina hobbled across the dining hall, expecting the Immortals to stop her. But Sinan had told them only to stop her if she tried to escape or interfere with his work. She crossed the dining hall and stopped where Tanzir and Mahdriva sat bound to their chairs. Mahdriva's face was numb and wooden, her cheeks wet with tears. Tanzir simply looked terrified.

Six Immortals followed her, their expressions impassive, scimitars in their hands.

"You're still alive," said Tanzir. "When that lightning struck you, I thought…"

Caina shrugged. "I suspect I did not annoy him as much as I thought."

Her skin tingled as Sinan began casting spells over his work table.

"You should flee," said Mahdriva, her voice a whisper. "Ardaiza met this fate, as did Ranai. It was foolish of me to think I could escape it. Go, before it is too late. Why should you die with me?"

"No," said Caina. "This isn't over."

"It is," said Mahdriva, bowing her head. "My father tried to save me, and you tried to save me…but it is too late."

"Forgive me, Ghost," said Tanzir, "but I fear that the lady is correct. You should go while you still can."

"A fine idea," said Caina, looking at the Immortals. "But I suspect they can outrun me."

The Immortals gave no answer.

She had to find a way to stall. Corvalis and Tomard were on their way. And she could not leave Mahdriva and Tanzir to Sinan's mercy. Nor could she leave the Imperial Guards, or Lord Titus or Halfdan himself, still unconscious and bound in their chairs. Gods, if only Caina could find a way to wake the unconscious Guards!

Tanzir licked his lips. "The…the netherworld. What was it like? It seemed like you were gone for less than a few seconds, but when you came back…you looked as if you had spoken to your own spirit."

"I did," said Caina. She did not want to think about that, not until she had found a way to beat Sinan. "Repeatedly, even."

Sinan's voice repeated an incantation over and over again, the arcane force in the air sharpening. A faint breeze stirred through the dining hall, tugging at Caina's shadow-cloak. Caina suspected the next phase of Sinan's spells would not take very long. Otherwise he would have withdrawn with Mahdriva to a more secure location.

Which meant he expected to complete his Elixir and kill Tanzir long before any help arrived.

If Caina pierced the skin of the sleeping Guards with her ghostsilver dagger, would that wake them? It might, but the Immortals would realize what was happening and kill her long before she awakened a useful number of Guards.

She stared at Sinan's back, watching as he summoned power.

At his unprotected back.

He was far away, but she thought she could put a throwing knife into him. One to wound him and get his attention. The next to plunge into his throat. Caina felt the weight of the blades at her belt. The Immortals would cut her down, of course, but with Sinan dead they would have no reason to harm Tanzir, and certainly no more reason to hurt Mahdriva. There was the possibility that Sinan had a warding spell to block steel blades, but he might have become complacent.

And a dark part of her mind murmured that it would be worth the sacrifice, if only to keep her from becoming the sorceress she had seen in the netherworld…

She started to reach for the knives in her belt, and Sinan threw out his hands and shouted the final words of his spell. Golden light blazed around him, and Caina felt a surge of sorcerous power. More golden light radiated from a crystal vial the size of a man's fist upon the table. The liquid within looked like luminescent honey, and Caina felt power rolling off it like the heat from the furnaces in Ark's foundry.

"Yes," whispered Sinan, holding up the crystalline vial. "Yes!" He turned and smirked at Caina. "You brought far more phoenix ashes than I needed, Ghost. Only a pinch is required. After I complete this vial, I shall have enough phoenix ashes left to over to create Elixir for centuries."

Caina said nothing, still weighing the possibility of hitting Sinan with a thrown knife.

"And now," said Sinan, putting down the vial of glowing liquid, "the final component."

He picked up a long dagger from the worktable and turned towards Mahdriva.

"No," whispered Mahdriva. "Please, no. Not this. Not my child. No."

Sinan ignored her and started forward.

Caina's hand fell towards her belt, and the nearest Immortals lifted their scimitars.

"Please," said Mahdriva, weeping. "I will do anything. Anything at all. Just spare my child. Please!"

"You two," said Sinan, pointing at a pair of Immortals. "Hold her still. This will get messy."

Caina took a deep breath, steadying herself. She would have only one chance to put a knife in Sinan's throat.

Sinan glanced at her and stopped, frowning.

"Actually," he said, "I have enough ashes that I have no further need of the Ghost. Kill her at once."

A dozen Immortals turned to face her, ready to strike with their scimitars.

Caina snatched a throwing knife from her belt and drew back her arm, ready to fling it at Sinan.

And as she did, the skylights overhead exploded.

CHAPTER 23
AMBUSH

The Immortals froze in surprise, and Caina dashed forward, dodging beneath the balcony to avoid the rain of shattered glass.

And as she did, she flung the knife in her right hand with all her strength. The spinning blade still struck Sinan in the face, and the impact should have opened him from lip to ear.

But instead the blade bounced away with a spray of sparks.

He had indeed warded himself against steel.

Caina saw dozens of militiamen ringing the broken skylights, crossbows in their hands. Corvalis stood in their midst, a dark shape in his shadow-cloak, and to her surprise she saw Muravin at his side. Tomard stood near them in his plumed tribune's helm, and Caina found herself grinning at Corvalis's cleverness.

He hadn't tried to dispel the mist or find a safe way through it.

He had simply gone over it.

She pulled up her mask and cowl, hiding her face from the militiamen.

"In the name of the civic militia of Malarae," thundered Tomard, his voice echoing through the dining hall, "and by the authority of the Lord Prefect of the city and the Emperor of Nighmar, I command the Alchemist Ibrahmus Sinan and his followers to lay down their arms! Surrender, and your lives shall be spared…"

Sinan roared in fury, the veins in his neck bulging. "Fool! You think to threaten an Alchemist of the College?" He leveled the fork, a spark flaring to life between its tines. "Then perish!"

"Tomard!" shouted Caina. "He can throw lightning! It…"

"Shoot him!" said Tomard. "Shoot him…"

Several things happened at once.

Scores of crossbowmen lowered their weapons and fired into the dining hall. Caina saw quarrels slam into the Immortals, saw blue-glowing blood splash across the gleaming floor. Yet the wounds only irritated the Immortals, who bellowed their inhuman battle cries. At least twenty bolts slammed into Sinan, the impact knocking him back, but the steel heads did not penetrate his warding spells.

And as he staggered, a dazzling blast of lightning erupted from his fork and slammed into the militiamen. Caina had seen Andromache conjure blasts that were far more powerful, yet the bolt from the Alchemist's enspelled weapon was powerful enough. Fingers of lightning chewed into a half-dozen militiamen, and the men screamed as they went up in flames.

Dozens of ropes fell to the floor, and Caina saw that the militiamen had driven grapnels into the roof. They slid down the ropes, and the Immortals hastened to meet them, even as Sinan raised his fork and the crossbowmen began to reload. Caina raced forward, yanking her ghostsilver dagger from its sheath. Sinan had warded himself against steel, but ghostsilver was proof against sorcery.

At the last minute the Alchemist pivoted to face her, his face twisted with hatred, lightning crackling between the tines of the fork. Caina threw herself to the side, dodging behind one of the stone pillars, and the fork spat out a lance of snarling lighting. It veered to the side and struck one of the Immortals and two of the militiamen, and all three men screamed in agony.

Another volley of quarrels hissed from the ceiling, rocking the Immortals, and the militiamen charged into the fray. Steel rang on steel, and men and Immortals screamed and cursed and died. Sinan shouted and loosed another blast of lightning. Caina had to stop him. If she did not, he would kill most of Tomard's men before the fighting was over.

But first, she had to make sure those men had not died in vain.

She slashed the ropes binding Tanzir to the chair, and then cut the ropes holding Mahdriva and pulled the girl to her feet.

"Go," said Caina, pushing Mahdriva towards Tanzir. "Find a quiet corner and hide. We'll find you when this is all over. Get out of here, now."

"But, Ghost," said Tanzir. "This…"

"Go!" said Caina, pointing with the ghostsilver dagger.

Tanzir swallowed, nodded, and he and Mahdriva hastened beneath the balcony.

Caina turned, intending to seek Sinan, and found herself face to face with an Immortal.

She ducked an instant before the scimitar would have taken her head. Caina struck back, lashing out with her ghostsilver dagger. The blade carved a blue-glowing furrow down his ribs, the handle growing hot in her hand. Smoke rose from the wound, and the Immortal threw back his head and screamed. Caina raised her arm for another slash, aiming for the Immortal's throat.

But the Immortal punched, and the back of his hand caught Caina in the temple. The sheer power of the blow spun her around, and she fell hard to the floor, her head ringing. The Immortal towered over her, and Caina seized a knife and flung it. The blade buried itself in the Immortal's stomach, but the hulking soldier did not even seem to notice. Caina scrambled backwards as the Immortal stalked after her…

The tip of a bloody blade erupted from the Immortal's chest, and the Istarish soldier stiffened. Caina saw a shape in a shadow-cloak spin around the Immortal, a dagger flashing. A line of blue-glowing blood appeared across the Immortal's throat, and the soldier fell upon his face.

Corvalis turned to face Caina, his eyes glinting green behind his mask.

She was glad to see him, so glad, and not just because he had kept that Immortal from killing her.

Her words from the netherworld echoed inside her head.

Caina pushed them aside. She could deal with them when she wasn't in a room filled with enraged Immortals trying to kill her.

"Good timing," said Caina, getting to her feet. Her head throbbed, and her arms and legs ached. She would pay a price for this much exertion over so short a time, she knew. But she could not rest, not until Sinan was defeated.

"It's a gift," said Corvalis, stepping to her side as the melee raged around them. Sinan loosed another stroke of lightning, sending militiamen tumbling from the broken skylights with a scream.

"How did you wake up Muravin?" said Caina.

Corvalis shrugged. "I dunked his head into a barrel until he came to. He told us what had happened, and I figured you could use the help."

"A safe assumption," said Caina, her eyes sweeping the dining hall. Mahdriva and Tanzir had retreated to the corner beneath the balcony. The militiamen struggled against the hulking Immortals in a confused, chaotic melee, blue-glowing blood falling to the floor. Sinan stood near his mirror, throwing arcs of lightning at the crossbowmen on the roof. Crossbow bolts hissed through the air, some striking the Immortals. Others hit Sinan himself, only to bounce away from his warding spell.

"We have to get at Sinan," said Caina.

"He's warded," said Corvalis.

"He is," said Caina, "but I'm pretty sure his spell won't stop a ghostsilver dagger."

"We'll have to get close enough for you to use it," said Corvalis.

"Let's get started," said Caina.

Corvalis nodded, started forward, and two Immortals rushed them.

A half-dozen crossbow bolts pierced the flesh of both men, but neither Immortal seemed to care. A black scimitar blurred for Corvalis's head, and he jumped back, ducking under the blow and striking back with his sword and dagger. The brutal training regimen of the Kindred families produced effective fighters, and Corvalis had been among their best. He danced around the Immortals' strikes, his weapons carving glowing lines in their flesh. Yet the Immortals shrugged off their wounds. They drove Corvalis back, pushing him towards one of the heavy pillars supporting the balcony.

Caina darted around the melee and drove her ghostsilver dagger into the knee of one of the Immortals, ripping into the tendon. Even with superhuman strength and resistance to pain, the Immortal's leg folded, and the soldier fell with a bellow. Caina struck twice more, glowing blood smoking on the ghostsilver blade, and finished off the Immortal.

The second Immortal roared and kicked the dying soldier. The Immortal slammed into Caina, and she lost her balance, stumbling onto one knee. The living Immortal knocked Corvalis to the ground with a vicious swing and stalked after Caina. She got back to her feet, dagger held out before her.

The Immortal flew at her like a storm.

A steely blur shot past her eyes and slammed into the Immortal's torso. The Immortal staggered with a groan, and Caina saw a trident jutting from his chest. A battle cry rang in her ears, and Muravin stormed past her, swinging his scimitar with both hands.

The Immortal's head jumped off his shoulder with a spray of glowing blood and rolled across the floor.

Muravin ripped his trident free from the corpse's chest. "My daughter, Ghost! Is she…"

"She is well," said Caina, shouting over the melee as Corvalis moved to her side. She jerked her head at Mahdriva and Tanzir in the corner. "But if we don't stop Sinan, she won't be safe."

"Then let this be the hour," growled Muravin, "that the blood of my daughters is avenged."

"Sinan has a ward," said Corvalis. "Steel won't touch him. We have a weapon that can harm him, but…"

"But you need to get close enough to use it," said Muravin. He gave a curt nod. "Come! Let us carve a path to our foe."

Corvalis nodded and lifted his weapons, and the two men charged into the battle, Caina following them. Corvalis fought with speed and grace, his blades flickering back and forth like a serpent's tongue. Muravin struck with power and raw strength, but he was no less effective. Together the two men forced their way through the press, blades rising and falling, Muravin's trident stabbing.

Caina stayed at their side, flinging knives and striking with her ghostsilver dagger whenever she saw an opening. Time and time again she wounded an Immortal, or drew the Immortal's attention, distracting the elite soldiers long enough for Muravin or Corvalis to land a killing blow. Caina struck another Immortal in the calf with a throwing knife, and the big man stumbled. Corvalis spun, his sword trailing blue-glowing drops, and slashed the Immortal's throat.

The Immortal fell with a heavy thump, and a strange silence fell over the dining hall.

Caina realized that all the Immortals had been beaten. She saw men in the chain mail and colors of the militia lying strewn on the floor, far more than she would have liked, but all the Immortals had been slain.

Sinan stood with his back to the mirror, teeth bared in a snarl.

"Back!" he snarled. "All of you, back!"

"It is over!" Tomard stood on the roof overlooking the dining hall, his cloak scorched. "Throw down your weapon and surrender!"

Sinan laughed. "Fool! You have no blade that can touch me!"

"Maybe steel won't touch you," said Tomard, "but your sorcery won't save you if we beat you into a pulp with our bare hands. You're alone, outnumbered, and that damned mist you conjured is dispersing. Soon we'll summon reinforcements from the Magisterium's chapterhouse, and your little tricks won't save you then."

"No!" said Sinan. "I am too close for you to stop me now!"

He reached into his robes, something glittering in his free hand.

"Take him!" said Tomard. "Stop him before…"

Sinan flung the vial. It exploded, and a column of thick white mist rose up, spreading in a pool across the floor. For a moment Caina thought it was similar to the mist he had conjured around the mansion, but then the mist rolled over a pair of charging militiamen. The metal of their armor sizzled and smoked, huge blisters forming on their skin. The men screamed as their hair and clothing caught fire.

The mist was acidic.

"Get back!" shouted Tomard, and the militiamen stumbled away from the mist as it spread across the floor. The floor itself began to smoke as the mist ate into it, and Caina backed away. Muravin snarled and turned away, crossing before the advancing mist.

Sinan turned towards his work table. Caina wondered if he intended to flee through the mirror into the netherworld with his vial of half-completed Elixir, or if he would simply launch another spell.

She never found out.

Muravin bellowed and sprinted forward, throwing himself into the air. He leapt over the pool of mist and landed at the very edge on the far side. His boots started to smoke, but sheer momentum carried him forward, both hands gripping the shaft of his trident. Sinan snarled a curse, Mahdriva screamed for her father, and Muravin stabbed.

Lightning erupted from Sinan's fork just as Muravin's trident rammed into the Alchemist's chest. Sinan's ward turned aside the steel points, but the power of Muravin's blow drove the Alchemist backwards and into the mirror. The great sheet of glass shattered into a thousand fragments.

Yet lightning still burst from his fork, clipping Muravin on the shoulder. The former gladiator bellowed in pain as blue-white fingers crawled up and down his chain mail, and for an awful moment Caina thought that Mahdriva would see her father die in front of her. Yet the lightning bolt had only clipped Muravin, its full force lashing uselessly against the wall. Muravin fell to one knee, his limbs trembling, his black eyes ablaze with hate as he stared at Sinan.

Caina ran to the edge of the mist as Sinan pushed himself away from the mirror frame, broken glass sliding from his shoulders. The fork began to spark with fresh lightning. Caina's mind raced, her fingers tight against the ghostsilver dagger's hilt. The acid mist was dissipating, but by the time it dissolved, Muravin would be dead. It was too far for her to jump, and...

The answer came to her.

"Muravin!" she shouted. "Catch!"

She threw the ghostsilver dagger over the pool of mist. The blade was not balanced for throwing, and the weapon flew at an odd angle. Yet Muravin's thick arm snapped out and caught the dagger, his fingers closing around the handle. Sinan leveled his fork, the lightning crackling to life.

Muravin plunged the curved dagger into Sinan's chest.

The Alchemist stiffened, the fork falling from his hands, his eyes bulging as his mouth fell open. Muravin yanked the dagger free and drove it into Sinan's chest once more, his massive hand closing around the Alchemist's throat. Sinan pawed at the former gladiator's wrist, but his efforts were useless.

"You slew my daughters and my grandchildren," hissed Muravin, "to live forever. Well, here is your immortality. Is it to your liking?"

He threw Sinan into the work table, knocking it over, and the Alchemist collapsed motionless to the floor with the clatter of breaking bottles and jars.

CHAPTER 24
REGENERATIONS

Caina let out a long breath. Muravin stood motionless, Sinan's blood dripping from the ghostsilver dagger. Sinan himself lay atop his broken table, his hands twitching feebly. Muravin seemed content to watch his enemy die.

"Remind me," muttered Corvalis, "never to irritate him."

The mist dissipated, and Caina headed across the acid-scarred floor towards Muravin, but Mahdriva beat her to it.

"Father!" shouted Mahdriva, throwing herself into his arms. "Father, you are safe. I thought...I thought..."

"I am glad you are alive and well," said Muravin. Caina walked to his side, and he passed the bloody dagger to her. Then both his arms went around his daughter. "That damned mist...I was sure that I was too late. I was certain that Sinan would do..." For the first time his hard voice broke, and he cleared to his throat. "Do as he did to your sisters."

"He would have," said Mahdriva, looking over her shoulder at Caina, "but the Ghost came and delayed him. The Ghost...the Ghost was very brave."

"Indeed," said Tanzir, picking his way over the scarred floor. "I, too, would have perished."

"Are you well, my lord emir?" said Tomard, hurrying over with a dozen militiamen.

"Er...yes, all things considered," said Tanzir. "It could have been," he looked at the dead Immortals and militiamen and swallowed, "it could have been much worse."

Tomard nodded and turned to his centurions. "Get the wounded comfortable, and start waking up those Imperial Guards." Both Halfdan and Lord Titus straightened up, groaning, as the militiamen cut their ropes. With Sinan dead and the mist dissipated, it seemed the sleep spell would not last much longer. "My lord Titus, are you well?"

"Not particularly," said Titus with a scowl, climbing to his feet. "What the devil happened?"

"Yes," said Halfdan, looking at Caina and Corvalis. "What happened?"

"It seems the Alchemist went berserk and tried to kill the lord emir," said Tomard.

"Ah...tribune?" said Tanzir.

Tomard didn't seem to hear him. "The Alchemist put an enspelled mist around the mansion, and sacrificed the Bostaji to hold our attention. Fortunately, the Ghosts realized what was happening, and we came to your aid."

"Tribune?" said Tanzir again.

"Capital work," said Titus. He looked at Caina. "It seems I owe my life to your friends among the Ghosts once again, Basil. This Balarigar of yours is quite useful."

"Tribune?" said Tanzir, fear on his face.

"Tomard," said Caina, using her disguised voice. "The emir has a request."

Tomard turned. "My lord emir?"

"Er," said Tanzir, blinking. He swallowed, looked at Caina, and then drew himself up. "Sinan was brewing a vial of bright golden fluid. I suggest you find it and destroy it at once."

"He didn't finish it," said Caina, looking at Mahdriva.

"Well, no," said Tanzir. "But it's still incredibly dangerous. I urge you to find and secure it."

"Of course," said Tomard, turning to his centurions. "Delegate some men to find the damned thing. We want no sorcerous relics tormenting our city."

"Treat it carefully, tribune," said Tanzir, glancing at Mahdriva. "Master Muravin saved my life from Sinan...and Sinan used the ashes of Muravin's grandchildren to create that Elixir."

"Gods," said Tomard. "Damned sorcerers. Well, I..."

He turned, and Caina saw Sinan.

To her shock, he was still alive. He lay slumped against the broken table, his white robes wet with blood, but he was still alive.

A crystal vial shone with golden light in his right hand.

And even as she looked, he lifted the vial to his lips.

"No!" said Caina. "Stop him! He..."

Sinan swallowed the incomplete Elixir in a single gulp.

The empty vial fell from his shaking fingers.

"Oh, no," said Tanzir. "Oh, no. That's very bad."

"Why?" said Caina. "The Elixir was incomplete."

Muravin backed away, one arm raised to shield Mahdriva, his scimitar pointing at the prone Alchemist.

"Well, yes," said Tanzir, "but incomplete Elixirs…there are stories. The results are apparently very bad. It…"

Sinan managed a croaking laugh. "This is your doing, Ghost. You drove me to it. You…"

He groaned, twitching like a dying fish. Perhaps the unfinished Elixir would simply kill him outright.

Then his face began to glow.

A golden gleam shone from his mouth and nose and eyes, spreading across his skin. His hands start to glow, wisps of golden radiance dancing around his fingers. Sinan's trembling grew more violent, golden light shining from his collar and sleeves. The militiamen and the others stared at him, stunned. Caina remembered the Sacellum of the Living Flame, remembered the phoenix spirit descending to the shallow niche.

Remembered the golden flames erupting from the phoenix spirit.

Suddenly she knew what was going to happen next, even as she felt the crawling tingle of powerful sorcery around Sinan.

"Get out of here!" she said. "All of you, out! Now!"

"Why?" said Titus. "What is happening?"

"Go!" said Caina. The golden light around Sinan brightened. "The sorcery in him is going to burn this mansion to the ground. Run! Move, damn you!"

"I suggest," said Halfdan, "that you do as she says."

Sinan sat up, his robes smoldering.

"Go!" said Tomard. "Everyone out, now!"

The militiamen fled for the exit, an escort falling around Tanzir and Titus. Muravin urged Mahdriva forward, one arm around his daughter's shoulders. Caina looked back at Sinan. The Alchemist stood, his face a rictus of agony and terror beneath the golden glow, smoke rising from his robes.

He began to scream, and his robe burst into flames.

"We have to go," said Corvalis, grabbing Caina's shoulder and turning her towards the exit.

Sinan went rigid with another scream, his head thrown back, his arms outthrust. The pressure of sorcery against her skin doubled again.

"It's too late," said Caina. A high-pitched keening noise came from Sinan, drowning out his agonized screams. "Behind the pillar. Now!"

She darted behind one of the thick pillars with Corvalis as the last of the militiamen hurried out the dining hall doors.

And then Sinan exploded.

Gouts of golden flame erupted in all directions, blasting over the floor and walls. The pillar shielded them from the fire, but the blast of hot air washed over Caina like a giant fist. The floor shook and heaved beneath her feet, the roar of the flames filling her ears. Wave after wave of sorcerous power crawled over her, and for a horrible instant the dining hall reminded her of the river of molten metal flowing through Tower of Study in Catekharon...

The flames died away.

Caina stepped around the pillar, coughing. Muravin and Tomard walked back into the hall, as did some of the militiamen. Charred corpses and heaps of misshapen, half-melted armor littered the floor. Rubble lay heaped here and there, portions of the ceiling blasted away by the fire. A smoking crater lay on the far end of the room, all that remained of...

Shock rippled through Caina.

Ibrahmus Sinan stood naked and untouched in the crater.

No, not untouched.

Younger.

Before he had looked about forty, his thinning hair touched with gray. Now his hair and beard were thick and black, and he was muscled like a god. The wounds Muravin had carved in his chest had vanished.

Sinan looked at himself, at them, and started to laugh.

"All this time," he said, striding out of the crater. "All those years. It was a trick, wasn't it? No, another test. The ashes of the children of three sisters. But that was a lie. Three sisters were not required." He spread his arms wide. "Two seemed to serve, did they not?"

Muravin growled. "Just as you stole their lives, so shall yours be taken!"

Sinan laughed. "Try, worm!" He lifted his hands, and Caina felt a surge of sorcerous force. "Try! I have been reborn...and my powers have been reborn with me!" Caina slipped a throwing knife into her hand, wondering if Sinan's ward against steel had survived the upheaval of his rebirth. "I shall melt the flesh from your bones." He stepped forward. "Get on your knees and beg, and I shall..."

Caina raised her arm to throw, taking a good look at Sinan.

She recoiled in disgust.

Caina had seen more horrible things than she wanted to remember. Maglarion's experiments in the vaults below Aretia. Men burnt alive by sorcery in Rasadda. Andromache's face twisting in horror as Scorikhon's spirit claimed her flesh. A woman turned to stone by an enslaved spirits.

But she had never seen anything quite as unsettling as the thing upon Sinan's right hip.

The Alchemist glanced at her, eyes narrowed.

"Oh, gods," whispered Caina.

Sinan smirked. "Yes, beg for your..."

"You idiot!" said Caina. "Look at your hip. Look at what you've done to yourself."

Sinan glanced down, and his eyes widened.

The left arm of an infant jutted from his right hip, the tiny fingers opening and closing over and over again. Sinan jerked back in disgust, as if trying to pull away from his own flesh, and turned in the process.

The face of an infant bulged from the back of his right thigh. The child's mouth contorted in a silent scream, the tiny eyes clamped shut. Something dangled from the back of Sinan's knee, and Caina saw the leg of an infant, the toes twitching.

"You did this!" hissed Sinan, glaring at Caina. "You did this to me, you sabotaged the ashes..."

"You drank the Elixir before it was ready," said Caina. "You murdered Muravin's daughters and stole the lives of their children. You did this to yourself."

"For the gods' sake!" said Tomard. "Kill the damn fool and put him out of his misery."

The militiamen charged, and Sinan cast a spell. A column of air before him congealed into mist, and two of the militiamen went down, screaming as their skin and flesh melted. Caina flung her knife, and it sank into Sinan's leg, sending the Alchemist staggering back.

His ward against steel had not survived his transformation.

The surviving militiamen attacked, and Sinan charged with a scream, his hands hooked into claws. He seized one of the militiamen, lifted him, and swung the man like a club, battering the others to their knees. Sinan threw the unfortunate man to the ground, his eyes wild, blood leaking from the wound in his leg.

It seemed the unfinished Elixir had also given him inhuman strength.

Caina flung another knife, opening a second wound in Sinan's side. The Alchemist turned to face her, face livid with rage, and both Corvalis and Muravin raised their weapons.

"Shoot him!" said Tomard.

Three of the militiamen had crossbows, and they took aim. The bolts slammed into Sinan's stomach and chest, and the Alchemist fell to his knees, breathing hard. He glared at Caina, hands hooked into claws as he tried to cast another spell, but Corvalis and Muravin plunged their swords into his chest.

Sinan fell upon his back, his blood pooling around him.

Blood that began to glow with golden light.

"Get back!" said Caina. "It's happening again." Sinan's entire body shone with golden light, his limbs twitching. "Run!"

The surviving men raced for the dining hall's double doors. Caina scrambled after them, and a second later a sheet of golden fire erupted from the hall, so powerful that it tore the massive doors right off their hinges, so hot that the mosaic floor cracked. Caina pressed herself against the wall, wondering if the golden fire would chew threw the stone itself.

But at last the fire faded away…and a hideous groan came from the dining hall.

Caina spun around the doorway, ready to attack.

Sinan stood in the center of the hall.

Or, at least, the thing that had once been Ibrahmus Sinan.

He stood upon six legs, their lengths corded with muscle and bristling black hair. Two arms jutted from each of his shoulders, his chest misshapen and bulging. Two heads rose from his torso. One looked young and healthy, though its expression was twisted with terror. The other was a grotesque mockery, its eyes white and sightless, its jaw hanging open, a moan coming from its throat. The creature twitched back and forth, pawing at itself with its four hands.

"Gods," breathed Corvalis, more horror in his voice than she had ever heard before.

"You did this to me!" shrieked Sinan, his misshapen bulk shaking. "You did this to me! You sabotaged my Elixir, you…"

"This is the judgment of the Living Flame," said Muravin, and even he sounded shaken, "for your terrible crimes, for…"

Sinan charged at them, looking like a colossal insect wrought of human flesh.

"Kill it!" shouted Tomard. "Cut off its head. Cut off both of its heads! But I want that thing dead!"

The militiamen hesitated. They had killed Sinan twice before, and both times he had risen again. They hesitated, but Sinan did not, and the mutated Alchemist crashed into them. He caught one man, lifting him with his four arms, and tore him in half. Two of his legs stamped out, crushing a militiaman. But the remaining men found their nerve and attacked, their blades biting into Sinan's rippling flesh. The Alchemist screamed, throwing back both of his heads in pain.

Caina raced forward, Corvalis and Muravin at her side, and struck. Her ghostsilver dagger sank into Sinan's leg, and the wound sizzled. Sinan shrieked, his misshapen head rotating to face her, and two of his arms reached for her. Muravin yelled and swept his scimitar before him, and two of Sinan's hands fell to the floor. The Alchemist stumbled back, both of his heads screaming, and a bold militiaman plunged his spear into Sinan's torso. The Alchemist staggered backwards and collapsed to the ground.

For a moment Caina hoped the fight was over, that Sinan had been slain at last.

Then his wounds began to shine with golden light, the glow spreading over his skin.

"It's happening again!" said Caina. "Run, all of you!"

Tomard, Muravin, Corvalis, and the surviving militiamen sprinted for the mansion's front doors, Caina at their heels. She risked a glance over her shoulder, saw Sinan thrashing and screaming, saw golden light wreathing his body.

Then he exploded in golden fire for the third time.

The force of the blast slammed Caina to the mosaic floor. She landed with a grunt, all the breath exploding from her lungs. A pillar of brilliant golden fire whirled before the dining hall, chewing into the walls and ceiling and floor. Corvalis helped her to stand, and Caina regained her feet as the golden flame faded away.

Bile rose in her throat.

The thing that squatted before the ruined dining hall was a grotesque parody of human life, a creature congealed out of nightmares. Sinan was now size of a bear, a huge mass of dripping flesh crouched upon a dozen muscular legs. A score of heads rose from the thick stump of his torso, some of stunning beauty, others of hideous appearance. Dozens of arms jutted at random places from the creature's flesh, and Caina saw that some of its organs were outside of its skin. Two hearts beat atop Sinan's torso, and she saw four brains and several lungs pulsing and throbbing in his hips.

An all the while, half of the heads screamed, while the other half cursed and snarled in Istarish.

"Run!" said Corvalis.

Caina saw no reason to argue.

She sprinted for the main doors alongside Corvalis. Sinan pursued them, his legs driving his huge, misshapen body with a drunken wobble as he bounced off the walls. Despite that, he moved with terrifying speed, his mouths hurling curses.

Caina raced out the mansion's front doors. Tomard and Muravin waited outside, surrounded by the surviving militiamen. A mob of Imperial Guards stood behind them, weapons drawn, Halfdan and Titus and Tanzir at their head.

"What's happening in there?" said Titus.

"Shut those doors!" said Corvalis. "Barricade them! Right now!"

Titus took one look at the creature charging up the entry hall and his face went white.

"Do as he says!" he shouted.

Militiamen and Guards leaped forward, closing the doors and bracing them with spears and shields. Caina heard a thump, and the doors trembled as Sinan pounded against them, his dozen voices raised in insane fury.

Those doors would not hold him for long.

"Gods," said Titus, "what sort of creature is that?"

"Sinan," said Corvalis. "Or whatever is left of him."

Even Halfdan looked stunned. "What happened to him?"

"I don't know," said Tomard. "Something in his sorcery went...awry. Seriously awry."

"Demons," said Muravin. "Demons have inhabited his flesh, summoned by his wickedness."

"No," said Caina. "He's a copying error."

"A copying error?" said Titus, incredulous.

The doors thumped again, some tiles sliding free from the mansion's roof.

"Don't you see?" said Caina. "It's like a scribe copying a book and making an error, and then another scribe making a copy of the same book with the first error, while making mistakes of his own. The errors compound themselves over time. Every time we kill Sinan, the power of the Elixir rebuilds his body. Except...except he didn't finish the Elixir. That must be why he needed the ashes of three unborn children, to stabilize the Elixir. It's rebuilding his body, over and over again, but..."

"But it's making mistakes every time," said Corvalis, "and it turned him into that thing."

"The Ghost speaks true," said Tanzir, gazing in fear at the mansion. "There are stories of Alchemists who botched their Elixir Rejuvenata, who transformed themselves into horrid monsters." He shivered. "I do not think he will be Mother's favorite Alchemist any longer."

"Those stories," said Halfdan, "do they say how Sinan can be killed?"

"Er," said Tanzir. "No. Unfortunately."

"Every time we deal him a mortal wound," said Tomard, "that golden fire appears and heals him."

"Sooner or later the power of the sorcery will fade," said Corvalis.

Another thump, and Caina saw the doors splinter.

"Aye, but how many more mortal wounds can he take?" said Titus. "A dozen? A score? He might well kill us all before we can even inflict that much damage. Or, worse, he'll escape us and rampage through the city!"

Again a thump came, Sinan's voices screaming threats, and a new crack appeared in the doors.

"Perhaps if we dismember the corpse," said Muravin, "cut out his heart before the fire comes..."

"We can't," said Caina. "Anyone who tries will get burned to cinders."

Fire. That was the key, somehow, the phoenix fire.

"We are overmatched," said Titus. "I will dispatch a messenger to the Magisterium's chapterhouse, and bid them to send magi to deal with Sinan. We shall have to hold him here until the magi arrive."

"The Guards and the militiamen may not be able to hold the creature," said Halfdan. Another thump, and another crack appeared in the mansion's doors. "It will be a slaughter, and the magi may not even come.

They may well be content to let Sinan slaughter Tanzir."

"You and you," said Titus, pointing at a pair of Imperial Guards. "Take the lord emir to the Imperial Citadel, and keep him safe. The pregnant girl as well – that Alchemist might kill her simply out of spite. The rest of you, form a battle line. We will kill that damned Alchemist as many times as…"

"Wait," said Caina as an idea came to her.

Titus scowled at her. "What?"

"The fire comes from the phoenix ashes," said Caina.

"Phoenix ashes?" said Titus.

"Don't ask," said Tanzir.

"That's the source of the power that heals him," said Caina. "It's based in fire. If we are to kill him, we need to douse the fire."

"And where shall we get that much water?" said Titus. "It…"

Caina pointed. "The reservoir pool behind the Lord Ambassador's residence. It's twenty feet deep. If we dunk Sinan in that, I think that much water will counteract the fire of the phoenix ashes."

"He will simply climb out again," said Tomard.

"Not if we wound him badly enough first," said Caina, "and trigger the healing."

One of the panels in the door smashed apart, and Caina saw Sinan's glistening flesh. The Imperial Guards hurried forward, shoving additional shields and spears against the doors, but they would not hold for long.

"So you want to lure out Sinan, wound him, and then push him into the pool?" said Titus.

Caina nodded.

"Madness," said Titus.

"Probably," said Caina, "but there isn't any other option, my lord. When he breaks out, he'll kill us all, and no matter how badly we wound him, he'll heal himself. We'll kill him eventually, but not before he kills many, many innocent people."

"The Ghost nightfighters know their business," said Halfdan.

Titus gave an irritated shake of his head. "And just how are we to get Sinan into the pool?"

"Trust me, my lord," said Caina. "He'll follow me."

"You?" said Titus, and she saw Corvalis stiffen in alarm.

"Me," said Caina. "He's…rather irritated with me, and I know how to make him angrier."

Titus sighed. "Very well. Centurion!" Tylas hurried over, his face wary behind his helm as he looked at Caina. "Array your men near the pool. When the Ghost lures Sinan near it, strike with your javelins to wound him, and then use your shields to shove him into the water."

"Is…is that wise, my lord?" said Tylas, glancing at the crumbling door.

"Probably not," said Titus, "but I have no better ideas."

Tylas banged his fist against his cuirass in salute, and the Imperial Guards hurried to obey. Ten men moved around Tanzir and Mahdriva and Muravin, escorting them away from the chaos, while Tomard and the militiamen moved to seal off the surrounding streets. Titus fell back, flanked by the Guards, leaving Caina alone with Halfdan and Corvalis.

"You are sure about this?" said Halfdan.

"No," said Caina, gazing at the door. "Go already."

"As you command," said Halfdan with a bow that held no trace of mockery, and then he went to join Lord Titus.

"This is madness," said Corvalis. "He will kill you."

"He will try," said Caina.

She would have sent Corvalis away, but she knew he would not listen.

Corvalis laughed and shook his masked head. "Look at you."

"What?" said Caina.

One of Sinan's fists smashed through the wood.

"You've got a lord of the Empire and an emir of Istarinmul hopping to do your bidding," said Corvalis. "You'll rule the Empire yet."

She felt a chill at his words. Yet it reminded her of the attack upon the House of Kularus, when she had taken command of the defense. Was the vision from the netherworld her future? Could she become like the sorceress she had seen?

Of course, Sinan might rip her head off her shoulders, and then she would have no future at all.

The militiamen and the Guards fell back from the doors, and a moment later Sinan bashed them open. The creature staggered onto the mansion's stairs, all twenty heads shrieking curses and looking for fresh victims.

Caina stepped forward, raising her voice. "Ibrahmus Sinan!"

A shiver went through the hulking creature, and all twenty of its heads rotated to face her.

"The Ghost," rasped one of the heads. "The clever, clever little Ghost."

The creature took a few skittering steps towards her.

"Do you have anything to say," said another of the heads, "before I tear you to shreds?"

Caina stared at Sinan. "You deserved to be a slave."

A furious ripple went through the hulking mass of deformed flesh.

"You're pathetic," said Caina. "You thought you could be a Master Alchemist of the College. But a former gladiator and a pregnant girl escaped you, and you couldn't even catch them. You were too much of a coward to enter the netherworld and take the phoenix ashes for yourself. You tried to become a Master Alchemist...and look at you now. You murdered those women and their children for nothing. The College would kill you on sight. You weren't fit to be a Master Alchemist. You weren't even fit to be an Alchemist. You were born a slave, and you deserve…"

All of Sinan's heads loosed an earsplitting shriek, and the vast creature charged at her, its bare feet slipping and sliding over the ground.

Caina waited to the last instant, and then threw herself to the left, Corvalis dodging to the right. She hit the ground and rolled, coming back to her feet, the ghostsilver dagger a blur in her hands as she struck. The blade bit into one of Sinan's many legs, the wound sizzling, and the Alchemist's heads howled in unison. Corvalis struck at Sinan's right side, his sword digging a gash, but Sinan ignored him.

The Alchemist's fury was focused upon Caina, and his many arms reached to seize her.

Yet she eluded them. The Elixir had bestowed Sinan with superhuman strength and speed, even in his mutated form, yet Caina suspected the Elixir had not bestowed superhuman agility to match. His legs tangled around each other as he tried to turn, and often his own arms blocked his attacks. Caina danced around him, darting out of his reach, hitting his flank with the ghostsilver dagger. Corvalis struck him over and over, but Sinan ignored him.

Whatever remained of Sinan's mind wanted Caina dead.

And she drew him around the edge of the mansion, towards the aqueduct reservoir.

She ran around the mansion's corner. The pool gleamed in the moonlight, a wide concrete basin filled with rippling water. Dozens of Tylas's Imperial Guards waited near the edge, shields on their arms and javelins in their hands.

Caina backed towards them.

Sinan staggered around the corner, bleeding from a dozen wounds as Corvalis struck again and again, and the twisted Alchemist's eyes widened at the sight of the Imperial Guards.

"Now!" shouted Tylas.

In one smooth, well-drilled motion, the Guards drew back their arms and flung their javelins. Caina ducked, Corvalis moved away, and a rain of razor-tipped steel hurtled towards Sinan. The Alchemist screamed, and dozens of the javelins slammed into him, driving him towards the pool.

His wounds, all of them, began to glimmer with golden light.

Caina scrambled to her feet, getting out of the way.

"Shields!" said Tylas. "Get him into the water."

Golden haze flickered around Sinan's misshapen form.

The Guards surged forward, dozens of them, driving their shields against Sinan. The Alchemist bellowed and thrashed, knocking several Guards to the ground.

Golden fire blazed around his wounds.

Sinan shrieked, his heads snarling, and shoved himself at the Guards, scattering them. He was going to heal himself...and the inferno of his healing would kill dozens of men.

"Sinan!" shouted Caina, running at him. She buried her dagger to the hilt in the wet flesh of his side and ripped the blade free, the golden light shining from the wound. Sinan whirled to face her, ignoring the Guards, ignoring the javelins jutting from his flesh, ignoring everything but her.

And his desire to kill her.

Caina shoved her dagger into its sheath and jumped into the pool.

The shock of the cold water filled her, and she started swimming for the lip of the pool. Sinan threw himself in after her, and Caina felt his fingers grasp for her legs. But she kicked herself free, the wave of his impact carrying her forward, and she half-swam, half-thrashed for the pool's lip.

Below she saw a golden glow fill the reservoir, felt the water heat up around her. She wondered why Sinan did not pursue her, and after a belated moment realized that his misshapen body prevented him from swimming. He moved back and forth beneath twenty feet of water, the golden light growing brighter and brighter. Terrible heat soaked through her clothing as the water started to boil around her.

The golden light filled the world. She glimpsed the edge of the pool, but it seemed so terribly distant.

Sinan was going to die, but he was going to cook her alive.

The golden light blazed, and Caina lunged for the edge of the reservoir.

It was just out of reach.

A pair of black-gloved hands seized her wrist and wrenched her out of the steaming water with such force that her left arm almost popped out of its socket. She gasped and fell forward, her head spinning from the hot water, and landed hard against Corvalis.

"Go!" said Corvalis, urging her forward.

Caina half-ran, half-stumbled forward, and then the reservoir pool exploded.

A wave of hot water smashed into her like a burning fist and knocked her to the ground. Caina rolled over, grabbing at Corvalis and digging her boots against the rough street to keep from being washed away. A plume of steam erupted from the reservoir, lit from within by a golden radiance. Caina's skin crawled with the presence of terrible arcane force, nausea twisting her stomach and pain stabbing in her head.

But the power faded away, the golden light winking out, and the only noise was the steady hiss of steam rising from the reservoir pool.

Caina felt a hand upon her shoulder.

216

"Are you all right?" said Corvalis, helping her to stand.

Caina blinked, lightheaded, and leaned on Corvalis as the world spun around her. "I've never been better. Tonight I've almost been stabbed, shot, set on fire, consumed by giant fish-monsters, burned alive, and then boiled. Truly, it's been delightful."

She was babbling, she realized, but was too woozy from the heat to care.

"Fish-monsters?" said Corvalis.

Armor clattered as the Imperial Guards climbed to their feet, their black cuirasses glistening with condensation. Tylas shook his head, his helm's plume hanging limp against his armor. Caina stared forward, Corvalis following her.

"Ghost," said Tylas.

"Centurion," said Caina. "Be ready to shoot Sinan if he is still alive."

But she looked into the reservoir and realized that would not be necessary.

Almost two-thirds of the water had boiled away in the backlash of power, and what remained of Ibrahmus Sinan floated in the rest. The half-completed healing had twisted him further, transforming him into a creature that looked like a random assortment of body parts. Dozens of black eyes glared up at Caina from a score of heads.

All of them unblinking and dead.

"Gods," muttered Tylas. "If an Alchemist ever offers me a vial of that damned Elixir, I'll cut off his head first."

"Good choice," said Caina. "He was afraid to die. But he was wrong. There are worse things than dying."

"Clearly," said Tylas.

Lord Titus, Halfdan, Muravin, and Tanzir joined them at the edge of the pool.

"Is it over?" said Tanzir.

"Aye," said Caina. "He's dead."

"A dire way to die," said Muravin. "I would not wish it upon any man." He spat upon the misshapen corpse. "But after what he did to my daughters, he deserved no less."

"By the Living Flame," said Tanzir. "I owe you my life, Ghosts. It is just...I cannot believe it is over and I am still alive. I was certain I would die here."

"Everyone dies," said Caina, "but we won't die quite yet."

CHAPTER 25
THOSE WHO WILL CARRY ON WHEN WE ARE GONE

Caina collapsed soon after returning home with Corvalis. At first she thought the heat of the reservoir had dehydrated her. But she did not know how long she had spent in the netherworld, and the experience had drained her strength.

Caina slept for the better part of two days, strange dreams flitting through her mind. She saw the Sacellum of the Living Flame again, the phobomorphic spirits, the Keeper taunting her as it wore her face. Sinan appeared, screaming and cursing as his body reshaped itself in golden fire.

She awoke drenched in sweat, got up long enough to drink some water, and then fell into a black and dreamless sleep.

Late she awoke with the sun in her eyes. It was well past dawn, to judge from the light streaming through the balcony doors. How long had she lain abed at home? Two days? It...

She blinked again.

When had she started thinking of this townhouse as home?

The door opened, and Corvalis strode into the bedroom, again wearing the black coat and trousers of a prosperous merchant. One of the maids walked behind him, carrying a tray of food. The maid set the tray beside the bed and hurried away, leaving Caina alone with Corvalis.

"How do you feel?" said Corvalis, sitting on the edge of the bed.

"Sore," said Caina, examining the tray, "and hungry enough to kill a horse with my own hands." There was bacon and cheese on the tray, along with a mug of steaming coffee. "Thank you for bringing me breakfast, by the way."

She took a drink of coffee and started on the food.

"There's more if you want it," said Corvalis. "Given how long you were asleep. And…however long you were in the netherworld."

Caina hesitated, nodded, and took another drink of coffee.

"How long were you there?" said Corvalis. "Tanzir said it took an instant, but Claudia told me that time flows differently in the netherworld."

"It does," said Caina. "I don't know how long. Maybe a day? Maybe longer. It's…not a good place, Corvalis. Sinan was a coward and a murderer, but I understand why he didn't want to go there."

"I am just glad," said Corvalis, "that you are safe." He hesitated. "I should have not let you go alone."

Caina laughed and ate a piece of bacon. "That was my decision. You couldn't have stopped me."

"I suppose not," said Corvalis. He looked at her, face grave. "It is all because of you, you know."

"Because of what?" said Caina, taking another sip of coffee. Gods, but Shaizid made good coffee.

"That I am still alive," said Corvalis, "that Tanzir Shahan is still alive, that Muravin and his daughter and his grandson escaped from Sinan."

Caina shrugged. "We were lucky. We could all be dead just as easily. And if not for you, the Immortals or the Kindred would have gutted me any number of times."

"Aye," said Corvalis, "I have the stronger sword arm, Caina Amalas, but not the stronger brain. Your mind puzzled this out. If not for you, Tanzir and Mahdriva and her son would be dead, the war with Istarinmul would continue, and Sinan would be immortal."

Caina laughed. "You are flattering me."

"No," said Corvalis. "I'm not." His hand, strong and hard with calluses from sword work, took her free hand. "I am many things, but a flatterer is not one of them." His green eyes looked almost haunted. "This will sound strange…but watching you go with Muravin to the Lord Ambassador's mansion was one of the harder things I've done."

"Why?" said Caina, puzzled. "As it turned out, it was the right thing to do."

"Because I love you," said Corvalis, "and I don't want you to die."

Caina looked away, her eyes stinging.

"I love you, too," she said, "and you are too kind to me. Too kind by far."

She loved Corvalis, loved him as she had not loved anyone else…but her answer to the Keeper of the Sacellum of the Living Flame had been a true one. She loved Corvalis, but if he betrayed the Ghosts, if he sided with the Magisterium, she could kill him.

Corvalis laughed. "Why do you think I am too kind to you?"

"Because I am a killer," said Caina.

Corvalis snorted. "So I am. And a darker one than you. You were never a Kindred assassin."

"The Keeper asked me a question," said Caina.

"The Keeper?" said Corvalis.

"A spirit I saw in the netherworld," said Caina. "It asked me a question, and I had to answer it truly or perish."

"What did it ask?" said Corvalis.

"If I could kill you if you betrayed the Ghosts," said Caina, the words tumbling out of her. "And I said yes."

She stared at Corvalis, waiting for his reaction. She expected him to get angry. Or for his face to go blank, the way it did when he was hurt. The Kindred had taught him to mask his emotions, to ignore them when necessary.

Instead he only laughed.

Caina blinked in surprise.

"Of course you could," said Corvalis. "I love you, but you frighten me a little. I know you could kill me if I betrayed the Ghosts." He laughed again.

"Why are you laughing?" said Caina, annoyed. "It's not funny!"

"It is," said Corvalis. "You don't understand. My father and the Kindred turned me into a weapon, and I have become a weapon for the Ghosts. But I'm not loyal to the Ghosts. Or to Halfdan. Or to the Emperor and his Empire, and certainly not to the Magisterium and the Kindred."

"Then who holds your loyalty?" said Caina.

"You do," said Corvalis. "I serve the Ghosts as long as you do, Caina, because…well, because I suppose you own my heart now. If you want a man's head on a platter tomorrow, I'll bring it to you with an apple stuffed in his mouth."

Caina felt herself smile. "Don't do that. It would be a waste of a good apple."

They looked at each other in silence for a moment, and Caina squeezed his fingers.

"We should stop talking about this," said Corvalis. "You're weeping, and you'll lose too much water and pass out again."

"I am not weeping," said Caina, and she rubbed at her eyes. "How is the House of Kularus?"

"Almost repaired," said Corvalis. "Shaizid hired men from the carpenters' collegium to rebuild the doors. He'll get a good price out of them. Gods, but that mouse has some acid on his tongue when he thinks someone is trying to cheat you." He grinned. "I told everyone that Sonya Tornesti was so overwhelmed by the vandalism that she took to her bed and has not stirred from it in days."

"Good," said Caina. "Where is Tanzir staying? I suppose the mansion was wrecked?"

"It was," said Corvalis, "and half of it burned down anyway. Tanzir's staying at the Black Cuirass Inn, with some of Tylas's men keeping watch over him." Caina nodded. The Ghosts secretly owned the Black Cuirass Inn, and Tanzir would be safe there. "The negotiations are finished, and Tanzir and the Emperor will formally declare peace tomorrow at the Praetorian Basilica."

Caina nodded. "And Mahdriva. She…"

She frowned, working through some of the things that Corvalis had already said.

"Gods!" said Caina. "Mahdriva had her baby, didn't she? A son! And you didn't tell me?"

Corvalis grinned. "Why? I don't need to tell you anything. You figure it out on your own, don't you? But, yes, Mahdriva had a son. She's staying with Ark and Tanya at the foundry. Feels safer there. Both Mahdriva and the child are healthy." He shook his head. "The boy can scream, though…I didn't think anything that small could be that loud."

"I'm glad," said Caina.

And she was. Sinan might have claimed Ardaiza's and Ranai's children…but he would never touch Mahdriva's son.

The next day the House of Kularus reopened, having repaired the damage from the peculiar burglary attempt. The tribune Tomard of the civic militia had inspected the damage and the corpses, and declared that two rival gangs of thieves had tried to break into the House. Anton Kularus and his workers were clear of all wrongdoing.

Merchants and lords packed the tables and booths, all of them scheming. Now that peace with Istarinmul had come, the trade routes to Anshan, Alqaarin, and Istarinmul itself were open once more, and a bold man might reap a fortune.

Caina watched the crowds, wearing again the rich gowns and jewels of Sonya Tornesti. She stood at Corvalis's side as he spoke with Shaizid.

A short time later their guest arrived.

"Master Anton," said Tanzir Shahan, Halfdan and a trio of Imperial Guards trailing after him. "It is good to see you again."

"And it is good to see you healthy and well, my lord emir," said Corvalis. "I heard you suffered some most…vigorous attempts on your life."

"I did," said Tanzir. "But I had the help of some capable benefactors." He looked at Caina and smiled. "Without them I would be dead. Or I would have given up and waited for my foes to slay me."

Caina smiled back. "Your benefactors, I am sure they were only doing their duty, yes?"

"Indeed," said Halfdan. "Shall we sit?"

They took their table, the Imperial Guards watching for attackers, and Shaizid's maids hurried forward with a tray of coffee.

"I confess I shall miss this place," said Tanzir, sipping from his cup. He sighed. "It is certainly more pleasant than most of Istarinmul. And Mother and Morazir will be disappointed I survived." He grinned. "I look forward to seeing the expressions on their faces." His smile faded. "Though I suppose they will simply try to kill me again."

"You should do something about that," said Halfdan.

Tanzir shook his head. "I don't know what I can do."

"You could have them killed," said Caina.

Tanzir looked at her, shocked. "My mother?"

"You are the emir of the Vale of Fallen Stars," said Caina. "You know they tried to have you killed. You would be well within your rights to execute them. And if you do not want that...well, you have done a great service for your Padishah, have you not? I think he would be inclined to do you a favor."

Tanzir opened his mouth to argue...but Caina saw something harden behind his black eyes. He nodded, stroked his beard for a moment, and then nodded again. "I believe, Sonya Tornesti...I believe you are right. As you have been right about many other things."

"Perhaps," said Caina. "Living is fighting. And I do not think you are ready to die just quite yet, my lord emir."

"No," said Tanzir. "No, I am not." He smiled at Caina, and then looked at Halfdan. "Master Basil, you should know that I am grateful for my life. Know that the Ghosts have a friend in Istarinmul. I will not betray my nation, of course..."

"Nor would I ask it of you," said Halfdan.

"But you now number an emir of Istarinmul among your friends," said Tanzir. "And there are many men like Rezir Shahan and Ibrahmus Sinan in the Padishah's lands. Should you need my help against them, you need only ask."

"There is," said Caina, "one favor you could do us."

"Of course," said Tanzir.

"I understand that there are many coffee plantations in the Vale of Fallen Stars?" said Caina.

Tanzir nodded. "For centuries. Do not let the Anshani fool you. Istarish coffee is the finest in the world."

"The Empire has never shown much interest in coffee before," said Caina, "but you have seen the House of Kularus, and now that there is peace with Istarinmul...well, there is an opportunity here. I think you might sell your coffee to the House of Kularus, and we both shall profit."

And the Ghosts would gain that many more eyes and ears in Istarinmul.

"Of course," said Tanzir, "but...should I not be speaking to Master Anton of this?"

Corvalis laughed. "You might be an emir, my lord, but you're not terribly observant."

Tanzir frowned, looked at Caina...and then comprehension spread over his face.

"Ah," he said. "Well. Shall we haggle, then?"

Later that afternoon Caina walked into Tanya and Ark's guest room.

Mahdriva lay propped up by pillows, face tired and wan but...satisfied. Content, even. Muravin stood near the window, and he, too, looked as close to happy as Caina had ever seen him. Tanya sat next to the bed, talking with Mahdriva.

Mahdriva's son lay in her arms, black eyes darting back and forth.

"Mistress Sonya!" said Mahdriva with a smile. "You came. Are you well? After the...the fighting at the emir's mansion, I feared you would not recover."

"Just in need of some rest, that's all," said Caina. "How are you?"

"Tired. But well," said Mahdriva. "My son, he does not like to sleep through the night."

Tanya laughed. "They never do."

"The birth was very hard," said Mahdriva. "I thought he would rip me in half..."

"I heard," said Muravin. "There were men in the fighting pits who did not scream so loud."

"But then I heard him crying, and it was over," said Mahdriva. "Or it was just beginning." She raised the baby. "Would you like to hold him?"

Caina smiled. "I would."

She took the child in her arms, cradling his head in the crook of her left elbow. He looked at her solemnly, reaching for her with his stubby arms. Caina held out her right hand, and his small hand wrapped around her fingers.

"He has a strong grip," she murmured.

Muravin laughed. "He is my grandson."

"I named him in your honor," said Mahdriva, voice quiet. "Sonyar."

Caina looked at Mahdriva in surprise.

"For Sonyar would not be here, if not for your help," said Mahdriva. "None of us would. Thank you."

Caina nodded and looked away, blinking. Gods, but she had become as weepy as a child lately.

"I shall have to find work," said Muravin. "I have a daughter and a grandson to support properly."

"Fear not," said Caina. "The Ghosts will find a place for you. We have many friends in the city…and we could always use a few more. You will help us as we move against men like Sinan."

"An easy enough price to pay," said Muravin.

Sonyar tugged on Caina's hand and stuck her finger into his mouth.

"Ah," said Tanya with a laugh. "I think he's hungry."

"Here," said Caina, handing the boy back to Mahdriva. "He is a beautiful child."

Mahdriva smiled. "He looks like his father. Oh, but I wish he could have been here for this."

"As do I," said Muravin. "Still, his son shall carry on his memory."

Caina nodded, spoke with them for a few moments longer, and then left.

Corvalis awaited her in the sitting room, sharpening one of his daggers.

"Ah," he said, looking up. "You're smiling. The baby is well, then?"

"He is," said Caina. "They named him for me."

Corvalis grinned. "I know."

"And you didn't tell me?"

"I thought you would enjoy the surprise," said Corvalis.

Caina laughed, kissed him, and threaded her arm through his as they left the foundry.

Her thoughts turned to the future as they walked through Malarae's streets. She need not become the Moroaica's ally or the sorceress she had seen in the netherworld. There was another path open before her, that of the Ghost circlemaster. Of a woman who used her influence and knowledge to save others, to help those like Muravin and Mahdriva and Tanzir.

Mahdriva's son was alive because of her, and that knowledge made Caina's heart feel lighter than it had been in a long time.

Someday, she knew, she would stop being a Ghost nightfighter.

But not quite yet.

EPILOGUE

Tanzir Shahan, emir of the Vale of Fallen Stars, strode into the solar of his family's mansion in the heart of Istarinmul.

His mother reclined on pillows, attended by a pair of slaves. Even in her late forties, the amirja Ashria was still beautiful, with skin the color of bronze and long, glossy black hair. But the black eyes that turned towards him were cold and hard as obsidian knives.

"So," she said, voice dripping with disdain, "you have returned from groveling before the Emperor's throne? Pitiful. Send Sinan to me. I would have words with him."

Tanzir quailed before the scorn in her voice, and wanted to leave the solar and hide in the library.

He started to turn, but then he remembered the words of the blue-eyed Ghost, and nodded to himself.

"Angry that he failed to kill me, I suppose?" said Tanzir.

Ashria's eyes narrowed. "I don't know what you mean. Cease this foolishness and tell Sinan to attend me."

"He is dead," said Tanzir.

For the first time, a hint of surprise went over her face. "What? How did he die?"

"Of his own folly, as it happens," said Tanzir. He took a deep breath. "Mother, you are under arrest for plotting the assassination of the emir of the Vale of Fallen Stars. Namely, myself."

Ashria laughed with disdain. "How amusing! Do you think to threaten me, boy? You cannot lay a hand on me."

"I cannot," said Tanzir, "but the Immortals the Padishah loaned me think otherwise."

He clapped his hands, and a half-dozen of the Padishah's personal Immortals strode into the solar.

"What is this?" said Ashria, her voice rising to a screech as the Immortals hauled her to her feet. "Do you think this is a joke? Morazir will never stand for this!"

"They arrested Morazir on our way here," said Tanzir.

"Unhand me!" shrieked Ashria, clawing at the Immortals. "I command you to unhand me at once!"

"The penalty for hiring assassins is traditionally death," said Tanzir, "but I persuaded the Padishah to show leniency. You are being exiled to the monastery on the Isle of Seven Stairs. I understand the monks consider physical labor to be cleansing for the soul. I do hope you enjoy tending gardens, Mother."

She screamed curses at him, threatened him with death and mutilation and worse, but the Immortals dragged her from the room, and her threats faded away.

Tanzir let out a long breath, his heart racing, sweat dripping down his face.

He saw his mother's slaves staring at him in shock.

"Ah," he said. "Yes. Um." He thought for a moment. "That silk hanging there, by the window. Could you take it down? I really never cared for it."

The slaves leapt to do his bidding.

It really did improve the look of the rom.

Tanzir had never asserted himself before...but he thought he might come to enjoy it.

Darkness fell over the Imperial capital of Malarae. The burned-out ruins of the Lord Ambassador's residence jutted against the night sky, like blackened bones rising from the earth.

It reminded the Moroaica of the pharaohs' pyramids rising from the sands of the Maatish desert.

She stood outside the mansion, gazing at the ruins. Her spirit still wore the flesh of Mihaela the Seeker, and she had kept Mihaela's preferred costume of leather vest, trousers, and heavy boots. Much as the Moroaica preferred skirts, she had come to appreciate the trousers' freedom of movement.

She had grown Mihaela's black hair out, though.

The pharaoh's priests had shaved her head, long ago. They had embalmed her, bound her spirit to her undead flesh, and sealed her within a tomb, condemning her to serve the pharaoh as a drudge for all eternity.

Jadriga felt her lips curl into a smile.

The priests were all dead, and the souls of the pharaohs had been bound upon the desert wind to burn screaming for all eternity.

How they had begged for mercy!

They were all dead...and she was not. They had paid for the pain they had inflicted upon her.

But there were more to repay.

The gods themselves would pay for what they had done.

Caina Amalas would have said that was madness, but she did not understand. Some of Caina's memories flooded through the Moroaica's mind, and she remembered lying in Corvalis's arms, his mouth against hers, their bodies pressed together...

A wave of longing went through the Moroaica, sharper than anything she had felt in centuries.

She pushed it aside with annoyance. The memories were not hers.

Jadriga looked against at the mansion, focusing upon the reason she had come to Malarae.

"Well," said the Moroaica to the woman standing next to her. "What do you think?"

The woman was eighteen years old and beautiful, with long red hair, bright green eyes, and curves of hip and bosom accentuated by her close-fitting green gown. Her eyes were full of hatred as they stared at Jadriga.

"It seems," said the young woman, "that your guess was correct, mistress." Her voice was hard and confident beyond her years. "The Alchemist failed utterly."

"Indeed," said the Moroaica, examining the emanations of spent sorcery that echoed around the ruined mansion. "He underestimated the child of the Ghosts. He should not have done that."

The young woman scowled. "You should kill her immediately. That wretched..."

Jadriga looked at the other woman.

The woman lowered her eyes at once. "Forgive me, mistress. I spoke out of turn."

The Moroaica nodded.

"But you can see," whispered the red-haired woman, her voice filled with loathing, "why I wish her dead."

"I can," said Jadriga. The woman standing at her side – or at least the spirit wearing the woman's body – had betrayed her. But Jadriga never cast aside a useful tool, and the woman would be useful to her yet.

There had been no particular reason to bind the spirit of Ranarius, once the preceptor of Cyrioch, to the body of a woman.

But even with all the centuries Jadriga had seen, watching Ranarius's discomfort at his new form was still amusing.

A dark shadow emerged from the mansion's broken doors, and Jadriga walked forward, Ranarius trailing after her. A short man in a black cloak walked from the ruins. A hint of moonlight touched the face beneath the cowl, revealing a ghastly patchwork of scars. One eye was a sulfurous orange-yellow, while the other was a pale blue.

He must have replaced it recently.

"Mistress," said Sicarion with a deep bow. He looked at Ranarius and grinned. "And you, my lovely lady."

"Be silent," hissed Ranarius.

"The Ghost killed you the first time," said Sicarion, his rusty voice dripping with mockery, "but perhaps I'll get do it the second time."

"Enough," said Jadriga, voice calm. "Did you find it?"

Sicarion bowed again. "Indeed I did, mistress."

He handed her a metal flask carved with blue-glowing sigils. At once she felt the tremendous power within the flask, the latent energy in the gathered phoenix ashes.

"Good," said Jadriga. "Very good. The fool Alchemist used only the smallest part of the ashes. Prudent, if futile. But all the more convenient for us...and for the great work."

She had the Staff of the Elements. She had the phoenix ashes.

And now she needed one more thing, just one more, and she would remake the world.

And make the gods themselves pay for their cruelties.

THE END

Thank you for reading GHOST IN THE ASHES. Look for the next book in the series, GHOST IN THE MASK, to appear in the second half of 2013. If you liked the book, please consider leaving a review at your ebook site of choice. To receive immediate notification of new releases, sign up for my newsletter, or watch for news on my Facebook page.

ABOUT THE AUTHOR

Standing over six feet tall, Jonathan Moeller has the piercing blue eyes of a Conan of Cimmeria, the bronze-colored hair a Visigothic warrior-king, and the stern visage of a captain of men, none of which are useful in his career as a computer repairman, alas.He has written the DEMONSOULED series of sword-and-sorcery novels, the TOWER OF ENDLESS WORLDS urban fantasy series, THE GHOSTS series about assassin and spy Caina Amalas, the COMPUTER BEGINNER'S GUIDE sequence of computer books, and numerous other works. Visit his website at:
http://www.jonathanmoeller.com

Printed in Great
Britain
by Amazon